SILVERADO PRESS PRESENTS

WESTERN STORIES BY TODAY'S TOP WRITERS

Volume 1

Edited and with an Introduction by
Jeffrey J. Mariotte

ACKNOWLEDGMENTS

There are so many people to thanks for helping to make this book a reality.

First, Silverado Press cofounder and writer extraordinaire Howard Weinstein. Without him there would be no Silverado.

Robert Greenberger, another exceptional writer and editor, helped us launch the project on Kickstarter, and has been an avid proponent of Silverado Press since the very beginning. He and the rest of the Crazy 8 Press crew are all brilliant and talented folks.

My wife, author and poet Marsheila (Marcy) Rockwell and our family kept me sane and grounded while working on this project.

Of course, the book wouldn't exist but for the authors who contributed stories. Some are friends, some are folks I've never met, but all of them are incredibly talented writers whose stories, I believe, will wow you.

Extra-special thanks go out to Lila Havens and Glitch in Normality for their support.

CONTENTS

Introduction: The New Old Frontier

Jeffrey J. Mariotte

At the Columbian Exposition in Chicago in 1893, historian Frederick Jackson Turner declared the American frontier a thing of the past. The nation had shifted, Turner argued, from an agrarian society into an industrialized one, and the westward expansion that had marked American life had come to an end. The settlement and colonization of the West had formed the American character and differentiated it from our European forebears.

Turner was right, but he was also wrong. Notable frontiers — physical, scientific, and emotional, continue to be identified and attacked. Gene Roddenberry, in his highly influential TV series *Star Trek*, called space "the final frontier." I believe that's wrong — humans in general and Americans in particular have always, and will always, set their sights on what's over that next mountain range, across that mighty river, or around the bend.

Turner and Roddenberry both minimized the cultures of the Indigenous people who already lived at "the frontier," instead focusing on the expansion of the numerically and technologically advanced newcomers, but that's a discussion for another time.

Like Turner's frontier, the frontier of western fiction — whether it be in stories and novels, in comics, on television, or on the big screen, has been declared over and done with more times than we can count. But in the same way that new frontiers are continually identified and explored, western fiction continually reinvents itself. When I was growing up, western TV shows could be found on all three networks, and it was easy to catch Roy Rogers and Hopalong Cassidy and Gene Autry on the tube. Every film studio put out western movies along with their mysteries and comedies and melodramas, and actors like Gary Cooper, John Wayne, and Clint Eastwood seemingly had no problem getting work. Western comics and novels were omnipresent.

Since those days, the western has been written off more times than I can count, but it always comes back around. Most general bookstores still have a westerns section, even if in the last decade or so it has shifted from mostly Louis L'Amour to mostly William Johnstone. (My local Barnes & Noble insists on shelving Erich Maria Remarque's *All Quiet on the Western Front* in the westerns section, no matter how many times I move it back to general fiction. I don't know if it's a running gag or just booksellers who don't know history, or their own stock.)

This anthology is Silverado Press's way of saying "Don't hang up those spurs just yet." The traditional western, we insist, is alive and well. To prove it, along with stories by acknowledged and award-winning authors primarily known for their western books and stories, we have nearly as many writers who mostly write in other genres, including science fiction, fantasy, and horror. As soon as the book was announced, we were approached by many of these writers, all of whom love westerns and wanted to try their hand at it. Some of the writers here are old hands, some are young up-and-comers. Additionally, despite the traditionally male image of western writers, fully half of our stories are written by women (in two cases, women and their husbands writing together).

I think their stories here will prove that there is indisputably plenty of talent out there — that fictioneers have new, different, and compelling stories to tell within the general framework of what we consider "western fiction." For this particular collection, the writers were asked to choose a specific event in the history of the American west around which to set their story. Not that the event needed to be central to the story, but that the stories had to reflect a certain time and place by virtue of the chosen event. You don't mind learning a little history while you read, do you?

Yes, the western changes, and recent decades have seen an explosion of westerns combined with other genres, most notably romance, horror, and science fiction. Don't worry — as much as I enjoy reading (and writing) them, you won't find any of those genre-bending tales in this book. You will find traditional western stories written by a diverse and enthusiastic group of talented scribes.

Saddle up and get ready to be entertained.

The Incident Above Mentioned

Rod Miller

I will tell you what happened and to hell with you if you don't like it.

I was there and can vouch for the *how* of it, but if it is the *why* of it that you're after you will have to go somewhere else for your answer. You're not likely to find satisfaction, sad to say, on account of anyone and everyone else who might know is a heap of dry bones lost in the brush somewhere, else they're moldering in a grave. There ain't none but me. I'm the only one left. And you're damn lucky I give the lie to the threescore years and ten the Psalmist gives us. Hell, I even outdid his fourscore years by a damn sight — but it sure ain't by reason of strength like he claims. He's right about the sorrow, though. I've suffered my share of it and then some. And a good bunch of that misery, I'd say, started that day you're wondering about.

That day. . . .

That day, where "once the embattled farmers stood and fired the shot heard round the world." Of course, there weren't no shots fired that day so it ain't exactly like that Longfellow poem, but it amounts to the same thing. And whilst most of the world don't know a thing about it, what started that day was sure as hell heard round our valley — hell, all of Utah, come to that — and the echoes of it ain't gone yet.

Since you keep asking about it, I'll tell you the truth of it.

Ninth day of April, it was. Way back in 1865. I ain't likely ever to forget that day. That's when it started.

I say it started that day, but the truth of it is that it had already been going on for years, one way or another, since about the very first day Brother Brigham sent us down here to settle the Sanpete. Seemed like the Indians — the Utes — was all right with us coming in here, at first. But when it all finally went to hell that day there wouldn't be any going back. Well, I guess there was, in a way — going back where we came from, that is. But after that was over, we came back here again, so I guess we went back and came back, which is both going back, sort of, I guess.

But I will get to that. Anyway, when it all broke loose it was like when a weak spot in a water gap gives way and the ditch water comes rushing out in a flood. And whilst it had been building up everywhere, it might never have broke loose like it did had not John Lowry filled his belly with more whiskey than was wise that morning.

In most ways, John Lowry was no different than a hundred other men thereabouts at the time. But he was different than most in that he was given to imbibing strong drink in excess, despite the advice of the elders and the Book of Commandments. But his being drunk ain't no excuse, it's just the way it was that day.

I suppose the same could be said of that Ute Indian Black Hawk, even though there wasn't any liquor involved on his part so far as I know. Still, he had an awful hate built up in him and that can muddle a man's mind every bit as much as drunkenness will. And that day it all come down to what was going on in Black Hawk's head as much as John Lowry's.

See, Black Hawk was a youngster when the Mormons first showed up in this country. The bunch he lived with spent most of the time just over the divide from Salt Lake Valley, there along the shores of Utah Lake. Them Utes was suspicious of us Mormons moving in but never raised much of a fuss — at least not at first. But when the white folks started catching all the fish they lived on, killing off all the game, and pushing them off land where they had lived forever, well, that led to trouble.

There was a fight that ended up in a rocky canyon there by the American Fork River when Black Hawk wasn't but a boy, and from what I was told, some of his kin was killed and he saw it happen. Then, later on, when there was that mess they had in the winter at Fort Utah down by the lake, it got even worse. That was way back in 1850 — February, as I recollect, but in the dead of winter for damn sure. They fought there at the fort for a time till the Utes left off across the lake ice and holed up on a benchland over there, a place called Table Mountain. Some militia followed after them and overran the camp, killing a bunch of the Indians, including some more of that boy Black Hawk's family.

Worst part of it was, some men led by some doctor went over there afterwards and cut the heads off of most of them dead Utes. Said it was in the interest of science or some such nonsense. Anyhow, that didn't sit well with Black Hawk and the other Indians, as you might imagine. And who the hell can blame them? Thing is, that Black Hawk, he wasn't too fond of white men at all after that.

Now, don't be settin' that pencil of yours aside. I know I tend to wander off the trail now and then, but bear with me. If you don't pay attention, you might miss something.

Back to what you asked about.

When John Lowry did what he did here in Sanpete that day, Black Hawk wasn't a boy anymore. Oh, he was still a young man, but he wasn't no boy. Them Utes had a whole lot of respect for him, and they listened to what he had to say and followed his lead. Not only just his band, but Utes all around. So he was here that day. I suppose word had got around amongst the Indians that there was to be a parley that day and Black Hawk came to see what the white men had to say. Indians, too, I guess.

But it wasn't Black Hawk who took the lead when them Utes showed up to talk. And it wasn't him that caused the trouble. Mostly, he just sat there horseback and watched and listened. Hell, looking back, I don't think there was many of the town men that was there that even knowed who he was, if any of them did. Just another Indian, far as they knew.

The one who caused all the trouble — the one besides John Lowry, I mean — was this Indian that went by Jake Arapeen. Oh, I suppose he had some other name with the Utes that white folks couldn't get their tongues around, so he was known by us — and maybe amongst them as well — as Jake Arapeen.

What happened was, there had been troubles for some time, what with Utes making off with a cow now and then, sometimes a few head. See, they didn't think nothing of it. If they were hungry and there was food to be had, they took it. Same as they would an elk or a deer. Hell, even a jackass rabbit, come to that. That the cow might belong to someone didn't make no difference to them, see. Far as they was concerned nobody owned anything — it was all there for the taking by whoever needed it.

But that ain't the way it works whenever there's white folks involved. Everybody's worried about who owns what, and if you want something somebody else has got, you pay for it. 'Course that never mattered when it come to taking land from the Indians, but that was the way of it. I guess you can see why them Utes thought there wasn't nothing wrong with taking a cow now and then.

The white folks weren't having it, though. And that's why there was this meeting that day. Lowry and some of the men from the town and some of the Utes had agreed to meet at a certain time and place and try to work out some kind of arrangement — that meaning that the Indians wasn't to steal any more stock or there would be hell to pay. Most likely the Utes already knowed there wouldn't be anything in it for them, as there never was when it came to parleying with the white men. All give and no take, is what it was for them.

And the Utes was ready to give that day — they brought along a horse to give to Lowry to pay for the cow of his they took. But he wasn't having none of it. He wanted his cow. In a way you couldn't blame him. If you'd been around back then you'd of seen that the loss of one cow could make a hell of a difference to some of the settlers. Most all of us was poor and barely getting by, so it ain't like we could stand seeing any of what we worked hard for disappear without so much as a by-your-leave.

Now, maybe you're wondering what it was I was doing there at that meeting, what with me being nothing but a kid. See, with cattle getting drove off the grazing grounds, the men had started sending us boys out to watch the herd.

Maybe I had best say something about cow herds and how it worked back then. See, the Mormons did things different when they settled country than what most folks did. Nobody — well, hardly nobody, there was always a few who wouldn't go along with the program — lived out on their farms. Everybody lived in town, and the farm fields was laid out outside of the town and given to each family according to what they could take care of. Out beyond the fields is where the town cow herd was kept. There wasn't any particular piece of property given to one man for his cows to graze — they was all run together in one big bunch.

Most times, someone from the town would just ride out every day or so to check on the herd and maybe push them onto better grass. But whenever the Indians took it in mind to take a few head for their cooking pots, the cows would be kept closer to town and watched over, especially at night. We never worried about it so much in the daytime as the men working the fields could more or less keep an eye on the herd.

But to get back where I was, that day was a Sunday, so no one was working in the fields. Everybody was at church meetings most all day. But they wanted somebody to keep watch on account of the cows that was getting stole, like I said. That day it was just my turn, I guess. Not that I minded. Most times them church meetings went on so long you could get rump sprung sitting on them wooden benches, so being out on my old horse wasn't no cause for woe — fact is, I liked it fine.

Anyway, the men who were assigned to meet with the Utes came riding out of town and I just kind of drifted along with them when they rode on to the meeting place. I could tell John Lowry must have missed going to church on account of it was clear that keeping one leg on each side of his horse took some effort. Even with me being a kid and not having been around liquor much at all — my old man didn't hold with it and there never was a drop of it in our house — I knew enough to see that Lowry had been at the bottle. It was a wonder why they never sent him back to town, what with his temper and all. Things sure would have turned out different if they had sent him home, that's for sure. But like I said — did I say so? — one of the cows that got took had carried the Lowry brand, so I guess maybe they figured he had a right to be there.

Things started off about as you'd expect. Lowry did most of the talking. He cussed the Indians up one side and down the other for their thievery. An old Indian we called Old Joe talked for the Utes mostly, with some others pitching in now and then, with that Jake Arapeen being the loudest of them.

Anyway, Old Joe, he told of how the cows and horses and sheep the settlers had brung in was using up all the grass, and all the elk that used to be there had been scared off, and how them elk and the deer had been ran off into the high country — them that hadn't been shot, that is — where it was hard to hunt them. He said all the plants and seeds and such the Utes used for food had been plowed under, or trompled into the ground by the stock. And that their people wasn't allowed to pitch their tents where they used to as they moved around the valley, on account of the white folks's towns, and no matter wherever they set up camp the white folks would come along and push them off.

All that was true, I guess, both what Lowry said about the Indians stealing, and what that fellow Old Joe said about the white folks. Still, there wasn't either side making any headway, and as the palavering went on things started in to getting heated.

One thing, though. While Jake Arapeen and some other Utes sometimes stuck their noses into the argument, Black Hawk never said a word. He just sat there on his horse calm as a cornstalk on a day when the wind don't blow. You'd never of guessed what kind of hell he'd raise on account of that meeting. For years afterward, he led them Utes in a war against the settlers like you never seen the like of. Hell, not only the Utes, of which he used every band there was in his fight, but he also recruited some Navajos and Paiutes and even some Apaches from time to time.

Not all of them was in on the fighting. Some of them he used to move the cow herds he stole. See, all through that Black Hawk War them Indians raided herds all over this valley and most all the rest of the territory. They made off with thousands of head of stock. You no doubt heard tell all them stories about cowboys trailing herds out of Texas starting about that same time. Well, them Texans never had nothing over Black Hawk and his Utes. Oh, the Indians never herded as many cattle, maybe, but they had just as good a system. Mormon cows they drove off went from tribe to tribe, getting passed along till finally getting sold down in Santa Fe, or maybe Mexico. They even drove herds as far as Los Angeles, way out there in California.

So it was mostly a war where the Indians would sweep in and run off with stock. Oh, it ain't like there wasn't any shooting. Whenever them raiders would find anyone out on their own, or traveling in small bunches, they'd run them down and kill them. Now and then they would come into a town and shoot up the place, but not that much. Still, from what I've been told, there was dozens and scores of settlers killed by Indians.

There was plenty of Indians killed, too — more than whites, they say. But what they won't say is that a lot of the Utes that got killed was women and old folks — even kids. There was times the troops — we called them troops, but what they was was just men from the towns organized into militia type of outfits — maybe I ought to say something about that.

You might of thought the government would send out the army to put down the Indians like they did everywhere else. But it wasn't that way here in Utah, most times. We — meaning the Mormons — never did get along with the United States government. Our folks had been at odds with them ever since our troubles back in Missouri in the thirties, and in Nauvoo after that.

And the government never trusted us, either, what with some of the stuff Brother Brigham and some of the other head men in the church was always saying. It damn near came to a shooting war between us and them when they sent the army out here in '57. Them troops left once the War Between the States started up, but pretty soon there was other soldiers sent into here from out in California to keep watch on us so we didn't side with the Southerners or start a fight of our own.

So there was soldiers here when Black Hawk took up his raids, but the army wanted nothing to do with it. And Brigham Young never wanted them sticking their noses into anything to do with us. Anyway, any Indian fighting that got done got done by those militias I told you about. "Nauvoo Legion" is what they was called. But like I said, they was just the men from each of the towns — including my pa and my uncles and even granddad now and then — who was called up to be part of it even though they never had much in the way of military training or anything like that.

Still, they went about their work like they meant it and whenever there was any hint of Indians being around, they'd saddle up and take after them. Mostly they just chased the Utes around from Dan to Beersheba and from hell to breakfast and hardly ever caught up with them. But now and then they'd get to fighting and there'd be some Indians killed and some militia men killed. Still, it wasn't like there was big battles where lots of Utes and lots of Mormons faced off against one another to shoot it out. Mostly there were just running fights — and more running than fighting.

But before it was all over, the Utes had managed not only to drive off most of the stock over hundreds of square miles, they'd managed to drive off most of the settlers, too. Brother Brigham sent down word to abandon most of the towns and fort up in them that was easier to defend. Around these parts, Fountain Green, Fairview, and Moroni was shut down. Farther south, them that had settled Richfield, Salina, and Glenwood pulled up stakes like the folks in Marysvale and Circleville had done. Hell, even Panguitch got abandoned. So did Glendale and Long Valley and Mount Carmel. Bunch of other towns, all the same. There was a few years there where Black Hawk and his people had all but driven the Mormons plumb out of this country.

Well, hell, I've wandered off the trail so far I can't even recollect where I lost the track. Mark my words, sonny, getting old ain't no Sunday School picnic. How I've held on this long is a mystery — most folks my age has been feeding worms for years by now. You get old and your body turns on you, and your mind gets so full of holes you can't even remember when last you had a sit-down in the backhouse, and between losing your mind and losing control of your bodily functions you might miss out on a trip to the outhouse altogether — and that's a hell of a mess, not to mention downright embarrassing. . . .

Now, where was I?

Oh, right, that meeting with Black Hawk and them when all hell broke loose.

Like I said, I ain't altogether sure *why* it happened like it did. Lowry being drunk had something to do with it, I suppose. That Indian Jake Arapeen being hotheaded, too. Between the two of them being the way they was that day, I guess it wasn't no surprise trouble would come. Nobody expected it, though, and nobody seen it coming. There had been plenty of such parleys between our people and theirs before, and there never was any trouble like what there was that day.

Like I said, Jake Arapeen got all het up when he wasn't happy with the way Old Joe was handling things for the Indian side, so he started in to hollering and cussing. That threw a few logs onto John Lowry's fire and he started in to hollering and cussing right back.

After a few minutes of that, Jake Arapeen lifted an arrow out of his pouch and fitted it to his bowstring, his bow having been hung over his shoulder all this time. When he did that, he made Lowry even madder. Lowry kicked his horse in the guts and rode right up beside that Indian and reached out and grabbed him by the hair of his head and yanked him plumb off his horse.

Then he bailed out of the saddle and took ahold of Jake Arapeen and started in to beating him about the head and shoulders. Some of the town men stepped down, and so did some of the Utes. They managed to pull Lowry off of Jake, but not before that Indian was bleeding from his nose and had his bottom lip split apart, so his teeth was all bloody, too.

Now, I don't know what all you know about Indians and their ways, but giving an Indian man a thrashing like that was worse than killing him. They just didn't cotton to having their pride damaged, see, and for one man to do that to another was considered downright cowardly. Either kill a man or leave him alone was their way of looking at things.

By that time, me and Black Hawk was the only two out of the bunch still horseback. Everybody else was dismounted — Lowry and Jake on account of the fight, and the rest of the Utes and the town men from trying to stop it. Me, I just sat there not knowing what to do and halfway scared to death.

But Black Hawk — well, to look at him, which I did, you'd never know there was anything untoward going on at all. He just sat there looking on, not saying or doing anything. But when he turned to look at me, there was a fire deep in his eyes like nothing I had ever seen before and ain't never seen since.

He reined his horse around and rode off. Them other Utes got Jake Arapeen back aboard his horse and they mounted up and rode off after Black Hawk.

What's that you say? Lowry?

Well, after he sobered up, I guess he maybe felt kind of bad about what happened, but not too much. He was about as pigheaded as a sulled-up old cow, so it never bothered him too much about what he set loose when he beat the tar out of Jake Arapeen that day.

Here . . . .

Here's a piece I tore out of the newspaper years back where Lowry spoke his mind about it. He didn't get all the details right when he told this years later. Some of it might be on account of how memories fade and get muddled over time. Some of it might of been him trying to make hisself and his part in it sound better that what it was.

Anyhow, go on and read it. Be careful, that paper's old and brittle, but you can still read what it says all right. Make of it what you will. I'll be damned if I know any more about it than what I've said.

I agreed to meet with them at Manti about the eighth of April and talk the matter over of their killing our cattle. Accordingly, the council took place. It appeared the difficulty would be settled amicably, but a certain young Indian continued to halloo and make demonstrations. I told him a time or two to let me finish my talk. Just then someone called out "lookout, he is getting his arrows!" I rode up to him and turned him off his horse, and pulled him to the ground. The bystanders interfered and we separated. I believe they started hostilities sooner than they would have done had not the incident above mentioned occurred. But the trouble would have come just the same. I have patiently borne the stigma placed upon me, for I knew the facts, and to those who still persist in looking upon me as guilty of precipitating the Black Hawk War I will say this, that I appeal from their decision to a higher court — Our Creator, who will ultimately judge all men. —John Lowry

#

For a variety of reasons, primarily owing to the insular nature of Mormons who settled the region, much of Utah's history gets little notice. Although the Black Hawk War, which ravaged the territory from 1865 until 1872 and essentially depopulated much of Utah of white settlers and their livestock, it is little noted in histories of the West. The protracted struggle also resulted in significant depredations and the deaths of numerous Mormons and Paiutes alike. There are stories there worth telling.

—Rod Miller

Rod Miller writes novels, short stories, poetry, history, and magazine articles about the American West, with some two dozen books and scores of magazine articles to his credit. Recognition for his work includes four Western Writers of America Spur Awards, two Western Fictioneers Peacemaker Awards, two Westerners International Poetry Awards, and the Academy of Western Artists Poetry Book of the Year award.

Raised in a cowboy family in a small town in Utah, Miller rode for the Utah State University Rodeo Team. He has worked as a cowboy, ranch hand, farm laborer, in an underground hard-rock mine, as a radio disc jockey, in television broadcasting and production, and spent decades as an advertising agency copywriter and creative director. Now retired, he spends his time writing about the West.

TREMORS OF THE PAST

NIK JAMES

*D*enver, Colorado
November 7, 1882

Henry Jordan stood across the street from the office of the *Rocky Mountain News*, Denver's largest newspaper. Pulling up the collar of his elk-skin coat against the cold wind, he screwed down his black, wide-brimmed hat a little tighter. The silvery disk of a sun had disappeared a couple of hours earlier. But on each of the three floors, every damn window was ablaze with light, and the building glowed in the November darkness.

Just looking across at the place stoked the anger that had been simmering inside him for too long. Maybe he was tired and hungry. Maybe he was thirty-one and feeling every one of those long years in the saddle.

Or maybe he was just feeling like it was time to settle the score. It had been sitting in his craw for almost five years now. And that was long enough.

Henry took the leather wallet from the inner pocket of his coat and pulled out the yellowed news clipping. Unfolding it, he held the paper up to the brand new electric streetlight and studied the name of the sonovabitch who'd penned the slander. *N.J. Hawk.*

Yes, Henry had been in that damn fight. No, he hadn't started it. Still, he'd served jail time and paid his dues. And since then, he'd worked hard to be a respectable citizen of Elkhorn, running a cattle ranch with his friend and partner Caleb Marlowe. This article had been written a year after the fight. And what for?

Henry glanced up at the windows across the way, hoping Mr. Hawk was sitting at his desk right now. The fella was about to get a visit from the past. And he wasn't going to like it much.

Putting the paper back in his pocket, Henry crossed the street and marched into the building.

The small lobby was lit by a chandelier, and two sets of stairs led to upper floors. Straight ahead of him, the newspaper's name was painted on the pebbled windows of large double doors. He strode across the lobby and pulled one open.

Before he could enter, though, a woman suddenly backed out, bumping into him.

With gleaming black hair pinned up on the back of her head, she was wearing a high-necked white blouse and a long black skirt. Under each arm, she was carrying folders stuffed with papers. The collision staggered her, and she clutched at the slipping folders.

Henry reached out to help her, but she righted herself and backed away.

"I have them," she said. "Thank you."

He tipped his hat.

Without another word, she crossed to a door by the stairs, pried it open, and disappeared.

As Henry turned back toward the office, he stepped on a folder.

When he picked it up, a page slipped out, and a few words on the paper jumped out at him. Pushing it back in, he followed her and went through the door and found himself at the top of a wooden stairwell. It was fairly dark, but he could see a dim light down below.

He descended and at the bottom found a wooden door with the words 'Records - Private' painted on it. It was slightly ajar, so he pulled it open and went in.

The musty smell of old paper and ink hit him square in the face. A single bulb dangling over a large wooden table illuminated the room. The cellar was a storage area for old editions. Rows of shelves stretched out into the darkness. An ancient printing press sat in pieces by one wall.

The woman was alone, standing at the table, staring at him, alarmed. Her folders were stacked in front of her, and she had one in her hand.

"You dropped this, miss," he said, holding the one she'd dropped out to her.

Josie Sinclair's pulse quickened as the door at the top of the stairs creaked open. She heard the thud of boots coming down the wooden steps, each one deliberate, as if whoever was coming knew exactly where they were headed.

She'd planned to be down here at an hour when there was little chance of running into anyone else. A news office is naturally populated by nosy people. But in this cellar space, she was safe from curious glances and prying eyes.

This research was personal, and what she hoped to eventually write about would be frowned upon and possibly rejected by her superiors.

But two generations of keeping secrets had taken a painful toll on the women in her family. Josie was the first one in a position to expose the lies that had been told and retold. Her ancestors were long gone, but she'd be damned before she'd see them erased from history.

And if the men upstairs refused to print the truth, she'd find another paper in this country that *would* print it.

Josie's eyes darted to the door of the record room as it swung open, and she recognized the tall man she'd collided with in the lobby.

"You dropped this, miss."

She had no chance to take it. As Josie started to reach for the folder in the stranger's outstretched hand, the table began to shake violently. The floor beneath her feet rolled like the deck of a small boat on river rapids, throwing her off balance. The piles of papers on the table spread out and spilled onto the floor, and the crash of shelves behind her raised a cloud of dust.

The walls shuddered and groaned in protest as a low rumble filled the air, and the sound of falling furniture somewhere above reverberated dully. The packed dirt floor rolled again, and the door behind the stranger slammed shut with a bang.

A second later, the light above the table flickered with a rasping buzz and then died completely.

Josie felt like she'd suddenly been thrown into the black abyss of a bottomless hole. Her heart raced as she grabbed for the desk.

Once again, the floor rose and fell beneath her feet like a living thing, and she held on for dear life.

The man's voice was calm in the darkness. "Earthquake. Hold on. It should stop soon."

Then, as suddenly as it began, the shaking and rolling stopped.

"I've never felt anything like that," she gasped, her heartbeat still a loud drum in her ears. "Terrifying."

"The brick walls are standing," he said. "Reckon the building is solid enough."

Josie listened intently to his tone. Low and almost conversational.

The building trembled again, but this time, it wasn't an earthquake. The rumbling came from above. Panic-stricken people rushed to flee.

"Let's get out of here," she said, listening to the furor.

"Yup. Not a bad idea." There was an odd tranquility in his words, as if the situation didn't faze him in the slightest. "That door's over here somewhere."

"There's a lamp." Josie felt for the end of the table, pulled the oil lamp from its hook, and set it on top.

"I got a match," he said.

In the darkness, she couldn't see his face, but there was something about him — something so steady — and his composure wrapped around her like a blanket on a cold night.

A sharp *scratch* cut through the room, and flickering matchlight illuminated his face. Her fingers closed around the base of the lamp.

For a second, their gazes locked in the soft glow, and she recalled her first impression of him upstairs. Extremely handsome, but there was more. There was a quiet confidence in the way he moved.

He reached across the table, and his fingers brushed against hers as he lifted the glass chimney and put the match to the wick. The flame caught.

He shook out his match and went to the door.

Josie began to gather up the files, adding the one he'd dropped on the desk. The room felt too small. The dust was settling, but the air was suffocating.

She watched him try the door. He turned the handle, but it wouldn't budge. He put his shoulder to it. Nothing. He stood back and hit it harder, putting more weight into it. Still nothing.

"It's jammed," he said. "But we'll be alright."

Josie thought about Amna, who lived with her in a small house close to the newspaper office. A wave of panic clenched her stomach. Their neighbors would likely check on her grandmother's wellbeing, but Josie needed to get home to her.

She had reason to worry. As her grandmother aged, she dwelled more and more on the past. Amna would often talk about people long gone — and in particular, people lost in an earthquake she experienced in her childhood. Those stories were actually the reason why Josie was down here, digging for information long buried with the passage of time. Another surge of worry brought Josie to the edge of panic. She had to get home.

And then the walls began to shake again.

No matter how hard Henry slammed his big body against the door, it wouldn't give. Either the wall had shifted, or something heavy had collapsed behind it. And there was nothing in sight he could use to force it open. The sound of the exodus above had faded, and he cast a glance over his shoulder. Even in the dim light, the tension in the woman's face as she stood by the desk was unmistakable.

He couldn't blame her. They were caught in a building that could come down around their ears at any moment. Plus, she was trapped alone in a room with a strange man. Not a comfortable situation in either case.

The ground shuddered again, and she gripped the desk with both hands. Thankfully, this tremor was brief and far less severe than the last one.

"You can't get it open?" she asked.

"Jammed. Or something's blocking it on the other side." He needed to calm her, so he lied. "People in the lobby saw me come down. Someone will look for us soon. We'll get out."

"Those same people most likely ran for their lives. What happens if no one comes?"

"They'll come for us. I'm sure." Henry said gently, his voice steady and reassuring. He glanced at the folders, searching for a distraction. "So what do you do at this newspaper, Miss . . . Miss . . . ?"

"Sinclair. Josie Sinclair."

"Henry Jordan. Pleased to meet you." A chair sat next to the door, so he placed it closer to the table. Not too close, though. He didn't want to make her any more nervous than she was. "Might as well make ourselves comfortable."

With a glance at the door, the woman frowned slightly. Then she nodded and righted a chair that had tipped over behind the table. Henry sat down, and she followed suit, sitting ramrod straight on the edge of the seat.

"What do you do at the paper, Miss Sinclair?" he repeated.

"Why did you come down here, Mr. Jordan?"

"That folder you dropped," he reminded her.

"Yes, thank you. But you could have handed it to anyone who works at the paper. Why follow me down here?"

"Good point." He admired her directness, her lack of hesitation. He respected smart women who didn't turn dreamy-eyed in his presence. "Well, I accidentally noticed the mention of the Acjachemen people on a paper that slipped out of your folder."

One shapely eyebrow arched as her eyes met his. "You can pronounce the tribe's name."

"Actually, Miss Sinclair, I'm sorta familiar with some of their history."

Her eyes widened, and she tilted her head as if reconsidering him. "I'd like to hear what you know about them, Mr. Jordan."

Henry turned his chair a little so that he could keep an eye on the door, then settled back. "They're one of the tribes along the southern coast of California. All ranch lands now, and not many of them left, but those folks lived there since before the Spanish ever set foot in the place and long before we took it all and made a state of it."

"I find your knowledge of them quite remarkable, Mr. Jordan. Very few people here in Colorado have ever heard of the Acjachemen." Her eyes narrowed. "So, how is it that you know so much?"

Henry considered his answer before he spoke. Most people who knew him were unaware of his parentage. But at this point in his life, he didn't care what people thought.

"I have a personal interest in the Indian nations." He held her gaze. "You see, I'm half Crow myself. Through my mother."

"I see."

"But if most folks round here don't know about Acjachemen people, Miss Sinclair, why are *you* interested? And you've been holding your cards close to your vest about what you do at this newspaper."

Josie wasn't about to admit anything regarding her job to this stranger.

Not that what she did on a daily basis had anything to do with the collection of letters and articles and notes that sat on the table between them. But seeing how easily Henry Jordan spoke of his roots made her feel comfortable enough to share something no one working upstairs knew.

"I too have Indian blood, Mr. Jordan. I am a descendant of the Acjachemen."

"You don't say." He sat forward and planted his elbows on his knees. "We're a long way from California. How'd you end up in Denver?"

"My grandmother, my Amna, was sent away when she was a girl. Oddly enough, after an earthquake. She was just only twelve years old at the time, and that quake killed her mother."

"I'm sorry to hear that, miss."

"Thank you. It happened seventy years ago, back in 1812, but she still likes to tell the story as if it happened yesterday."

He gestured toward the door. "Well, we have some time, I reckon. And I'd like to hear her story and yours, if you don't mind sharing."

Josie considered it. Amna's life wasn't the most uplifting story, given their current situation, but Henry Jordan seemed genuinely attentive. Besides, he was the only person outside her family who showed any interest.

Maybe this was her chance to practice retelling some of what she'd long wanted to write. She took a closer look at the man before her. Amna always said Josie had a gift for reading someone's character and intentions right from the start — a gift passed down through generations. They'd only just met, but she felt at ease with him. Even trusted him.

"What I share goes no further."

"I'm no reporter, miss."

"All right," she started. "You probably know this, but like other European explorers, the Spanish came for conquest and riches. Starting in Mexico, they pushed northward in search of gold and silver, bringing Franciscan priests along. Together, they built a series of missions that had barracks for soldiers. Well, they didn't actually build them. At each site, the soldiers rounded up the local Indians and forced them to build the missions, while the priests busied themselves converting the natives to Christianity. It worked out quite well for the conquerors. The missionaries got ranches, farmland, mines, and laborers to work the land, while the soldiers gained forts to control the region."

"And the Acjachemen were among those tribes," he put in.

"Yes, my own people were called Juaneños by the Franciscans because they belonged to the mission at San Juan Capistrano." Josie placed a hand on one of the folders. "That's where an earthquake in 1812 destroyed the stone church in the middle of a service. It killed forty Acjachemen people. Women and children. No white people died that day. None. Only my people."

She'd spent years researching, even traveling to California once and listening to first-hand accounts of that earthquake. But as she stared at the pages of notes on the table, raw emotions tightened in her throat.

"And your grandmother was there."

"She was one of four children in the church who survived."

"Four." The man whistled softly. "How old was she?"

"Twelve years old."

Josie thought of her Amna, seated by the fireplace, sewing as she told the story. With age, forgetfulness had begun to creep in, and the older woman was terrified of losing the memories — of not passing on the truth of what happened.

"Let me tell it the way she told me," Josie said, pausing to listen as she gathered her thoughts. Still, there was no sound of rescuers. She took a deep breath and began. "My Amna never liked the priests. Never trusted them. . . ."

I never liked the priests, my Josita. Never trusted them.

Our people were peaceful. Our village was one of the largest along the shore. It was called Toovanja. Hundreds lived there along the bluff where the river reached the sea. At one time, it was a thriving place. Fresh water flowed down from inland mountains, clean and lifegiving. The sea and the land fed us all.

I heard the stories as a little girl, events that came before me, whispers of our history, told by the old women with cautious glances. They had to speak in whispers. If the padres heard them, the punishment was harsh. Days in the stocks without even a drop of water. Whippings. And worse.

For generations, there had been no war, no disease. We hunted deer and elk and mountain lion. When one of the great whales washed onto our beaches, we roasted the meat. Our *nota* — the village clan chief — would declare it a time of great feasting. Indians who lived on the islands nearby — especially the one the Spaniards called Santa Catalina — would see the clouds of smoke and come in their wooden boats. In exchange for dried meat, whale bones, and the baskets we weaved, we would receive the skins of seal and otter, colorful abalone shells.

Before the Spaniards arrived, other Indian people visited us in the summers, camping along the beaches. They traveled through the mountain pass from a great lake far inland, bringing goods to trade. When the autumn fogs descended, they would return to their homes.

It was a good life.

When the white men came, everything changed. Even though we welcomed them, the soldiers ravaged our village on the shore while the padres looked the other way. Men were killed or taken to work. Women were assaulted and raped. I was born after my mother was forced by one of the soldiers from the garrison there.

In my earliest memories, the village was a dying place. We were no longer allowed to fish or hunt, and most of the food we gathered was taken by the leather jackets. Sickness spread, and many of our people died. But it was still our home.

Then, one afternoon, our *nota* was dragged from his hut and staked to the ground. He had defied the padres, and they could not abide that. We were forced to watch as he was tied to the ground and gutted like an animal. After that, all we had been taught about how we should live was banned. Our community. Our rituals of life and death. Our language. All crushed by the white men. It was a time of great sorrow.

We soon learned the plan of the padres and the soldiers. They came with a sword in one hand and a cross in the other. They were building mission after mission — and a chain of armed garrisons — until they controlled a vast empire in the name of Spain and their God. When the native people resisted, they faced steel blades, powder, and shot. They were slaughtered in the land their fathers and mothers had inhabited since the beginning of time.

So one after another, the missions were built. As each one was finished, the padres and the soldiers drove some of the younger laborers farther up the coast to build the next.

The Mission San Juan Capistrano was built a short distance from our village. The construction was still going on when I was a small child. I remember clearly our people being rounded up before dawn each morning and forced to walk up the trail along the river to quarry the stone and bring the oak timbers down from the surrounding hills.

One spring night, without warning, the village was put to the torch. Our people were driven like cattle up to the mission, and our new life began in earnest. The land around the mission was planted with Spanish crops. We had never been farmers, but we labored at it now. Horses and cattle were raised for trade, and we became herders, as well.

The land changed and suffered, but the padres paid no heed. The ancient oak trees were cut down, and the grasses and plants that remained turned yellow and brown, and every summer, the fires burned the dry land all the way to the mountains. Except for the times when the floods came, our river became nothing more than a small stream.

The padres had a plan for our spiritual lives, too. Once our own rituals were outlawed, we were forced to learn about and practice their religion. There was no choice in the matter. Land and wealth for the king; our souls for God.

Most of our people did not believe in the new religion. But to survive, they pretended. The padres had very little patience for those who resisted them. I remember many times when men would be whipped or beaten with canes outside the church door for refusing to go in to worship. One time, I heard a padre tell a soldier, "Break the man and save the soul."

Our souls were important to them, so long as we worked. We had elected a new *nota* who told the people to stop working. It was summer and very hot when the leather jackets brought him out to a field not far from the mission. While they beat the *nota* with sticks, a calf was killed and skinned. The young chief was sewn into the skin and staked in the sun for the whole day. He died before sundown.

Our souls. When we had an outbreak of smallpox, many men, women and children died. The padre in charge of the mission said that "their souls were a great harvest." But after that, they became worried that there would not be enough Juaneños to work the fields and care for the livestock.

Husbands and wives were encouraged to have more children, and when they didn't, trouble began. One husband was beaten nearly to death when he refused to couple with his wife in front of the padres to prove they were trying. When the woman refused to let the priests examine her private parts, she was given fifty lashes and then made to stand holding a wooden baby doll in front of the church for nine days.

But in their eyes, we were truly seen as little more than the animals we tended. A kind of monkey, one padre liked to say. We were only capable of mimicking superior men.

So the padres prospered, and our souls were 'harvested' for their God.

And the work went on. The missions were built from stone and blood. Our blood.

It was winter when the earthquake happened. I was twelve years old. I'd lived most of my life inside the mission. It was only when another terrible fever broke out in the *monjerio* — the separate quarters where girls were kept until marriage — that I went to stay with a family by the river, where many Indians were now forced to live.

The morning was cold and clear, and the sun was just rising over the mountains when I took the family's three children to the mission for Mass. We had to go to the early service because the High Mass later on would be only for men.

When we entered, the padre in charge on the mission was standing by the heavy oak door, his iron keys hanging from his belt. Two soldiers from the garrison were with him, making sure no one tarried outside. We were the last ones in, and the door closed behind us. I heard the padre's iron key turn in the lock.

Two of them were saying Mass on the altar, with only Acjachemen women in the church. As children, we had to stand at the back. I was looking for my mother and had just spotted her on the far side when suddenly the ground shuddered and began to shake. Pieces fell from the walls and candles tipped over on the altar.

Before anyone could move, a crack opened in the wall beside me, and I heard bells crash to the ground outside.

Women were screaming. The padres grabbed silver chalices and candlesticks. They ran for the side door. They told a different story later, of course, but they were the first to flee the church.

The shrieks were loud, and some women had been hit by falling stone.

A portion of the ceiling fell near the back of the church, close to me. The ground was still moving, but I grabbed the children and pushed them toward the front. I could see the side entrance where the padres ran out was open.

We were not allowed to use that door. It was only for their use . . . and for important Spaniards who sometimes came to the mission. But the roof and walls were falling around us.

Before we could reach the front of the church, a young padre reappeared in the door. He dashed to the altar and grabbed the gleaming silver crucifix. He pushed us aside and ran out as another padre slammed the door shut.

We pulled at the door and cried out, but it wouldn't open.

I turned to see the rest of the women crowded at the back of the church. They were clawing and beating at the heavy oak door, and it would not open. Women were screaming. The padre had locked it when we came in.

The ground shook hard again — harder than before — and the stone tower crashed onto the roof. It was then that everything at the back of the church, roof and walls, came down on the women.

And then, the ground stopped shaking.

The stunned silence that followed was surely like that of the grave. All those women, my mother included, were buried beneath stone and timber and dust. And there was not a sound.

I was still standing by the side door with the three children holding tight to me. We were choking on stone dust. The youngest child was pulling at my skirts and wailing.

The door never opened, so we climbed through the remains of a wall into the cold morning air.

It took weeks and weeks to dig out all the bodies of the dead. The Acjachemen people did the digging, of course. As the work went on, the padres were nowhere to be found. Finally, one of them came out and prayed over the one large grave where they laid the women and children.

More souls were harvested. More souls.

Not long afterward, I was sent north to Mission Santa Barbara and then San Luis Obispo.

But you must remember what happened, Josita. You must keep it in your heart. For your great-grandmother and the others, you must remember. . . .

Henry was struck speechless. He had no words that could soften the crushing weight of the grandmother's memory, nothing he could offer to ease the pain the story clearly stirred in Josie . . . or in himself. He had no doubt that the record of that earthquake and the church's ruin had been carefully tailored to absolve the guilt of those priests on that morning. But this story told a different tale. One that rang with hard, bitter truth.

Across the East, the West, the Plains — all across this vast land — native peoples had suffered since the first Europeans set foot here. Their ways of life and histories had been swept aside, made small and destroyed by those who saw themselves as rightful owners of lands held by these tribes for generations. Sickness, war, hunger, and the merciless pushing of tribes from place to place had been the weapons of the white man. The freedom of those who were still surviving, still fighting, was being stripped away.

On the reservations, Indians of every nation were struggling to stay alive and hold on to the remnants of their pride and their way of life. Their communities had been scattered, their traditions torn asunder, but Henry knew there were so many still standing against a world that was determined to take everything they held dear, piece by piece.

"Are you going to do something with your grandmother's story?" he finally asked. "Have someone write it down? Publish it in this paper?"

"Something like that."

He jerked a thumb upward. "The wolves who write for this rag are only interested in selling papers. They're not in it for the truth." He couldn't hide the skepticism in his voice. "What are you doing with all these files?"

"Right now, I'm gathering any accounts or articles that have been published since the earthquake."

"And what have you found?"

"So far, not much. A lot of it is like this." She pulled out a news-paper, yellow in the lamplight. "An article written in a San Francisco paper seven years ago. It reported that nearly a hundred people died . . . and the journalist never thought it worth mentioning that those who lost their lives were Acjachemen. "

"History is written by the victors."

She arched her brow and then nodded slightly before straightening the papers.

Henry's eyes wandered over the piles of pages Josie had collected. He'd become a reader since settling down in Elkhorn. The main reason for it was Sheila, Caleb's New York-educated wife. After his friends had married, two wagonloads of books had arrived from back East for her. "Maybe this could make a good novel."

She shrugged.

"Know anybody who could do it? Make it a book, I mean."

"Maybe."

Josie leapt to her feet, as distant voices could be heard. Henry went over to the door, shouted, and banged hard with his fist.

Men's voices came from the top of the stairs. "Anyone down there?"

Henry answered, and boots clomped down the steps. Gruff commands and grunts accompanied the sound of wood scraping on the other side.

There was little he could do to help, but a minute later he was told to push against the door. Putting his weight against it, he managed to shove it open a crack. Immediately, Josie Sinclair slipped past him, her arms full of files, and disappeared into the darkness.

After putting out the lamp, Henry squeezed through, looking for her. She was nowhere in sight.

Three men stood on the other side, one of them holding a lantern. A floor joist had fallen and blocked the door, and when Henry told them there was no one else in the Records Room, the men started back up the stairs to continue searching for anyone else who might still be trapped in the building. They told him most of the regular workers in the newspaper office had gone home to check on their families.

Henry went up with them, hoping Josie would be waiting for him. But she wasn't at the top of the stairs. Nor was she in the lobby. The rescuers left him and continued up to the second floor.

Shattered shards of the pebbled windows bearing the newspaper's name lay scattered across the lobby floor. Beyond the open doors, a few people were moving about, picking up overturned furniture and papers that were strewn across the floor.

Henry stood in the lobby peering in, wondering if Josie might be in there. There was no sign of her.

Then again, it was more likely she went right out that front door, he thought.

He still hoped to see her, but it didn't look like that was going to happen tonight. If ever.

A stocky bull of a fellow wearing a black bowler and a silver vest came out from the newspaper office, clutching a stack of paper in his hand. He had a fat, unlit cigar clenched in his teeth, and he fixed a glare on Henry with the look of a man who owned the place.

"Can I help you?"

"Don't think so."

"Then what are you doing here?"

The newspaper article that had brought him into the building had nearly been forgotten.

"Maybe you can help me. I'm looking for a reporter named —"

"If there's a reporter left in this building, I can promise you they won't be working here by morning. They're all out getting stories for tomorrow's edition." He paused. "Who are you looking for?"

Henry touched his pocket. "N.J. Hawk."

The man pulled a watch from a vest pocket and glanced at it. "She just left. Surprised you missed her."

"*She?*"

"That's right," he said. "She was stuck down in the Records Room. Thankfully, someone went down and found her. Come back tomorrow."

Without another word, the newspaperman went up the stairs, and Henry watched him go as the information sank in.

N.J. Hawk. Josie Sinclair.

Henry strode from the building and stood on the sidewalk. At least a half dozen fires were burning in the distance, their flames climbing high over the city. He barely saw them.

Josie Sinclair. N.J. Hawk. One and the same.

Well, hell.

#

Living near the historic San Juan Capistrano Mission, Nikoo and Jim are drawn to the complex history of California and to the role the Spanish missions played in shaping that part of the Old West. In writing this story, they wanted to explore the profound impact of these missions as instruments of conquest and control, bringing to light the human stories behind a period marked by both expansion and exploitation.

—Nik James

Nikoo Kafi and Jim McGoldrick are the bestselling writing duo behind the pen names Nik James, May McGoldrick, and Jan Coffey. With backgrounds in engineering and literature, they've combined their talents to create over fifty historical, contemporary, and Western novels, captivating readers with their vivid characters and action-packed plots. Their work has garnered numerous awards, including a Will Rogers Medallion, a Daphne DuMaurier Award, and a Connecticut Press Club Award for Best Fiction. Their novels have been translated into over a dozen languages. Based in California, they continue to write stories that resonate with readers around the world.

Five Miles from Yank's Station

Mary Fan

"We are not enemies, but friends. We must not be enemies. Though passion may have strained, it must not break our bonds of affection. The mystic chords of memory, stretching from every battlefield and patriot grave to every living heart and hearthstone all over this broad land, will yet swell the chorus of the Union, when again touched, as surely they will be, by the better angels of our nature."

Abraham Lincoln
First Inaugural Address
March 4, 1861

I'd always loved riding fast, and riding far. Was always small for my age, too. Which was why, when I saw those Pony Express posters looking for riders, just a few months after Pa followed Ma into the grave, I knew it was me they were looking for. Took them a little longer to catch on, though. Somehow, those fools got it in their heads that a boy having brown skin had something to do with his ability to ride.

But that was June of 1860, right around when I turned 14, and the war with the Paiute Indians had killed a bunch of riders and spooked a whole lot more into quitting or refusing to sign up. So the company couldn't afford to be picky.

Besides, I was a damn good rider.

In March of 1861, I was among those tasked with delivering President Lincoln's Inaugural Address across a shattering nation. Despite all I'd heard about the South wanting to secede because they'd rather cleave the country in two than consider someone like me a whole person, I was still somehow hopeful. I remember imagining each hoofprint my ponies left behind, as we carried the president's words, to be stitches that might sew America back together.

No history book would record that Carlos Castillo — called "Carlitos" by my friends and "Charlie" by everyone else — rode a hundred miles at top speed for twenty straight hours, pausing only to change ponies at each relay station. And few know how close we came to losing one of the most famous speeches in American history, or how wrathful the man who tried to silence the president became when he failed. In fact, most don't believe the story when I tell it.

But I'm gonna tell it again anyway.

By the time I reached Yank's Station, California's easternmost remount station, I was so exhausted, I could barely see straight. Part of me was disappointed that I wouldn't get to be the one to finish the job, but a greater part was looking forward to a break.

When I saw Bill Walker and his pony silhouetted by the afternoon sun, waiting by the station's low buildings for the hand-off, a sigh of relief escaped me. With my pony still galloping at top speed, I grabbed the mochila containing Lincoln's speech, plus a few other pieces of mail.

I must've ridden a hundred mounts in my time at the Pony Express, and for the most part I didn't know their names, or whether they even had them. This one, though, this little brown fellow, with a white cluster of spots on his left flank, I recall. His name was Arrow.

Before I could reach Bill, a gunshot went off.

Startled, Arrow reared. I leaned forward against his back and managed to stay on. My pulse thundered. I'd been shot at before — that was part of life when you lived out West — but it wasn't exactly the kind of thing you got used to.

I looked around wildly, wondering who had fired, and why.

"Get the bag, boys!" a gruff voice called out. A brawny white man — who looked three times my size — with brown hair and a thick horseshoe mustache rode toward me, leading half a dozen others. Everything he wore was brown, from his hat to his trousers, except for his red kerchief. He pointed at me with a shotgun. "Don't let that rider get away!"

Except "rider" wasn't the word he used.

Not everyone wanted California to hear the president's plea for unity.

My eyes flicked down to the revolver strapped to my belt, then over to Bill. I set my jaw and, still clutching the mochila in one hand, urged my pony forward. I had a job to do.

Jeff Giese, one of the men who worked at the station, rushed out and fired at my attackers. He was tall — maybe six-foot-four, with olive skin and dark hair and eyes. In between shots, he called toward the building, "Hurry up and get out here!"

Soon, several other men joined him. Gunfire rang out all around me, but I had no idea what was coming from where. I tried to focus only on the hand-off, and it seemed to me that Bill was doing the same. He rode toward me with one hand outstretched.

I'd just managed to toss him the mochila when a terrifying *bang* sounded right in my ear. Gasping, I whipped my head to the side and saw the mustached man a few yards from me. But he wasn't paying attention to me anymore. Instead, his gun was trained on Bill, who was now rapidly galloping away.

Fury shot through my veins. I seized my revolver and fired.

I didn't think I hit him, but I spooked his horse. The poor animal let out a great cry and bucked. The man flew through the air and landed in the brush by the road.

"*Pa!*" A panicked voice cut through the din. One of the other mounted attackers rode toward the man — a boy who looked about my age. He was pale and lanky with brown hair, and I couldn't help noticing that his kerchief was yellow, same as mine.

"I'm fine!" The man picked himself up.

"Charlie!" Jeff shouted. "Get inside!" He nodded toward the building, then took aim and fired toward the mounted gang.

Still clinging to Arrow's reins, I shouted back, "Do you know who that is?"

"Isaiah Davis — goes by Buck. He and his band have always been trouble." Even from some distance, I could hear the disgust in Jeff's voice.

"Outlaws?"

"Not exactly — he owns some land a few miles out. Thought he and his bunch ought to be the law in these parts and, well, there's no one really to oppose 'em. Now, they've got it in their heads that California should secede and that cutting off the mail's part of that fight, especially since we all knew the president's speech would be coming this way. They've been attacking us for days. We keep driving them off, and they keep coming back."

I looked over at where Buck had fallen. He was still shooting down the road, but Bill had vanished into the distance. Apparently realizing Bill was out of reach, Buck let out a frustrated cry.

A satisfied smile tugged at my lips. Whatever happened next, the most important part of my job was done, and the president's speech was on its way to Sacramento.

I started to steer my pony toward the station when Buck caught my eye. Hatred burned behind his scowl. That was when I noticed the blood trickling down the side of his face, and the pulpy mess where an ear should have been. *Guess I hit him after all...*

"Forget the rest!" he yelled to the others. "Get this one!"

Except he didn't say "one."

If it'd been Jeff or Bill or any of the others who'd shot him, he'd still have been plenty angry, but I don't know if it would have triggered the same explosive rage. The way he looked at me . . . it was like I wasn't even a person anymore. Only prey.

Half a dozen pairs of eyes zeroed in on me, and though most of the gang was some distance away, I suddenly felt surrounded.

"*Charlie!*" Jeff waved urgently. "I said, get inside!"

I started to ride toward him but stopped. *It's me they want...*

Miles and miles of forest stretched all around Yank's Station, much of it already green even though winter's frost still dusted the mornings. Surely I could draw Buck and his band in there, away from the others, and lose him among the trees.

I twisted the reins and urged Arrow off the road. He whinnied in protest but obeyed.

"After him!" Buck hollered.

I rode deeper and deeper into the wilderness, crashing through branches and taking whatever opening I could find in the dense woods.

By now, exhaustion was catching up to me so badly, my head was starting to swim. The tall trunks seemed to sway, and the sky seemed to tilt. I couldn't tell what was moving because of my pony's frantic leaps and what was only in my mind.

Yet Buck and his band persisted. The sounds of their horses fumbling through the trees, punctuated by the occasional gunshot, only got louder the farther Arrow ran. Normally, he would've been a whole lot faster than their horses, but he was tired, too. I tried to fire back, hoping to drive them off. The revolver slipped from of my weary fingers.

The smell of smoke wafted past me. I wondered if that meant someone was nearby.

But I didn't have much time to think about it before my poor, worn-out pony tripped on a root. If I hadn't just ridden a hundred miles, I probably would've stayed on. But I was too damn wiped to react in time.

The next thing I knew, I was lying in the brush and my pony was scampering away.

Meanwhile, the sounds of Buck and his band kept getting closer.

That's it, I thought. *I'm a goner.*

Then, out of nowhere, a series of shots rang out. They sounded close, but I couldn't tell from what direction they'd been fired.

I must've hit my head when I fell, because black splotches were fast taking over my vision. The last thing I remember is glimpsing a small figure holding a shotgun in both hands.

"Helldamnfire! Thought you'd couldn't weigh much, since you're so skinny, but you must have bricks for bones."

I blinked, confused. All I saw were treetops and the darkening sky above, and I realized I'd been loaded onto a small hand wagon and was being dragged through the woods. All I could see of the person pulling the wagon was a shock of curly red hair sticking out from under a beat-up black hat.

I sat up with a start. "What's happening?"

The person stopped. Because of the short hair and trousers, I thought for a moment that it was a man, but then she turned to look at me. She was older, with bright blue eyes and a fair complexion with rosy undertones. A narrow mouth cut across an oblong face, with distinct lines that deepened each expression.

"Oh, good, you're awake," she said. "That means you can walk, and I don't have to drag you any farther."

I climbed over the edge of the wagon and hopped onto the ground. The revolver I'd dropped earlier sat in one corner; the woman must have found it and picked it up. "Who are you?" I asked warily.

She put her hands on her hips. "You first. I scared off Buck and his bunch of ruffians because I never much liked them, but I'd like to know whose hide I saved."

"Call me Charlie." I rubbed the back of my head. "I'm a Pony Express rider. Buck and the others tried to keep me from handing off the mail, and I shot him in the ear to save the other rider."

"Charlie, huh?" She arched her brows. "Charlie what?"

"Castillo."

"'Castillo'? Isn't that Spanish?"

"Yeah. My pa's family was from Mexico, until the borders changed and suddenly they were from Texas."

"How'd he end up calling you 'Charlie'?"

"I guess he didn't." I shrugged. "He called me 'Carlitos.' But it's easier to say I'm Charlie."

"Well, nice to meet you, Carlitos." She stuck out her right hand. "I'm Peggy Flannigan."

I accepted the handshake. Though her weathered fingers were slight, her grip was surprisingly strong. "Thank you for helping me out back there."

"You're welcome. So, where was your ma from?"

"Virginia. My grandpa was a freedman who eventually bought my grandma's freedom, too, and the whole family made their way out west when my ma was a girl." I glanced back. Jeff and the others at the station had to be wondering what had happened to me. "I'd better be on my way."

"Yeah, you'd better. The sooner you get going, the sooner you can get lost in the darkness and eaten by wolves." She snickered. "Your pony has run off, and it's gonna be pitch black in less than an hour. Do you really wanna risk your life after all that trouble I went through to save it? You'd better come with me, kid." She gestured forward, and I glimpsed a small log cabin maybe thirty feet ahead.

Realizing she was right, I nodded. "Yeah. Sure. Thanks."

"And you can pull that wagon, now that you don't need to be lying in it anymore."

Nodding again, I grabbed the handles and pulled it behind me as I followed. "It's just you out here?"

"Yes, indeed. Been that way for half a century. My pa tried to make me marry a brute of a man when I was about your age. I ran off and never looked back. Been happily on my own ever since." She glanced back. "What do your folks think of you riding all up and down the country?"

"Nothin'. They're dead." I stared at the ground. "Fever took Ma two years ago. Pa was never the same after that. Always angry. There was a man who worked on the same ranch as us that was always lying and cheating, and one day, Pa had enough and challenged him to a duel. He lost." A wry smile curled my lip. "I don't even remember what they were really fighting over. I couldn't stay at the ranch after that, so I struck out on my own. Started riding with the Pony Express about nine months ago. Feels like I've been doing it my whole life. In fact, I hope to do just that."

Peggy shook her head. "Nothing lasts forever. And at some point, you gotta figure out who you are, instead of always running away."

"You just told me *you* ran away."

"I did, and that's how I know. I ain't runnin' anymore." We reached the cabin, and she pointed at a spot by its door. "Leave the wagon there."

I did as she asked, grabbed my revolver, and stuck it into my belt. Guilt bit at me. Buck and his band were still out there and might attack again. But if he had a grudge against me specifically, was it better to stay away from the station?

I clenched my fists. It wasn't right that Buck should get away with what he was doing. We got lucky today — me, Jeff, Bill, and the others who were just trying to make an honest living. If some of those bullets had strayed just an inch or two, I might not have been standing there. I had no idea how the others at the station were . . . someone might had gotten hurt, maybe even died. Had we been in some big fancy town, we might've been able to get a sheriff involved. *But there's no such justice out here.*

Peggy opened the door to reveal a one-room cabin just big enough for a bed, a table with a single chair, and a fireplace, which had a steady flame going. A large trunk stood in one corner. Tools and hunting weapons sat on shelves built into the walls. She paused under the doorframe. "What's got you looking so sour all of a sudden?"

"I can't let Buck keep attacking the station." I yanked the revolver from my belt. "I've gotta find him and stop him."

"Oh, is that what you've gotta do?" A sharp laugh escaped her.

"It ain't right, what he did!"

"So, you're gonna hunt him down and shoot him dead by yourself? Do you really think you can do that? Do you really think you should? What gives *you* the right?"

My nostrils flared, and I whirled. "I've gotta try. I've gotta…"

Darkness pressed between the trees ahead. I could barely see more than a few feet ahead of me. Even if I could, even if I made a torch or waited until the morning, I had no idea where I was. And I certainly didn't know how to track someone. Buck and his men lived in these parts. They must have known the woods like the backs of their hands.

My shoulders slumped. *What do I do?*

Maybe it really would be better to stay away from the station, to keep Buck from targeting the others in an attempt to get me. That was why I'd taken off in the first place, after all.

Ma had always hated violence. I hadn't realized until after she'd died how much she'd been soothing my pa's temper. She must have given him an earful when he met her in Heaven. She would have been furious if she'd known what I'd hoped to do to Buck and his men.

Sighing, I turned back to Peggy. "I know I just met you, but I have a huge favor to ask. I . . . was hoping I might lie low with you for a little while before heading back to the station. Maybe Buck will give up on me, and things can go back to normal. They won't be happy with me having missed a few rides, but I think they'll understand. In exchange, I can . . . help out around here. Whatever you need. I used to be pretty handy back on the ranch."

The older woman gave me an appraising look. "You're fooling yourself if you think Buck will let things go, but I like this plan better than your last one. Sure, you can stay." She trundled into the cabin. "Come on in."

Staying with Peggy was a lot different from the life I'd become accustomed to. I couldn't remember the last time I'd spent as many consecutive days in one place. I felt . . . still . . . in a way I hadn't in a long time. With only my own two feet to carry me, instead of the fleet hooves of a pony, I couldn't move very fast, or very far. Without a pony, I felt like a bird with clipped wings, grounded and stuck. I tried to hide my frustration — Peggy was doing me a great kindness by allowing me to stay with her, sleeping on blanket in the corner by the fire — but she sensed it anyway.

That was why she tasked me with taking some pelts to a man who lived maybe three miles down the river behind her cabin, with instructions to trade them for bullets. It felt good to get away for a bit, and to interact with someone other than her, even though the man barely spoke two words to me.

Having made a successful trade, with the bullets sitting in a bag slung over my shoulder, I made my way back up the river, whose gentle babble floated past my ears. The afternoon sunlight glittered off its clear surface.

I was about halfway back when I glimpsed a brown creature drinking from the water. I stopped in my tracks and blinked. I could have sworn it was a pony. But that couldn't be right. . . .

Surely, my eyes were playing a trick. . . .

I carefully made my way closer. No mistake — it was a pony all right. With white spots on his left flank . . . the same pony I'd ridden into the woods nearly a week earlier.

A grin crept onto my lips. "Well, howdy, Arrow. I've missed you."

The pony looked up at me. Even though we knew each other, I moved slowly to make sure I wouldn't spook him.

Arrow blinked placidly as I approached. His saddle was askew but still secure, and he didn't move as I adjusted it, only tossed his head.

"I know, it can't have been comfortable wearing that for so many days." I climbed onto his back. "We'll just have a quick ride, and then I'll get it off you, okay?"

I gave his sides a kick, and the pony raced off through the woods.

A laugh escaped me. I'd missed it so much — the feeling of flying, the freedom and joy. We galloped through the trees and leaped over rocks and bushes. I whooped in delight.

A movement caught my eye. My gut warned me not to ignore it, and I yanked the reins.

A boy on horseback stared at me from between the trees. The same boy who'd been riding with Buck Davis, who'd called him "Pa."

I seized the revolver from my belt. He grabbed his at the same time. But though we aimed at each other, neither one of us fired. Looking back, I like to think it was our better angels holding us back. But I'm pretty sure the truth was we were both too scared to make the first move.

"What're you doing out here?" I demanded. "Who the hell are you anyway?"

"Name's Benny Davis," Buck's son answered. "I was lookin' for you. I ought to shoot you for what you did to my pa."

"You can certainly try," I scoffed. "You can call me Charlie, by the way. In case *I* end up shootin' *you*, I figure you oughta know whose bullet is inside you."

Benny scowled and raised his revolver. Alarmed, I pulled my trigger, thought my shot missed by a mile. He fired too, and it wasn't until after the weapon went off that I realized it was aimed at the sky.

"*Pa!*" he cried. "I found him!"

The sounds of distant shouts peppered the air. If it were just Benny, I might have stood my ground, but I wasn't stupid enough to think I could fight half a dozen men by myself.

Benny turned his revolver toward me. I fired in his direction with one hand while yanking the reins with the other. I gave Arrow a hefty kick, and we took off.

I flattened myself against the pony's back, expecting to hear more gunshots, yet none came.

At least Benny had the decency not to shoot someone in the back.

Seven days on his own didn't seem to have slowed Arrow any, and it only took a few minutes to make it back to Peggy's cabin.

As I approached, she stood from the stump she'd been sitting on, and the knife she'd been sharpening glinted in one hand.

"Welcome back, Carlitos," she said. "I see you found your pony."

"Yeah, but that's not the only thing I found." I swung my leg over the saddle and hopped off. "Buck and the others are still lookin' for me. I ran into his son, Benny, but I got away."

"And you came right back here?" Scowling, Peggy shook her knife at me. "Idjut! You don't have to be a master tracker to follow *that* trail!" She gestured at the mess of hoof prints, snapped twigs, broken branches, behind me. "You led them right here! Bet the only reason they aren't on us yet is because they're regroupin'."

My heart sank. "I . . . I'm sorry. I panicked, I guess. I'll leave, lead them away from your place." I put my foot in a stirrup, preparing to jump on, but Peggy grabbed the back of my kerchief with her free hand and pulled me back.

"You'll do no such thing." She shoved the knife into a sheath on her belt. "Think Buck'll leave me alone when he finds out you're not here? Nah, he'll know I sheltered you, and you and me stand a better chance of dealing with him than each of us by our lonesomes. Besides, I've had enough of him. A man that mean doesn't deserve to walk this earth. You got them bullets?"

Nodding, I took the bag off my shoulder and held it out to her.

She grabbed it. "Good. Now, it won't be long before they're here. We'd best be prepared."

Turned out, Peggy kept an armory in that trunk of hers, and it seemed to me like she had as many guns as the U.S. Army. Since my one little revolver would probably have run out of bullets before Buck and his gang were finished with me, she lent me two more — both Colts — which I'd tucked into my belt.

She herself opted for a rifle, which presently sat perched on her shoulder as she crouched behind the stump she'd been sitting on earlier. I'd turned the wagon on its side and ducked behind it for cover. In the past several minutes since returning, I'd also made sure to take note of every detail around me—the pile of firewood that could be useful cover if I was forced out from this spot, the large rock maybe fifteen feet to my right, which trees looked thick enough to stop a bullet.

I held my revolver by my side, doing my best to stay calm, to breathe steady. It was one thing to get shot at and run away. It was another to lie in wait for a gunfight you weren't sure you could win, that you had no business provoking in the first place.

I'd never been a great shot. So why was it the one time I hit a tiny moving target, it had to be Buck Davis's ear?

The golden light of late afternoon glowed between the trees. Yet the birds chirped on, oblivious to what was about to happen. Arrow was tethered to a small tree nearby, nickering softly. I swallowed hard, wishing for the hundredth time that I hadn't panicked and led Buck Davis and his band here.

"They'll be following your tracks from the river." Peggy's voice came low, sharp. "Keep your eyes open, and don't shoot unless you're sure."

The words were barely out of her mouth when a cacophony of hoofbeats and crunching foliage struck my ears, quiet at first but quickly growing louder. Shadows moved between the trees, and then they came into view: seven riders in total, with Buck Davis at the front and Benny not far behind.

Peggy fired first, the crack of her rifle shattering the air. The dirt in front of Buck's horse exploded, and the startled beast reared with a shriek. The rest of the gang stopped in their tracks. Benny and the others started to raise their weapons, but Buck held up his hand.

"That was your one and only warning shot, Buck!" Peggy yelled. "Get off my land!"

"Crazy old Peggy Flannigan." A mocking laugh colored Buck's voice. "So you're the one who's been shelterin' that little shit. I ain't leaving without him. You'd best hand him over if you wanna live to see tomorrow."

"You think I'm scared of you, boy?" Peggy made a derisive noise. "Come and try me."

"I've got no beef with you, ma'am, so I'm giving you this one last chance to change your tune."

"Well, I've got beef with anyone whose soul's as ugly as yours. 'Bout time someone cut you down to size."

"Suit yourself."

Two gunshots cracked the air. I couldn't tell who'd shot first, only that Buck's bullet embedded itself in the stump while Peggy's flew past Buck's shoulder. Probably would've hit if Buck's horse hadn't startled.

Buck kicked his heels, spurring his mount forward. "Get 'em, boys!"

Benny and the others scattered. They were going to try surrounding us. I gritted my teeth and raised my revolver.

I fired at the nearest rider. My shot went wide, chipping bark off a tree, but it was enough to make the rider pull up short. Another shot rang out — Peggy's — and the man toppled from his saddle, clutching his arm.

The wagon's wood split as a bullet hit it. Another man broke through the trees on the far side, trying to circle behind us. I pivoted, taking aim, and squeezed the trigger. I think I grazed his leg — he yelped and dropped his reins. His horse bolted into the trees.

But someone else was coming that way, and from this angle, I was exposed.

I darted out from behind the wagon and over to the rock I'd eyed earlier, wedging myself between it and a thick tree, and fired again.

Wood splintered as bullets ripped at the cabin's walls and roof. Peggy's curses cut through the chaos, and I heard a man scream. She must have got him.

Shards flew from the rock I was ducked behind. I kept firing at the man who was after me. One of my bullets struck his mount, which screamed and bucked in pain, throwing the rider to the ground. The man didn't get up — must've been knocked out. I wasn't sorry he was down, but I did feel bad for the horse. He didn't do nothing.

I caught Benny's eye through the trees, his pale face clear against the deepening shadows. He looked like a kid playing at being a man. In hindsight, he probably thought the same about me.

Buck appeared from between two trees, his shotgun aimed right at me. Terrified, I ducked up against the rock and fumbled at my revolver.

"Over here, ya yellow-bellied sonuvabitch!" Peggy stood and aimed a rifle at him — a different one than she'd held originally, I noticed. She must've run out of bullets in the first.

Buck glanced toward her as she pulled the trigger. The bullet struck the saddle, which snapped off, sending Buck tumbling. His panicked horse ran off before he could climb to his feet.

Peggy kept her gun trained on him. "You must be real proud of yourself, picking on old women and young boys. This the kinda man you're teachin' your son to be?" She nodded toward Benny. "Only reason you're still standin' is 'cause I don't think it's right to be killin' a father in front of his kid, but if you keep coming at me and Carlitos, I'll have no choice."

Buck glowered and looked around. All but one of his men had been shot, unhorsed, or both, and two of the mounts had vanished into the woods.

"Fall back!" he barked. He jumped onto Benny's horse, grabbed the reins from the boy's hands, and retreated. The others followed, one of them pausing to scoop up the unconscious man.

For a long moment, the only sound was the pounding of hooves fading into the distance. Then Peggy dusted her hands off and slung the rifle over her shoulder.

"That'll teach 'em to mess with me," she muttered.

She started to step out from behind the stump, but her leg collapsed beneath her. She caught herself with one hand, a string of curses flying from her mouth.

"Peggy!" I rushed up to her.

Blood trickled down one pant leg, and I gasped.

She gave me a withering look. "Don't gawk at me like I'm dyin', kid. Think this is the first time I've had lead under my skin? Just help me get inside."

"Yes . . . yes, ma'am."

Peggy leaned against my shoulder, and I helped her into the cabin and onto her bed. She rolled up her pant leg and sucked in a breath. "You remember that cluster of boulders about a quarter-mile up the river? With the big one kinda shaped like a triangle?"

She'd showed me that spot three days earlier, explaining that it was where she hid some extra supplies in case she ever had to flee her cabin.

"Yeah," I replied. "Need me to fetch something?"

"Moonshine." She leaned back against the cabin wall. "There's a few bottles in the trunk I buried there. Bring two — one to clean this wound and one so I don't feel it so bad."

"Got it."

I grabbed a shovel, untied my pony, and took off at a gallop.

The sun was pretty low by the time I arrived at the spot Peggy described. I dismounted, tethered Arrow to a nearby branch, and dug as fast as I could while the shadows thickened around me.

I'd just managed to uncover the top of Peggy's hidden trunk when Arrow let out a panicked neigh. I looked up in time to see Buck rush at me, his gun raised. To this day, I have no doubt that pony saved my life.

I ducked, and the bullet whizzed over my head. I dropped the shovel and grabbed my revolver, but when I tried to fire, I found its chamber was empty. I cursed, my mind briefly flashing to all the loaded guns back at Peggy's cabin, and all the bullets I'd traded for earlier that day, all of them useless to me now.

I leaped behind the cluster of boulders as Buck fired again. I looked around for something, anything I could use.

Several large gray stones sat at my feet. I picked up one about the size of my head, held my breath, and waited.

A second later, Buck rounded the cluster. Using both hands, I threw the stone as hard as I could, and it struck him square in the gut.

He fell backward. The gun went off. He cried out in pain, and a bloodstain appeared on his boot.

I grabbed another rock — just a fist-sized one this time — and leaped at him. I smashed that stone into his head, stunning him, and seized the shotgun from his grip.

With a cry of rage, I stood and aimed down at him.

"*No!*" Benny's scream rang through the woods.

I looked up to see him standing a few feet away, holding the reins of his horse, his eyes wide and trembling.

Was that the look on my face the day I watched my pa duel another man and lose? I can't for the life of me remember what they were even fighting over, and frankly, I don't care. Did Benny even know why his pa hated me so? That it was about more than a shot ear, but who I was, what I looked like, what he thought I represented? Did it matter?

I glared down at Buck. He was probably still seeing stars from that blow to the head. There was no honor in shooting a man when he was down. At least my pa had died on his feet.

I knew what my ma would have said if she'd seen me in that moment. I had faith that someday, at the end of my time, I'd see her again. She'd know what I did — angels see everything, after all — and I could already picture her disappointment.

Buck was the kind of man to never let go of a grudge. So was my pa. *Look where that got him.*

I wasn't gonna let myself become the same. And maybe, by seeing me choose the better path, Benny wouldn't either.

I crouched down beside my wounded enemy, the shotgun still aimed at his chest. "Buck . . . Isaiah . . . Davis. Are you a God-fearing man?"

He glowered. "'Course I am."

"Look, I lost my pa because of a gunfight. I don't much feel like doin' the same to Benny. Like Peggy said, it ain't right to shoot a father in front of his kid. So I'll make you a deal: I'll let you go if you swear before God that you'll never fight again."

Buck chuckled with disgust. "If you think —"

I pressed the barrel into his chest. "Even I can't miss from this close, Buck. Swear you'll give up fightin' forever, and you can walk away."

Benny took a few steps closer. "Do it, Pa," he said, his voice shaking. "*Please.*"

Buck's expression darkened. His eyes flicked to the gun, and he nodded. "Fine."

I clenched my teeth. "*Say it.*"

He glared. "I swear before God that if you let me go, I'll never fight again."

For a moment, I remained still. I didn't want to let him go, didn't want to let him live.

But I reminded myself of the better man I hoped to be, and I lifted the shotgun and stood up straight. As soon as I did, relief poured through my chest. I hadn't realized how tight my muscles had been until they'd released their stranglehold on me.

"Go on, get outta here." I backed away, though I kept the shotgun.

Buck looked ready to explode with anger, but he stood and stumbled toward Benny. I waited until they were both walking off before turning away, heading back to the trunk and Peggy's moonshine.

I'd barely taken two steps before a loud *bang* sounded behind me, followed by a gruff cry.

Gasping, I whirled and raised the shotgun. I thought I'd see Buck coming at me again.

Instead, he was lying unconscious on the ground several feet away. A small revolver sat in one hand.

Benny stood over him, holding a branch. "He was gonna shoot you in the back." He dropped the branch and knelt beside his pa. "I couldn't let him break his oath to God so easily. And I'm gonna do my best to make sure he never does. It's not worth it — any of this."

I lowered the shotgun. "Thanks."

Benny grabbed Buck by the arms and dragged him toward the horse.

"Need a hand?" I asked.

The other boy hesitated, then said, "Yeah."

I helped Benny get Buck onto the back of the horse, and then he rode off. Part of me wondered if I was being a fool by letting Buck go, but I chose to believe I'd done the right thing. I chose to hope that a better person lay within all of us.

I finished digging up Peggy's moonshine, then reburied the trunk, hopped on my pony, and rode back to the cabin.

She'd already dug the bullet out of her leg with a knife when I arrived and had gathered a needle and thread to stitch up the wound.

"Took you long enough." She held out a hand, and I gave her a bottle. "What happened?"

"Ran into Buck Davis."

"And?"

"I had him, but I let him go."

A smile curled her lips. "Seems you've figured out who you are, kid." She sucked in a breath as she poured the clear liquor onto her wound.

"Anything I can do?" I asked.

"Yeah, get the hell outta my house first thing tomorrow." She looked up with a smirk. "You must be eager to get back to Yank's Station, now that the danger's past. Back to ridin' like the wind across the country, just to make sure people get their mail."

I smiled. "That I am."

Yet part of me didn't want to leave. I had a strange feeling that even though my time with her was brief, Peggy had changed my life, and that once I was gone, I'd never see her again.

Thanks to the Pony Express, President Lincoln's Inaugural Address reached Sacramento in seven days and 17 hours. Some say his words convinced California to stay in the Union. I believe it.

The day after the shootout at Peggy's, she told me how to navigate back to Yank's Station. Turned out the whole time, I'd been less than five miles away. I rejoined the Pony Express and spent the next several months going back to what I did best: ride fast.

But it didn't last long. A few months later, the company dissolved, and I was left on my own yet again.

This time, though, I wouldn't keep running. I wanted to stand for something.

So when the war between states heated up, I joined the Union army, first as a drummer boy, and then, when I was a few years older, as a soldier.

The fractured nation managed to hold together, but just barely. To this day, it often still feels like it's about to crumble again. And a big reason why is because large swaths of folks will never see people like me as equals.

A few years after the war, Wild West shows became all the rage in America, and plenty of them were looking for talented riders with exciting backgrounds. What could be more exciting than riding for the Pony Express?

I had more fun than I had any right to, galloping and jumping about to thrill audiences, doing tricks on the backs of ponies. Each time I did, I hoped to remind them that not all heroes looked the same, that someone like me could be one too. By then, I'd stopped going by "Charlie" and only answered to "Carlitos."

One day, I received a letter from Benny Davis. Our show had passed through the town he was living in, and he'd recognized me from one of the posters. He told me that Buck had broken his word and joined the Los Angeles Mounted Rifles only a few days after our encounter, fighting for California to secede. So Benny had taken it upon himself to live out the oath of nonviolence on his father's behalf. He'd refused to fight in the war and was studying to join the priesthood. It seemed like a small thing compared to all that had happened and all that was to come, and yet it made me feel better to know that one choice I'd made, one moment in which I'd let my better angels win, had helped shift the balance of the world toward good.

Before the Pony Express folded, my route took me past Yank's Station a few more times, and I made a point of dropping in on Peggy when I could. Her leg had healed up faster than expected, though she walked with a limp.

After I joined the army, I wasn't able to make it back to California. Finally, more than ten years after I'd first crossed her path, the tour for our Wild West show took me back that way.

But when I rode out to her place, all I found was an empty cabin that looked to have been abandoned some years ago.

#

When I first set out to write this tale, I just wanted to compose a Pony Express yarn. Fast horses, daring rides, youthful adventures — what's not to like? But the Pony Express wasn't an event . . . it was an era. A very short era, sure, but an era nonetheless. Then I learned that they were the ones who delivered Lincoln's inaugural address to California when the country was on the cusp of the Civil War, and I knew I had my moment in history. Because those words — those immortal words — about unity and better angels, are as relevant today as they were in 1861.

—Mary Fan

Mary Fan is a sci-fi/fantasy writer hailing from Jersey City, NJ. She is the author of the *Jane Colt* sci-fi series, (Red Adept Publishing), the *Starswept* YA sci-fi series, (Snowy Wings Publishing), the *Flynn*

Nightsider YA dark fantasy series (Crazy 8 Press), and *Stronger Than a Bronze Dragon*, a YA steampunk fantasy (Page Street Publishing). She is also the editor of *Bad Ass Moms*, an anthology from Crazy 8 Press. In addition, Mary is the co-editor (along with fellow sci-fi author Paige Daniels) of the *Brave New Girls* young adult sci-fi anthologies, which feature tales about girls in STEM. Revenues from sales are donated to the Society of Women Engineers scholarship fund. Her short fiction has appeared in numerous anthologies, including *Thrilling Adventure Yarns* (edited by Bob Greenberger), *Magic at Midnight* (edited by Lyssa Chiavari and Amy McNulty), and *Mine! A Celebration of Liberty and Freedom for All Benefitting Planned Parenthood* (from ComicMix).

The Truest Story Ever Told

Steve Hockensmith

L t. Diehl lay stretched on his bed in the room he'd been sharing with Capt. Zimmer, staring at the ceiling, waiting.

Someone would come for him soon. Maybe Zimmer. Maybe Sgt. Hoop. Maybe Zimmer *and* Hoop, with a couple H or J or K Company troopers as escort.

Or maybe it would be men from the 15th Infantry. They may have been guests at Fort Duncan, but they'd know the way to the guardhouse as well as anyone.

Diehl lifted his right hand and inspected the knuckles. They were still a little red, still a little sore. But he hadn't broken his hand.

Small favors.

The front door opened. Footsteps — from a single pair of boots — approached. A figure appeared in the doorway to Diehl's room. Diehl looked over.

It was one of the black troopers from his regiment, the 10th Cavalry. Cpl. Thompson.

Thompson came to attention and saluted.

"Sir — the major wants to see you in his office," he said.

Diehl sat up slowly, gave his hand a shake, then returned the salute. "I'll be right there."

Thompson pivoted crisply and marched out.

So it would be like this. A tongue-lashing from the old man first, *then* the march to the guardhouse. Then the court martial, then . . . Diehl didn't know. Dishonorable discharge? Hard labor at Fort Leavenworth?

The things they don't prepare you for at West Point. . . .

Diehl stood, straightened his tunic and the gold frogging across the front — he'd already put on full dress — then picked up the envelope that had been beside him on the bed and stuffed it under his sword belt. Then, reluctantly, he put on his helmet.

Diehl hated the full-dress helmet. It made him feel like a little boy pretending to be a knight by putting a pot on his head. Which would've been bad enough, but it was August and this was south Texas, half a mile from the Rio Grande and the Mexican border.

The second Diehl had the helmet on he could feel his scalp start to sweat. By the time he'd walked from his quarters to Major Crowe's cramped, oven-like office beside the quartermaster's store it felt like someone had dumped a cup of lukewarm coffee over his head. And the first thing the major did, of course, was glare up at him from behind his desk and snap, "Oh, take that silly thing off."

Diehl saluted and did as he was told.

Rivulets of sweat ran down his face and beaded along his already soaked collar.

"Reporting as ordered, sir," Diehl said.

Crowe got right to the point. As usual.

"Well? What's this business between you and Lt. Steelhammer?"

Though Diehl thought of Crowe as "the old man," he really wasn't old. Just older — an Illinois volunteer during the Rebellion who'd gone regular army afterward. Whatever C. Kermit Crowe had been before the war, Diehl couldn't imagine him going back to it. He was a hard, sharp little man with all the warmth and bonhomie of an icepick.

"May I be permitted to begin at the beginning, sir?" Diehl said.

"Oh, by all means. Tell me your life story," Crowe snarled. "Keeping you from in front of a firing squad is exactly how I intended to spend my whole day."

Firing squad? Diehl thought.

He hadn't even considered that one. Surely Crowe was joking.

Only . . . did Major Crowe joke?

Crowe drummed his stubby fingers on his desk.

"Oh, go on, will you?" he said. "Begin wherever you must. Just *explain.*"

"Yes, sir. Well. . . ."

Diehl cleared his throat and forced the image of himself standing against a wall wearing a blindfold out of his head.

"Lt. Steelhammer was a couple years behind me at West Point," he said. "We weren't friendly, but we were acquainted. So, this being his first assignment on the frontier, when his detachment from the 15th arrived I took him aside to offer a little friendly advice. . . ."

"Jesus, Sam — ease up," Diehl said. "Being a hardass isn't gonna earn you anyone's respect any faster."

He and Steelhammer were under the broiling sun a thousand yards from the waterhole they'd been assigned to watch with their men.

Off to the right, crouched along a dusty ridge, were Diehl's twelve troopers — buffalo soldiers from K Troop, 10th Cavalry. To the left were Steelhammer's fourteen infantrymen from the 15th Regiment.

And somewhere off in the distance before them, in Mexico (for the moment), was Victorio, Warm Springs Apache chief, with his band of renegade warriors. They'd killed dozens on both sides of the border over the last year. It was the 10th Cavalry's job to put a stop to it, with a little help from the 15th Infantry.

And *little* help was certainly what it looked like to Diehl — at least what there was to see of it here at Waterhole #8, Cresta Amarilla. Sunburned replacements fresh from the cities to the east, most Irish, some German or Italian, several barely able to speak English, all with "How did I get here?" easy to read in their fear-filled eyes.

And in charge of them: a gangly shavetail lieutenant so eager to prove he should be taken seriously he'd spent the last minute berating a cowering private named Schweinsteiger for not saluting properly.

"I'll handle my men how I see fit," Steelhammer told Diehl.

He had a warbly, high-pitched voice and a haughty curl to his thin lips, both of which Diehl remembered well.

Diehl had befriended several underclassmen at West Point. The ones like Diehl himself — middling students, unmotivated, most definitely *not* bound for glory, full of their own brand of *How did I get here?*.

Samuel Steelhammer he'd steered clear of. The kid seemed like a prat.

"Of course, Sam," Diehl said to him with a little smile. "I'm not trying to undercut you. It's just that, though I haven't been out here long, it's been long enough to learn a thing or two. And one of them is you need to work *with* your men, not just bark *at* them. That way they'll listen better when the barking really needs to be done."

"So that's what you've learned in two years on the line? Mollycoddle the men? Well, you can save your advice."

"I didn't say mollycoddle," Diehl started to say.

"Like I'd want to follow in *your* footsteps," Steelhammer went on, "and end up in charge of a bunch of monkeys."

"Ah!" Major Crowe said, tightening a fist on his desktop. "So that's why you did it!"

"No, sir," said Diehl.

Crowe furrowed his brow. "No?"

"No. Not exactly," Diehl said.

"Well, get to the exactly! He didn't respect the 10th, and . . . ?"

"And he made that plain, sir. Repeatedly. Both to me and my troopers. But I did my best to ignore it."

"Yes, yes. I understand. And then . . . ?"

Diehl took a deep breath.

"And then, sir," he said, "Mr. Bethune arrived."

"And you've been in a scrape or two with this 'Victorio,' have you, Lieutenant?" Bethune asked.

He mopped his face with a handkerchief. There was a lot of face to mop, and a lot to mop off it.

Bethune was a big, broad, moist man in a white seersucker suit that was going sweat-yellow in the back. Diehl had been shocked to learn that Major Crowe was allowing Bethune — a correspondent from the *New York Weekly* — to accompany the detachments headed out again to watch the waterholes along the border. But then the major had sent Diehl off with seven words that explained it.

"You're a talker. Make a good impression."

The U.S. Army didn't get much respect. The 10th Cavalry got far less. Major Crowe was hoping that Thomas Jefferson Bethune could help change that.

"Well," Diehl told Bethune, "I haven't run into ol' Victorio myself so far. But the 10th Cavalry has. You've heard about the Quitman Canyon fight . . . ? And the battle at Rattlesnake Springs . . . ?"

"Oh, yes, yes. Of course," Bethune said. But he lifted up the little notebook he carried around with him and jotted down "Rattlesnake Springs."

"K Troop hasn't gotten its licks in yet," Diehl said. "But it will. And we'll make them count."

"Ah," Bethune said.

He wrote "K Troop" and "licks" and "Deal."

Diehl would find a subtle way to correct the man's spelling later.

He looked away — at his troopers along the ridge and the 15th Infantry detachment nearby — so it wouldn't be obvious he was reading Bethune's notes.

"I know what the public thinks of the 10th, Mr. Bethune," Diehl said, lowering his voice. "I see it all the time. Sneers. Jeers."

He focused on Lt. Steelhammer, who was kneeling by the ridge gripping the field glasses Diehl wouldn't let him use during the day. A glint off the lenses would be visible for miles.

"But there's no better regiment," Diehl went on. He nodded at Steelhammer's infantrymen. "Half those men will have deserted by Christmas. But the 10th has the lowest desertion rates in the Army — despite getting the worst horses and gear and food. You won't find better soldiers anywhere on the frontier."

Steelhammer seemed to sense that Diehl was talking about him and his men. He sent a glare over his shoulder, then stood and started toward Diehl and Bethune.

"You take Hoop there," Diehl said, no longer whispering. He pointed at a tall trooper with a carbine in his hands and chevrons on his sleeves. "A couple months ago, he and two other K Company men ran into a little band of Mescaleros making a break for Mexico to join Victorio. And you know what he did? Whipped one in a hand-to-hand fight, then talked the rest into turning around and going back to the reservation. *That's* the kind of story about the 10th Cavalry that ought to be in the papers, Mr. Bethune."

Hoop studiously ignored Diehl's words, but some of the troopers lined up beside him looked over and smiled proudly.

Bethune nodded and scribbled some more in his notebook.

"Excellent, excellent," he muttered. "This is exactly why I'm here, Lieutenant. To uncover the stories that paint a true picture of what's happening in the West."

"Like Ned Buntline?" Steelhammer asked as he walked up.

Bethune stopped writing and gave the gawky young officer a sour look.

Diehl kept his expression neutral.

He'd told Bethune he was an avid reader of the *New York Weekly* — he'd actually never picked up a copy — and he didn't want to get caught in a lie. And "Ned Buntline" sounded vaguely familiar.

"Yes. Like Ned," Bethune said. "He's made quite a splash with his stories about Buffalo Bill Cody. Discovered the man himself in Nebraska a few years back. Well. . . ." He threw Diehl a glance and a wink. "There are heroes in Texas, too."

Steelhammer gave Diehl a glance, as well — the dismissive, contemptuous kind that he usually gave him.

"I can't imagine, Mr. Bethune," Steelhammer said, returning his attention to the reporter, "that your readers would be interested in 'heroes' who are barely more civilized than the savages we're here to fight . . . or the second-rate officers assigned to lead them."

"So that's why you did it!" Major Crowe blurted out, giving his desk a thump. "Well, I'll admit that I sympathize, but . . . what?"

Diehl was shaking his head.

"That's *not* why you did it?" Crowe asked.

"No, sir. Not quite."

"Diehl, . . . " Crowe growled.

"You recall the incident of August 17th, sir?" Diehl said.

"Of course."

"Well, my report, sir . . . it wasn't entirely . . . comprehensive."

"You lied?"

Diehl winced. "I expurgated."

"Diehl, . . . " Crowe growled again.

Diehl went on explaining — without expurgating this time.

"Is it Indians?" Lt. Steelhammer whimpered.

A bullet pinged off the boulder he was cowering behind, and he began to weep.

Private Schweinsteiger patted him on the shoulder.

"Should we *scheißen*, Herr Steelhammer . . . ?"

"'Lieutenant,' Friedrich!" said another infantryman — an Italian named De Luca who had his back pressed against the rock beside

Steelhammer. "Call him 'Lieutenant'! And it is 'shoot.' You do mean 'shoot,' yes?"

De Luca mimed firing a rifle. He'd dropped his twenty yards off after the first shot had whipped away Lt. Steelhammer's campaign hat.

"*Ja*, yes, *danke*, Carlo," said Schweinsteiger.

He froze for a second as two more shots zipped by overhead, then went back to patting Steelhammer's shoulder.

"Should we *shoot*, Lieutenant?"

"Is it Indians?" Steelhammer asked again. His voice rose to something just short of a shriek. "*Is it Indians?*"

"It's Indians, Sam!" Diehl said.

When the shooting had started — from somewhere behind them — he and Sgt. Hoop and the other 10th Cavalry troopers had scrambled over the ridge onto the rocky slope beyond. That gave them cover from the shots coming from the north, but now their backs were to the waterhole in the distance — completely exposed.

"Damn it . . . they can start picking us off whenever they want," Diehl said. He squinted to the south, expecting to see puffs of rifle smoke. He didn't. "Why aren't they?"

"Cuz there ain't nobody over that way. They know it's where we been watching," Hoop said. "And the ones that are doing the shooting ain't here for a fight."

There were more shots from the north, and most of Steelhammer's infantrymen stopped milling around in confusion and rolled over the top of the ridge to join the troopers on the slope. But a couple of them — Bethune with them — ran to the boulder and tried to press in beside Steelhammer and Schweinsteiger and De Luca.

"Get *back*! Don't *shove*!" Steelhammer cried.

Another shot ricocheted off the rock, and all six men huddling behind it yelped.

"Stay down!" Diehl told them.

He resisted the urge to add "And shut up!"

Steelhammer had started crying again, and it was distracting.

"You think it's a feint?" Diehl asked Hoop.

Hoop nodded. "If this was Victorio and his whole bunch, we'd've seen 'em, and there'd be a hell of a lot more shooting right now. No — there's probably just a handful of 'em out there. One or two keeping us busy while the others — "

"Go for fresh horses," Diehl cut in. "Damn. Kerr and Gore."

Diehl had left two of his troopers three hundred yards back with their mounts.

Another shot kicked up dust on the ridge above the infantrymen's heads. Steelhammer's men instinctively cringed, and two more of them dropped their rifles and let them go clattering down the dry, rocky grade.

"Ain't heard no carbines from the rear," Hoop said to Diehl.

Diehl nodded grimly.

Kerr and Gore were probably already dead.

"Either way," Hoop went on, "the Apaches'll have to take the horses west to get 'em outta that arroyo we left 'em in. Gives us a chance to stop 'em."

"Good thinking."

There was a loud *snorp* from the boulder thirty feet away. Diehl glanced toward it but couldn't see what it was thanks to Bethune's seersucker-covered ass and the crush of other men pushed in there. He had a guess, though.

Steelhammer had stopped crying and was sucking the snot out of his nose.

Diehl tried his best not to judge the man. Diehl had only come under fire for the first time a year ago himself. He'd managed not to burst into tears, but it took him some practice to keep his thinking straight when bullets were whizzing past.

"Why aren't we shooting back?" Steelhammer asked, voice shaking.

"There's been no order to," Diehl said.

"Well, shouldn't we — ?"

"In a second, Sam!" Diehl snapped.

Steelhammer went quiet for a moment, then muttered, "He shouldn't speak to me like that."

Diehl didn't hear him. He was talking to Hoop.

"Pick who you want to go with you. We'll provide cover when you're ready."

Hoop nodded, turned, and started moving slowly, hunched over, along the ridge, careful to kick up as little dust as possible as he went down the line. He tapped four troopers on the shoulder, and they rose and followed him.

"Prepare to fire," Diehl told the remaining troopers. He looked over his shoulder at the infantrymen. "You, too."

The cavalry troopers cocked the hammers on their Springfield carbines.

Some of the infantrymen — the ones who were still armed — did the same for their rifles.

"*Ich erinnere mich nicht. Haben wir diese bereits geladen?*" one of them said.

I don't remember. Did we load these already?

"Yes. When we got here," the man beside him replied in German. "And watch where you're pointing that thing."

Another shot smacked into the boulder.

"Fire!" Steelhammer cried.

The soldiers rose up and squeezed off shots, though none of them could see anything in particular to shoot at.

Hoop had just reached the western end of the line with the troopers he'd picked to come with him. He glanced back at Diehl.

Diehl sent him off with an exasperated flap of the hands.

Whether he gave the order to commence firing or Steelhammer did didn't matter now. Hoop had his distraction. Now he had to make the most of it.

He hurried off with his little squad, quickly disappearing around the ridge as it arced northwestward.

"Continue firing at will!" Diehl called out. He lowered his voice before throwing in an addendum for this troopers: "But don't pour it on too hard. You'd be wasting ammunition."

He didn't bother telling that to the infantrymen. Several of them were clearly struggling to remember how to reload their rifles.

As his troopers kept up a slow but steady fire, Diehl rose just enough to look for movement or gun smoke from the rocks and gullies and mesquite to the north. He saw nothing.

Now that they had the soldiers shooting back, distracted, the Apaches who'd been firing at them had probably cleared out, racing to catch up to their friends with the horses.

Diehl let his men keep shooting at nothing — which would hopefully convince the Apaches that their plan had worked.

Three of the infantrymen crouching with Steelhammer leaned out to add the occasional shot of their own, and Bethune went down on both knees with fingers in his ears.

"It's so *loud*!" he said.

Diehl didn't bother telling him that war usually was.

He could see Steelhammer again now. The other lieutenant was still sitting with his back to the boulder, teary eyes wide.

"I want my hat," Diehl heard him say.

A volley of shots erupted from the northwest, quickly followed by the scream of a horse and a return shot that sounded like it came from a pistol.

"K Troop — with me!" Diehl called out.

He dashed off toward the sound of gunfire, and the remaining troopers followed him. The infantrymen spread out along the ridge looked at each other, then half of them followed as well.

"Where are they going?" Steelhammer said. "Are we retreating?"

There was more carbine fire from the northwest, and the charging troopers with Diehl put up a hoarse, wordless war cry as they swept toward it.

"I know I'm not a military man," Bethune said, "but I don't think it's a retreat if you're running *at* the gunfire."

Private De Luca nodded sagely. "Si, Signore. That is correct."

Private Schweinsteiger turned to Steelhammer. "Should we go, too, *Lieutenant*?"

"Oh." Steelhammer shrugged but otherwise didn't move. "If you want to."

For the first time since the Battle of Cresta Amarilla began, Bethune pulled out his notebook and started writing.

"That *is* different than your report," Major Crowe said.

"Just a bit more complete, sir," Diehl replied. "At the time, I guess I thought I was being loyal to a fellow officer. If his . . . performance was going to be exposed, it wouldn't be by me."

"And the four warriors you claim your men killed recovering the horses . . . ?"

"Not a claim, sir. That's fact. They *were* Warm Springs Apaches from Victorio's band. Sgt. Hoop will confirm it."

"As he'd confirm what you're saying about Lt. Steelhammer?"

Diehl nodded.

Crowe did, too.

"And *that's* why you did it," he said.

Diehl switched to shaking his head.

"Oh, for god's sake, . . . " Crowe said.

Diehl slid a hand down to his side and pulled out the envelope tucked beneath his belt. He opened it and removed a large, folded sheet of paper.

"I received this today," he said. "From my father."

He unfolded the sheet, revealing it to be a full page from a newspaper. He handed it across the desk to the major.

Crowe snatched it away and looked down at it.

It was the front page of a recent *New York Weekly*. The layout was dominated by an illustration: a drawing of a soldier holding a guidon pole in one hand and a revolver in the other. The American flag waved from the pole. The soldier — an Army officer — was gazing at something off to his right, his expression resolute.

Crowe began reading the story that looped around the drawing.

Lt. Samuel Steelhammer

Fighting Lion of the Southwest

The Wildest, Truest Story Ever Told

By Thomas Jefferson Bethune

Chapter I.

Apache Ambush!

An orange-tinted dusk on the desert — a vista of vast and desolate beauty — a bluff overlooking a lonely waterhole. Here we find the gallant men of the 15th Army Regiment. And none more gallant —

more tall and straight and well-formed, with noble brow and deter-mined expression etched into manly features — than young Lt. Samuel Steelhammer.

They have come here to find the Apache fiend Victorio and his pack of bloodthirsty disciples. Find . . . and kill!

Suddenly . . . BANG! BANG-BANG!

Gunfire! But not from the waterhole over which the stalwart soldiers have kept a vigil lo these many days. No! From behind them!

"The cunning devils!" exclaims a soldier — stout and true Sgt. Smith, ever at the side of the lieutenant he has quickly grown to cherish like a beloved son. "They have slipped around behind us with thoughts of wiping us from the earth as we sought to do to them!"

"Take cover, men," Lt. Steelhammer says. "But fear not! This is but a ruse!"

There are more shots as Sgt. Smith and the other men conceal them-selves behind rocks and trees. But one figure remains erect, unbowed, unhidden. Lt. Steelhammer! Alone he strides toward the bluffs from which leaden death hurtles their way.

"Lieutenant! What are you doing?" Sgt. Smith cries.

Lt. Steelhammer continues his solitary march toward the enemy. He spies but six skulking redskins taking aim at him — and six Indians he can handle!

"I am going to convince these so-called 'braves' to surrender," he de-clares.

"But how?" Sgt. Smith asks.

"By talking to them — or whipping them!"

"Twaddle," Major Crowe muttered.

He began skimming.

Lt. Steelhammer defeats Victorio's (nonexistent) sub-chief, "Blood Wolf," in hand-to-hand combat.

Lt. Steelhammer recovers a herd of stolen cavalry horses.

Lt. Steelhammer rescues a wagon train bound for Oregon (through south Texas?) from Victorio's warriors, saving the honor of a captured maiden in the process.

Lt. Steelhammer and Sgt. Smith infiltrate Victorio's village by darkening their skin with ochre and putting on feather headdresses and loincloths.

"Tommyrot," Major Crowe said.

There was one notation on the page: a penciled "This you?" beside an arrow. The arrow pointed to a passage in which a "cowering, craven cavalryman" named "Deal" begs Lt. Steelhammer to save him and his panicky black troopers ("Lawd! Dem Injuns gon' scalp us!") when they're surrounded by Victorio's murderous hordes.

Crowe slowly lowered the page.

"The 10th is never mentioned by name," Diehl said. "Fortunately."

"But I don't understand. Did Bethune and Steelhammer become friendly?"

"No, sir."

"Did they have some prior connection?"

"No, sir."

"Did . . . ?" Crowe flapped his hands in flustered frustration, unable to think of another plausible explanation. "Did Steelhammer *bribe* him?"

"I doubt it, sir." Diehl nodded down at the newspaper page now resting on the major's desk. "I don't think Lt. Steelhammer's even aware of that yet."

"Then you insulted Bethune somehow! You sent him away with a seething hatred of the 10th Cavalry!"

Again, Diehl shook his head. "Mr. Bethune and I parted on excellent terms, sir."

Crowe jabbed a pointed finger at the newspaper page. "Then why would he do this?"

"I have a theory, sir."

"Well? Spit it out!"

"Lt. Steelhammer has a good name."

"What do you mean? The boy had no reputation at all before this."

"I don't mean his reputation, sir. I mean his *name*. Samuel Steelhammer. It's memorable. It sounds . . . mythic."

Crowe blinked once, twice, taking that in.

"Plus," Diehl added, "he commands white troops. But 'Samuel Steelhammer' — I think that's what really made the difference. Bethune came west looking for a hero to write about, and when he didn't find one that suited his editors he created one from the best material at hand."

Crowe nodded slowly. "And *that* is why you punched Lt. Steelhammer."

"No, sir."

The major scowled, his face reddening.

"I punched Lt. Steelhammer," Diehl went on quickly, before the major could snatch the saber hanging from its peg on the wall and run him through, "because he's here, and Mr. Bethune isn't."

"Ahhh. . . ."

Crowe eased back in his chair, his gaze sliding to the side, resting on nothing in particular.

Diehl remained at attention before his desk for half a minute before Crowe spoke again.

"Dismissed," he said.

"Dismissed?" Diehl repeated, surprised.

He'd been expecting "Capt. Zimmer will be your advocate at the court-martial" or "Report to the guardhouse" or at the very least

"You are confined to quarters until further notice." Yet when Crowe continued, he said none of these things.

"Stay away from Steelhammer, Lieutenant. And don't speak to anyone about what happened between the two of you."

"Yes, sir."

Diehl looked down at the newspaper still spread across the major's desk. Crowe hadn't mentioned it, nor was he offering it back. So Diehl just saluted, spun around, and marched out, leaving the *New York Weekly* behind.

When Diehl was gone, Crowe allowed himself a moment of humanity: a weary sigh. Then he began drumming on his desk with the fingers of his left hand.

Lt. Steelhammer was part of a small detachment temporarily assigned to Fort Duncan. His superiors in the infantry were hundreds of miles away. So, he'd reported the punch to the nose — delivered by Lt. Diehl outside the privy behind the officers' mess, unwitnessed by anyone except perhaps a few horseflies and jackrabbits —to Major Crowe. And now it was up to the major to decide what to do with Diehl . . . and what to tell Col. John W. Forsyth, commander of the 15th Infantry Regiment.

Diehl was young and callow and a bit of an odd duck. But he was finding his footing, and he didn't resent his assignment to the 10th Cavalry like some officers. He'd learned to keep his cool. He cared about his men. He had potential.

From the moment Crowe had met him, on the other hand, Samuel Steelhammer had struck him as a hopeless ass.

If the Army had to lose one or the other, Crowe knew which he'd choose.

The major stopped drumming his fingers and picked up the newspaper page on his desk. Slowly, methodically he balled it up in his hands. When it was no bigger than a crabapple he dropped it into the wastepaper basket beside his desk. Then he opened a drawer, took out a sheet of cream-white paper, and spread it out before him. He picked up his pen, but he didn't dip it in the inkwell. Not yet.

He still had to come up with the right approach. One that would keep the Army from making a bad trade: losing an asset, keeping a liability. It would be tricky, especially now that Steelhammer would be (briefly?) a celebrity. But there had to be a way . . . though it might be a bit distasteful.

Major Crowe didn't like lying in a report, but there were bigger goals and values — larger truths — to protect.

When he'd thought up a story that just might work, he began to write.

#

When the first chapter of Ned Buntline's story "Buffalo Bill, the King of the Border Men" appeared in the Dec. 23, 1869, edition of the *New York Weekly*, it ran with a subhead: "The Wildest and Truest Story I Ever Wrote." And it certainly was wild, telling "Buffalo Bill" Cody's origin story as a determined young man sworn to avenge his father's murder by rebel raiders. The story didn't just turn Cody into a superstar. It created an unquenchable appetite for frontier heroes that would show no signs of letting up for nearly a century. It was the birthplace of the Western genre — the little log cabin in which some of our most cherished American myths were born. Was it Buntline's "truest" story, though? Well. . . . Buntline did go to the West looking for material — once — and did meet Cody there. But Buntline was a prolific peddler of hooey — a fabulist and liar (and lecturer on the evils of alcohol who frequently stumbled up to the podium drunk). "Buffalo Bill, the King of the Border Men" was melodramatic B.S. designed to sell newspapers — the clickbait of its time. And though almost no one reads it anymore, its legacy lives on all the way up to today. Oh, and by the way, there was a Steelhammer in the 15th Infantry after the Civil War: Capt. Charles Steelhammer. Let's say Lt. Samuel Steelhammer is his disappointing nephew. No offense intended to the Steelhammers for associating them with a doofus. Like Ned Buntline and Thomas Jefferson Bethune, I simply couldn't resist a good name.

—Steve Hockensmith

Steve Hockensmith's first novel, the mystery/Western hybrid *Holmes on the Range*, was a finalist for the Edgar, Shamus, Anthony, and Dilys awards. He went on to write several sequels as well as the tarot-themed mystery *The White Magic Five and Dime* and the *New York Times* bestseller *Pride and Prejudice and Zombies: Dawn of the Dreadfuls*. He also teamed up with educator "Science Bob" Pflugfelder to write the middle-grade mystery *Nick and Tesla's High-Voltage Danger Lab* and its five sequels. A prolific writer of short stories, Hockensmith been contributing to *Alfred Hitchcock Mystery Magazine* and *Ellery Queen Mystery Magazine* for more than 20 years.

POINT OF IMPACT

VONN MCKEE

The little girl clung like an iron clamp to the front door frame of the Peterson home. Blue-green eyes blazed in her reddened, sweaty face. Wheat-colored curls plastered against her forehead. From outside the open door, on the porch, her mother tugged vainly on the girl's waist. The father stood planted on the entry hall's geometric tiles, sweat forming at his sideburns and under the band of his straw boater.

"I don't want to go!" shrieked the child.

Father spoke more calmly than he felt. "But, Louise, you will enjoy it once we get there, I promise. We will get to ride a train! And there will be carnival games and wonderful things to eat."

"The train is going to crash!" wailed Louise. "I heard you say so!"

"Oh, no, no, no. Not our train, darling." Father soothed. "Once we arrive, there will be a show. Two old engines are going to run into each other, but it has all been planned. No one will be on the trains when they meet. No one will be in danger. Just a big loud crash, that's all."

"I don't want to hear a big loud crash!"

Mother stopped tugging and folded her arms. "Mother will cover your ears. And you may turn your face away," she said. "Come along now, Father has already bought our tickets and paid a handsome price. Stop being foolish."

Father squatted to his daughter's level. "Louise. Look at me."

Louise kept her hands and feet fastened to the wood molding but turned her head. The lace ruffles at the front of her dress rose and fell with her quick breaths.

"Your friend Colleen is going," he said. "You could sit together on the ride there and back if you promise to be ladies. Would you like to take your dolly along?"

Louise seemed to consider the proposition, then screwed her face into a frown.

"I will be afraid when those engines crash."

"There's nothing to fear, poppet. We will sit far away." Father's voice was not deep, but its softness was reassuring. Louise's hands relaxed.

With his thumb, Father caressed a drop of perspiration from her brow. "I bet there will be ponies. You're such a fine rider. Would you like to ride a spotted pony? Colleen could ride another one."

"Colleen won't. She's frightened of riding." Louise's serious gaze met her father's. "Are you certain there will be ponies?"

"Well, not one hundred percent certain, I cannot lie. But what kind of a carnival would it be without ponies?"

Louise released her hold on the door frame and wiped her forehead with a dimpled hand. "I think I'd like a brown pony today. Not a spotted one."

Five minutes later, the Petersons closed the front gate behind them and walked toward the train station. Mother held a picnic basket, and Louise cradled a porcelain-faced doll in a time-softened blanket. Seeing Colleen with her family at the corner, Louise quickened her steps.

"You have a way with her," said Mother, staring straight ahead as Louise embraced her friend. "It infuriates me to no end."

William George Crush closed the door to the office tucked under one end of the newly constructed grandstand. The room held only a planked table strewn with documents and handbills hawking the "MONSTER CRASH!"

"I've never seen anything like it!" A skinny man fanned himself with a handbill. "The trains are still arriving from all over the state, just as you hoped. People are riding on the roofs of the cars! I tried to estimate the crowds but gave up the effort. At least twenty thousand, maybe thirty, and I do not exaggerate." The man laughed. "And how does it feel to have a Texas town named for you? The Crash at Crush!"

Crush smiled faintly. At first, he had not taken the foreman seriously when he said, "We have dug two water wells and built enough seating for the World's Fair. Why not declare it a town for a day?"

Now that the day had come, Crush felt subdued and anxious. He had thrown himself into preparations for the staged train crash over the summer. It astonished him when the Missouri-Kansas-Texas Railroad brass bought into the wild idea — from himself, a passenger agent, no less! — to wreck two aging locomotives as a public spectacle. Engines 999 and 1001 were painted brightly, one red and one green, and they made whistle-stop tours of Texas towns to advertise the event.

He had chosen a shallow bowl-shaped valley outside of Waco. A four-mile spur was laid along the regular track, its ends backing up the slopes at each end of the valley. Workers had furiously toiled to erect the enormous grandstand, a viewing platform for the press, and to clear space for a carnival midway.

Even P.T. Barnum got involved, lending an enormous tent to serve food to the spectators. Crush marveled at how quickly Barnum's crew tilted up and fastened the poles and unfurled what seemed like acres of canvas.

Thirty thousand people at two dollars for a round-trip rail ticket from anywhere in Texas! Crush mentally calculated the numbers — far beyond his hopes.

As long as the viewing stands and crowds were held two hundred yards away from the track, the mechanical engineers assured him that the collision of the trains was controllable. Well, all the engineers except Adam Lovell.

Crush had asked plenty of questions. "But what about the boilers? Might they explode?" He had been with the M-K-T, called the "Katy," Railroad long enough to know the horrendous outcome of such a disaster.

"That's highly unlikely," said the lead engineer. "When two loco-motives meet head-on — and there have been other, similarly staged events — the noses dip into a V-shape on impact. The boilers are located far enough back to avoid rupture, and they are elevated above the point of impact."

Adam Lovell cleared his throat. "If I may point out . . . during the crash staged in Ohio last May, the engines did the opposite. They impacted in an inverted V. In other words, numerous variables make it impossible to predict the results of impact between two thirty-five-ton locomotives."

Crush had seen newspaper photographs of the Ohio crash and recalled the locomotives, tilted against each other, front wheels locked in a macabre embrace.

"For instance," Lovell continued, "the terrain at the Ohio site was relatively flat. The engines were spaced one mile apart and pulled four cars apiece. What you propose is a starting point of two miles apart, with each engine pulling six box cars — not four — and those filled with railroad ties.

"Then there is the slope at each end of the track to consider, which will increase their speed. I fear the impact will create far more force than the Ohio collision."

Lovell glanced down at a bound notebook, open to a page of sketches and calculations. His colleagues frowned in disapproval, but he took a deep breath and held up the notebook. "With due respect, I am not convinced the outcome will be as my esteemed peers predict."

There was an uncomfortable silence. Crush was the first to speak.

"Very well. Thank you, gentlemen, for your observations and . . . recommendations. I will make a final decision by day's end."

That evening, as his wife Katherine knitted in the chair beside him, Crush sipped on a brandy.

Three engineers in accordance and a cautious one.

He swirled the amber liquid, watching it streak the insides of the glass.

There will always be anomalies, but statistics are based on the largest number of as-predicted outcomes, are they not?

Crush took another sip of brandy and felt it burn his throat on the way down. Katherine's knitting needles clicked softly. Setting his mouth in a hard line, he nodded, to no one.

He decided to proceed with the Crash at Crush.

The Petersons stepped onto the rail platform at the temporary town of Crush and were instantly engulfed in a sea of pressing bodies.

"Here. Let me hold you, Louise."

The girl reached up to her father with one arm, the other clinging to her blanket-wrapped doll. He cradled her high on his forearm and she buried her face on his shoulder.

"Elaine, stay close," he said to his wife, who already clutched his free hand. They pushed through the crowd and threaded their way toward the looming grandstand a few hundred yards from the tracks. The aroma of food drifted from a striped big-top tent. Everywhere, people lined up at lemonade booths and souvenir stands. A top-hatted, croak-voiced politician stood on a small platform, pontificating to a few onlookers.

"Where is Colleen?" Louise wailed. "I lost her when we got off the train."

"We will find her, poppet. Her father and I arranged to meet at the north end of the grandstand. Then we will see about that brown pony."

Louise raised her head. "I see them, Father! Ponies! There, beside the big tent."

"Yes, yes. I see them, too. And look, there are carnival rides just as I told you. As soon as we find Colleen and her family, we'll go exploring."

"Back! Everyone back!"

A line of uniformed men pressed against the surge of spectators who spilled past the safe-distance markers. As the time for the crash grew closer, so did the crowd's level of frenzied excitement.

Engineer Adam Lovell stood outside the Crash at Crush office, arms folded. The unruliness of the crowd only added to his apprehension. The man of the hour, William George Crush, approached him.

"We cannot begin until the spectators are on the grandstand," Lovell shouted over the din. "It isn't . . . safe." He wasn't sure Crush would heed his warning, given that his earlier safety concern had been ignored.

Crush nodded. "I'll ride out and make an announcement. If they will listen. . . ."

His white gelding was tethered at the rear of the stands. Crush mounted and circumvented the mass of people. Once he was between the police and the railroad tracks, he rode back and forth, yelling at the crowd.

"We will not hold the event until you move back! Do you hear me? We will not hold the event! Please, move now!"

By the time the spectators gave up and filled the grandstand benches, many standing in throngs for lack of seating, the Monster Crash was running an hour late.

Jarvis "Joe" Deane, head bent, checked the settings on the three Novelette Triplex cameras lined up on the press platform. His brother, Martin, and assistant, Louis Bergstrom, hovered nearby.

"Brilliant idea, Joe, utilizing three cameras," said Martin.

Joe said, for the tenth time that day, "Don't forget the order. Martin, you're in charge of the — "

"I know, brother. You will take the point-of-impact photograph, and I will take the shot immediately after the crash. Louis is to capture the aftermath."

"Yes, yes. They will be seconds, perhaps fractions of a second, apart. Be mindful! And be prepared to advance and keep shooting."

"We will be mindful," said Martin.

Joe straightened and gave his arms a stretch. "I'm sorry, fellows. I can't help feeling nervous. I know you won't disappoint."

Since he had received the telegram announcing he was chosen as the official photographer for the Crash at Crush, Joe had planned and replanned every detail a thousand times.

Locomotive engines 999 and 1001, which had been idling a distance apart for hours, huffed to life and began a slow approach to the viewing area.

"Ah, the handshake!" said Joe. "I will take this one."

The engines moved closer and closer, setting off cheers and whistles from the packed grandstand. They slowed to a creep, the gap between them narrowing until they stopped. The massive engines gently touched cow catchers.

Joe opened the shutter and the Novelette clicked, capturing the moment. He immediately advanced the film for his next shot, when the engines would meet at a much higher speed.

"Look, Father! They just kissed!" said Louise, clapping her hands. The Petersons sat near the bottom of the grandstand. Colleen's family, the Brights, sat directly behind them, one row up.

"They did indeed!" Father let Louise stand on his lap for a better view. "Now, Louise," he spoke close to her ear, "when the trains back up and meet again, there will be a very loud crash, remember? I will hold you close, and Mother will cover your ears. Right, Mother?"

"Yes, I will cover them, just like this. . . ."

Louise smiled, satisfied with the arrangement.

After the formal gesture, the trains, each pulling box cars emblazoned with the names of sponsors — the Oriental Hotel, Ringling Brothers, the "Katy" Railroad — began to back away from each other. Again, the police had to form a line to force enthusiastic viewers away from the tracks.

Crush, on horseback, rode to the edge of the tracks. He watched 999 and 1001 recede until they were in position, two miles apart on the spur. He removed his hat and waved it high as a signal. Within seconds, each locomotive's stack spewed a dark cloud of smoke, and they began to move.

As agreed, the engineers blew the whistles, then waited until the driving wheels rotated four times before leaping from the trains.

Adam Lovell checked his pocket watch. In less than two minutes, the "Monster Crash" would shake the ground and air of Crush, Texas. The two-hundred-yard space between the viewing stands and the track suddenly seemed miniscule. He tried to envision the shrapnel flying from the collision. Around him, families watched expectantly. He noticed a particularly pretty little blonde girl, standing on her father's lap. He closed his eyes, said a prayer that pieces of the wreckage would not travel this far.

First came a faint rumble as the trains gathered speed. Charges had been placed on the tracks at intervals to add drama, and they exploded like muskets as the engine wheels rolled over them. With every report, the spectators shouted.

The trains were now a half mile apart and closing fast. Lovell winced. A final speed of 45 miles per hour was predicted, but he could swear they were already moving at a higher rate.

"Ready, boys?" Joe Deane was practically dancing behind his camera. Louis and Martin were poised at their stations, eyes darting from one locomotive to the other.

The rumble became a deep churning now, as driving wheels pounded the rails. Within seconds, the churning turned to a roar. If there were crowd cheers now, Joe could not hear them. Two fingers resting on the shutter lever, his eyes were focused on the point where the great machines would collide. When they were about fifty yards apart, Joe took a deep breath and held it.

With timing perfected by years of photographing squirming children, nervous lovers, and large families who couldn't sit still at once, Joe felt, rather than saw, the precise moment. The trains were mere feet apart when his finger dropped the shutter mechanism. In that millisecond, he delighted in the blur of red and green, in the way the two opposite streams of black smoke trailed like mourning veils over each train, at the wholeness of mighty machines that were about to become nothingness. He somehow knew he had taken the most important photograph of his life.

Neither Joe, nor anyone present, could have predicted the sound. As if mountains collided, or planets, a deep boom seemed to emanate from the core of the earth, sending a long shudder through rock and soil, and the structures built on it. There was first a hot, percussive wave of displaced air, then the physical evidence of the explosion. An enormous cloud of black smoke, filled with millions of wood splinters and pulverized train parts, quickly engulfed the crowds.

Joe let out the breath he'd been holding. His head jerked back violently.

And everything went black.

The explosion pushed Lovell back ten feet and buckled his knees. In the milliseconds following, spinning bits of timber whistled by his ears. Hot pebbles and cinders pelted his face.

Then, an eerie quiet fell. Before the crowd had time to gasp or cry out, another explosion rocked the ground. This one sent bolts and portions of driving wheels, gears, rods, and random chunks of iron screaming through the air.

Lovell scarcely formed the thought before he was knocked flat . . . .

"The boilers! Oh, dear God. . . ."

Although stunned by the force of the blast, Martin Deane knew he had caught the explosion from the train crash on film. And he was confident that Joe had tripped the shutter on his camera as the engines met head-on. Wiping grit from his eyes, he realized Joe lay on his back on the platform, as did Louis, who had apparently been hit by a flying piece of wood plank. The assistant was already scrambling to his feet, tossing the board aside, determined to take photographs of the wreckage.

Martin knelt beside Joe's still form. "Joe, we got it! Joe! Are you all right, brother?"

Joe was breathing.

But Martin choked back a sob when he saw a dark, bloody hole where Joe's right eye should have been.

"Aw, no. Joe! Aw, no, no. . . ."

An acrid, metallic odor thickened the air. Sections of the grandstand were twisted and splintered and the bodies of the fallen lay draped over its benches. Some had landed on the grass underneath the structure. Everywhere, there were groans and whimpers.

But, Lovell realized, almost all the bodies were moving, stretching their limbs, many standing unsteadily, coughing, dusting themselves off. Dusting others off.

A wailing child, clutching a doll, stumbled against Lovell's leg.

Mother! Ohhhh, Father! Where are you?" The rest was a garbled cry of distress. Lovell recognized her as the little blonde girl he'd seen standing on her father's lap.

"Here, now," he said, stroking her dust-covered hair. "We'll find them. Hold my hand, child. They can't be far away."

Lovell thought, grimly, that the parents might be badly injured or even dead and hoped he could prevent the girl from seeing them in such a state.

He looked at the wreckage of the trains, trying to take in the destruction, and shook his head in disbelief.

The engines were not tilted in a V-shape, inverted or otherwise. They had collided and, astonishingly, telescoped into each other. Two 35-ton locomotives were reduced to unrecognizable fragments in a grotesque pile.

Already, several men clambered through the debris, picking up souvenir bits of the trains. Lovell saw them fling their treasures aside, as the hot metal seared their hands.

Off to one side, William George Crush sat on the white gelding, silhouetted against the dissipating smoke.

Still holding the girl by the hand, Lovell muttered, "You, sir, have sacrificed your fellow man on the altar of commerce."

"Louise! Louise!"

A slim, bearded man crawled from under the grandstand, his arm around the shoulders of a distraught young woman.

"We will find her, Elaine. We will. Louise!"

The little girl holding Lovell's hand twisted her head toward the sound. "Mother! Father! Here I am! Oh, here I am!" She rushed to the couple, who dropped to their knees and pulled her close.

Relief washed over Adam Lovell. He turned away from the smoldering heap of rubble on the tracks and began to walk, in search of water to wash his face, his hands. He took a last look at little Louise, reunited with her parents, and smiled sadly.

These three souls, at least, did not die on Crush's altar today.

#

Miraculously, only three people died as a result of the September 15, 1896, "Crash at Crush" — one, when he fell to his death on the train ride home. The "Katy" Railroad fired Crush immediately, but he was rehired the following day based on overall positive publicity as a result of the event. Jarvis "Joe" Deane lost his right eye when it was pierced by a flying bolt. He continued his career as a photographer. Other principal characters are fictional.

—Vonn McKee

Vonn McKee brings deep storytelling to the Western genre, rich with emotion and vivid pictures of a beautiful but unforgiving land and the hardy, spirited people who settled it. She often weaves real-life historical events into her writing, adding realism and intimacy to the characters and storylines. Her short stories have twice been named Spur finalists ("The Songbird of Seville," "Wren's Perch"). "The Run for Ruby Camp" was Western Fictioneers' 2023 Peacemaker Award winner. Her work has been published in multiple anthologies, as well as in a collection of her own, *Comanche Winter*.

Roy Earll's Debt

Jeffrey J. Mariotte

The men came two days after Roy Earll's body was consigned to the earth, and his spirit to the Lord.

Amelia still grieved for her loss. She moved around the house like a wraith, managing to feed the girls but not herself. On this afternoon, she heard the dogs barking and went to the window and looked out through aching, red eyes and whirling snow and saw three men on horseback riding toward the house. The dogs scampered around the horses now, nipping at their ankles. One of the horses kicked out, catching the shepherd in the ribs. The dog winced and backed away, but the two smaller dogs kept up the harassment.

Tightening her apron strings, Amelia started toward the door.

"What is it, Mama?" Ruth Ann asked. "Another visitor?"

Both girls were tired of visitors. Truth to tell, so was Amelia. They wanted only to be left in peace, Amelia to mourn her husband and try to figure out what came next, how she would provide for the girls until they were of marrying age, and Ruth Ann and Grace Louise to think of their father and weep and remember.

Amelia opened the door and stepped outside. Wind-whipped snowflakes stung her cheeks, but the heat from the stove inside warmed her back. "Can I help you?" she asked. She recognized none of the men. "Are you lost?"

"Not if this is Roy Earll's place," one of them said. He was gaunt, with hollow cheeks and dark eyes set beneath a jutting forehead. It looked to Amelia like two caves below a massive cliff face, with a dying fire inside the mouth of each.

"My husband isn't here," she said.

The men brought their mounts to a halt about six feet away from her. The man off to the first speaker's right started to laugh. Gold flashed in his open mouth. She saw a rifle in a worn leather scabbard hanging from his saddle. "Course he ain't here," the man said, between guffaws. "He's dead, ain't he?"

"He is," Amelia said. "But I'm afraid I don't see anything funny in the situation."

The man stopped laughing. The third one, a few feet behind the others, urged his horse forward at a slow walk. He stopped no more than four feet from Amelia and leaned forward in his saddle. He was a big man with a bushy black beard and long, black hair flecked with snow. He wore a black coat of animal furs, and the snow had fairly caked it. A derby hat shaded the narrowed slits of his eyes. Amelia read menace in them.

"I don't reckon you would. You're Mrs. Earll, are you?"

"I am. I don't know you, and I'll thank you to leave this property. Certainly any business you might have had with my husband is over now."

"Thing is, seeing as Roy's gone, that turns our business with him into our business with you."

Roy Earll had been a carpenter, and a good one. He had helped build Bisbee, from the days when it was a tiny settlement called Mule Gulch to the growing town it was today. He had a small workshop behind the house, and a larger one in town. He had no debts of which Amelia was aware. "Do you owe him some money, then?" she asked. "Did he do a job for you?"

"For us?" the bearded man asked. He gave a laugh and said, "No, no. He done a job *with* us, though."

"Building a house? Or a store?"

"Nothing like that." This was the first man again, his eyes glowing embers in the shadow of that brow.

"Roy done a *job* with us," the gold-toothed man said, still chuckling. "Only we ain't had a chance to split the . . . uhh . . . profits, I expect is the word. Roy got it all, and we still need our shares."

"I'm sure I don't know what you're talking about. If you haven't any business with me, then I would appreciate it if you would leave now."

"What's going on, Mama?"

Amelia looked over her shoulder. Grace stood there, still in her black dress. At fourteen, she was the older of the two girls. Dark brown hair like her mother's. Behind Grace, little Ruth Ann was just visible inside the house. She took after her father, with pale, freckled skin and light-red hair. "Nothing, Grace. These men are confused. Go back inside, the both of you."

When she turned back to the men, she saw them looking at Grace with something like hunger in their eyes. Grace stepped back and closed the door. "Go on, now. We've nothing to discuss."

The bearded man urged his horse a few steps closer still, and he leaned almost out of his saddle. "I reckon if Roy didn't tell you where he put the proceeds, we could take it out in trade," he said. As he did, his eyes flicked toward the doorway where Grace had just been standing.

"You three should be ashamed," Amelia said. "Trying to take advantage of a widow woman. Well, it won't work. You likely never even met my husband, and your stories are ridiculous. I'll thank you never to set foot on my property again."

"Our business ain't finished," the man in black said. "We'll leave, for now. Give you a little time to think on what Roy done with our money. When we come back, we'll expect our shares, or else we'll find another way of claimin' what's ours."

He turned his horse around and snatched off his hat, waving it once at her and then pointing the way back toward Bisbee with it. The other two stared at her for several more seconds, then followed. Soon, they were lost in the blowing snow, and Amelia went inside to stand by the stove.

When Roy built the house, he insisted that Amelia needed a fireplace. And so there was, but it was cold and empty. Roy had always taken care of the firewood, but he hadn't done much about it since before Christmas, and the woodpile was down to sticks she had to keep for the stove.

She looked at the framed photograph on the mantel. The image of the two of them had been taken shortly after their wedding. She was standing, once again wearing the dress she'd been married in, behind Roy. He sat stiffly in a chair, the shoulder that might have been touching her stomach pulled forward slightly as if to demonstrate some distance between them. His hair was combed and greased, and his bushy orange mustache hid most of his mouth, except for the slight curve of his lower lip. His eyes were wide, giving him a startled appearance.

The photograph told a truth she had never noticed before. Ever since they'd met — certainly since they'd been married — she had been behind him. He had been the one who set rules, the one who earned and spent money, the one people turned to with the most important questions. It was as if he had been a person and a half, and she only the other half of him, rather than a whole person of her own.

And he had been acting a bit distant, lately. Away from home even more than usual, and barely present when he was there. In his workshop, mostly, or in the barn. As if he had become a stranger to his own family.

She shivered, and it wasn't entirely from the cold.

Not wanting to leave the girls home alone in case those men came back, she took them with her the next day when she hitched Spooky, their strongest mule, to the old buckboard and drove it toward town. Along the way, she made a slight detour to the Bergin spread. Both girls were close friends with Elena Bergin. They were always happy to see her, and they would be safe there in case those men returned.

The journey was only a few miles, but the road wound through the hills surrounding Bisbee, and it took hours. Amelia wore a fur hat and gloves and coat, and the girls were similarly attired and wrapped in blankets. Still their cheeks were reddened from the wind and snowflakes clung to their eyelashes and dusted everything in white. As expected, the Bergins had a warm fire going inside and welcomed Grace and Ruth Ann. Elena was delighted to see them, and after visiting with the family for a few minutes, Amelia climbed back into the buckboard alone and continued on her way.

Once she reached Bisbee, Amelia left the wagon outside W. B. Scott's mercantile store near the mouth of Brewery Gulch and walked up the hill to the constable's office. She was surprised to see so many people in the streets, surprised as well by how many were already intoxicated at a little before noon, whooping and laughing, slapping one another's backs, and firing pistols into the air. It felt like a celebration, though she was unaware of any holiday.

Constable Meriwether had white hair, parted in the middle and plastered to his scalp, and a mustache styled to match, its waxed ends curling up toward full cheeks. When Amelia walked into his office, he looked up from a ledger book on his desk and smiled. "Mrs. Earll," he said. "This *is* a surprise. I hope you're well, all things considered."

She ignored his comment, utterly exhausted by telling people that she wasn't crushed by Roy's death. It was an obvious lie, and continuing to pretend made it all the worse. "What's going on, Cary?" she asked. "Everybody's outside raising a ruckus like I never seen."

"Oh, you haven't heard the news? I suppose you've had other things on your mind. My condolences again, ma'am."

"Never mind that. What news?"

He smiled again, more broadly this time. A potbellied stove in one corner made the office too warm, and the aroma from a coffee pot sitting on top of it almost — but not quite — blocked out the stench of stale tobacco smoke. "Why, you're no longer living in Pima County," George said. "We're a county unto ourselves. *Cochise* County. It became official yesterday. Johnny Behan's to be sheriff, and the county seat will be up in Tombstone."

"It's named after that awful savage?"

"Cochise weren't so bad," the constable argued. "He was friends with Tom Jeffords, after all. Weren't for him negotiatin' peace, I reckon we'd still be at war with the Apache. Old Geronimo would still be kickin' up a fuss. Anyhow, we did take their land, so you can't rightly blame them for bein' unruly."

Unruly seemed an understatement. But she and Roy had been in the territory for years, and although Apache warriors had stopped by their place sometimes, they'd never posed any threat. Usually, they wanted to trade for a couple of sheep to feed their families with. Her enmity for Cochise was instinctive, based on stories she had heard and not on any personal interactions.

Cary studied on her for a few moments, then said, "I don't guess you stopped in just for that, Mrs. Earll. How can I help you?"

Amelia swallowed, looked around the office and back toward the door, as if those men might be standing nearby. When she spoke again, it was in low tones, leaning toward the lawman. "Yesterday three men came by our place," she said. "I didn't know them, but they were rough-looking types. They said they and Roy had done some kind of a job, but Roy had taken all the money they were to be paid." She paused, uncertain of how to continue. Then she decided she just had to soldier on.

"Well, Roy hadn't brought home any pot of money, so of course I don't know what they were talking about. And I confess I'm still not entirely clear on how he died."

"Why, it was a kick from a horse, like you been told," Cary said.

"What horse? Why was it enough to kill a strong man?"

"Can you describe the men who came to your house?"

"Are you going to answer my question, Cary?"

"After you answer mine."

He appeared determined, and Amelia was too upset to argue. The shooting outside never stopped, and it was fraying her last nerve. "Three men," she said. "I only got a good look at one of them. Skinny, and with a forehead like you could plaster handbills on. One had a bunch of gold teeth in his mouth, and one was big and hairy. Thick black beard. He wore a derby hat."

Constable Meriweather nodded as if it all made sense to him. Then he reached toward her, as if to take her hand, before pulling his own back and resting his fingertips on the edge of his desk. "Amelia, if I may call you that?"

"Certainly."

"Four men robbed a mine payroll about a week ago. Them three you just described sounds like three of them. The fourth one? Well, the paymaster said he had reddish hair and a long mustache."

"You're saying it was Roy?"

"I'm saying I don't know that for a fact. But the paymaster, he got off one shot as the men was riding away. He was sure he hit one of them. When Roy was killed two nights later, he had been drinking down in the Gulch. Drinking, Homer Carson says, like he was trying to bury some pain. After that he went stumbling outside, lost his footing on some ice, and fell into some horses tied to a rail. One of them kicked out and caught him just over the eye, then kicked him twice more for good measure. When Doc Sheehan checked him over, there was a scrape along the side of Roy's ribs and holes in his coat and shirts. Doc says it looked like a bullet had skinned him there."

Amelia couldn't believe what she was hearing. "You're saying Roy helped rob a payroll? Then came home wounded and I never knew it? That's not possible."

"I showed the paymaster his body," George admitted. "He couldn't say for certain that he was the fourth man, on account of how bundled up he was. But he thought it might be."

Amelia thought back to the last time Roy had been home. He had been up in Bisbee for a few days. Working on a new house, he'd said. The way the town was growing, new houses and stores were going up all the time. He had looked a bit pale, and he'd walked a little funny. She had asked about it, and he claimed that he'd hurt his leg jumping down from the second story of the house.

Roy wasn't the type to consort with thieves, though. And he had been making enough money doing carpentry that he had no need to steal a mine's payroll.

But then again, he had been drinking a lot, recently. Daytime drinking even around the house, which wasn't like him. Would a drunk carpenter be hired to build anything meant to last?

She guessed there was much about her husband she didn't know, despite their sixteen years together. The last year, or a little more, he had been ever more distant. Coming in late, leaving early. She and the girls had been doing more of the work around their little homestead. He'd said it was because of the town's rapid expansion, that he couldn't spend much time at home because he was always needed here.

There might have been truth to that. Bisbee had certainly boomed since she had last been here.

But there might have been some lies mixed in with the truth.

"Cary, they say Roy took all the money. Maybe he had the best place to hide it until they could split it up. I don't know anything about it, but I'm scared. They threatened my daughters, threatened me."

"I knew who or where they was, Amelia, I'd already have 'em locked up, and that's a fact. You just be careful. Keep a loaded gun handy, and keep your door latched when you're in the house. I'll keep tryin' to track those men down and I'll get Sheriff Behan to help."

Amelia knew Homer's Saloon, deep in the gulch. She went there next, keeping her eye out for those three men all the while. When she walked in, the place was dark and relatively quiet. A couple of card games were underway at different tables, but the players were solemn-faced, eyes fixed on their cards or their opponents' hands. At the bar, the men drinking seemed to take that work just as seriously. She saw one prostitute, an older woman named Nellie, sitting alone with a drink she'd probably had to pay for herself.

Homer was behind the bar, polishing glasses with a bar rag that looked as if it had been in service for a decade or more. He was balding, with just a fringe of hair wrapping around his scalp from one ear to the other. His nose was prominent and about the color of the scarlet globemallows that bloomed around home in the spring. He recognized her as she approached and put down the filthy scrap of cloth.

"Mrs. Earll," he said with a sad smile. "What can I pour for you? It's on me."

"Nothing, thank you," she answered, hoping her voice came across as glacial as she was trying for. "Roy drank in here the day he died?"

Homer swallowed, rubbed a knuckle against his nose, and studied the path of a lazy fly that was buzzing around him. "Well, I can't say for certain, but I think he might could've been."

"The constable says he was."

"Well, he's a right smart feller. He would know, like as much."

"Was he or wasn't he?"

"I don't like to speak ill of the deceased, ma'am."

Amelia held her temper in check, but just barely. "Your business is serving liquor to people. If you think drinking liquor is a sin, then perhaps you ought to take up a new trade."

"Well, yes," Homer relented with a shrug. "I believe I did serve him a drink or two that day."

"Or ten or twelve?"

Homer knuckled his nose again. "Possibly."

"And the days before that? He was in here quite a bit, wasn't he?"

"I'd say I got to know him right well."

"Who did he drink with?"

"Well, whoever was around. 'Specially if they were buyin'.'"

Three men? One with gold teeth, a burly fellow with a fur coat?"

"It's hard to say exactly, Mrs. Earll. When it gets busy in here, I'm scramblin' ever which-way. Don't really see who's drinkin' with who."

"Do you know the men I mentioned?"

"Might know 'em if I saw 'em, but not from what you said."

"But he was here a lot, Roy? Drinking during the day instead of working?"

"Unless somebody was payin' him to drink, he weren't workin' much of late."

"That's the idea I'm getting. Thank you, Homer."

She turned on her heel and headed for the door. Homer said something to her back, but she didn't hear it and didn't care to have him repeat it.

Roy Earll had been lying to her, possibly for months. He was drinking instead of working. Still managing to bring money home from time to time, though. Did he make it gambling? Or was it from other crimes, ones not as flagrant as the mine holdup?

Her husband had been a proud man. And when a proud man, a good provider, loses his living and his pride, she expected that drinking might instead fill his days. He could pretend to be going into Bisbee to work, spend a few days getting good and snorted, then sober up and come home with a little money in his pocket.

The mine payroll, though — that sounded like a substantial crime. They would have had to use guns, threaten the paymaster and anyone else around. From the sound of it, they made off with a good bit of folding money.

Which Roy took — maybe because he was the 'respectable' one, known around town as a hard worker — until they could divide it up. And with Roy dead, those three men wanted it all.

She was suddenly fearful for the girls. She rushed back to Scott's Mercantile and collected the wagon. She had intended to do some shopping, but without Roy's wages she would have to watch her spending even more than usual. All she wanted now was to get back to the Bergin ranch. The sky looked dark and threatening, like molten lead, and she wanted to get back home before the next storm hit.

Come morning, their little spread was encased in white. Out the window she could see trails crisscrossing the property, probably coyote, javelina, jackrabbit. Deer, maybe. She had been looking at them for a few minutes, trying to identify their makers, when an idea occurred to her.

She was certain that Roy hadn't brought any large amounts of money into the house. She would have seen that. But there had been tracks heading out toward the barn a few days ago, left in old, half-melted snow and mud. Those tracks had been larger — the size a man's boots might make. She pulled on boots of her own and wrapped herself in a coat and went outside into the still air. The blanket of snow seemed to erase most odors from the air. She couldn't smell the privy or the little creek running behind the barn. That was probably iced over, anyway.

When she'd sensed snow in the air, she had herded what remained of their little flock of sheep into the barn. Roy would have chided her for being soft-hearted, pointing out that each one wore his own wool coat, but she hadn't wanted them wet and cold. As she neared it now, trudging through crusted, ankle-deep snow, she caught their scent, and when she pulled open the door it hit her full-on, the wet wool and sheep droppings confined in a small space making her eyes water.

Inside the barn, the air was cold, and it seemed darker than usual compared to the brilliant white outdoors. Amelia stood in the doorway, looking about, trying to figure where Roy might have hidden something he didn't want anyone to find. She decided she couldn't put herself in her husband's mind, so she would just have to do the work. She navigated through the livestock, looked behind and under bales of hay and coils of rope, under saddles and tack and behind tools.

Finally, she eyed the ladder leading to the loft and started climbing. There, she saw an old Indian blanket draped over something lumpy, with a saddle sitting on top. She moved the saddle and pulled back the blanket, finding four burlap bags with leather closures and brass hardware.

They were heavy.

She opened one and found more currency than she had ever seen at one time in her life. Possibly more than she had seen throughout the duration of her life.

And she knew those men weren't going to give up. Not on this much money.

Not a chance.

They came that afternoon. The air had remained bitterly cold, and when Amelia heard horses approaching, she looked out the window and saw them blowing steam from their muzzles, the riders bundled in furs and canvas coats, scarves wrapped around throats and faces. She recognized them just the same.

She took the rifle down from over the fireplace and handed it to Grace. "Shut the the dogs in your room. Take Ruth Ann and go around the corner. When I come back to the house, I'll call out. If anybody else comes in, don't ask them any questions. Just point this and start shooting."

Grace chewed her bottom lip, swallowed, and nodded. Tears glistened in her eyes. She looked like she wanted to say something, but if she opened her mouth she would start bawling, so she kept it shut tight.

"Ruth Ann, you stay well back of Grace," Amelia said.

Then she tucked a revolver into the pocket of her apron, pulled on one of Roy's heavy coats over it, and stepped out the front door.

The same three men. Apparently, Constable Meriwether had not located them.

"I found your money," Amelia said when they were close enough. "You were correct, Roy brought it here."

The big, bearded man spoke for them. "Figgered as much. Pleased to see you've come to your senses and ain't tryin' to hide it from us."

"What would be the point?" Amelia asked. "You'd just take it from me, and you might hurt me or my girls in the process."

"We might have us some fun with them girls," the gold-toothed one said. "But we wouldn't hurt 'em much."

Amelia spread her feet wider on the snow-crusted earth, squared her shoulders. "I need your solemn word that you won't touch my daughters, or I'll never show you where the money is."

The big man twisted in his saddle and looked at the younger one. "You keep your mouth shut." Then he faced Amelia again. "I apologize for that fool," he said with a dry chuckle. "Truth is, Jimmie wouldn't know what to do with a female if he had one. Might be we'll take some of our money up to Tombstone and buy him a woman who can teach him somethin'."

"I don't find that very amusing, sir. And I don't like the looks of you. Let's finish our business so you can be on your way."

"All right then, where is it?"

"It's in the barn," Amelia said.

"Show me."

"Well, come along, then."

She stalked toward the barn through drifting snow. The bearded man said, "Jimmie, you wait here, make sure nobody comes outta that house. Bent, you come with me."

"Bent?" Amelia asked over her shoulder.

"Name's Bentley," the big one said. "But he don't like the whole thing. Thinks it makes him sound soft."

"He's not wrong."

"Hey, now, lady —" Bent began.

"Quiet!" roared the bearded man. "Let the little missus show us our money."

"Quiet would be a blessing," Amelia said.

She reached the barn door. Before she could open it, the big man climbed down from his horse. "Hold up!" he said. "Bent, you go on inside and make sure this ain't some kind of trap."

"Me?" Bent asked.

"You heard me."

Bent dismounted, drew a pistol, and started toward the door.

"I gather you're the man in charge," Amelia said. "These others sure snap to when you bark orders."

"Because they know what's good for 'em."

"I'm sure they do."

Bent slipped inside. Amelia heard him stomping around, likely trying to shake the snow from his boots or clear a path through the sheep.

A moment later he reappeared in the doorway. "I don't see nobody in here, Calvin. Just a lotta sheep."

"Calvin?" Amelia echoed. "And you think Bentley sounds soft?"

The big man scowled at her as he climbed down from the leather. "Just get in there and show Bent where it's at." He raised his voice and added, "We'll stay out here and keep watch, Bent!"

Amelia shrugged and followed Bent inside. In the half-light of the barn, that giant forehead shadowed his eyes so much that they seemed to have vanished altogether. "Well?" he asked.

"Up the loft," Amelia said.

Bent eyed the ladder. "You first."

She sighed. "Very well, then." She pushed through the flock to the ladder and climbed it quickly. "Nobody up here but me," she said. "And some spiders and mice, like as not."

Bent looked uncertain about the whole business, but he gripped the ladder and started climbing.

He paused as he neared the top, looking this way and that. Amelia pointed to an Indian blanket bunched up over something, with a saddle on top. "It's right there," she said.

"Show me."

"Come up and look for yourself."

He shrugged and kept climbing. When he was halfway off the ladder, but still holding onto the floor, Amelia drew the revolver and charged toward him. His mouth dropped open and he pawed at the floor and the ladder, trying to keep his balance.

She swung the pistol's barrel at the best target available, that massive cliff of a brow. It struck him and he cried out, then tipped over backward. Screeching and flailing his arms, he dropped to the barn's dirt floor, landing with a heavy thump. Sheep scattered, *baa*ing their terrified hearts out.

"Bent?" Calvin called from outside.

"He fell!" Amelia shouted. "I think he's hurt!"

Calvin stormed toward the door, kicked it wide. He saw Bent on the ground and Amelia above, and although she tried to hide the revolver she might not have been fast enough. Calvin spun around and left the doorway. "Jimmie!" he screamed. "Get those girls and bring 'em down here!"

She could hear JImmie heading for the house.

"Here's your blood money!" Amelia cried. "Take it!"

She rushed to the pile, shoved off the saddle and yanked the blanket aside. She hurled one of the money bags down. It slammed against the door, pushing it open a little wider, and fell to the ground. When it landed, a seam split and currency spilled out.

Calvin must have seen it, because he muttered something, and she heard his boots coming closer again. She shucked off her heavy coat and scurried down the ladder. At the bottom, she jerked her white apron around, so the strings were at her belly, and brought the lower part over her head to hide her dark hair. Then she squatted down among the sheep, pistol in her hands. The stink made it hard to stay still, but terror held her in place.

When he came in, the big man seemed to fill the barn's entrance. He had a revolver in his right hand and the money bag in his left, bills falling out and fluttering down like autumn leaves in a strong wind. He scanned the loft, then started forward.

"I know you're up there, lady," he said. "Throw down the rest of that money and we'll leave you be. You don't, you won't want to see what Jimmie and me do with them daughters of yours."

Amelia crouched amidst the livestock and held her breath, afraid to move.

"You don't show yourself right now, we'll make you watch every minute of it. Then we'll cripple you instead of kill you, so you won't escape the memory by dyin'."

How could Roy have become entangled with men so evil? she wondered. Had she ever really known her husband at all?

Calvin pushed farther into the barn, nudging sheep aside as he came. He hadn't seen her yet, to him she was just one more meaningless, near-white shape, and what he wanted was in the loft.

But he was almost upon her. She realized her mistake — ducking down when she was between the door and the ladder, instead of off to one side. Only two of the animals stood between them now. In another moment he would have her.

Then a gunshot sounded from the direction of the house.

Calvin stopped in his tracks, looked over his shoulder. "Jimmie! I didn't say to shoot —"

He paused mid-sentence, possibly realizing what she already knew: that had been Grace shooting, not Jimmie.

Or so Amelia desperately hoped.

"Damn you," Calvin said. He hesitated in that awkward pose, seemingly unsure of whether to continue toward the ladder or return to the house to see what had gone wrong.

Amelia took advantage of the moment. She reached the heavy revolver forward as far as she could, jammed its barrel into the man's groin, and jerked the trigger.

The shot seemed at once like the loudest sound she had ever heard, and yet surprisingly soft, more of a *crack* than a *boom*. Even before she pulled her hand away, Calvin's blood jetted onto her hand, her arm, her face, and the darkened steel of the old firearm. The sheep scattered, leaving just Amelia and Calvin at the center of the barn. He screamed and buckled over, folding himself almost in two, grabbing at his crotch and cursing between clenched teeth. Saliva sprayed her, flecking her forehead and mixing with the blood there.

Then his gaze focused on her, and he seemed to remember the gun in his hand. As he was swinging it toward her, she fired again. This time her bullet tore through his chin and out the back of his head, filling the air with a fine red mist. He toppled forward, and she barely scrambled away before he landed on her.

Amelia realized that she hadn't counted the bullets inside Roy's old pistol before she carried it to the barn. Not wanting to be caught short, she snatched up Calvin's, righted her apron, and stuck Roy's in the pocket. Calvin, she guessed, was a more experienced gun hand, and would not go around with his weapon half-loaded. So armed, she started toward the house.

"Grace!" she hollered as she approached it. "Ruth Ann! It's me!"

The door stood open, and Jimmie lay half-inside, his head toward her, eyes open, mouth gaping, a ray of sunlight catching his gold teeth. Inches below that was a bloody tear in his throat. His blood was still pooling around him, a lake of red so dark it was almost black except where the sun glinted off it.

"Grace!" Amelia called again.

She saw the barrel of a rifle appear first, around the corner from where the girl's bedroom lay. Then Grace followed it into the main room, with Ruth Ann clutching her shoulder. "Mother!"

"Are you hurt?" Amelia asked. "Did he —"

"He never got near us," Ruth Ann said. "As soon as he came in, Gracie shot him."

Grace was trembling, tears cascading down her cheeks, sucking in her lips to keep from blubbering. Amelia stepped around Jimmie's corpse, took the rifle from her and leaned it against a wall, then wrapped her arms around both girls and wept with them.

They found every bottle of liquor that Roy had squirreled away in the house and splashed it on the floors and walls and furnishings, along with all the lamp oil, cooking oil, and grease they had. Hitching both mules to the buckboard — Amelia worried that the outlaws' horses might be too easily recognized, so left them behind — they loaded it with every necessary the three of them owned. They helped themselves to provisions and weapons from the outlaws' belongings and added those to the wagonload. The two smaller dogs would ride in the wagon, and the shepherd would follow, as he always did unless he was tied up.

Amelia dragged Calvin's and Bentley's bodies up from the barn by herself, not wanting her daughters to share in such a grisly chore, and she left them on the floor with Jimmie's.

Some of the money from the torn bag had blown away on the wind, but most of it was there, and the other three bags were intact. Those were secreted on the buckboard, inside a trunk and under their clothing, where no one was likely to come across it. Amelia thought it was enough money to start a new life, some-place where no one had heard of the Earll family. They might buy a farm or a store, earn an honest living. The mining company made enough from pulling ore out of the ground to replace the miners' pay, so she didn't worry that anyone would go hungry on her account.

The fire, she hoped, would dispose of the outlaws — Roy's compatriots, she knew now. Her husband had hidden so much from her that he felt like a stranger, like someone whose life had intersected hers for only a moment and then passed out of it.

Amelia wrapped a good-sized stone in one of Roy's old kerchiefs and soaked it in alcohol. When Amelia struck a match and touched it to the cloth, it burst immediately into flames. She hurled it through the open front door. She didn't feel that she was ending something. She barely felt anything at all, except perhaps a slight sense of relief, as if an ache that had troubled her for days had miraculously vanished upon awakening in the morning.

She climbed onto the buckboard's spring seat, nestled between her daughters, and clucked at the mules. By the time the smoke could be seen from Bisbee, across the hills, they would be miles from here and heading east, away from the sunset, and toward tomorrow and all the days after that.

#

I lived in Cochise County, Arizona from 2004 to 2016 — most of that time, on 40 acres of what had been open range, used by the Erie Cattle Company, among others. It's a big, sprawling border county, as large as the states of Rhode Island and Connecticut combined, but sparsely populated. Sierra Vista was, and remains, its largest city. Other towns of comparatively significant size are Benson, Douglas, and Willcox. Tombstone's population is small, but its hold on the American imagination is strong.

Until February 1, 1881, there was no Cochise County. In its early days it was part of Pima County, of which Tucson was and is the population center. But the distance between Tucson and the towns of Cochise County made managing affairs and enforcing Pima's laws problematic, so Cochise County was carved out from Pima's eastern side, and Tombstone declared the county seat. Johnny Behan was appointed sheriff of the new county, with an office in Tombstone, where Virgil Earp was already the city marshal and a deputy U.S. marshal. If Behan and the Earps hadn't had different ideas about enforcing the law—Behan sided with the Cowboys—would the October 26, 1881 gunfight near the O.K. Corral have ever taken place? Cochise County — particularly Bisbee and Tombstone — was the site of much crime and violence in those early days, and that's what my story is about.

—Jeffrey J. Mariotte

Editor, author, and Silverado Press co-founder Jeffrey J. Mariotte is the award-winning author of dozens of books, including the *Major Crimes Squad: Phoenix* procedural thriller series, historical Western epic *Blood and Gold: The Legend of Joaquin Murrieta* (with Peter Murrieta), the *Cody Cavanaugh* Western series, *Tarzan and the Forest of Stone*, the *Deadlands* novel *Thunder Moon Rising*, and many more in various genres. He's also known for his comics and graphic novel work, especially the long-running Weird Western series *Desperadoes*. Three of his novels have won Scribe Awards for Best Original Novel, presented by the International Association of Media Tie-In Writers. He's also won the Inkpot Award from the San Diego Comic-Con, is a co-winner of the Raven Award from the Mystery Writers of America, and he has been a finalist for the Spur Award from the Western Writers of America and the Peacemaker Award from the Western Fictioneers, among many others. He has worked in virtually every aspect of the book business, including bookselling, editing, and publishing. He lives in the desert with his wife, author and poet Marsheila Rockwell, and their family.

THE BUFFALO

SHARON FRAME GAY

I t's easier to talk about it, now that time brushed the clouds of doubt away and replaced them with wonder. This ain't just a yarn. It's my heartsong. The ballad of an old man who sits here by this river and whittles his words for you, so you can see 'em carved into your imagination. Sit down and have a listen. It just might touch your soul, the way it did mine. I swear to you, every word is true. . . .

The year was 1865. Like so many men, I was a shadow of myself when the Civil War ended. Now, I suppose, you want to know what side I fought on. I ain't gonna tell ya. You might think you can figure it out because of my accent, or where I lived before the war started, or where I live now. That's up to you to decide. Because in my mind, that war didn't matter one way or another, who fought for what side. All that really mattered was, we turned on each other like rabid wolves. Every one of us should have had more sense.

I didn't have a home to return to after I mustered out. Both my mother and father died while I fought on distant battlefields. I had no stomach to go home. I had no other family. No woman waited for me. To tell the truth, I don't think I wanted one, anyway. I yearned to be free and follow my dreams.

It didn't take me more than an hour to decide I was headin' west. I didn't know where, but I figured my heart would tell me when I got there. So, one bright morning I started out fresh as paint on my horse, Ranger. I rode straight and confident in the saddle, and Ranger pranced beneath me like a circus horse on our way to a new start.

Within a week, the journey lost a bit of its luster, the way your boots do when they need shining, but you don't have the time. They get mud-caked and wrinkled and will never have that sheen again. That's how I felt. Like my entire being got worn down until all that was left was a touch of scrappiness that I knew to be the last gasp from a stubborn soul.

We made good time, though, even though my enthusiasm got dropped along the trail right outside of St. Louis. The rest of the journey was just a prairie-swept gauntlet we ran, day after day. I thought my future was waiting for me over the next hill. But all I saw was another hill, then another, until my eyes ached. The stubborn part of me decided that instead of turning back, I'd cast my net towards Montana Territory.

Now, I imagine you're asking yourself why I didn't just stake out some land there on the Great Plains and build myself a sod hut like a lot of men were doing. I thought of it. But I decided I wanted to see those tall mountains in Montana I'd heard about. I pictured them clean and blue and forgiving, and I needed plenty of forgiveness after what I'd done in the war. So, I pushed on.

Sometimes I'd see Indians in the distance, and my heart quickened. I'd heard many tales about these people, and a lot of it was downright upsetting. They never got close enough for me to find out. They were always far away, the way a mirage is, somethin' shiny in the distance that disappears if you ride up on it.

Once I reached Montana Territory, I felt something uncoil inside, the way a spring feeds a lake and renews it. This was going to be my new home. Now I just had to figure out where.

Well, the Crow had other ideas. I saw them one morning up on a ridge, trailing along in single file and lookin' down at me the way a predator stares into a tide pool, just waiting to pick out the fish that's trapped in there.

My hand pulled on the rifle like a baby to a teat all day long. It was my comfort. I figured if they attacked, I'd die anyway, but at least I had something to hold on to when they dispatched my sorry hide.

That night, I hardly slept. *This is when they'll swoop in and scalp me,* I thought, but in their native wisdom they let me simmer in my own juices of worry, while they probably slept in peace.

There was no peace for me. I mounted at first light and swiped Ranger with my spurs, just to let him know we needed to step up our pace. My head swiveled around like an owl all morning long, but I didn't see a single soul, red or otherwise.

That afternoon, I saw movement down by a wide river that appeared along the horizon like a fat snake. It wound its way through a valley, pretty as a picture. I figured nobody would kill me in such a heavenly place, tied Ranger to a tree, and walked to an outcropping of rocks to gaze at the scenery.

I peered over the ledge and gaped in awe. In a clearing below was a herd of buffalo. Nowadays you folks call them bison, but to me they'll always be buffalo, and so that's what I'll call 'em. At least forty of them grazed in the tall grass, moving their wooly heads back and forth like a scythe, cutting through the meadow. If they saw me up on the rocks, they didn't seem to care.

But I cared, when I looked across the banks and saw a hunting party of Crow on the other side of the water. They were making gestures with their arms and pointing at the herd. The men split up and spread out along the far shore, then crossed the river. Their horses thrashed around and lost their footing, then launched into a swim. Then they clamored up the bank and on into the valley.

The buffalo lifted their enormous heads and gazed at the Indians coming their way. One or two snorted and raised their tails. But most of 'em just kept yanking on the grass like nothing was amiss.

Maybe they were right to think that way, because once the Crow caught a gander at me, they forgot about tracking those animals. I could tell the instant they switched from hunters to a war party. One man raised a spear over his head and let out a blood chilling whoop. The others followed suit.

I scrambled off the rocks, pulled myself up on Ranger, and turned his neck so fast I swear it could have snapped right off his shoulders. Startled, he gave a little crow-hop, then burst into a gallop. I rode low over his neck and prayed for deliverance.

Damned if those Indians didn't sound like a mountain lion with all their screaming and hollerin'. It was enough to make my hair turn white. You don't believe me? See this lightning streak right over here next to my ear? It turned white that very day. I once had hair black as a raven's wing. You wouldn't know it now that I'm an old feller. But if you look real hard at my head, you'll see the streak standing out among the gray.

The buffalo decided they didn't like all that ruckus. One after another, they followed me across the valley in a panic, the Indians right behind them.

There we were, me riding low on Ranger and praying he didn't step in a prairie dog hole, the buffalo bearing down on us like the hot breath of the Devil, and behind them the Indians, their war cries cutting all the way to the heavens.

The stampede closed the gap between us alarmingly fast. Ranger's ears were flat against his head, eyes rolling in terror. My heart was beating so hard in my chest it felt like it was going to climb right out.

An arrow shot past my shoulder. I heard it sing its death song as it flew by. Right behind it was another. Then another. One of 'em struck Ranger in the haunch and he leaped ahead, taking the bit in his mouth. It felt like sitting on top of thunder as his hooves hit the ground hard. We raised up a dust devil, and when I looked behind, I saw nothing. Just a big cloud with the eerie sound of hooves and hollerin' coming out of it, the way the wind whistles down your chimney on a winter's night.

"Help me"! I shouted to nobody. My cries of terror turned into something I can't describe. I just kept howling and praying as we swept across the land.

All of a sudden, the ruckus slowed behind me, then stopped and grew quiet. I thought for a second that I'd lost my hearing. Looking back, the dust was clearing. Still, I heard nothing. More curious now than petrified, I pulled on the reins and Ranger slowed to a frightened jog. I dared to take another look.

The Indians were gone. Vanished. Settling in the sunlight of a cloudless day roamed the buffalo, calm as they were before, going about their business.

I pulled Ranger to a halt. His sides were heaving, and he pawed at the ground. If I didn't see the arrow in his haunch and the blood trickling down his leg, I would have thought it had never happened. The arrow hadn't done much but poke his hide. I tugged it out and snapped it in two.

The meadow was empty except for the herd. I strained to see, as there was still some dust in the air from the stampede. I wondered if the Indians were invisible behind it, and then they'd reappear right in front of me like magic.

Now here's the part you ain't gonna like much, because you'll think I'm spinning a tall tale. Let me take a swig of water before I continue, because my throat's parched and tight, thinking about that day. I need to tell it just right.

Stepping out of the cloud of dust like a damned ghost was a huge buffalo. He snorted and shook his wooly head, then circled the herd like a general, giving orders with his grunts and nudgin' em with his muzzle. I could tell he was their leader. The animals meandered through the grass, swishing their tails, hides twitching like they were knockin' off flies, just as peaceful as they were by the river.

But here's the amazing part. That lead buffalo bull was white as milk. An albino. Or maybe a spirit animal. The sun shone on his thick hide as if lit from within by a thousand candles. His horns were dark as pitch and gleamed. He towered above the other buffalo, maybe half again as big.

I know you've heard plenty of stories about white buffalo, and maybe you've had your fill of 'em. But this testimony is straight from a witness. Me. I was just about as doubtful as you probably are now, but that creature was white as could be. He stood out in the meadow like snow.

"So that's what chased those Indians off," I muttered, relief flowing through me. I shivered as all my nerves shook loose the fear they were housing, and grabbed on to the saddle horn so I wouldn't swoon.

The white bull reached down and tore out a piece of grass and chewed on it. Then he turned his head and fixed his eyes on me. It felt like he put me in a trance.

He started walkin' towards us in slow, measured strides. The kind of steps a king might take. Sure of himself. Arrogant. Beautiful in his own way.

And me? Why, me and Ranger just stood our ground like he'd hobbled us with his mind or something. Frozen, we watched as he approached. Ranger snorted and stepped back, breakin' the spell. But by then it was too late. The buffalo stood only a few feet away.

He rolled his eyes and snorted, then took a step closer. If we moved in any direction, he'd try to kill us.

I swear he came right up to my leg and sniffed at it, his breath warming my thigh. I could have reached out and touched his shaggy skull. A rope of saliva spilled along his jaw, and when he shook his head, the spittle covered me like a summer rain. I didn't move.

He bumped my horse with his head, but Ranger stood his ground. Then he bumped him a little harder and Ranger started walking. The buffalo walked beside us. Craning my neck, I saw the whole herd fall in behind.

So there we were, this parade of sorts, with me and Ranger and the big white bull, leading his herd to God knew where, and I let him push me along, too.

We walked like this for what seemed like hours before I found my voice. It sounded rusty in my throat and high as a little girl's.

"Thank you," I said. I don't know how he did it, but that buffalo saved my life. Somehow, he chased off those Indians, and now he was ambling alongside me as gentle as walking to church. And maybe we were. Maybe he was God or somethin' and if I blinked my eyes, he'd disappear. Only we just kept walkin', and so did the herd. Ranger relaxed under the saddle. I even hummed a tune under my breath, the way you do when you finish up a battle and you're not quite over feelin' jittery, but realize you still have all your parts.

At nightfall, I worked up the courage to climb off Ranger and lead him over to a tree. I took off the saddle and tied him to a limb, then tended to his injury. After that, I slid to the ground with my blanket and huddled as close to the trunk as possible.

The white buffalo settled in beside me, so close I could hear him breathe. He stood there all night. I know he did, because I didn't sleep a wink. The next morning the huge bull went about his business with the herd while I saddled Ranger and mounted.

You won't believe this either, but that herd walked with me for days. I lost track of how many days, to tell you the truth. But long enough for me to grow so used to it I sometimes got off Ranger and walked with the bull, talkin' to him. He'd toss his massive head and snort as though he were listening. Or maybe taking my measure.

Things got serious one morning when I talked about the Civil War. I told him how I cried like a baby almost every night, and the only way to find the courage to go to battle the next day was because there was no other way out.

The buffalo grew quiet. He rocked his horns from side to side and his eyes looked straight into mine with such compassion that I sat down right there in the middle of the grass and wept. I showed him my boots and how they were worn-out from battle, the soles stuffed with paper. I pulled a bible out from my coat pocket and told him how it caught a bullet, right through the page that said "thou shalt not kill." Then I told him about my horse, and how Ranger once belonged to a soldier from the other side. I chased after him when his rider got shot right out of the saddle and died. Poor Ranger bolted in terror, but I hung on to his reins. He dragged me ten feet before he calmed down.

It was me who killed that soldier and took his horse. I ain't never told anybody that before. Just the buffalo. And now you...

I even talked to that buffalo about a girl I once loved. Why, she never knew I hankered for her. Her name was Sally, and I swear her red hair blazed like an autumn leaf at dawn. Before I went to war, I must have paraded past her house a hundred times, just hopin' to get a glimpse of her. Only I seldom did. And right before I was foolish enough to join the other men to go off to battle, she married the son of a local shopkeeper. I thought my heart would break, and now I carry that pain with me, too. Every time I see a sunset, I think about her hair, and how I would have given up ten years of my life just to run my fingers through it. Just once.

Clearing my throat, I let him know I was an orphan now. Both my parents were dead. "I hope you never lose your family here," I said, looking around at the herd. For the first time, I reached out and patted his nose. He didn't back away. "I have no next of kin. No wife or children to carry on my name. I have nothing but Ranger here and my saddle, and a wanderlust that was just about to slake until you walked out of the clouds and saved my life."

I was to find out later this wasn't true at all. The buffalo didn't save my life. He was prayin' I'd save his.

One morning, I awoke to find myself and the herd surrounded by a party of Crow. I jumped up, then sank back down on my knees, prepared to beg for my life. The white buffalo shook his massive head and stamped his hoof, pacing between me and the Indians in a menacing way. They shrank back. All but one. A tall Indian with a jagged scar across his face and feathers in his hair stepped forward and faced us.

"I talk English. We aren't here to fight. We're here to see the great buffalo."

Now, you might think I was a fool, but I believed the man right off, and sighed in relief. I held out my hand in peace, but he stepped back, like he was afraid or somethin'.

"The buffalo is your friend," he said.

I nodded.

The Indian shook his head in wonder. "You have strong magic to have such a spirit as your friend. We came to see who this white man is. What is your name?"

"Me? Why, I'm James Swift. I ain't got no problem with you folks. I hope you let me pass through your land in peace." Then I remembered my shaggy guests. "And the buffalo, too. They're on their way somewhere, and I think it's important."

The Crow nodded, then sank to the grass cross-legged. I did the same. The white buffalo stepped aside and grazed while we talked.

It weren't much of a conversation, but the upshot was the Indians thought we were part of the spirit world. The leader gave me this beautiful pouch I wear every single day on my belt. See here? Those colorful beads are all sewn in a design that means something to the Crows. And this feather I keep in the pouch came straight out of that Indian's braid. It's black as night and must have been powerful, because he gave it to me with the most solemn expression on his face I've ever seen.

They brought me food, and we sat and talked a while more before he rose and made a signal with his hand. His men mounted and turned their ponies towards the east.

"You will be safe going through our land, James Swift," he said. Then he swung up on his pony and let out a little whoop. They galloped away so fast Ranger yanked at his reins on the tree limb and snorted, all excited and wanting to join them.

The Indian spoke the truth. For days, our strange caravan passed through the territory in peace. Wherever we went, natives lined up to watch us on our way. Sometimes they raised their arms to the sky and cheered. Other times, they knelt like they were in the presence of God. The children had eyes big as saucers as they stared and chattered among themselves. Old folks often wept.

I'm telling you right now there was a majesty about that buffalo and his herd. He walked with dignity and bowed his head as we passed by the Indians like he was blessing them. There was somethin' holy going on, I figured, and I was a part of it, like a Magi. Bit by bit I felt my burden lift, and I knew that God or the buffalo or something was telling me it was okay. Maybe at last I'd find forgiveness.

Winter was in the air. I smelled it one morning when I rose from the campsite and led Ranger down to the stream to drink. I'd hoped to find a homestead before then, but nothin' felt right. I kept thinking I might find something better. I pictured a ranch, a wife, and the whole herd living with us on our land. Maybe I trekked on longer than I should have, but I still harbored that stubborn soul.

When the peace shattered, it happened all at once, the way your horse will shy and buck in front of a rattler. There was no time to think. No time to figure anything out. It was just there.

A line of riders appeared over a hill, bearing down on us. At first I figured it was the Crow again. But then I realized they were white men. Lots of them. My heart leaped with happiness to see them after all those lonely months, but as quick as I felt comfort, dread set in.

The bull lifted his head and let out an angry bellow. His herd stood stock-still for a moment, then took flight, the men chasing them. I barely got the saddle on Ranger when the first rifle shots rang out as they bore down on the beasts.

"No!" I screamed. "Stop!!"

I jumped on Ranger and headed towards the massacre, waving my arms and shouting at the men.

The white buffalo galloped beside me, then lowered his massive head and passed us like we were standing still.

One by one, the buffalo were killed. They hit the ground hard, raising clouds of dust as they fell. Calves turned in circles, bawlin' for their mothers. They were cut down, too. As I raced past, the scent of blood in the air was so strong I thought I was back at Gettysburg.

Then the hunters turned their attention to the white bull. The men pointed and hollered among themselves. They aimed their rifles. I raised mine.

I shot at 'em and they shot back. The first bullet struck Ranger in the neck, and he went down, sending me flying into the grass. Another bullet ripped into my shoulder and back out again like it was just visiting. Pain seared through my body.

The white buffalo spun on his heels and placed himself between me and the white men. They bore down on us like a flash flood. I fired my rifle at them, but I was no match with my torn shoulder. Within seconds, they had surrounded the great bull.

That buffalo was brave. He stood his ground and pawed at the dirt in fury as several slugs slammed into his hide and brought him to his knees. Even then, he didn't give up. He thrashed and hollered and lunged as the men dismounted and approached him.

"No!" I screamed. Then that was all I knew because a hunter jumped off his horse and hit me square in the back of the head and knocked me cold.

When I finally opened my eyes, I wanted to close them again. I crawled over to Ranger. He was dead. The hunters cut the saddle off and hauled it away, along with my rifle. I patted his neck. My good companion. Gone. I placed my head on his noble belly and cried.

All around me was a field of death. The hunters had skinned the buffalo, cut out their tongues and taken their hides. They left the meat behind. It was already rotting in the sun, flies buzzing in droves. I shook my head at the waste.

The white buffalo was missing his hide, and his mighty head, too. Only his milky tail and great size were recognizable. I bowed my head in anguish. He wasn't magical or a spirit animal. He was flesh and blood like the rest of us sorry souls, after all. Whatever power he possessed was taken from him under the knives of the hunters.

Bleeding, I staggered back to the tree and wrapped myself in a blanket. Then I fell into such a deep sleep I figured I was dyin'.

The next morning, the Crow rode on to the battlefield. Their yips and shouts shook me out of my dark dreams. They rattled their lances and screamed towards the sky. Then they approached, their faces etched in sorrow. All we did for a while was just stare at each other.

One warrior walked over and nudged the white buffalo with his toe. He knelt and pressed his hands into the blood and drew war paint on his face. Then he painted some on his pony, too.

The Indians lifted me up and put me on a horse. We rode through the woods to a village where I stayed for months as I healed. I learned their ways. They learned mine. We grew to trust each other, and they treated me with more kindness than I deserved.

They didn't understand when I said I needed to leave. They wanted me to stay with them, and I have to tell you, I did, too. But I decided I had to tell my story to folks from Montana Territory, through the Great Plains, and all the way back east about what I witnessed. They needed to know how the buffalo were slaughtered and wasted. Hunters needlessly killed millions of those magnificent animals. The Crow, and all the Indian nations, were robbed of their food and their destiny. The buffalo were robbed of their future. And this country was robbed of its integrity.

I figured this is what that white buffalo wanted from me. He wanted me to speak for him, and it was my honor to do it.

The Crow gave me a horse and followed me out of their village in a gentle procession that raised my spirit and gave it wings. My horse tried to turn around three times and go back to them. It took every bit of my resolve not to let him.

I wound my way through this country, talkin' to anyone who'd listen, begging for help for the buffalo and the Indians. I think it fell on deaf ears most of the time. But I had to do something. That buffalo counted on me.

In 1867, the Kansas Pacific Railroad hired William F. Cody to hunt buffalo for meat to feed the railroad workers. Before long, there were rivers of men flooding the Great Plains, killing the buffalo by the droves. My heart sank straight into the prairie as I passed carcass after carcass rotting in the grass on my way to the next settlement. I swear there were times when I felt the ghost of that white buffalo walkin' beside me, shaking his great wooly head in sorrow.

Hope lifted as a representative from Illinois, Mr. Ford, introduced a bill on January 5, 1874. The bill was to prevent the slaughter of buffalo. *'Finally'*, I thought, *'the killing might stop'*. Although the bill passed through the house and senate, it expired on President Grant's desk.

I was in Omaha the day I read about it in a newspaper. Trembling with disappointment, I stood in front of the bar at a local saloon and spoke to the crowd. Some of the men grumbled, shaking their heads. Several rose from their chairs and glared across the room. Then, two buffalo hunters walked up, grabbed me by the collar, and hauled me through the swinging doors.

"Shut your damned mouth if you want to keep your *own* hide, stranger," one man hissed, his filthy fingers digging into my neck. "Yer talking about our livelihood. Leave town before someone shuts you up for good."

The other man pressed a pistol into my back, then shoved me off the walk into the dirt. I struggled to my feet as they turned and stalked back into the saloon. The music started up again and voices filled the night, a dismal light from the saloon pouring into the road where I stood with fists clenched by my side. Nobody could make me stop, no matter what they did.

I kept on talking wherever I went until my voice gave out, and eventually my legs did, too. Years rolled by, and the weavers of time turned me into a threadbare old man. I ended up here along this muddy river, livin' in a home for old soldiers. It ain't a bad place to live. There's plenty of food and a soft place to sleep. The folks around here are kind.

They all say I'm crazy, though. None of 'em believe me, even though they hear this tale every day. Most of 'em think I bought this beaded pouch from the ancient Indian who sits in front of the dry goods store, or I found the feather lyin' on the ground somewhere. Some even said I never went out west at all, that I'm muddled from the war and dreamed it all up. "Crazy Jim," they'd mutter, and wink like I have the brains of an otter. Then they walk right past like I'm invisible and go about their day.

This is why I perch here along the banks of the river each morning, and why I'm tellin' all this to you. I hope that someday, maybe someone will believe my story and set my spirit free. I can tell you right now that I'll feel it, wherever you are, when you believe. Then maybe things will change. I'll know because the moon will shine overhead, even in the middle of the day, and I'll see the faces of Ranger and that white buffalo in the clouds.

That's when I'll be set free and join them for a journey among the stars. Until then, I only ask that you listen, then make up your own mind.

#

"The Buffalo" is a fictional story, as seen through the eyes of a man who traveled to the Montana Territory in hopes of making a better life for himself. Instead, he witnessed the greatest massacre of animals in American history.

The end of the Civil War in 1865 brought an influx of settlers and growth to the Great Plains and the West. In 1867, William F. Cody was hired by the Kansas Pacific Railroad to hunt buffalo in order to provide meat for the railroad workers. Thus began the near extermination of the American Bison, resulting in an impact on the Native Americans who relied on them as a primary source of food. In 1874, a federal bill was introduced to Congress in an effort to stop the slaughter, but President Grant "pocket vetoed" the bill.

Millions of bison were killed, irreparably changing the lives of the Native Americans.

—Sharon Frame Gay

Award winning author Sharon Frame Gay grew up a child of the highway, playing by the side of the road. She has been internationally published in anthologies and literary magazines, including *Chicken Soup for The Soul*, *Typehouse*, *Fiction on the Web*, *Lowestoft Chronicle*, *Thrice Fiction*, *Crannog*, *Saddlebag Dispatches*, Owl Hollow Press, 5-Star Publishing, and others. Her work has won awards at Women on Writing, *Rope and Wire Magazine*, Pen 2 Paper, and The Writing District.

Sharon is a 2021 recipient of the Will Rogers Award for excellence in Western Writing (short fiction) and a finalist for the 2024 Peacemaker Award (short fiction). She has been nominated several times for the Pushcart Prize, as well as the Washington Science Fiction Association Award, and Best of the Net.

Her collections of short stories, *Song of the Highway*, *The Nomad Diner*, and *The Wrong End of a Bullet* are available on Amazon.

The House of Evening Entertainment

Del Howison

Inside Ainima's room, darkness was a twenty-four-hour companion. This was her room. She told time by sound — vendors shouting their wares, the saloon next door, and Della checking in on her.

"Somebody is going trip over something in here and knock their brains out on your bedpost, Ainima," Della said.

Just prior to the house opening each evening, Della made the rounds of her girls and their rooms. She was a good mother, ran an honest house and tolerated no tomfoolery when it came to the business. She had a reputation to uphold. She managed with a tight fist and a touch of kindness for her workers.

The house madam always had one of the boys with her. Anything Ainima needed before the start of business would be taken care of when Della stopped in to check on her. She'd bring Ainima food and the boy would switch out the laundry. He would arrive with fresh bedding and remove the soiled sheets and clothing.

Della pulled the curtains open so the boy could see to clean up.

"Gauzy or not gauzy, that curtain material still blocks light. Pull them aside once in a while. Maybe open a window and get some fresh air."

Ainima didn't want to open the window and let the dust and heat from the mining operations enter her room. Light alone meant nothing to her. Yet, it remained hot in her second-floor room.

"Oh, can you see through them? Maybe there is still too much light. I keep the advantage when I can." Ainima smiled toward the wall. There was no mirror. There was no need.

Ainima turned back around facing Della, who stood in the doorway.

"It's close in here. Too hot," the madam said,

"Doesn't make any difference to me. They will all still want me. Everyone will be sweating in no time. They like that."

"That's the way men are," Della said.

Ainima smiled large.

"Am I beautiful, Della? Am I really beautiful? Or am I only another body, a female who is mostly a vision in their minds?"

"You are something special, Anna. There's no doubt."

Ainima cocked her head, listening to the music from the building next door.

"The dance hall is starting to kick up. Must be time for us to go to work," she said.

"I'll talk to you later," Della said. "Shout for Hector if you need anything. Now I need to gather up the other girls and parade them downstairs for tonight's reveal."

As she walked down the hall, she knocked on each door.

"Come on girls. It's showtime."

Ainima went to her window and pulled the curtains back across the glass. The shadows returned to her room of mystery.

Ainima stood in the middle of her room in darkness. He would be coming soon. She wanted to make sure everything was perfect for him. Only for him.

She removed her atomizer from the top of her bureau and spritzed the perfume to make the closed-up room more welcoming. She was the house favorite, even though most clients couldn't afford her. She was a mystery and needed to keep up that illusion. Ainima had a select clientele. He was her most select. In her mind she was a courtesan. In the minds of the patrons, she was a beautiful, consenting woman who understood their physical and emotional needs.

Her men managed the mines and the banks, making more money than anybody else in town. Except, possibly, her. She would work those she called *her boys*. She loved servicing her select group of bosses and politicians. She had no pangs about keeping the high rollers to herself. The other girls could fight for their own clients. This was the only time in her life that she'd felt special. The rest of her life she had only felt different. Her power came with the price they paid. Rich and powerful. She had everything.

Her downfall came with her heart. She was also in love. She would give up everything she had if only it was reciprocated. For someone in her position, love was not an option. Like everything else in her life, it was a dream one way or the other.

Cripple Creek was booming, with hundreds of gold mines and a population of more than 50,000. She had wound up there by a lucky break. It was one of only two lucky things that Ainima could remember ever happening to her.

Even more importantly, tonight was *his* night. He was the other stroke of good luck she had experienced. Though he paid the most money, it didn't matter. She would have given herself to him for free.

He was her island of comfort in the sea of confusion that lay right outside her window. She smiled, remembering the street fight a couple of months ago when a bullet had come through from outside and struck the framed picture of Jesus on the opposite wall. She was crying by the time he'd arrived. Not for the loss of the picture — she didn't know — but from fright, knowing it could have just as easily been her and not Christ who'd been hit in the heart. So maybe that was a third lucky thing.

He'd held her against his chest for almost an hour, making deep comforting sounds that whispered and rumbled like a distant thunderstorm, until she'd fallen asleep in his arms. He spoke to her softly and wiped tears from her face.

The last thing she remembered him saying was, "Jesus was a broken man anyway."

When she woke up the next morning he was gone. She could smell him, lingering in her hair. He also smelled of the oil paints he used to render pictures on canvas and the turpentine he cleaned the brushes with. He would lay in the bed with her and describe the scenes and colors. His visions splashed across the wood and canvas panels. It almost brought it to life for her when he described them. Over the years, her memories of colors had faded to grey. She loved to listen to him speak. Ainima never wanted to remember too much. She felt better without a past and only a future to live for.

Thinking of him made her smile. So did the sound of his boots coming down the hallway. She walked to the bureau and turned, facing the door. His walk stopped and he knocked, a firm but polite entrance.

Tonight, when her sweat beaded up, the clear liquid on her skin sat like dew drops on the bell flowers of the lilies of the valley, smooth, clear, inviting. It called to him, not only the lust from a sexual act, but the joy of being with a beautiful female who only wanted to spend time with him. For those evenings he was special. But he knew it was business, only an illusion, like his artwork. She always was there. For a fee she would be his for a lengthy time. He even kept a photograph of the two of them in his hat. Like a French postcard, her naked, offering the gifts of a thousand treasures only for him, and him standing behind her in dominance of the beauty. Her voice was earthy with a touch of choke. Something that would be hers forever since the fire and smoke when the wagon had burnt, taking away the light frailty of her voice along with her sight.

He slowly ran his soft artist's hands up the inside of her thighs. It teased her skin like a spider climbing to find a great spot to catch the insects that became entangled in its web. She moved and writhed, turning the slight irritation into a performance of desire and finally release. She imagined him seeing her contours, folding and unfolding her shape for a great piece of art he would create. He would immortalize her. She was in love.

"I was afraid you wouldn't come tonight," she said. "I was starting to panic."

He leaned up on his elbow as he spoke, playing with a strand of her hair.

"Never panic. Despite how frightening a situation may be, don't panic."

"There is excitement at the edge of panic, don't you think?"

"When panic wants to set in always stop and think first." He lay back down, looked up at the ceiling. "It could save your life."

"Oh really?"

"I have seen a herd of antelopes run themselves to death in panic. They died of fright. They panicked. They would have lived had they not spooked."

He was convinced she charged him more because she couldn't lie with another on the same evening, needing time to recover from their passionate encounters. That was part of his illusion. She was something special. She may have been the cleanest of all the women he had ever slept with. Best of all, he never got lice from her bed.

"I would love to paint your voice," he said.

"You can't paint sound."

"You can't see paint. I would love to try."

"I would love to hold you inside for the rest of my life," she responded.

He smiled at her and kissed the bottom of her earlobe, gently holding it between his teeth for a moment, then releasing it as he inhaled her scent. *Hell*, he thought, *for a whore she's the sweetest thing I've ever smelled*. He was going to miss her. He knew she would have no trouble finding others. Blind, she was exotic. Beautiful, she was a unique treat. Her healed purple scars created novelty.

She always led with her fingers instead of her mouth. You had to be clean to be a client. Della made sure of that. But you needn't be good looking. She was an ugly man's first prize. As long as she worked there, Ainima would never be alone, and she would never be out of money. He would miss her skill, but he doubted if she would even remember him after he'd been gone a fortnight.

From the street below a small choir from the local church sang "How Great Thou Art," being matched by drunken hollering and threats from the dance hall of sending them to their personal hell if they didn't go away. It was her turn to laugh. She rolled over, facing him so she could smell his warm breath on her face.

"It's the Salvationists," she said. "Who've come to save the world again. Getting to be damn near every night since they got that wagon to haul their asses back and forth with that band. They must think they are playing on stage at the Music Hall in New York City."

She laughed and wrapped her arms tighter around him, pulling him in as close as she could.

"Let's see if we can drown out their singing with the sound of our passion."

She giggled and kissed him hard.

Leaning her head back, she said, "Now that's a good start."

She paused.

"How come you've never hit me?"

He watched her face. She was serious.

"Why? Do most men hit you?"

"Some. I'm an easy target. Makes them feel strong. But I don't like it." She traced her finger along his jawline. "You never hit me."

"Hmm," he said. "I like your smile. I wouldn't want you to lose a tooth like some of those girls in the dance hall next door. And I like the color of your skin. It's white as snow with the purple crags of mountain rock showing through. Don't need it marred up with additional bruises."

He smiled and gave her a look of fake concern, though he knew she couldn't see it. "Have you done something wrong for which you need to be punished?"

She laughed. "I am flawed."

He pulled her close and kissed the skin covering the hollows of her eyes.

"You are perfect," he said. "Nobody has to tell you that you're beautiful."

She reached up and touched the side of his lips with her fingertips.

"Really?"

"Yes, really," he replied.

Shouting and yelling from the dance hall intermingled with the outdoor choir, which by now had moved on to "Swing Low Sweet Chariot." It was a strange juxtaposition with the out-of-tune piano from inside the bar and the two horns and a drum from the wagon stage. The two lovers paused to listen. Some yelling. Then a couple of shots. Everything went quiet.

"Cripple Creek creating new cripples," he said.

"What about me?"

"What about you what, Anna?"

He called her Anna, his shorter lover's name for her. She didn't know what her real name was, at least her white-girl name. The Blackfoot Indians had named her Ainima after they had pulled her from the charred wagon rubble. They had named her after the one thing she no longer had, sight. As a child she lived with them for a decade before finding her freedom. But they'd been kind.

"Am I crippled?"

He laughed. "Not the way you're working it tonight. I'd say you're magical. Nothin' broken I can tell of."

She laughed and ran her fingers through his hair. Then she slid the palms of her hands down along his cheeks, scuffing back and forth on his stubble and played with the inside of his ears. He grabbed her wrist and took her hand away.

"Stop it. You're tickling me."

Ainima sighed. "I want to see you. I want to set every feature on my brain like one of your paintings. I want to map you in my mind. Why should you have the advantage?"

"Because your eyes are blind." He kissed her fingers as he held her wrists.

She jerked her hands away.

"They aren't blind! They aren't even there," she said, and rolled out of the bed on the opposite side.

"I'm sorry. I was really hoping for a better night, on this of all nights."

"What?" She turned and faced him full. "What is it about tonight?"

"Well, it ain't the music," he said, referring to the cacophony below and trying to lighten the mood.

He sat there and watched her, framed against the light from the party next door. He had come to talk and now he couldn't get the words out. "Onward, Christian Soldiers" filled the air from below with the steady beat of their old Army marching drum and the tinny blaring of a horn. Sometimes it didn't sound like they were all working on the same tune. Their conversation was beginning to feel the same way. She knelt back on the bed.

"Oh, don't tell me how the story ends," she said.

At times, the way she tilted her head in the darkness, he imagined she could actually see. It was spooky, off-putting.

"Please let me continue to dream."

"Even dreams have endings," he said.

Now he rose from the mattress and turned away. She continued to face him, pulling her emotions inside herself. Ainima picked up a pillow and wrapped her arms about her in a self-hug.

"You've put the Devil in the room," she whispered, pouty. "Now we're done with good things."

He watched her. She kept turned towards the sound of his voice.

"The commission is over," he said. "The painting is complete, and my client is satisfied. The time has come for me to go back East." He sighed. "I'm sure I have work waiting for me that has been neglected while I created this project."

He clapped his hands together.

"I'm finished here."

She held a long pause and moved across to his side of the bed. As he stood there, Ainima reached over slowly and took his hand in hers. He watched her as she played with his hand, making small circles and then tracing the creases in his palm. She turned her face back up and smiled.

"Lately, I cry easy."

She turned her attention back to his lifeline. She stayed silent a moment as she ran her finger the length, detailing it in her mind.

"I'll be remarking about a person or maybe something I heard that wasn't particularly sad."

She smiled as she spoke.

"It could, in fact, be a good thing, like somebody has won a race or overcome a sickness and I'll have to stop for a moment and catch myself from speaking before choking up. I don't want to make a fool of myself."

"The sun will come up every day, whether I'm here or not," he said softly.

"Couldn't you have used longer, slower strokes?" She smiled to herself. "I know you have it in you."

He closed his eyes and smiled, tipped his head back and a breath escaped him.

"I can't . . . I have to go." He pulled his hands away. She could hear him as he removed his pants from the back of the chair and started pulling them on.

"Take me with you! I can change."

She'd climbed back into the middle of the bed and raised up on her knees. She was holding her arms out towards where he stood.

"I would never want you to change," he said.

"I can let go of my past. I've been real good about it, saving myself for only your visits," she lied. "But . . . I can't let go of my future."

She stopped, catching her breath before she sobbed.

"You can't come with me! Christ, Anna. I'm married. I'm not your future."

He took her arms and pulled them down by her side.

"No, no, this is where you belong."

He was trying to calm her. He watched her as he finished dressing.

"This is where your future is. My future is out there."

The conversation was shattered by a gunshot from the saloon next door. Then the screaming voices and angry tones continued out onto the street and a voice yelled, "I'm going to wrap that horn around your head iffen you don't shut up."

She folded her legs beneath her and slowly settled down on her calves, her hands flat on the tops of her legs. She turned her head towards the window.

"Do you ever get blue?" she asked of the curtains.

"I'm blue right now." He jerked on his other boot. "Just thinkin' about leaving."

He stood up and took a couple of bills out of his wallet, stared at them and then took out another. He folded them in half. Laying them on the wooden bureau top, he patted them a couple of times to make them stay folded. He reached into his shirt pocket and pulled out a small strip of canvas. Unfolding it, he smoothed his hand across its surface to make it lie flatter. On it was a charcoal drawing of the side of her forearm and hand. It caught it all, the gentleness and the strength, the river of scars running its length, and the fact that her hand was empty.

Reluctant as he was to leave, he knew that staying would only make things harder. He wanted it to be over. He'd grown too fond. She heard the click as he shut the door and then his boots down the hall. She could always tell his walk.

He stepped out on the sidewalk and stood still while two fellas punched themselves past him. Once they were beyond him, he moved down onto the dirt and walked towards the hotel. There he would grab his bags before heading to the stable, loading his rented buckboard, and heading off to Colorado Springs for the train.

In the dance hall, now behind him, there was a boom and a flash as a lantern shattered in the wooden room and the flames shot across the dance floor. He did not turn back to the sound. He was lost in his own emotions, fighting the confusion of his heart, forcing himself to march on to his destination.

Upstairs, in her room, Ainima soon smelled the burning wood, as vivid as any small fire inside the teepees of her youth. She walked to the window, keeping the curtains between her and the panes. The shouts and screaming were clearer there. The people were rushing in vain to smother the spreading conflagration. The screaming and the sound of the running crowd flowed up out of the street. She placed her hands flat on the curtains, pressing them against the window. By now, she could begin to feel heat through the glass.

She turned her head back toward the room door, hoping for the sound of his boots coming to get her. Everything was drowned by the noise from out of her window.

In her room the temperature rose as the floors below her burst into flame. On the bureau the scorching linen had a smell of its own as the canvas began to brown and the charcoal lines smoked, the edges of the folded money began to singe. The bills slowly opened and lay flat, allowing them to ignite. Within minutes they'd be fully engulfed.

As he snapped the reins and pulled his conveyance out of the stable, the horse stopped and whinnied at the smoke. The pumpkin-orange light reflected off the sheen of the beast's coat. The heat was strong from the burning buildings, and he drove the horse towards her, only to be stopped by an animal smarter than himself. The buckboard would be pulled no closer.

Her building was a celebration of flame. She was there, up high above the street in the window, not moving, with the palms of her hands pressed flat against the curtains and glass.

"Don't panic," she thought.

Suddenly the material between her and the glass exploded in a bright red hue and her image disappeared behind the sheet of flames.

He turned the horse away with little effort. The horse was ready to run. As he rode out of town through the push of people rushing in to help, he wondered if empty eyes were actually able to cry.

"Goddamned Cripple Creek," he said, and gave the reins a snap.

In April of 1896 the gold-mining town of Cripple Creek, Colorado lost most of its buildings when a kerosene lamp started a fire during a fight in a dance hall. Half of the town burnt to the ground. Four days later a grease fire in a hotel spread to its storehouse. The hotel had been storing half a ton of dynamite. Forty blocks of Cripple Creek were laid flat.

—Del Howison

Del Howison is an author, journalist, actor, and the Bram Stoker Award-winning editor of the anthology *Dark Delicacies: Original Tales of Terror* and *The Macabre by the World's Greatest Horror Writers*. He has written articles for Fear.net, Cemetery Dance.com. and *Writers Digest* among others. His western short story "The Lost Herd" was turned into the premiere (and highest rated) episode, "The Sacrifice," for the series *Fear Itself*. His dark western novel *The Survival of Margaret Thomas* was shortlisted for the Peacemaker Award given out by the Western Fictioneers. He has been shortlisted for over half a dozen awards, including the Shirley Jackson Award and the Black Quill. He is the cofounder and owner (with his wife, Sue) of Dark Delicacies, a book and gift store known as "The Home of Horror," located in Burbank, California. The store won the "Il Posto Nero" award from Italy and has been inducted into the Rondo Hatton Hall of Fame.

STAY

CHERYL PIERSON

There was a wagon where there shouldn't have been—

Randel Mason halted on the gentle rise overlooking the scene below. The wagon was close to Little Tree Creek where the occupants probably had stopped to make camp. Yet, there was no sign of a cookfire having been made recently. Rand edged forward slightly, taking a quick glance around.

The wagon stood motionless in the dry stillness of the April afternoon. *No horses.* The traces had been cut, hanging uselessly, with not a bit of movement. There was no sound from inside.

The wagon sat in eerie silence in the lengthening shadows of late afternoon. Sweat trickled down Rand's neck. He had become many things in his thirty-one years, but heartless wasn't one of them. With the recent land run taking place a few days ago here in Indian Territory, it looked like someone could need some help down there.

His horse, Mollie, grew restive and gave a snort. She'd sensed the water ahead, and Rand couldn't blame her for wanting to get to the creek and drink her fill. What was left in the canteens was tepid, and there wasn't much of it.

Rand tipped his hat back and took a swipe at his forehead. *Might as well get on down to that wagon and see what's going on.* He was ready to call it a day, even though it was earlier than he usually liked to settle in for the night.

The heat had let up some, but it was still hot for an April day. Mollie walked slowly, picking her way as if she sensed danger, too — or smelled death.

Rand drew up the reins a few feet away from the deserted prairie schooner and listened for any sound from within. There was no sign of life, either from tell-tale rustling inside the wagon, or from any movement that he could see. He dismounted and started forward, leading Mollie.

There was no way to use surprise to his advantage. A chill crept up his spine in the late April sun. *Was this a trap? But how?* No one could have planned on a lone traveler coming this way . . . discovering this wagon at a specific time of day.

The well-publicized land run here in Indian Territory took place five days ago — on April 22nd. *Someone must have tried to claim this acreage and run into trouble.* With no thought, the .44 was in his hand. He gave Mollie a quick pat and started forward.

They watched him from the woods on the far side of the clearing.

"What's he doin', Del?"

Del turned to his younger sister, Bethie, and put a comforting hand on her shoulder. "Don't you worry. I'm keepin' a good eye on him."

"I wish we could see, too," the youngest, Charlie, said. "Maybe you and Bethie could lift me up. . . ."

Del shook his head, not looking at Charlie. "Naw. . . ." Watching this man was serious business. It was up to him, as the oldest, to decide if it was safe to make their presence known. He was responsible. Miss Ella had said so often enough.

When they'd been attacked by the three men, Miss Ella had shot two of those outlaws. But the third one had kept on coming. Miss Ella had shouted for Del to run. He wasn't a coward . . . but what chance did he have against a full-grown man — and a big one, at that? *He had to get Bethie and Charlie to safety.*

Though he was only ten, he knew what bad men did to women. Having been raised in a whorehouse, he knew the difference between what happened when a man paid to be with a woman and when he took what he wanted against her will.

Besides, those other two weren't completely dead — at least, *one* of 'em hadn't been. He'd been yellin' for one of the others, Mr. Bill Wright, to hurry up and kill Miss Ella so Wright could get him to a doctor.

Finally, Wright had come out of the wagon wiping his knife blade on his pant leg. Del had covered his eyes. He'd felt like he was going to puke when he'd seen that. Miss Ella had been shouting right up to the very end. When she'd stopped, Del had known she was kilt.

Now, he watched as the lone cowpoke entered the wagon with his gun drawn and ready for trouble. *If he'd only been a half-hour sooner!*

Sudden tears stung Del's eyes, but he blinked them back fiercely. He had to be the strong one. He was the oldest. Bethie and Charlie wouldn't have a chance without him.

Somehow, he had to figure out a way to keep them all safe and together.

They'd set out from Fort Smith four weeks ago, headed right here to Indian Territory. Miss Ella said they'd have to go through some rough territory to get here, but she'd said it would be worth it — for them to have their own land. Right now, Del didn't feel *anything* was worth what had become of Miss Ella . . . and what might become of Charlie, Bethie, and him.

The overpowering smell of blood made Rand swallow hard. So much blood from one body . . . how could that be? And . . . the black, flowing cloth the woman wore suggested . . . .

He gently turned the body over, steeling himself for whatever he might find.

A nun? Someone had murdered a nun?

Rand let go a long string of curses as he tried to look past the crimson splatters. Her wimple had been ripped off and tossed to the side, freeing the woman's blonde hair.

Rand was no Catholic, but somewhere in the back of his mind, he had the idea that nuns wore their hair cut short. This woman's was long — long enough to curl and fall down around her face.

He pulled his knife and held it under her nose, not expecting to see any sign of life. But when a fine sheen of condensation formed on the blade, he sheathed it and quickly searched her body for the wounds she'd suffered.

The woman's chances of surviving were slim to none, but he was well familiar with duty — and there was no choice for him. His grim task was to stay here with her and see her through it — one way or the other.

He finished ripping the material of the habit she wore to be able to see what damage her injuries had caused. A deep knife wound in her right side still bled profusely. He quickly began to tear strips of cloth from the bottom of the garment she wore. Gently working it under her, he snatched up a piece of clothing he found lying nearby on the floor of the ransacked wagon, making a pad of it to soak up the blood. He tied the strip firmly in place, his mind racing.

It was stifling inside the wagon, but did he dare try to move her? He could easily carry her to the nearby stand of trees that bordered the creekbank. At least it would be cooler there. But that wouldn't matter one whit if she died from being moved.

Water . . . had the marauders taken all of it with them?

He hated to leave her, even for a moment. A person or beast shouldn't have to die alone. He would be here with this woman if she lived or died — whether she realized he was here or not. *He* would know he'd done all he could.

"Listen to me," he said quietly. "I'm here to take care of you, Sister. Your job is to just . . . try to survive."

He cast a quick glance about for a piece of cloth he might be able to wet and use to wipe the blood from her face and hands.

There was nothing in her expression to indicate she'd heard him. Her left eye was purpling and swollen, and there was a long gash across her forehead. He needed to examine her more closely, to see if there were other wounds . . . but damn, this wagon was close, and the stifling odor of fresh blood was enough to make a person sick, even without the sight of it everywhere.

"I'm going for water . . . I'll be gone for a few minutes, but I'll be back —"

At that, the woman's brow seemed to furrow in consternation, and Rand went on. "I'll hurry." He paused, then touched her cheek. "I won't let anything happen to you. Just rest."

Beside him on the floor lay a child's shirt. He stopped and looked again, then bent and picked it up. It was a white shirt made of soft material . . . looked as if it would fit a young boy of maybe eight or nine. . . .

What would a nun be doing traveling with a child? Had the would-be murderers stolen the boy? With a low curse, he moved through the wagon entrance into the fresh air. A quick check of the barrel of water tied to the side of the wagon turned to disappointment as he realized there was very little left.

Well, this would have to do for now, he thought, unstrapping it and tipping it toward the side to wet the cloth he carried. *The child's shirt. That poor young'un might never be seen again.* He had to find out where they'd taken the boy — and what had become of him.

Rand climbed back into the rank-smelling wagon, clearing a path as he made his way back to the woman. He wiped the blood from her face, along with a good deal of what looked like . . . *face paint.*

He scowled as he worked. Something wasn't right about any of this. A nun wouldn't paint up like an actress or a whore — not unless she was trying to somehow disguise herself. And a nun wouldn't be traveling with a child. A nun wouldn't have an enemy who'd kill her, or *try* to . . . .

This woman was not what she appeared to be — with each passing moment, he felt it more strongly. Nothing added up the way it should.

She groaned and tried to turn, but he held her in place effortlessly. She hadn't the strength to turn onto her uninjured side, he didn't believe, even had he released her shoulders.

There was something that touched him about her vulnerability. *He was all that stood between her and certain death.* And Rand wasn't at all sure *he* was enough. This woman was as near death as anyone he'd ever seen — but she fought to live. *By God, he was going to do whatever he could to help her.*

Suddenly, as if she'd sensed his thoughts, her lids fluttered, and she looked directly at him with eyes as blue as the turquoise skies of an early summer morning. Pain filled her expression for a moment, and then she muttered, "The children. . . ."

There was no mistaking her words. She wasn't out of her head with fever. And Rand *had* used a child's shirt to wash away the blood as best he could from her face and hands.

"I'll look for them," Rand responded, more to set her mind at ease than anything else There was not much chance that there were any children alive nearby — not with the viciousness of this attack. But he didn't want to say that. He would do whatever he had to do to save her life.

At his response, her face softened.

He didn't want to have lied to her, but he saw no point in leaving her alone for the time it would take to walk into the woods in search of the children she'd mentioned. Children he didn't expect to find.

He started to think she'd slipped back into darkness once more. Then, "Please. . . ." she whispered, when he made no move to leave.

"'M goin', ma'am," he responded, rising reluctantly and heading out of the wagon once again. He'd go, but he wouldn't be long — and he wouldn't leave Mollie behind. Unsure of what had happened here, it would be foolhardy to be separated from his mount. With reluctance, he swung into the saddle and headed toward the secrets of the beckoning woods.

"*Oh, donkey dang, he's comin'!*" Del exclaimed softly. "Bethie, you an' Charlie get over yonder behind that big ol' tree. Don't make any noise, no matter what."

"What're you gonna do, Del?" Bethie asked.

"Stand 'im off, best as I can," came the determined reply.

"Don't'cha get caught," Bethie bossed.

Del didn't call her on it. There wasn't time, and she and Charlie were already heading for the tree. Del hunkered down where he was, close beside a fallen log.

The man rode near to the trees, then urged his horse to enter the cool shadows of the woods.

Del hadn't had a chance to think about what would happen to them if Miss Ella was dead. All he cared about right now was the stranger. It was up to him to decide if this man would help them, or if he was a danger.

"Children! If you're in there, come on out and save me some time," the man called. "I need to get back to the — the lady in the wagon. She's hurt bad, but she's concerned for you."

"Miss Ella ain't dead?" a small voice sounded from behind Del.

Bethie!

Del's head swiveled around, but at least Bethie had the sense to stay hidden.

The man didn't come any closer. He only tipped his hat back on his head and relaxed in the saddle. He looked surprised when Bethie had spoken, but now, he only looked tired.

"No, she's not dead," he said, his eyes scanning the oak tree. "But she's badly injured. She needs — our help."

"I want to help," Charlie said, coming out from behind the tree. "I don't want Miss Ella to die."

"Me, either." Bethie stepped out from their hiding place to stand by Charlie. "Are the bad men gone?"

"*Well, double donkey dang!*" Del stood up angrily, looking at his sister and brother. "I told y'all to stay behind that tree and be quiet! Now, we're in a heap of trouble."

Rand stood down from the saddle and took Mollie's reins in hand. He schooled his expression to one of calm reassurance.

"Come on over here," he said, motioning for the oldest boy. For a moment, defiance turned the child's features mulish, but he came, anyway, and stood gazing up at Rand with fierce determination.

"I mean you no harm, boy. I just came up on the wagon back yonder, with no horses, and discovered a wounded woman inside."

A million questions hovered on Rand's lips, but seeing the varying expressions on these three waifs' faces, he knew he'd have to wait for answers.

"Now . . . can you tell me your names?" He turned and led Mollie back the way he'd come, the children falling into step behind him.

After a pause, Del said, "I'm Del Jackson, and this here is Bethie and Charlie."

"I'm glad to meet you." Rand stopped briefly to turn and put a hand out to Del, struck by the resemblance the boy bore to him. "I'm Randel Mason —" He broke off when the boy flinched and stepped back to keep his hand from making contact.

"I'm a lawman . . . ." he said quickly, trying to soothe the youngster with a half-truth. *I was a lawman. . . .* In his heart, he still was — and would be again. But young Del didn't need to know all those particulars. The worry in the child's eyes spoke of uncertainty, but the fleeting look of shock at the recognition of his last name was what caught Rand's attention.

Del recovered himself well, reaching to grasp Rand's offered hand firmly in his. *Strong grip for a kid. . . .*

Rand released his brief hold and started toward the wagon again with a quick step. "Del, when we get to the wagon, I want you to take a couple of canteens and go get me some water to tend Miss — Miss Ella with." He didn't like the idea of sending the boy off alone — not knowing what had transpired here — but the youngster seemed cagey enough to manage.

Del nodded. "I will."

"What can I do?" Bethie asked plaintively.

"And me?" Charlie piped up. "Don't forget me. . . ."

Rand smiled at Charlie's eager note of reminder not to forget him. "We'll find something for you and Bethie to do, Charlie," Rand promised vaguely.

They'd reached the wagon, and Rand turned to the children solemnly. "I don't want any of you coming in this wagon. Wait here for me." He jumped up onto the wagon and went inside, quickly locating a canteen that had been poured dry and left on the floor. He wiped it quickly to remove any blood and handed it out the opening to Del, who waited below. "Get my canteen from Mollie's saddle and take it, too. Try not to go too far."

Del nodded. "I won't."

"Bethie, you and Charlie go — go pet Mollie and keep her company, will you? She's traveled a long way." The two of them hurried off toward the horse, and Rand ducked back inside the wagon.

The woman hadn't moved. He quickly checked the wound. The bleeding had stopped, thankfully. He tried to adjust her clothing to make her more easy. Finally, he gave up. Unsheathing his knife, he gently began to cut the material away from the woman's body. She shivered as the warm air touched her skin, and Rand could tell it was from fear rather than cold.

He glanced around, looking for something to cover her with as he removed the blood-soaked material of the black habit she wore. He pulled a quilt from the bed and wrapped her in it, then carried her to the back of the wagon, lifting the flap. He held her close against him, his eyes scanning the prairie around them for any sign of whoever had done this woman such harm.

She seemed to weigh next to nothing as he carefully lifted her down from the wagon and started toward the creekbank with her.

Bethie and Charlie were gingerly petting Mollie, but they both started toward Rand as he carried the woman. He gave a curt nod toward Mollie, and they returned to the job he'd given them.

In a moment, Del emerged from the tree line with two dripping canteens and headed toward Rand, then stopped abruptly.

Rand met his shocked stare with a look of compassion.

"Oh, Mr. Mason is — is she . . . *dead*?"

"No, but that might happen, no matter what we do for her. Walk with me a minute — I want to talk to you."

Del hurried to catch up with Rand's long-legged strides as he moved on toward the creek.

"I want you to go back to camp and make sure your brother and sister are safe. Don't get into any mischief. Don't go into the wagon, Del. I — I need to clean up some things before —"

"I can do that, Mr. Mason," Del volunteered eagerly. "I helped out with the cleaning in Fort Smith in . . . in the place I lived."

Rand noted the guarded way the boy finished his sentence. He'd ask more about that later . . . had he been the illegitimate son of an unwed mother seeking refuge at a convent? He pushed his thoughts aside and concentrated on finding a level place to lay the woman down by the rushing water.

"No . . . no, I'll clean the wagon, son." *There were some things a youngster should never have to witness. These kids had already been through enough — whatever it might have been.*

As Del started to protest, Rand felt his patience slipping. He held his emotions tightly in check. He didn't want to scare the boy. "Please. Just do as I ask, will you, Del? I need to see what I can do for Miss Ella. You can help by keeping a good eye on your brother and sister. Later on, I want to hear all about what happened here."

Del nodded and turned to go.

"One thing. How many men were there?"

"Three," Del answered. "But Miss Ella killed one of them and like to have killed another. He managed to ride off, though, and took the dead one with him. She . . . she wasn't able to get the best of the third one. I think her pistol must have misfired."

"How long has it been since they rode out?" Rand took his bandana from his pocket and reached to wet it in the creek.

"They left right before you came. We — we ran and hid in the woods."

"Okay, son. You go on and look after the little ones. I'll see what can be done here."

When Rand had cleaned the woman up and made her as comfortable as possible, he started back to the wagon, planning for Del to come sit with her for a while. He'd get on with the wagon clean-up, and he imagined the kids were hungry.

Del was more than eager to do what he could to help while Rand took care of everything else. The boy had taken Mollie to the stream for a drink and occupied Bethie and Charlie. Del was old for his years, but he, too, was still a child.

"I'll get some dinner started if you'll come sit with Miss Ella," Rand told him as he walked into camp. "You run get me if she comes to," Rand directed him. "Take one of the canteens and give her a little sip of water if she wakes, then come running."

"I will," Del promised, heading off at a trot toward where Rand had left the woman.

Rand took a chance on building a small fire in case he found anything in the wagon to cook along with his own remaining supplies.

April nights could be cold out here on the prairie, and he wasn't sure the wagon would be fit for them to return to by bedtime. No matter what, now that the warmth of the day was fading, he planned to move Ella back to camp so she could rest by the fire.

Finding a can of peaches on the floor of the wagon amidst the ruins, along with some canned milk and a tin of flour, he figured they'd have themselves a feast tonight. Hardtack, biscuits, beans, and bacon, the makings for gravy, along with these peaches — at least they wouldn't go to bed hungry.

The shadows were lengthening. It was time to go get Ella, and hope for the best. Tonight would be a critical time for her survival. She seemed strong, but she'd lost a lot of blood.

As he reached the place where she lay, he noticed Del's expression of relief at seeing him. "Any trouble?" he asked.

Del shook his head. "No, sir. It's just — well, it's startin' to get dark. I — didn't have a lantern. I'm sure glad you came."

Rand smiled at him, then bent to gently gather up the woman and move her back to camp, with the boy following him. He slowed his steps so Del could keep up.

"Del, do you have any idea why those men attacked Miss Ella?"

By the way the boy shifted his gaze away, Rand figured he had to have some inkling of what the motivation had been.

"I need to know what we're dealing with. Every last piece of it. So don't lie, and don't leave anything out." Rand kept walking, not looking down at Del. "I want to help, but I can't if I don't know what's happening."

Del gave a long, shuddering sigh and Rand could feel his indecision. Trust was something this boy had a hard time believing in, and Rand couldn't blame him.

"There . . . there's a letter in the wagon that explains everything. Miss Ella only told *me* about it, not the little kids. She said in case anything bad ever happened to her to find someone I could trust and give them the letter. She told me to find a lawman . . . or a *good* preacher."

Rand quelled the smile he felt at that statement. He wanted to ask how Del would know a *good* preacher from a bad one. In his eyes, most of them were insincere charlatans.

"Are you . . . *really* a lawman?" Del's question was posed earnestly. It broke Rand's heart. Yes, he was — he *had* been — but any man Del asked could have answered in the affirmative. *How would the boy ever have known the difference? He had so much to learn, and no one to teach him.*

They'd reached camp and Rand took that moment to kneel and lay Ella on the ground near the fire, making sure she was wrapped and covered with the quilt.

When he looked up at Del, he nodded. "Yes. I am. I'd like to see that letter if you can tell me where to find it." He'd managed to clean most of the blood away, and he would burn the bloody remains of Ella's habit later when the children went to bed, but the wagon was still not a place he wanted the kids to enter. Not yet.

"Under the floor. There's a board you can take up —"

"Okay. You come with me. We'll go in and out quick, all right?"

Del shrugged, then nodded seriously. "All right. But I've seen blood before."

They went in together and Del retrieved the letter, immediately handing it over to Rand.

Outside, they sat beside the fire near Ella, while Bethie and Charlie contentedly ate bacon and hardtack. Rand opened the envelope and began to read the neat handwriting.

If you are reading this, I've either passed on or am close to it. We are traveling to Indian Territory for the land run. It's a fresh start for all of us — I hope.

The children are Del Mason (full name, Randel Raymond Mason, like his father)— Born July 4, 1879; Beth Jackson (father unknown) — Born March 23, 1881; and Charles (Charlie) Jackson (father unknown) — Born November 1, 1883. All have the same mother — Delinda Jackson. Their mother passed away in 1888. They are orphans, but all wonderful children.

It was my hope to reunite Del with his father at some point. The other children's fathers are not known, and it's my greatest desire that they shall all remain together.

I am Ella Eileen Reagan, also in need of a fresh start — hence, the land run. It's been said this will be an opportunity for all to start anew, with a bright future ahead. We set out from Fort Smith with high hopes for such a place.

With nearly two million acres waiting for new settlers to make of it what they will, I'm hoping for the very best for the children, even should I not live to see what comes of my claim. Should I pass on, my claim is theirs to settle on as best they can. Please, treat them fairly and kindly.

With all my gratitude,

E.E. Reagan

Rand sat quiet, not trusting himself to speak yet. *He had a son. A son!* He felt like someone had gut-punched him. Finally, he folded the letter and put it back in the envelope. *He had to make this right.* He remembered Delinda Jackson quite well. He'd visited her often. But he'd never known about Del. *Why hadn't she told him?*

"Can we have some gravy?" Charlie asked, bringing Rand back to the present.

"Sure." He dished up the rest of the meal for all of them, and there were smiles all around.

Rand ate in silence, listening to the ebb and flow of conversation around him, and noting that Del was quiet, as well. The boy didn't know what the letter contained, but he was aware Rand was his father. That was obvious by his reaction when Rand had introduced himself.

A son. He had a son, and he'd never known. And this boy, his son, was in danger . . . .

"Del, do you have any idea what those men wanted?"

"Sure. They wanted our claim. Said they'd been wantin' this piece of land ever since they heard about the land run. Only, they didn't get to the starting line on time. So, they decided to just come on in and take it anyway." He reached for another piece of bacon, then stopped himself. "Miss Ella might be hungry when she wakes up."

Rand nodded absently. "Yeah, maybe so. . . . What did Miss Ella say to them?"

"She said, 'You're not taking this from me. Move on. I have big plans for this land, and I'm not giving it up to a passel of . . . jackasses'."

Rand's lips quirked. "So, she's not *really* a nun."

Del shook his head. "No. She's — she *was* our mother's best friend, back at Miss Thomas's Elegant Pleasure Parlor for Men. She promised Mama she'd take us and we'd all get a fresh start. But . . . it looks like that won't happen now."

Rand laid a hand on the boy's shoulder. "You've carried a lot of weight on your shoulders, but that's all over with. I'll take care of things now."

Del nodded, then asked in a low voice, "Are you my . . . my father?"

Memories flooded over Rand. Delinda Jackson had been someone he could have loved if he'd allowed it. If they'd both been older. Ten years ago . . . it seemed like five lifetimes. He smiled. "That's what Miss Ella says in the letter. Your mother — she — well, she must have told you who I was. I know you recognized my name when I introduced myself." Del nodded and Rand went on quickly. "I didn't know, Del. If I had known about you, your life — and mine — would have been a lot different. But this is — really a miracle, that we should meet up like this. I'm gonna see it as a second chance — for both of us."

Mollie whickered, and Rand's grip tightened slightly on the boy's shoulder. "Go inside and take the others," he said in a low tone. "Do it now, but don't rush. Someone's here."

Del nodded and did just as Rand asked with no argument. Rand reached to put his bandana in his hand, quickly covering the gun he'd drawn and held under his dinner plate. He stood up and moved toward the shadows of the wagon, close to where Ella lay.

"Hey, mister, can I come in and get some grub?" a rough voice called from the gathering darkness.

Rand gave a slow nod, making sure he was in a good position before he replied. "Come and get it."

I'm ready. . . .

The stranger came into the light, his eyes widening at the sight of Ella, wrapped in the quilt beside the fire. Rand had to bite back his words. *This man had been the one who'd tried to kill her. He was surprised to find she still lived.*

"Shore am hungry," the stranger said with a greasy smile. "I thank ya for sharin' with me." His eyes shifted to the front seat of the wagon and the darkened opening to the interior.

Just then, Charlie's head emerged, followed by Del, snatching him back inside. The stranger's face quickly changed from smarmy affability to anger. He swore softly.

Rand knew from the boy's gasp of recognition he had the final proof he needed for his own conscience. This would be settled now, tonight. No other justice but what he meted out to this would-be murderer would be sought.

"Get inside, Del," Rand ordered softly, not looking away from the stranger.

The man stood still. There was no doubt he understood that he'd been found out. "This woman, here, she kilt my little brother and our cousin earlier today. Lucky I had a knife. She went plumb loco! I — I had to save myself —"

"But you didn't. You just put your fate off until . . . *now.* I need your name." Rand dropped the tin plate and bandana to the ground, revealing the six-gun in his hand.

"My — my *name?*"

"Yeah. I need to know what to carve on your grave marker."

"*Wait — I —*"

"*Draw.* You're a dead man, either way, but I thought I'd give you a better chance than you gave her." He nodded at Ella's still form.

With a feral growl, the man made a desperate grab for his gun. Rand fired sure and true, the bullet finding its mark in the man's chest. He fell to the ground with a groan of pain and shock. Rand walked toward him, his .44 still smoking.

Standing impassively silent over the stranger, he offered no word or expression of emotion. "Your name? I'm gonna need it."

"Bill . . . Wright. . . ."

Rand nodded. "Where is the team for this wagon?" he asked curtly.

"I'm not . . . tellin' . . . *you.*"

Without a word, Rand put his boot heel over the bloody hole in Wright's chest and pressed down. "You won't be able to die fast enough if you *don't* tell me."

Wright wheezed hard and groaned, and Rand worried he'd die before he could divulge the location of all he'd taken. It could be crucial to the survival of these people, out here, alone, on the prairie.

But Wright gasped deeply once again and said, "'Bout two miles back . . . down the river. I — I buried both . . . cousin . . . brother. . . . Can you bury me there . . . the horses — that's where they are. . . . Please. . . ."

Rand gave a slow nod. "I will. *If* I find those horses."

"They're there . . . mister . . . I swear. . . ." The life left his eyes, and his body relaxed as death took him.

Rand turned back toward the wagon. Three terrified faces stared owlishly out at him. He motioned for them to come out, and they hurried to him, standing a few feet away from the body.

"Thank . . . thank you. . . ." Ella's soft voice sounded in the stillness as Rand held the three children in his arms.

They all turned to look at her.

"Careful, now," Rand cautioned. "Y'all walk over real slow, and don't touch Miss Ella — not yet. There'll be time enough for hugs when she's feeling better."

They all approached slowly, and Rand thought Ella's gentle, loving smile was the best thing he'd seen in a very long time. He took her hand, crouching beside her, unsure of what to say.

"Thank you for . . . finding them. Please . . . just see that they get to bed . . . they've had quite the day —"

"Ella," he said in a quiet voice. "I'll see to *everything*. You just rest and get better. Let me take care of things, now." He reached to take her hand.

She nodded weakly, her eyes closing again as she faintly squeezed his fingers. But the last thing she whispered before she slept would not leave him. *"Stay . . . ."*

Stay. . . . He'd not put roots down anywhere in his entire life. He'd had a son he'd never known, but now . . . that had changed. And so, his life was going to have to change, too.

Ella's letter had spoken of this new land opening being a path for a second chance. *And she'd asked him to stay.* This could be a new beginning for all of them — if he dared to take that gamble . . . and if she really meant it.

He gently caressed her hand, knowing she couldn't hear him, but promising anyway. "I will . . . *stay.* I'll be here . . . as long — as long as you want me." He looked around the camp, taking in everything that he'd gained in one day —everything he'd never known he wanted or needed.

There was no finer piece of land than this — Ella had chosen well. But more than anything, he had the gift of his son, and these two other little ones who all needed a family. The bounty of shining hope of this woman who was looking for a second chance and a new beginning kindled that identical desire within him.

He'd been searching for the same thing for a very long time, though he'd not realized it.

With one word, his life had been transformed. What he had been missing for so long had revealed itself. A day of miracles, this had been; all brought about by one quiet word. . . .

Stay . . . .

#

Growing up in Oklahoma, we were taught about the Land Run of 1889 from elementary school on through high school — the "settler side" of that event. The Native American side was quite different. This was the first land run to be held, and the most historically significant, though there were seven land runs in all. People came from all over the country to race to stake their claim in the western portion of Oklahoma, in the Unassigned Lands of Federal Indian Territory. My character, Ella Reagan, was one of those people who was looking for a second chance, and was willing to risk everything, even her life, in hopes of finding a new life, better than the one she was leaving. With close to two million acres up for grabs, you'd think there'd be room for everyone who wanted to enter — but of course, greed always stood ready to step in.

Another cause for hardship for many was that there were only seven weeks from the time the land run was announced until it happened.

Luckily for Ella, she lived in Fort Smith, Arkansas, so was able to gather what she needed to make the trip and get to the starting line in time. But many didn't have that much advance notice to gather supplies and funds, much less time to make that journey if they lived a good distance away. What could entice people to give up everything they knew and undertake such a trek to a lawless, dangerous place? Imagining all the scenarios that would tempt people, whether it was from their dream to start over somewhere new or simply to get away from the troubles they were leaving behind, the desire to better themselves was a common catalyst. Participating in the Land Run of 1889 was, most likely, the biggest gamble any of those settlers had ever taken — and there was no way of knowing how it would turn out.

—Cheryl Pierson

Cheryl was born in Duncan, OK, and grew up in Seminole, OK, both small towns. Reading and writing her own stories were her favorite pastimes as far back as elementary school, which led to earning a B.A. in English from the University of Oklahoma. Writing westerns and western romance is in her blood, having been born and raised in Oklahoma, the product of at least five generations of proud Oklahomans who lived there when it was still Indian Territory. She has also served as the President of the Western Fictioneers, a professional organization for western authors. Three of her stories have been nominated in the Best Western Short Fiction category of the Western Fictioneers Peacemaker Awards. Cheryl and her husband have lived in the Oklahoma City area for the past 40 years. She has two grown children and two fur babies.

THE DEVIL'S ROPE

PAUL KUPPERBERG

"Sweet Lord above," Willie said in a soft, stunned voice as dry as the creaking branch of the old Texas red oak from which dangled the pale body of a young cowhand from Arkansas, suspended by a noose around his neck. He'd hired Ben Wilkins two weeks back.

The grizzled old foreman had to force himself to look away from the lifeless youngster, barely twenty years old. The oak was on his boss's side of the fence line, its triple strands of barbed wire cut, and the posts trampled into the sludge of mud and bovine excrement by the herd that had been run through here.

"Weren't no call to kill the boy," one of the hands riding with him rasped.

"What kind'a monster does this?" another man asked in a tight voice.

Willie knew the answer but all he said was, "Cut the boy down."

Willie could tell something in Judah was off the first time he laid eyes on the toddler. The boy was smart, no doubt, already speaking in full sentences at a year and a half and able to read and cipher better than Willie before he was five. But some are born bad, damaged in ways that makes them need to damage everyone around them, and Willie saw that in Gus Hunnicutt's firstborn son. Gus saw it, too, and nurtured it with paternal indifference and endless criticism. He told Willie that was the way you made young men strong, the way his old man had done with him.

They didn't start calling young Matt Hunnicutt "Bull" until he was eleven years old. His father hung the name on him after he'd been in a brawl with four older boys and refused to go down no matter how hard they pummeled him. He believed moments like those decided what kind of a man a boy would grow to be, whether he could stand up to the blows delivered him or crumble under them. Matt was staggered and bloodied but never felled. He hurt two of the aggressors bad enough that they quit the fight, but the other two had to finally grow tired of poking at the dark eyed boy who wouldn't stop coming at them and walk away.

"The kid's a bull, ain't he?" he said to Willie, who he'd had to order to stand back and not break up the fight.

Fourteen-year-old Judah hadn't needed to be told to keep out of the melee. It was usually him beating up on his younger brother, but he didn't mind seeing others getting their blows in. They could do a lot more damage to Matt than he would ever be allowed to get away with, even by the largely disinterested Gus. Judah had on a few occasions gone too far, leading to his brother's broken bones and scarring wounds and Gus repaying Judah in brutal kind. Judah took the lessons of those whippings to heart and changed his ways so that the torment of his kid brother would from then on only ever be felt but not seen.

Their mother died giving birth to a stillborn sister before Matt's second birthday, leaving their upbringing up to a stern Quaker housekeeper who saw to their physical needs but was indifferent to their emotional lives. The younger Hunnicutt found that complaining of Judah's abuses only ever earned him curses and a cuff across the face with the admonition to be a man and fight his own battles.

Bull just wanted to be left alone. For Judah, it was kill or be killed, a goal he nearly succeeded in achieving that time he dropped a noose from the barn rafters around his younger brother's neck and strung him up, dangling there with his feet off the ground, clawing at the rope around his neck choking off his breath while he kicked and gurgled like a cow with its throat cut in the slaughter chute.

Willie found the boy and cut him down just as he was about to pass out. Judah ran off when Willie appeared so they would never know if the older boy would have cut him down in time. But whether it was a cruel prank or a warning, Bull understood the harsh reality of his situation, and Willie swore to himself to always have the boy's back.

Willie always figured it couldn't be easy being the son of Gus Hunnicutt, the hardest son of a bitch in El Paso County. Judah was shrewd and tough, but not the kind of man to settle down and run a spread. He was a troublemaker, and the spark of humanity that burned in most men's hearts was missing in his.

Bull was a tougher nut to crack. Coming up bullied and forced by his father to be a man and fight his own battles, he became hard as well. But his shell was protective, not formed by resentment and bile like Judah's. The only thing Bull was afraid of was Judah. If the abuse by fist and word since infancy hadn't already done the job, Judah's near hanging sealed the deal.

Bull made Willie swear to keep the hanging incident a secret, equally frightened of Judah's harsh retribution for squealing as his father's punishment for letting himself be his brother's victim. But years later, even as a grown man, Bull would go cold at the mere sight of Judah and a noose.

"Judah *hanged* the boy, Willie," Bull snarled outside the bunkhouse where the murdered hand had just been carried, wrapped in blankets. "He's sending me a message."

"Don't let him goad you, Bull."

He spat again. "*Goad* me," he sneered. "Like we were boys and he's kicking me under the supper table to make me cry? Damn it, Willie, he *murdered* that boy."

Willie pulled off his hat and wiped a grimy handkerchief over his forehead. "You ready to start a war you ain't sure you can win?"

"We're already at war. He started it."

"Your brother don't back down 'till he's got the last word or drawn the last blood. One of you gotta keep a cool head or this ends bad all around," Willie warned.

Bull Hunnicutt nodded, his face a mask of stone. "Maybe it's time it did end. One way or another."

In the summer of 1878, a traveling salesman from back east came to town pedaling a miracle product he declared would tame the West, barbed-wire fencing. It was a thin steel wire studded at regular intervals with sharp, barbed knots, advertised as being light, durable, easy to install, and it would save on materials as well as man hours on installation and maintenance. Any fear the animals might injure themselves on the razor-like points of steel was dispelled by a demonstration in the town corral that proved even cattle, the dumbest of animals, quickly learned to keep their distance from the barbs.

Bull put in one of the first orders. There had been an outbreak of rustling in recent months, but the time and expense of putting up wooden or stone fencing to contain and safeguard the herd was prohibitive.

"All's a rustler needs to get through it is a pair of wire snippers," Judah objected.

"Rustlers will find a way around any fence we put up. Least the wire keeps the cattle where we can maintain a watchful eye on them," Bull said.

"You got any idea how many head we're gonna lose t'infected wounds on cattle too stupid to stay off the wire?"

"You didn't see the demonstration at the corral. A couple of cows got nicked, the rest of the herd got the message," Bull said.

"How gullible are you?" Judah yelled. "What you saw was rigged by a fast-talkin' salesman sellin' you snake oil. I'm telling you, you're gonna regret makin' a deal with the devil wire."

Gus, listening to the argument, slapped a hand on the table and announced, "The wire stays, boy," closing the book on the topic but not on Judah's anger. That he turned on his brother in a relentless campaign of abuse, including the childish tampering with Bull's saddle and ruthlessly hiding a rattler in his bedroll. And if all else failed, the sight of a noose fashioned from a length of rope or curtain cord would turn Bull's insides cold with the choking memory of his own hanging.

"He acts like the barbed wire done him dirty, the way he hates it," Willie said.

"I think it just might've," Bull said. "I wasn't going to say anything until I was sure, but lately we've been finding cattle with suspicious brandings mixed in with the herd."

"You sayin' what I think?"

"I'm not saying anything until I'm sure," Bull said.

Before Bull could confirm his suspicions on his own, the sheriff arrived at the ranch with a warrant for Judah's arrest. His gang had been running hundreds of stolen head with altered brands through the Hunnicutt herds before sending them south into Mexico for resale.

The old man was a tough, ruthless son of a bitch, but he was an *honest* ruthless son of a bitch who had no forgiveness in him for a thief, not even his own blood. His only concession was to give Judah a head start before alerting the law.

As he stood on the porch and watched his son swing into the saddle to leave the ranch for the last time, Gus said, "Why, Judah?"

Judah didn't flinch, looking the father straight in the eye and saying, "To have something of my own."

The father didn't flinch either. "Instead of stealing you could have waited a few more years. Half of this would've been yours."

"Guess I never did learn patience."

"Maybe that's on me, but I'm for damned certain I taught you right from wrong."

Judah snorted a laugh. "Only thing I learned from you, Pa, was to be tough and look out for myself."

Inside the big house, behind the drapes in the window of the front parlor, Willie watched the final filial exchange with a shotgun at the ready, in case Judah decided to take last-minute vengeance for his banishment. But all the boy took were last words before wheeling his horse around and riding away, leaving his father and his life behind without so much as a glance backwards.

Judah's departure seemed to somehow diminish Gus. He grew a little older, became a little less interested in the ranch and left its running more and more to Bull and Willie. It made no difference that his oldest boy had been nothing but trouble, growing into exactly the sort of man his father's cold, detached demeanor had nurtured. But when he left, he took with him any hope that one day he might show he *wasn't* the sort of man he finally proved to be.

Judah was missed nowhere else on the ranch or in town, and no one was happier to be rid of him than Bull. For the first time in his life, Bull could stop looking over his shoulder and be the man *he* was meant to be.

Barbed wire proved successful at keeping the herd in, but it couldn't keep rustlers out. Local ranchers continued losing cattle to theft, Judah and his gang now moving the stolen beef through other avenues. Hands were sent out to the ends of the Hunnicutt property to round up and drive the herd together to make it easier to watch over, still a daunting task with more than 60,000 head roaming over near 150,000 acres. When that didn't slow the rustlers down, the local ranchers banded together to hire extra guards and guns and post rewards.

Bull was all but living in the saddle, either on the hunt or riding fence lines on guard duty. Judah's boys were fast and efficient, experts at cutting a wide hole in the wire and stampeding the herd quickly through it, to be wrangled by their compatriots and whisked off, likely down to Mexico, where buyers didn't question the inartfully altered brands burned into their haunches.

At first, the rustlers had avoided confrontation with the ranchers and the law, but once shots were fired, the gloves came off. The more men thrown onto the field, the more likely the chance of clashes, especially with emotions running so high, erupting into an escalation in violence and body count.

The morning of the first autumn frost, Judah's men spread out along a quarter mile of Hunnicutt barbed wire and cut it while their compatriots rode onto the property to round up the cattle to drive through it. Instead, they found Bull and Willie and their men. The ranchers rode in hot, guns blazing, killing two rustlers and wounding at least the three they captured and turned over to the sheriff.

Two days later, Willie and his men discovered the body of the young cowhand from Arkansas hanging from the red oak.

Even before the boy could be buried, Bull assembled a posse of the best trackers and shooters money could buy and set out on his brother's trail. The rustlers usually had enough of a head start that they could disappear across the border by the time their actions had been discovered. Even when they were caught in the act, they rode in sufficient numbers to hold off pursuers with covering fire until the herd was safely away before melting into the surrounding terrain.

"Instead of waiting for a chance to chase them to wherever they're holed up, we start from where we know they been and work our way backwards," Bull told his crew of three trackers, nine gunmen, and Willie. "Good as they been about covering their tracks, they can't totally erase their trail, and they know the law can't follow them very far into Mexico. I'm betting they stop being so careful once they think they're safe on the other side."

The lead tracker was a weathered, one-eyed Cibecue Apache who called himself Colonel Eagle. He could detect hoofprints where other men saw only hard ground and was said to have once tracked a man six miles upstream through the rushing river waters of a spring thaw. The colonel rode point, often on foot, leading his horse by the reins, scouring the ground with his eyepatch flipped up, saying, "I see much better with this one since I lost it." Whether it was just some Indian mumbo jumbo or legitimate magic Willie didn't understand, there was no denying the old scout knew what he was doing. It wasn't his fault that the first few trails he picked up were dead ends to abandoned camps and corrals. Sooner or later, they would find the one that would lead them to Judah.

There were a few skirmishes along the way. Bull made it clear from the outset that he wasn't much interested in his brother's hirelings. "This isn't open season on rustlers. Give them the chance to surrender or run away, then do what you got to depending on their choice. But try and save a few that maybe we can get to talk." Most of the outlaws they encountered chose to stand their ground and resist, and whether by their natures or fear of Judah, all those left in any shape to talk told Bull to get hanged.

In those same words. Every one of them.

"Get *hanged*," they snarled or spat or growled.

"He's taunting me," Bull told Willie as they rode side by side under the harsh Mexican sun.

"You can't let him get to you. That's just givin' him exactly what he wants."

Bull said, "I'm not taking any more shots from him."

Every wrong path taken should have meant they were one step closer to the right one, but once Judah learned his brother was coming for him, he started leaving false trails that sent the posse off in circles or into dead ends marked with mocking reminders of the hunted man's contempt, like tangles of cut up barbed wire, a pile of rotting bovine carcasses or mounds of cow and horse crap. And always, hanging over it, a mocking straw effigy hanging by its neck.

Soon, trackers learned to recognize the planted signs and turned quickly back to the right trail. It was the Mexican scout called Juárez Jack who saw a possible destination on one trail to be Sierra de la Amargosa, a thirteen-hundred-foot peak on the Mexican Plateau in Chihuahua whose pass and the valley west of it was a frequent hideout for local bandits and rustlers.

Any doubt they were finally on Judah's scent was erased by the increase in encounters with his men the closer they got to the mountain. The rustlers struck like Indian raiders, with small, mobile parties appearing out of nowhere, inflicting damage, and riding off almost before the attacked posse could react. That damage was dear, including the lives of Colonel Eagle and three of the hired guns. But if the surprise attacks were meant to intimidate, they failed, instead hardening the posse's resolve which, coupled with Bull's promise of generous bonuses to those who stayed, kept them on the trail.

"Two ways through to where you want to go," Juárez Jack said as they rode toward the dusty gray range. "The hard way, through Pase Fuera de la Ley, or the *harder* way, through La Grieta."

"Pass'll be covered six ways from Sunday," Willie said. "What's this grieta, this crack?"

"Just what it say, Señor Willie. Wide enough for a man to get through on foot but *muy peligroso*."

"More dangerous than trying to ride through whatever gauntlet Judah's got laid out along that main pass?" Bull said.

Juárez Jack shrugged. "You ask me, is all the same."

According to Jack, the far side of the mountain, at the other end of the pass, opened into a valley that offered the outlaws easy escape for themselves and their stolen herds.

"It's pointless layin' siege to wait 'em out, and by the time we went around to come up behind 'em, they'd be long gone," the old man said.

"Judah's not going anywhere," Bull said with evangelical certainty. "He's gonna wait for me, right where he is."

The next morning at first light, the posse rode at full gallop into the Pase Fuera de la Ley.

"I'm tellin' you, if you think Judah's gonna fall for this, you're crazier than he is," Willie huffed as he clamored behind Bull over a pile of loose stones blocking the narrow crack in the Sierra de la Amargosa.

"There's nothing for him to fall for. He knows we're coming and unless we learn to fly, the only way to the other side is through the pass or this. Juárez Jack says we got enough of a head start that we'll be in place before the riders come through."

"*If* they make it past whatever gauntlet Judah's laid out for 'em along the way."

"I told you, he's been playing with us. We haven't been chasing him. He's been leading us on, drawing us . . . drawing *me* into a trap. As long as he thinks I'm riding into his hands, he's not going to move against them."

"Them men you sent into that pass better hope you know what you're talkin' about," Willie said with a derisive snort.

La Grieta was no place for a man who needed to be in open spaces. Sometimes just wide enough to pass through sideways, often obstructed by boulders or piles of fallen rocks, Willie was more than a few times forced to shove down the panic he felt at being trapped between the walls of the ancient fissure. But he kept his eyes on Bull, just ahead of him in the dim, suffocating granite channel, reminding himself over and over of his long-ago promise to have the boy's back against his brother.

Willie didn't know how long they had been squeezing through that mountain before they came to a bend in the crack where Bull paused, peering around it. When he looked back, he held a finger up before his lips, then pointed ahead. The old man got the message: they had reached the other side. He signaled for Willie to stay put and then inched around the bend, drawing his gun from its holster.

Willie pulled his own six-shooter and waited, listening to the soft scrape of Bull's boots on the rocky ground as he edged carefully ahead. He could hear his own breathing, shallow and ragged with anticipation. There was no turning back now. Whatever was coming would come fast . . . .

Too fast! Willie was caught by surprise by Bull's sudden shout, cut off just as suddenly by a loud gurgle and a scrabble of boots on the ground, and then nothing.

"Jesus wept," the old man grunted and without thought to his own safety, rushed the last yards to the mouth of the crack. But the final few feet to open ground were blocked by Bull, dancing convulsively at the end of a noose dropped from above, like a marionette.

Willie leapt forward, grabbing Bull's legs and lifting him up to give the rope some slack and take the weight off his neck. As soon as he did, the rope was released from above, dropping down on them like a monstrous snake from a tree, sending them crashing to the ground in a jumbled pile. With a gasp, Bull tore the noose from his neck, struggling to extricate himself from the tangle of rope.

"Settle down there, Bull boy."

Judah squatted atop a boulder a dozen feet from the mouth of the crack, grinning like a man who had just won a prize. Around him were three guns trained on the two new arrivals. A fourth man came scrambling down from the perch from where he had dropped the noose.

Bull didn't waste even a glance at the assembled gunmen. He threw off a coil of rope and stood up, defiantly facing his brother.

"Now what?" the younger Hunnicutt said, his voice low and defiant. "This's what you been waiting for since we were kids, isn't it? Just you and me, without Pa around to make you stay your hand."

Judah laughed. "You think that's it? Hell, I could've ended you any time I wanted, and a couple'a times I almost did and Pa never would'a knowed it was me, but it was more fun keeping you around to torment."

"You talk big with him a hundred miles away," Bull said with a sneer. "You'd be quakin' in your boots if Pa was here."

For an instant, Willie saw the grin slip from Judah's face and when it returned, it was changed, becoming forced and frozen in place.

"The posse's gonna be —" the old man started to say, but Judah cut him off.

"Delayed," he yelled. "That's what your posse's gonna be, Willie. De-*layed*!" The thought seemed to cheer him up again. "And I got baby brother and his big idea to thank for that. We got the pass tangled up with enough of his barbed wire to slow down an army. By the time they's through it all, me and my boys will be long gone. But I might just leave your bodies here for them to find." He laughed. "I told you the devil's wire was cursed, didn't I?"

Including Judah, Willie counted five men all told who'd stayed behind to deal with the posse. It must have been Judah's plan all along, to cut Bull out from the rest of his group and take him on, man to man. This was and always had been a blood feud, pure and simple, and it was a moment that he had been building to for a lifetime.

They had put up a crude enclosure some fifteen foot square by four foot high from dozens of strands of barbed wire stretched around stacked columns of stone. While Willie watched, off to one side under a double-barrel shotgun wielded by a scruffy blond boy in need of a shave and bath, Judah and another man threw a couple of horse blankets over a section of the wire.

"In you go, Bully boy," Judah said, nodding at the enclosure as he pulled on a pair of heavy leather gloves. When Bull hesitated, Judah laughed and said, "Don't fret. I'm gonna be right behind you."

Under the prodding of a pair of pistols, Bull climbed gingerly over the blanket, wincing at the razor-sharp points that poked through the thick wool at his hands and legs. Judah followed him over the blankets, which his henchmen then removed, effectively sealing the men inside. Then they stepped back, one of them hopping up on a nearby boulder for a better view, the other three jabbing at each other in excited anticipation of the beating they hoped to witness.

"Just you and me now, brother," Judah said with a mocking laugh. "No Pa to save you."

Willie couldn't tell whether Bull's roar as he sprang at Judah was one of rage or defiance to bolster his courage, but whatever its intent, it caught his brother by surprise, and they went down in a tangle of swinging fists and snarled curses. The men outside the ring cheered and the boy with the 12-gauge let out a whoop and hollered, "Smash 'im a good one for me, boss!"

As though in answer to the boy's request, Judah drove a gloved fist across Bull's jaw. Bull grunted, his head snapping back. His grip on his brother loosened, and under a barrage of vicious kicks and blows, he was forced to retreat.

Judah laughed again and wiped dust and blood from his mouth.

Bull roared and charged again. Judah stepped back and grabbed him by his shirtfront in both hands and stuck out his foot, tripping Bull. Bull stumbled face-forward into the dirt, falling just inches shy of the barbed barrier. He shook his head and pushed himself up on his hands and knees, but before he could get to his feet, Judah planted his boot against Bull's ass and shoved him into the strands of wire.

Bull twisted around to take the impact against his shoulder instead of his face. He growled at the pain of the barbs that tore through his shirt and snagged his flesh. He came back up, ducking Judah's right fist but catching his left on the side of his head. He staggered back, screaming when he fell against the fence. Willie had experienced a little of that pain once when he caught a barb in his leg helping lay wire, so he could only imagine the agony of being impaled on a cluster of the lethal steel knots.

Judah's men were hooting and hollering like it was Saturday night at the saloon, the drawing of blood increasing their fervor.

The younger Hunnicutt wrenched himself free as his brother came in swinging, trying to drive Bull deeper into the tangle of wire. Bull slid around the leather-clad fist and Judah lunged past him, exposing his back to the elbow Bull drove into his spine. With a pained gasp, Judah staggered, almost falling into the tautly stretched wire before his gloved fingers caught it and saved him.

A four-foot length of wire snagged on the leather glove and came free when Bull wrenched Judah's hand out. The violent action sent the wire whipping around, making Bull leap back out of its way.

Even at half a dozen yards distance, Willie could see Judah's angry expression contort into a sadistic smile as he gripped the wire between both hands, twisting it into a loop, a makeshift, barbed-steel garrote.

Bull saw it too, and for the first time since entering the ring, he hesitated.

"Yeah, we got some unfinished business, don't we, baby brother?" Judah taunted. "Always liked seein' you dance at the end of a rope, but this'll have to do. Remember I warned you you'd regret becomin' a disciple of the devil's wire?"

The men let out a fresh chorus of shouts, and Willie's guard raised his shotgun in the air like a flag of victory.

With a grunt, Willie threw himself at the young outlaw, jabbing an elbow into the boy's throat and reaching for the upraised gun. The boy choked and let go of the weapon to grab for his throat as he doubled over. Willie knocked him aside with the butt of the gun.

"Bull!" Willie roared and brought the shotgun to his hip.

The rustlers started to turn at Willie's call, reaching for their holstered six-shooters. Willie went first for the man atop the boulder, hitting him with the first barrel of #1 buckshot and knocking him from his perch, then turning the second barrel on the other three, dropping them in the spray of lead pellets like ducks in a hunt.

Willie wasn't sure if Bull also heard him, but it didn't seem like he could tear his eyes off the noose in his brother's hands. It took the twin echoing booms of the shotgun to break the spell, and he turned as Willie threw aside the empty weapon and stooped to pluck the boy's pistol from its holster.

Seeing what happened, Judah lunged at Bull to drop the wire around his neck. With nowhere to run, the younger Hunnicutt was forced to stand his ground and meet his worst nightmare head on. Willie thought Bull looked even more surprised than Judah when he burst suddenly into action, slamming headlong into his brother and wrapping his arms around his torso, catching the length of barbed wire between them. They were too close together for Willie to risk a shot and he'd never get over the wire in time to do any good.

Judah howled as the barbs ground between them, and he struggled to free himself, but it was as if something in Bull had snapped and unleashed a flood of savage strength that made him oblivious to pain. He slammed his head into Judah's face, blood spraying from the other man's nose and making his legs buckle. They went down in a pile, Bull raining a barrage of blows to Judah's already damaged face. Bellowing like a wounded beast, Judah reared to throw him off, scrambling to his feet, blood pouring from his face.

Bull was quicker, charging in and grabbing Judah by his neck and crotch to lift him off the ground and hurl him like a sack of dirty laundry into the wall of barbed wire.

Judah hung there, frozen in a moment of time, and then he started to struggle. When he did, the barbs dug into him and the deeper they cut the more he struggled and the more he struggled the deeper still they cut and the further into their razor sharp embrace he sunk.

Bull didn't hesitate. Tearing off his shirt, he ripped it in half and wrapped the pieces around his hands for protection to try and free his brother from the wire. But whether in a final act of hatred or an accident of the panicked moment, Willie would never know, the flailing Judah's boot heel caught Bull on the forehead and knocked him back down. Then, with a desperate grunt, Bull Hunnicutt made to wrench himself free, but he was tangled too deep into the wire and a strand caught Judah across the throat, a single barb tearing through his neck and unleashing a geyser of blood as his pounding heart pumped his life away in a matter of moments.

Willie looked away. He had no love for Judah, but this was no way to watch any man die, much less one he'd known his entire life.

Bull stood swaying in the barbed wire ring, bleeding from a dozen wounds, blankly regarding his brother's still form.

Finally, Willie said softly, "Bull? You okay?"

Bull nodded slowly. "Yeah, I'm okay, Willie."

"You sure? 'Cause you know it was him or you, Bull."

"I know. It don't make it any easier, but I know."

"Damned devil's wire," the old man said. "This whole affair made me regret the day I ever laid eyes on it."

"The wire's just a tool," Bull said, looking sadly at his brother. "It's the user that makes it one of the angels or the devil."

#

I've always been fascinated by transformative technologies, the inventions that changed the course of human history, everything from the prehistoric discovery of fire, the wheel, and the fulcrum and lever through to "modern" tech, from the printing press, electricity, and automobiles to the transistor and the PC. Barbed wire was a simple invention of razor-sharp knots at regular intervals along a steel wire to create a fencing material that drastically changed the landscape of the American southwest, playing a key role in the settlement of the Great Plains by effectively ending the open range system, and reshaping the cattle ranching industry. A fan of barbed wire wrote inventor Joseph Glidden, "It takes no room, exhausts no soil, shades no vegetation, is proof against high winds, makes no snowdrifts, and is both durable and cheap."

—Paul Kupperberg

Crazy 8 Press author Paul Kupperberg is a fifty-year veteran comic book writer. He has scripted hundreds of characters ranging from Archie to Zatanna (including his creations, Arion Lord of Atlantis, Checkmate, and Takion) in some 1,400 comic book stories. Paul has been an editor/writer for DC Comics, *Weekly World News*, and *WWE Kids Magazine*. He is the author of *JSA: Ragnarok, Direct Comments: Comic Creators in their own Words* (Buffalo Avenue Books), *Paul Kupperberg's Illustrated Guide to Writing Comics* (Charlton Neo Press), *Direct Conversation: Talks with Fellow DC Comics Bronze Age Creators, Direct Creativity: The Creators Who Inspired the Creators, The Devil and Leo Persky*, and *The Same Old Story* (Crazy 8 Press).

A Riverboat Detective

Richard Prosch

The homesteaders lined the riverbanks and cheerfully waved as the muddy Missouri foamed behind the steamboat *Arabia*, her enclosed wheel churning up leaves and sticks and chaff. On the aft lower deck, straddling the gate of an oakwood stall behind the whitewashed paddle box and under the curved ledge of the boiler deck above, I waved back with a feeling of satisfaction. Once again, I was on my way to glorious adventure.

Wherever life took me.

More or less lost.

But I wouldn't let it affect my mood!

"It's a beautiful afternoon for September," I told the skinny mule who swayed with the swells against my leg. "My name's Dart Emerson, what's yours?"

Irreverent brute, the mule tossed his knobby head at the fence, slinging a string of drool. I shooed a buzzing horsefly away and made up an answer.

"Son of an exotic mare called Princess Ell, heir to a donkey jack named Jake," I bit my thumbnail like the lady at Our Mission of Sorrows once warned me not to do. "I shall christen thee, Reuben, a knight of the Boonville docks."

Reuben batted his eyelids — irreverent, but likable.

The only friend I had on the *Arabia* — and why not? We'd boarded together, more or less, a few miles back at the last stop for uploading freight. Reuben was an official passenger on his way to a sawmill in Kansas. I crept in behind him like Ulysses and the sheep. Only instead of a way out, I was looking for a way in — as a stowaway.

That was sixteen year-old Dart Emerson of Hell's Kitchen by way of horse, wagon, and some well-meaning St. Louis nuns.

An orphan.

Now a free-spirit vagabond, a street Arab.

Balanced on the gate that way, I watched the river bluffs pass by, their pale limestone rock walls giving way to yellowing walnut, elm, and hickory trees as we traveled.

The steady boom of the boat's steam engine and the sloshing river water just a few feet beyond the edge of the deck soon made both me and Reuben sleepy. And sloppy.

We didn't hear the bearded man busy inside the adjacent cargo hold until the door next to me opened like a bursting shell.

"Hey, and what's that you're doing there, lad?"

The surprise action and accompanying voice knocked me off Reuben's gate, and sure as I landed on bare feet, calloused and thick from my western sojourn, I couldn't stay upright on the mule's dry, slippery bedding. I landed beneath the intruder's haughty gaze.

I had never seen a man of such size and girth. Framed by the burnished blue Missouri sky, he stood at least twelve feet tall and weighed in at half a ton. Caught in the autumn breeze his ebony beard was the wool of twelve sheep, and his hands were like lead anchors.

With nothing I could do to stop it, my lip poked out in defiance. "Who the hell are you?" I challenged, before I could still my rebel tongue.

I'd caught the villain off-guard with my tone, and he laughed in spite of his obvious outrage. "Who am I? Who are you?" A meaty paw swiped down toward my shirt collar, missing by a frog's hair as I ducked away.

Hardly frantic, but concerned for my immediate well-being, I searched for an escape. Reuben's pen and the paddle box blocked the way to the ship's fore, and behind the big man was the roiling mad wake of the river.

To my right was even more water, churning behind the wheel, bronze green, shallow to be sure, some said as thin as 15 feet, but dirty and vile.

To my left, the origin point of my foe, a pair of hinged double doors, strapped with iron, but open, leading into the *Arabia*'s rear cargo hold.

If I could slip inside, I could lose the giant amongst the boat's heavy freight. My eyes shot to the iron latch. All my pursuer need do was close the door.

Dart Emerson — not unlike a rat in a trap.

Frantic, after all, I considered giving myself up.

The big fellow understood my dilemma and laughed once more. "Caught like a bug, aint'cha?" Carefully, without turning his back to me, the man closed the cargo bay doors and locked the latch with a compact brass key. Arms crossed, he announced, "I'm Solomon Burke. I can see you've met the latest member of our crew."

He meant Reuben. I nodded.

Solomon said, "Filthy animal. His owner's a Kansas man, bought him sight unseen. I been taking care of him."

Once again my tongue rushed ahead of my thoughts. "Not too well, you ain't. He's hot and the flies are chewin' him something fierce."

"You know something about mules, do ya?"

I said I knew enough.

After a pause, Burke put thoughtful fingers to his beard and stroking it, said, "I don't wonder that you're onboard legal." He pointed a fat finger down at me. "I know a tramp when I see one. And I've half a mind to toss you into the drink."

I tensed, ready to run.

By now, I had a better plan than hiding in the cargo hold.

Once I got passed those bread-hooks Solomon Burke called hands, I'd scurry up the boat's aft stairway and get lost among the boat's multitude of cabins and wealthy, chattering passengers. I had reason to believe the Contessa Vanessa Drake was on board, an east coast Swan-singer who'd surely take pity on me, one of her own from back home.

But Solomon Burke didn't move. He had a different idea. "How far you figure on traveling?" he said.

"How far we going?" I asked

"The *Arabia*'s scheduled all the way up past Council Bluffs. We're carrying cargo for pioneers and pastors, farmers and merchants."

"We? Are you part of the crew?"

"You might say so." Burke looked around, then sniffed. "How about you stay down here in the cargo hold for the rest of the trip? Take care of the mule for us?"

"I'm not sure."

"That or I toss you overboard now."

The proposal seemed all the more sincere by evidence of Burke's impatience.

"You won't tell the captain?" I said.

"How do you know I'm not the captain?" he said.

Because I'd seen the captain, I thought without saying so to Burke.

Captain William Terrill, so addressed by others, had been busy back on the Boonville docks talking to a teamster who loaded twenty barrels of salt pork into the cargo hold next door to Reuben's pen. Terrill was rail-thin with well-cropped hair. The exact opposite of Solomon Burke.

"The captain wouldn't be taking care of a mule," I said.

"You've got me there," he had to admit, "and you're lucky I'm not the stickler for rules that Terrill is or you'd be swimming even now."

I nodded toward the cargo hold. "I'll need to get in there to access the grain closet. To get food and bedding for the mule."

Burke smiled and handed over the brass key. "This will get you in and out. Just be sure to lock up after yourself." I accepted the key with a nod of thanks.

As Burked turned to leave, my tongue got the better of me once more. "So, if you're not the captain, who are you?"

Burke glanced over his shoulder and grinned. "Simple," he said. "I'm a riverboat detective, and I mean to watch that cargo bay as if my life depended upon it. Because maybe it does!"

Then, almost an afterthought, he said, "If you should need me, I'm in Berth 21, right off the saloon."

"I'm a riverboat detective, son," Anderson Poe told me, earnest, full of authority, "and I'm counting on you to help me bring a thief to justice."

We sat across from one another at a covered dinner table for two on the boiler deck just above Reuben's stall, open to the elements, the afternoon air cool, the sun sparkling as it touched the tops of the tallest sycamore trees on the banks. We drank spiced tea from a silver set between us. I took a small bite from a nutmeg cookie and swallowed before answering. "What's the name of this arch criminal?"

Instead of an answer, I received a question from the small, clean shaven bald man. "What do you know about the *Arabia*, Mr. Emerson?"

I feigned complete ignorance. Munched my cookie.

Passengers strolled past on their way around the deck, moving from table to table in conversation. Men in fine slick suits and women in colorful dresses seemed jovial and well met. A bit behind and to my far right, the Contessa Vanessa Drake, her springy blonde curls tumbling down over an immodest neckline, opened her decorated ruby lips and her infamous laugh leapt forth.

At my table, Poe continued to speak. "This esteemed vessel was pegged together in Pennsylvania, you know. Sailed down the Ohio to the Mississippi. Thirty feet wide, 171-feet long. Hurricane deck with pilot house above us. So-called boiler deck here with passenger accommodations — aren't the cookies, fine, by the way? And the main deck below with boiler, engine, all sorts of cargo. By gum, even a donkey."

"A mule," I said.

"Yes, of course. As a city boy, I'm afraid I don't know the difference," Poe said, continuing his inventory. "Hardware and equipment for pioneers. All manner of foodstuffs in tin cans, glass jars, and bottles," he said, pausing for effect. "Even live entertainment."

"Well and good, but what's it to do with me?" I said. "Or does the *Arabia* buy afternoon tea for all its young stowaways?"

Poe lowered his head along with his voice. "I refer you to the woman sitting at your four o'clock. Notorious in New York theatrical society."

"Oh, I saw the Contessa at the Winter Garden," I said, not trying to show off, "before it burned down." Showing off a little.

Poe straightened up, trying not to show his surprise. "I didn't realize we were cut from the same cloth."

"Are we?"

"I've lived in the Bowery," he said, sipping from his cup, "met her backstage at the theater there. I'm quite familiar with Miss Drake."

"Like I said, I've only ever seen her on stage." I chanced a quick glance in her direction. Busty, with a dress two sizes two small, she sat forward with her elbow on the table, the heel of her palm propping up her double chin as she gazed at a slim gentleman dressed in black. As her jaw worked up and down, poetry fell out like clusters of summer blossoms. "She's a real Swan-slinger," I said.

"Er . . . uh, yes," Poe said. "A . . . uh, whooperup for certain." He put down his cup. "If you follow the Contessa, you must know about her missing *diamonds*?"

I turned back to my host. "Now you've surprised me, Mr. Poe."

"They went missing during the Contessa's engagement in Jefferson City." Again, he crouched down to lean across the table toward me. "We have reason to believe the stolen jewels are aboard *this very ship*."

I gradually pushed away from the table. "I assure you, I was nowhere near —"

Poe waved away my denials. "Not you," he said. "We don't suspect you."

"Who then?"

Poe locked his dark button eyes on mine. "Earlier, I saw you speaking with Solomon Burke."

I nodded slowly. "He said he was part of the crew."

Poe sniffed. "Burke is a man wanted by the authorities. And as such, you must ask yourself what he was doing inside the lower cargo hold?"

I held my tongue, waiting for the answer Poe was more than eager to offer.

"Why, don't you see, son? He's hidden the diamonds with the boat's inventory of freight."

"I think I understand," I said.

"I want you to find those diamonds."

I took a deep breath and thought about the heavy latch. "What if the cargo door is locked?"

Poe made a spectacle out of reaching into his trousers pockets. When his hand came up, he offered me a shiny brass key. "You should have no trouble," he said. "I'm in Berth 23. Near the saloon."

The lower cargo hold of the steamboat *Arabia* was dark, even during the mid-afternoon, and I carried a slim candle and holder I'd found just inside the entrance. My fire's feeble light threatened to flicker out in the occasional breeze, which truth-be-told was somewhat reassuring. Better that than an uncontrollable blaze.

Half the supplies I stumbled through would ignite with little more than a spark.

There were axe handles and wood pegs packed in sawdust. Yarn, thread, fabrics of foreign weaves. Buttons and iron buckles packed in straw.

I made my way through the main aisle of crates, some open, some closed, inspecting everything carefully, seeing as much as I could. The space was tightly packed and the air notably dry. At the far end, floor-to-ceiling shelves held clear jars of preserved cherries, blueberries, peaches, pickles — and diamonds!

But no. I pushed the candle close to the round white baubles drowning in their brine.

Onions.

Quietly, I moved on through the assorted dry goods, clothing of all kinds, china plates from England, shovels, picks, hardware and canned food.

Bear traps and fishing nets. Guns and knives.

And then, after less than three-quarters of an hour, I found the first jar: shoved between tin cans of tomatoes and beets, a slim bottle, eight inches tall, its contents glittering in my ever-waning light.

First jar.

Because five minutes later, and less than five feet away, I found a second container. On the floor.

Under a pile of Mexican saddles.

And then I found one more thing tucked between a stack of paper calendars and post office signs.

I wrote two simple notes and, careful not to be seen by Captain Terrill, paid a youngster of nine two nickels to deliver them to Berths 21 and 23. Then I sat atop Reuben's gate and waited for my summons to be answered.

It didn't take long for Burke to appear, overly affable and eager. "What is it, son? Something wrong with our mule friend?"

"Nothing like that," I said.

Burke's eyes slid one way, then another, watching the steam pour from the *Arabia*'s boiler stacks, flitting down to the river damp floorboards, then to Reuben, asleep in his stall, standing up.

Then he looked at me.

Doing his utmost not to show his interest in the open cargo room door. "Well, what is it?"

And just as he said it, Anderson Poe rounded the corner of the hold. "What goes on, son?" He was momentarily surprised to see Burke, but as reticent as the other man to show any emotion. "Er, that is . . . what's this about?"

Having secured both men's attention, I balanced on the top rail of Reuben's gate and held up the bottles I had discovered, one in each hand.

"The steamboat *Arabia* carries the most interesting cargo," I said with a smile. "Do these look familiar, boys?"

Poe jumped toward me. "Give me those."

"Ah-ah," I cautioned, making a wide gesture as if to throw the bottle in my right hand into the river.

Poe stopped abruptly. "You wouldn't."

My smile grew twice as wide. "I would." Then I shook the mule's gate under my rump. "Wake up, Reuben."

Burke's play was to pretend ignorance. "You're saying you found those bottles in the cargo hold? In there?" He slapped his forehead with an audible crack.

Reuben clopped toward me, expecting a scratch on the ear.

"Why, land of mercy," Burke said. "Those must be the stolen Drake diamonds. How on earth did they get in there?"

"Oh, fiddlesticks! As if you didn't know," I said. "Which one was yours? The food preserves?" I turned my head back to Poe. "Or did you hide your cut with the preserves, while he did the Mexican saddles?"

Poe glanced at Burke with a clenched jaw. Burke kept his eyes on the bottles in my hands.

Poe said, "I told you this beggar was a jewel thief. You've done the boat a great service, son."

Now Burke ripped his gaze away from me to stare at Poe. "Jewel thief? You told him that? What did you let fall out of your trap, Sam?"

Poe stepped into the question with a grim fury. "Poe," he hissed. "My name is *Anderson Poe*."

"Nope," I said. "It's not." Casually, I stuck one of the bottles under my arm and pulled my paper discovery from its front trousers pocket hiding place. I shook out the wanted pasteboard so both men could see it.

Then, motioning towards Poe, I said, "Your name is Sam Reynolds." Speaking to Burke, I nodded at his likeness on the poster. "And you are Billy Wyatt." Holding the bottles between my knees, I worked the cork out of both necks.

Then I poured the diamonds out across Reuben's upraised nose where they rolled off onto the wood planked deck. Casually the mule trod all over them.

And as he stepped and stomped, the diamonds crackled and broke.

"Those diamonds are as fake as the both of you," I said. Speaking directly to Sam's (Poe's) astonished expression, I said, "But then, you would have known that if you were really familiar with the Contessa Vanessa Drake."

Sam couldn't find the words. "I . . . don't understand?"

Neither did Billy (Burke) Wyatt. "We took those straight from her dressing room in Jeff City," he said. "Didn't we take 'em straight on from her room, Sam?"

"Shut up, Billy!"

"How come they ain't real?"

Keeping my attention on Sam, I said, "I knew you were fogging me when you claimed to be from the Bowery, but didn't know the difference between a donkey and a mule."

"You're the smart one, are you?"

"Smart enough to know what a Swan-slinger is. You mistook my description of Miss Drake for an insult. You agreed and said she was a whooperup."

"So what?"

"So a *swan-slinger* is a Shakespearean actor, while a *whooperup* is a horrible singer." I put both fists on my hips in triumph. "Somebody familiar with the theater would —"

But the decking fell out from under all of us then, and a concussive shudder ran through the hull of the *Arabia*. Abruptly the big paddle wheel slammed against its wood housing, and the clatter was only punctured by shouts and at least one scream of pure terror from the boiler deck above us. When I tried to regain my feet, I found the deck awash with river water and less than level.

Listing.

"I do believe we're sinking," Sam said, crawling to his feet.

"It felt like the boat hit something in the water," I said, making my way up to the latch on Reuben's gate. For his part, the kindly old devil was keeping as calm as could be expected, alternating with the lift of one hoof, then another.

Once I had the gate open, he clambered out onto the wood planks, slipping, sliding, and going down on his rump more than once.

"Get that beast away from me," Sam shouted as he rushed past Reuben directly toward the deck's sopping wet harvest of shattered fake diamonds. He reached out, catching flecks of melting white paste and slivered glass on his fingers.

"Fake. . . ."

I turned back to follow Reuben as he tried to navigate the aft deck but was brushed aside by the enormous bulk of Billy Wyatt, his long, dark beard framing his scarlet, blustering rage. "No!" he cried. "I won't believe it."

Sam said, "You hired the kid to find my share. You meant to cheat me out of my take."

"Didn't you do the same?"

They were both inside the mule pen, crouched on the teetering deck, oblivious of the unfolding drama taking place around them. Above us, the passengers were marching in orderly fashion toward the front of the *Arabia*. Even as I looked up, a face popped over the rail of the hurricane deck. "Hey, you, down there," the man called. "Climb up here! Hurry now! The *Arabia*'s in trouble."

No truer words were spoken, for even as he said it, the boat lurched again and half the paddle box was under water. Swinging around, I grabbed hold of the mule pen's gate, but Billy Wyatt, the giant who had called himself Solomon Burke, didn't find such a handhold.

Completely off his feet, his enormous bulk slammed into Reuben's plank fence and broke through with a splintering of wood. Desperately trying to right himself, his boot hit the submerged deck planking, and Bill fell backwards into the Missouri River. Before he could rise up, the swirling remnant of the paddle wash pulled him under the boat.

I spun around in time to see Reuben sliding toward me on all four hooves. At the last, he tried to avoid the water, but he couldn't stay dry any more than he could stop from careening into me.

My last view of the *Arabia* before the river took us both was to see Sam Reynolds, aka: Anderson Poe, clinging to the corner post of the mule pen like a wet kitten.

We pulled free of the rancid river near Parkville, Missouri, Reuben and I, on clay banks covered with sweet clover and mulberries. There was hardly any current. After assessing ourselves free of serious injury and a sufficient convalescence under the healing light of moon and stars, we made our way to a road house that offered breakfast. Water and a scoop of shelled corn for Reuben, coffee and a newspaper for me while my eggs and potatoes fried.

I'd missed supper, after all.

Later on, we read in the newspaper that the *Arabia* had been snagged on an underwater sycamore branch that ripped open her hull and pulled her down into the murky, sucking mud. All her cargo, all the hardware and dry goods and clothing were lost. All the foodstuffs destined to perish, forever entombed on the shifting, silt floor of the river.

The good news was that a headcount done after the rescue boats rowed back and forth a few times, showed none of the official passengers had been lost — a list that didn't include me or the two jewel thieves.

Only a lone mule, tied on the lower deck and forgotten about in the initial tumult, had perished.

"You look pretty good for a corpse," I told Reuben. and his knobby head swung back and forth in agreement. "A few good meals will get you back into trim," I said. "Me too."

And thanks to the Contessa Vanessa Drake's diamonds — the *real diamonds*, that is — and my good fortune at finding them in the cargo bay along with a cache of children's baubles and paste, we'd eat for a long time to come.

#

The Missouri River has long been a source of western trade, true tales, and legend. Growing up near the muddy flow and living on its banks now, the river continuously inspires me with its history. The sinking of the steamboat *Arabia* on September 5, 1856 is a particularly grand story, both for its Titanic-like drama (albeit smaller in scope) and its vast archeological trove more than 100 years later. Unlike so many wrecked ships, the Arabia saw her passengers all redeemed — except one, a no-name, forgotten mule doomed to the fickle deep. This was clearly unfair, and so, with "A Riverboat Detective," I've sought to remedy this egregious wrong, *i.e.* — in my version of history, the mule lives!   —Richard Prosch

Richard Prosch's work has appeared in *Mystery Magazine*, *Down and Out Magazine*, *Tough Crime*, *Wild West*, and online at *Boys' Life*. Winner of the Will Rogers Medallion and multiple Peacemaker-award finalist positions, Richard took home the Spur Award from Western Writers of America for short fiction, and his 2022 novel, *Pony Boys* was a Spur Award-finalist. As an anthologist, his book packages have garnered the Spur, Peacemaker, and Will Rogers Medallion for their contributors.

Midnight at Noon

Lisa Majewski

The young boy's legs pumped up and down, carrying his body forward. His black boots sank into soft snow only to reappear a moment later, kicking up small puffs of white behind him.

He veered left, barely averting a collision with the barbed wire fence.

"Faster, faster," he cried. His fingers curled into tight fists as his arms swung back and forth. "If I can but reach that bridge, I am safe."

He whipped his head around, eyes widening in terror.

He screamed and fell, landing face down in the snow.

A woman kneeled and surveyed the carnage. "The horseman again?"

Henry rolled over onto his back and opened one eye. "You really shouldn't be here ma'am. Sleepy Hollow is a dangerous place."

Rose Anderson stood, hands perched on hips, looking down at her seven-year-old son. She shook her head and wondered at God's wisdom of bestowing such energy on the young, who needed it only for play.

Grabbing a nearby shovel, she scooped up some of the fluffy snow and tossed it on his legs.

"Here lies Ichabod Crane . . . or what's left of him."

Henry crossed both arms over his chest and closed his eyes.

"Not the smartest fella in these parts by the looks of his dress," she continued, resting her arms on the handle. "Out and about in shirt sleeves with no coat or jacket to speak of."

Fanning his face, Henry said, "Cause it's a hundred and eighty out."

While not the inferno the boy claimed, the air was surprisingly warm. The bright sky offered a much-needed respite from the weather of late. *Let this be the January thaw*, she thought.

Their horse, Juniper, seemed to be enjoying the change as she trotted about flicking her tail.

Rose turned her attention back to the boy. "If you think it's a hundred eighty out then you surely need to be sittin' in a classroom learning a few things."

Henry patted his shoulders as if searching for something. "How can I learn anything when I haven't got a head?"

She felt the corner of her mouth start to turn up into a smile. Too smart for her, and more than likely too smart for anyone over at the schoolhouse. A secret best kept from him.

"Good point, Ichabod. But if you haven't a head, then you haven't a mouth to talk back with."

Henry groaned, stood up and dusted off his pants.

"Now go get some break — "

Before she could finish, he dashed by her into the house.

I swear, just watchin' that boy wears me out.

Rose followed through the door just as Henry snatched a biscuit off the table and catapulted onto the couch. He picked up a book from the side table, flipped to a page and started to read, pausing only to nibble on his breakfast and pull the quilt down around his shoulders.

He was wrapped in a lifetime of memories.

Her eyes drifted over the colorful squares; fragments of time joined together in a single place. As always, her gaze lingered on the snippet of heavy black wool stitched tightly to the piece of delicate off-white silk by its side.

"There never was, and there never will be, a finer looking bride and groom," Jack said proudly after they were declared husband and wife.

Rose's wedding dress lay tucked away in a box under the bed.

Jack's suit lay with him in a cemetery back in Utah.

Six plus years, and the ache throbbed just as fresh as the day of his killing.

"Can I have another one? But with a bunch of jam?"

The sweet voice soothed Rose. Henry, the only tonic for her pain.

"Yes, you may."

He scooted to the edge of the couch and stood up. "I'm going to eat jam every day for the rest of my life."

Rose laughed at her son's silliness. "Fine by me, but once you're married your wife might have a different opinion."

Henry's lower lip quivered, and his voice dropped. "But I don't want a wife. I want to stay here with you. Forever."

"Oh, honey." From the time he could walk, he shadowed her. And although she tried to reassure her little boy that she could take care of herself, Henry still thought of *himself* as her protector.

"I guess you better stay home *one* more day," she said, kissing the top of his head. "Help me out around here and make sure this place holds up."

"*Hooray.*"

"You're on barn duty today, mister."

"Ahhh, ma," Henry whined.

"No more dillying, Mr. Dally."

Henry laughed. "OK, Mrs. Dilly, I won't be dallying," he said, skipping out the door.

Rose sat at the table making a list of all the supplies she needed to get during their next trip to town. She massaged her temples hoping to ease the tension she could feel starting to build. It wasn't the first time she second-guessed her decision to pack up and move to the homestead Jack had only visited in his dreams.

Three weeks after she'd given birth, her husband sat her down for a talk.

"Things are not sittin' right with me, Rosie. Some days it feels like the bad guys outnumber the good guys."

She reached out and lifted his chin. "What's going on?"

"I don't want my son. . . ." Jack said, his voice cracking. He cleared his throat and tried again. "I don't want my son worrying every day that his father may not come home from work."

Rose would've never thought he'd retire; he loved the townspeople and being their sheriff. And they loved him something fierce in return. But their bundle of pure joy, weighing in at seven pounds six ounces, had changed everything.

They agreed homesteading in a new place sounded like just the kind of thing they were looking for and picked the Dakotas for their new life.

A few days before they were set to leave, Rose spent the afternoon helping decorate the Wilson's barn. It was the biggest one in town, and they had generously offered it up for the Anderson's farewell party. Rather than go all the way back home, she was going to get ready with Maggie Wilson.

At a quarter to five, Jack sauntered down the street to meet his wife and friends.

Movement in Miller's bank caught his eye — a robbery in progress. Although no longer wearing the badge, Jack remained a lawman at heart.

He entered through a side door just as one of the strangers pistol-whipped the clerk, Clyde, who also happened to be the bank owner's youngest son.

Years of experience had fine-tuned his skills, allowing Jack to get the drop on the thieves and the situation under control. The men were in the process of laying their guns on the floor when Clyde suddenly panicked and bolted for the back.

Startled, the gunmen opened fire.

Jack jumped in front of Clyde while pulling the trigger on his Colt. He shot one of the men twice in the right leg and the other in the groin.

Clyde, curled in a ball, was unhurt.

One of the gunman's bullets severed Jack's carotid artery. He was dead before he hit the ground.

The outlaws healed from their wounds only to have justice finish them off.

It made no difference to Rose; the other side of her bed was still empty at night.

Knowing she wanted to honor her late husband's wishes, the townsfolk (along with Clyde Miller Senior) raised enough funds for Rose to buy 320 acres in the Dakotas, outright. There was enough money left over for her and Henry to live comfortably. *That* was how much Jack was loved.

Rose walked outside. She didn't see Henry and wondered what exciting adventure he was undertaking now.

It really is a beautiful day, she thought. *Too beautiful to be whittled away to night with only chores.* She'd bring lunch out on the porch.

She stopped midstride. The gate was open.

Henry knew better than to be so careless when the horse was out of the barn.

A high-pitched, drawn-out whinny cut through her thoughts and sent a chill down Rose's spine.

She dashed across the yard as the sound escalated in intensity, knowing the horse was growing more frightened.

Juniper's head poked out from behind the barn, her ears flicking back and forth.

Rose opened her mouth to offer words of comfort when she saw a stranger walking next to the mare, a tattered rope going from his hand to her neck. Rose's stride faltered. He didn't see her right away as he was too busy bickering with someone.

His companion, who was trailing close behind, was no more than seventeen. He held on to the collar of Henry's shirt, who shuffled along making tracks in the snow. The young man jumped when he saw Rose and yanked on the boy, pulling him back.

"Aw shit, Charlie."

The man in front stopped, took a step back, stopped again and then stepped forward in such quick order he looked like he was doing a jig. He offered Rose the weakest of smiles and then out of the corner of his mouth barked a warning.

"Settle down, Samuel."

"What's going on?" Rose shouted, rushing over and pulling Henry out of the man's grasp.

Charlie winced at the sharp tone in her voice and nervously wiped the back of his hand across his mouth.

"Henry, are you OK?" Rose demanded of her son, scanning his body to see if there were any marks or wounds.

He nodded but shot Samuel a glare.

"He's fine, ma'am," Charlie said. "See, one of our horses turned her ankle."

"And what does that have to do with my son?" Rose spit out as she pulled the boy to her side.

Charlie scratched the top of his head as if the right answer might break loose from somewhere inside.

"Ahem . . . we were lookin' to . . . um . . . trade horses."

Steal is more like it, she thought.

"An afternoon social, and me without an invite," a voice said from behind her.

Rose whirled to see a man sitting high on a black Appaloosa stallion coming through the gate. He tipped his bowler hat as he looked her over from head to toe.

"I been watching you two run your mouths," he said to the men, while his eyes stayed locked on Rose. "What's the deal, Charlie?"

"Things went a bit off the rail, Ray" he said, his top lip twitching.

Ray cocked his head. "You don't say."

The words came tumbling out of Charlie's mouth so quickly they tripped up his tongue.

"Alright now . . . everything's . . . she . . . we." He took a deep breath and slowed down. "We're back on track. Told her about the, you know, trade," he said in an exaggerating tone, doing everything but winking.

"We're in the business of taking, not trading," Ray said, getting off the horse and making his way to Rose.

Charlie chewed on his upper lip and busied himself with twisting and untwisting the rope.

"I knew it," Henry yelled. "Dang horse thieves."

Ray laughed and ruffled the boy's hair. "Not by trade."

He leaned in close enough for Rose to feel his breath on her face. The proximity made her nauseous, and she swallowed back the bile at the opening of her throat.

"I need you to tell me two things. First, what's your name?"

She swallowed again. "Rose."

"Second, is there anyone else on the property?"

Rose raced through all the different scenarios and then decided. As she spoke, she struggled to keep her voice even.

"My husband."

Out of the corner of her eye, she could see Henry's jaw drop and then just as quickly, snap back into place.

"And his name?"

"Jack," she whispered.

He repeated the name while tapping his gun holster.

"And where would Jack be?"

"In . . . in the house."

He drew his gun and pointed at Charlie. "Got a simple assignment here. Watch these two while I check out the barn," he said, and then turned to Rose.

"Not that I don't trust you ma'am."

Ray strode off.

Samuel slapped his hand on his thigh. "Damn him."

"Watch your mouth. He hears you," Charlie snapped, "and he'll nail it shut."

"*Pfft*. You keep propping him up like he's the biggest toad in the pond, and I ain't seen it yet."

Charlie gave a look in Rose's direction and lowered his voice. "Got you set up for life, didn't he?"

Samuel rolled his eyes and threw up his hands. "And why are you whispering? He done told her we was stealing a horse. That's enough to get us some lead in the back."

"Oh, stop acting like a fool," Charlie said, but no longer keeping his voice down.

"Me the fool?" Samuel said, thumbing his chest. "I'm not the one who sent that four-flusher on ahead with all our cash and not more than a day's travel from disappearing."

Samuel ran his hand through his hair. "Now that's a fool right there."

"I recall you was at the table when plans were made. Not a peep outta you." Charlie chuckled. "'Course, I thought you were gonna wet your pants. Playing with the big boys and no mama's apron to clutch to."

Samuel stole a quick glance at Rose. The skin from his forehead all the way down to his neck reddened. He cleared his throat and jabbed his index finger in Charlie's direction.

"You don't remember nothing," he spat out. "Besides, I'm the fastest rider. I should be the one down at the Occidental knocking back a few, waitin' for you three slow pokes."

Rose pulled Henry tighter. Listening to Samuel go off at the mouth snuffed out any flicker of hope she might have had.

At the end of each day, Jack and Rose would share a whiskey and talk, her husband unloading the heavy burden of his job. She'd listen, ask questions, and offer advice. Once after a long discussion, he shook his head, saying, "I don't know if you'd make a fine deputy or one hell of an outlaw."

One dark day, two sheriffs from neighboring towns were killed. The men had fled through Utah and gone on to a place near Dirty Devil River. Jack said they would probably stay good and gone as law enforcement rarely chased anyone into those hideouts.

"The worst one's between the Bighorn Mountains and the Red Wall. "You could kill someone, have a drink at the Occidental and disappear within a day," he complained.

These men must have done some awful things, and she didn't think their plans included leaving any witnesses.

Ray returned and declared the barn clear of any "varmints."

"Alright, Rose, you're coming with me."

"Shouldn't we all go?" Charlie asked.

Ray shook his head. "Nope. You two are still on kid duty."

Rose wiped a wisp of hair back from her forehead, the skin slick with perspiration.

"You're gonna stay right in front of me the whole time. Your husband tries to be a hero, I'll put a hole where Henry slept for nine months."

They slowly walked over the melting snow, Ray pausing every few steps, checking for movement from the doors or windows. Once he was satisfied, she'd feel the gun in her back nudge her forward.

They stepped onto the porch, the wood creaking beneath their feet.

"Say something," Ray whispered, twisting her arm.

"Jack — " She choked back an unexpected sob as she called to a husband who would never answer. "Henry and I are in trouble . . . real bad trouble, and we need your help."

"Nice."

When there wasn't a response, Ray guided her to the threshold. His booming voice made Rose jump right out of her skin. "Jack, if you don't want to see every bit of your wife's blood spilling across the floor, I suggest you come out here with your empty hands in the air."

The house remained silent, revealing no secrets.

Slow and steady, she commanded herself, fearful she would dash at any moment to get away from Ray's touch. She might be able to control her feet, but her heart was another matter. Rose could feel it fluttering madly, her pulse darting at her temples and at the tips of her fingers, making them shake uncontrollably.

Just a few more steps.

"I do believe you lied to me, Rose. Nobody's here."

Ray spun her around and shoved the gun under her chin.

His eyes scanned the room and rested on the Winchester above the fireplace.

He holstered his gun and tilted his hat back.

"Did you confuse me with one of those coots out there?"

"What . . . no."

"Come on now," Ray said, turning her back in the other direction. He snaked his arms around her waist and rested his chin on her shoulder.

"On the wall up there."

She looked at the gun her husband taught her to shoot the first week they met.

Ray ended the embrace and moved to check out the rifle.

She backed away from him toward the couch.

"Sit down," he growled.

Rose did as she was told, pushing herself into the corner against the pillow, wanting to be as far away from him as possible.

He sauntered over to the fireplace and shook his head. "Rose . . . Rose," he chuckled, reaching up for the rifle. "You thought you were going to come in here and get the drop on me?" Ray said, swinging the finger lever downward, moving a cartridge from the magazine into the chamber.

Rose held her breath.

He laughed and ejected a round. "You had a better chance of catching a weasel asleep."

She exhaled.

Ray repeated the steps until he cycled the action and came up empty.

"Sorry I went and spoiled everything," he said, pulling the butt into the socket of his shoulder.

"Oh, Ray, what's that behind you?" he said in a high-pitched impersonation of a female voice. "Pow. Pow."

Rose reached over the side of the couch and grabbed the Remington from its hiding place at the same time she stood up. Its familiar weight steadied her, and she smoothly pushed the lever forward half a turn, revealing a round in the chamber. She aimed it at Ray who dropped the useless rifle from his hands.

"That's nearly as big as you. Are you sure you even know how to — "

Rose worked the lever, and the Remington's hammer pulled back with a well-oiled click.

"My husband always told me to have one for show, and one for go."

For the first time, doubt flickered in Ray's eyes.

"Put your hands up," Rose said.

Ray did as she asked, his hands coming up past his hips, before stopping below his shoulders.

The bickering voices of the other two outlaws wafted in through the window.

"You're buffaloed if you think I'm gonna sit out here twiddling my thumbs," Samuel said.

"I told you I was going to talk to him."

Rose chanced a quick glance out the window. Henry dutifully walked by Charlie's side.

She sucked in her breath.

Ray's smile reappeared, bigger than ever.

"Oh, Char*lie*," he yelled in a sing-song voice. "The missus has got a gun on me. Grab her kid, will ya?"

Charlie threw one of his arms across the boy's chest. With his other hand he reached behind his back and drew a Bowie knife out of the sheath attached to his belt. He pressed the blade against Henry's neck.

He whimpered as a small rivulet of blood trickled down his skin.

"Stopstopstoppleasestopplease," Rose begged.

"Your turn to drop it," Ray said, sharply.

She lay the rifle on the floor and took a step away from the weapon.

He moved to the door and leaned casually against the frame. "I'd like to give you a gift for all the hospitality you've shown us." Eyes fixed on her, he said, "Hey Charlie, take off the boy's head and toss it to Rose."

Samuel took a quick step back and fell.

Charlie gripped the knife and moved the blade.

A scream careened around in her head but somehow stayed inside, echoing.

Henry's eyes rolled to the left and heavenward.

"Hen Pen, the sky is falling."

Rose thought Henry had retreated to the past, when he sat on her lap while she read him *The Remarkable Story of Chicken Little.* Tiny hands touching her cheeks, fascinated with the sounds coming out of her mouth.

Rose teetered on the edge, ready to follow her son into madness.

Charlie's attention was suddenly drawn to what Henry spied in the distance.

"Ho . . . *ly* hell." The knife lowered and he let go of the little boy.

"What are you — " Ray shouted as he stepped outside.

"*Henry*," Rose screamed. "Run."

Her son took off, with Charlie in close pursuit.

Ray raised his gun.

A sound unlike anything Rose had ever heard before filled the air, blocking out all other noise. It was as if the Devil himself had unleashed a demonic stampede onto the open plain.

A rolling wave of snow and ice descended, wiping everyone from her view.

There was a sudden, whistling shriek from the fireplace, and a blast of icy air roared down the throat of the chimney. It battered the smoldering logs aside, driving soot and ash across the room in a billowing cloud as snow poured in through the front door and windows.

Rose seized the Remington and without hesitation, stepped out into the blizzard.

The wind pulled her violently into its embrace, spinning her halfway around before pushing her into another partner's waiting arms — Ray's.

It gusted from both sides, smashing their chests together. The gun pressed between them, the barrel pointing straight up.

Their eyes locked.

Rose's finger, already on the trigger, pulled.

The bullet ripped through the left side of Ray's face, a spray of blood hanging momentarily in the air. His hands flew up to a ragged flap of skin that whipped back and forth.

Rose drove the butt of the rifle against his head. It connected with a splintering crunch that she felt as much as heard, and Ray collapsed into the snow.

She tried to move forward, but for every advance she took, she was pushed two agonizing steps backward by the wind. She stumbled, and the rifle was suddenly wrested from her grasp, spilling from between her numb fingers and spiraling away into the blinding flurry. It too, disappeared.

Need to keep moving.

She squinted and headed off in what she thought was the direction of the barn.

If she couldn't see more than a few feet in front of her, then neither could they.

Please find a place to hide, baby boy. I'm coming for you.

Snow from the previous night spun into the air, and Rose's face was suddenly on fire. She screamed as jagged bits of ice peppered her cheeks like a swarm of bees with frozen stingers. She flung an arm up to protect her face and felt the fingers of her hand burn with searing pain before going numb altogether.

She tried to run, lurching through ever-increasing drifts. Rose couldn't tell where the sky ended and the ground began. *Had she been walking in a straight line or in circles? For two minutes or an hour?* A wave of dizziness hit, and she lost her balance, tumbling sideways, crashing into the barn.

She pulled herself along the side, feeling her way toward what she hoped was the open door. If it had swung shut, chances were good that she was going to die out here, with only scant inches of wood between her and safety.

After half a dozen steps, she stopped.

Ray lay flat against the building, his eyes squeezed tightly shut.

Was he frozen in place?

Then something struck the barn, hammering on the roof and walls.

And Ray opened his eyes.

Rose prayed he would let her be.

"She's over here," he whispered.

She shook her head and turned to run when he grabbed her hand.

This time he found his voice and yelled.

"She's over here. I've got — "

He suddenly dropped her arm. His mouth was wide open, but no sound came out. The powder snow poured in.

She watched as he tried to get a breath and couldn't. Rose backed away as he clawed at his throat, drowning in the open air. He pitched forward and was gone — just another drift of snow.

Rose hugged the barn as she walked, groping along until her hand fell into nothingness — *she had found the opening.*

She moved inside and a moment later the door slammed shut behind her with a thundering crash, casting the interior of the barn into complete darkness.

Outside, the storm lashed at the wooden structure, howling to get in. Ice shrieked through the narrow gaps in the barn siding, victorious.

Rose stumbled in the dark, arms stretched out before her, trying to find the heavy wooden support closest to the door. When one of her hands finally thumped against it, she ran her fingers over the splintered surface until she found the hanging lantern. Nailed next to it was a tin box. She reached inside. There was just a single match left. She carefully picked it up, sought out the bulbous tip, and raked it across the striking strip on the front of the box. The match flared into bright light, then guttered to a dim, flickering blue in the icy air. She cupped her hands protectively around the flame and used it to light the lantern.

Rose crept forward, holding the lamp out to light her way. When she reached the second stall, she peered over the railing and saw Henry lying on the floor. She cried out and rushed to him. She set the lantern down on the floor and drew him into her arms. *He's so cold*, she thought, looking down at his skin, so pale it was almost translucent.

"Henry? Wake up — please, wake up." He stirred, and she pulled him closer, praying that whatever warmth she had left would revive him. After a moment, his eyes fluttered open.

"Mama. . . ." he whispered.

"Yes, baby," she said, tears welling in her eyes. "I'm going to build you the biggest, grandest fire." She gently lay him back down and, as quickly as her body would allow, used the pitchfork in the stall to pull bundles of hay to the middle of the barn.

She had just set the lantern on top of one of the bales and placed the pitchfork against its side when the barn door swung open and Charlie bolted toward her. She rocked back on her heels, bracing herself for the impact. But it never came.

He skidded to a stop a full four feet from her and began to slap wildly at his face. In the flickering light Rose saw that his eyes were sealed shut with icy sutures.

She slowly extended a hand towards Charlie, waving it back and forth. No reaction. Rose turned to see Henry peering at her, and she quickly put a finger to her lips. He nodded and sat utterly still.

Charlie raked his fingers across his face. His left eyebrow split wide open, the flesh parting all the way down to the bone beneath, and hot blood coursed down his face. He swiped a hand, now sticky with blood, across his cheek, and the flesh tore away.

Rose took a step back and bumped into the pitchfork; it clattered to the floor.

Charlie spun in the direction of the sound. "Samuel?" he rasped. "Ray?" When there was no answer, he used his thumb and forefinger to pry open one of his eyelids. Delicate skin tore under his touch.

He looked at Rose. This time he saw her.

With a roar, he rushed at her. They tumbled over the bales of hay and fell to the floor. Rose tried to slip out from underneath him, but he was too big, too strong. He yanked a handful of her hair, and she screamed in pain. She tried to bat his hands away, but it was useless. He lashed a fist out at her. It clipped Rose on the chin and her head snapped to the side and thumped off the floor. Then his hands closed around her throat — squeezing. She couldn't breathe. Couldn't scream. Charlie suddenly grew heavier, the weight crushing down on her.

Somewhere, someone was screaming. The hands on her throat were suddenly gone, and Rose drew a ragged gasp of air. She looked up to see Charlie flailing at Henry, who had battened on to his back.

He was a wild thing, biting and scratching. Charlie got to his feet and whirled around. Henry lost his hold and fell to the ground, landing in a twisted sprawl. He scooted back toward the shadows. Charlie seized the lantern and began to swing it back and forth. Swiping blood out of his eyes with one scarred hand, he began to look for Henry.

Rose saw her son suddenly lit in the glow of the lantern. Charlie advanced on him, kicking savagely at the boy. Henry screamed in pain and clutched his side. Charlie stood over him in wounded triumph and raised one boot into the air over Henry's head.

Rose scrambled to her feet. Her hand fell upon the handle of the pitchfork, and she grabbed it. With a cry of fury, she ran at Charlie, who turned to meet her.

Just as he came around, Rose buried the tines of the pitchfork in his throat. The lantern tumbled from his grasp and shattered, spilling burning lamp oil across the floor. Rose saw his eyes bulging in their sockets. Blood poured from his throat in a steaming flood, soaking the front of his shirt. His hands pawed clumsily at the handle jutting from his neck. Then, his arms flopped to his sides, and he fell over backward.

He struck the door and pushed it partway open. Wind and snow barreled in through the gap, and the fire, which could have set the entire barn ablaze, was suddenly extinguished like candles on a birthday cake.

Rose stepped to Henry and hauled him to his feet. He screamed, arms clutching his wounded ribs. "We have to get to the house. Do you understand?"

He nodded.

She clutched his face. "Promise me you won't let go of my hand. No matter what."

He nodded again, meeting her gaze.

Their hands intertwined, Rose moved to the door. She helped him step over Charlie's body and together they ventured back out.

The ravenous storm swallowed them whole.

She tried to take a breath, but the air felt as if it was full of powdered glass.

They had only gone a few feet when she was hit broadside. The wind spun her halfway around, tearing at her repeatedly with icy talons. Henry's small hand slipped away.

She turned in the direction of. . . .

Where was the house? She swung around, searching for the barn, for a familiar landmark that would help send her in the right direction, and saw nothing.

Rose was tired and she didn't have much fight left in her. *Maybe it's time to give in and give up. Would that really be so bad? The two of us wrapped in a blanket of snow.* She collapsed to the ground.

Rose felt someone tugging on her dress.

Henry, please let me sleep.

Little fingers encircled her own, pulling them through the soft snow to the ground below. He guided her hand across the dirt, her finger dipping down into a groove —

The wagon wheel ruts!

She squeezed Henry's hand to let him know she understood. They could follow them all the way from the barn to a few feet from their front door.

She crawled on all fours, moving only a few inches at a time. Her knees and palms scraped raw with each motion, but she didn't stop. When the ground smoothed out, she sat back on her haunches. Henry stood less than twenty feet away, guiding Rose by waving his arms back and forth.

We made it.

Henry's gaze shifted from his mother's face to something in the distance. His eyes widened in terror and his fingers curled into tight fists.

Rose looked over her shoulder.

An apparition materialized out of the swirling snow. It came not from the innocence of a child's imagination, but rather the darkness of a mother's nightmare.

The black horse reared up; the rider now visible — Ray.

The left side of his face, a mass of ripped flesh and frozen blood.

He raised his gun and fired.

The blasts added their own note to the cacophony of the storm.

Rose barely felt the bullet graze her shoulder.

Henry ran toward her, arms outstretched.

She wanted to tell him not to worry; she wasn't in any pain.

The force of the wind increased in fury, suspending Henry in place.

A curtain of snow came down on the horseman's final act, blocking him from her view.

And when it went up, he was gone.

Suddenly there was a momentary calm. The wind died down and gently lay Henry on the snow.

Rose tried to stand, but the weakness in her legs and the fear in her heart prevented it. She pulled herself along and reached him.

A single bullet hole visible in the center of Henry's forehead. Blood pooled, forming a crimson halo around the crown of his head.

She gathered him in her arms.

The storm came back with ten times the force and there was nothing but white.

Rose's chest heaved and not even the blizzard could silence her scream.

Two weeks after the blizzard, the general store was filled with people bustling about for supplies and sharing stories of heroism and tragedy.

As Rose waited patiently at the counter for her purchases, snippets of conversations drifted past her. It was like an explosion . . . storm came out of nowhere . . . like a train going off its tracks . . . tied a rope around her waist and the children . . . heroine of the storm . . . face frozen to the ground . . . died two feet from his front door . . . wrapped in his older brother's arms . . . amputated both legs below the knee . . . lost most of her fingers . . . pneumonia . . . gangrene . . . beautiful day . . . bad feeling that morning . . . and your Henry?

"Mrs. Anderson?"

Startled, Rose looked up to see the shop's proprietor, Edwin Brewster, staring at her with a concerned expression.

"I'm so sorry," she said. "I was lost in my own little world there for a moment."

"I was asking after Henry. How is he?"

"Henry's at home," she replied with a slight smile, "wrapped up in a quilt, surrounded by his favorite books."

Once the clerk loaded Rose's supplies into the back of the wagon, she threw one of the horse blankets over everything, making sure to completely cover the new Winchester rifles.

As she slipped the additional Colt revolver into her leather satchel, Rose wondered how long it would be before someone stopped by her property. She'd buried Henry deep enough so that he wouldn't be disturbed. As for the other two, she left them where they fell and watched from the window every day as they were visited by coyotes and taken away bit by bit.

When the bank robbers killed her husband, they destroyed her past. When Ray murdered Henry, he stole her future. All she had was a string of todays; and today a storm was brewing.

You couldn't see it on the horizon or feel it in the air. It was raging deep within her.

And it was headed to Wyoming.

#

The morning of January 12, 1888, was deceptively warm, teasing a pleasant day ahead. Enticed from their homes by clear skies and rising temperatures, people across the Great Plains ventured out to run errands, do chores, and return to school. Then, without warning, a blizzard blasted through the area. In less than twenty-four hours, hundreds would be dead; many of them children on their way home from school.

Numerous survivors recounted how incredibly beautiful the day had begun. For me, the juxtaposition between this common recollection, and the sudden violent nature of the weather that followed, added another frightening layer to the tragic event. I wanted to explore those moments when the world shifts, and darkness comes to swallow the light.   —Lisa Majewski

Lisa Majewski graduated with honors from the USC School of Cinematic Arts. In addition to a career as a script doctor, she has also edited both nonfiction and fiction books. Her writing has appeared in award-winning anthologies and has been a finalist for the Peacemaker Award from the Western Fictioneers.

GODDESS OF WAR

KELLI FITZPATRICK

Clara Whitlock sat at the saloon table with a man who wanted to hire her and a man who wanted to kill her.

Neither of them had voiced their intentions, but after thirty years as a gunman, she knew what they were about the moment they sat down. The third man at the table, a store clerk lost in his drink, hadn't said a peep the whole evening. The four of them were partway through a game of euchre. Clara and the prospective client, a tall academic-type with glasses, led the killer and the clerk by four points. It was late at night and the saloon was mostly empty, only another card game in the corner and the barkeep wiping down tables.

Clara adjusted her black Stetson over short gray hair, then shuffled the cards to deal the next hand.

"I didn't realize folks played euchre in the West," said the client. He hadn't dropped his name. He looked a bit younger than Clara, maybe late forties, smartly dressed, elite Boston accent. "I've always thought of it as a Midwest game."

"Picked it up during the War," Clara said, dealing. "Taught each other games around the campfire. Not much else for soldiers to do at night."

"Too bad you fought on the losing side," the killer said. He was young, lanky, sweating, with a thick mustache and wild eyes. He hadn't asked to join the game. He'd told the previous player to beat it. "I heard you've never lost since."

Clara shrugged. "I'm good at what I do."

The killer was armed, a pistol on his right hip, knife visible in his left boot. She wasn't sure why he wanted to kill her, but she guessed it had something to do with a previous job. Clara's rifle lay across her lap, pistol holstered at her side.

The client looked at his cards. "What brings you to Houck, Arizona, Miss?"

"I go where there's work. New railroad means lots of stuff needs protecting on its way to wherever."

"You're a hired gun, then?"

"Something like that."

The killer laughed. "Don't you know this lady, mister? She's the Relentless Mother. Will neutralize anyone and anything that gets near whatever she's guarding. Consequences be damned. Ain't that right, Mother?"

"I ain't nobody's mother. Spades is up."

The clerk passed. So did the client and the killer. Clara turned the spade facedown. It went around again, but nobody called trump.

"We're playing stick the dealer, see?" the killer said with a sneer.

That meant she had to call trump, even if she had a lousy hand. She sipped her whiskey and looked at her cards: a red bauer, a black ace, and a whole lot of nothing. Her partner should be good for one trick. "Diamonds."

The killer shrugged. "Your funeral."

"I have always thought the diamond symbols looked more like stars," the client said.

It was hard to tell which one of them would make their move first. "You an astronomer?" Clara asked.

"Something like that."

The clerk raised his empty glass. The barkeep circled around and refilled it. Clara and the client took the first two tricks.

"Tell me something," the killer said. He sat across from her. "Why do you dress like a man? You look ridiculous in that collared shirt and trousers."

"I dress for the job."

"I bet you joined the Rebs because no one wanted you for a wife."

The killer was playing lousy. Clara wanted to either play cards for real or get on with whatever was going to happen here.

The killer eyed her. "You don't remember me, do you?"

She didn't. "I remember it's your turn to lay."

"The name's Frank Ballenbaum. You cost me the Sedona job. I worked three years on Tanner Carlson's crew before he trusted me with that heist. You mucked it up."

Sedona. That was two years ago. Clara had been hired to guard the transport of a jeweler's private collection by stagecoach. In the middle of the night in a river valley, two riders tried to jump the coach. Clara kicked one off his horse and shot the other through the gut. She never saw their faces. Apparently, one had lived to hold a grudge. It wasn't the first time someone got angry at her for doing her job. Wouldn't be the last. "We going to finish the game?" she said.

"I'm here to finish you." Frank stood, hand on his pistol. He didn't draw immediately. He was posturing. He clearly hadn't learned anything from their run-in two years ago.

Clara put her cards down and drained her whiskey. "Kid, you don't want to do that."

"I've got nothing left to lose." He stepped around the table to stand over her.

She leaned back, both hands on her rifle. "You're young. You never know what tomorrow will bring. Why don't you live to find out?"

The clerk got up from the table and ambled out the door. With a snap of his fingers and a thumb jerk, the barkeep directed the other patrons outside. The client didn't move. He watched them intently through his gold-rimmed glasses, looking from Clara to Frank.

"Why don't you go to hell?" Frank said.

Frank moved to draw, but Clara was faster. She jammed the stock of her rifle up hard into Frank's jaw. A loud crunch. He dropped his gun as he staggered backward. She stood and hit him again across the face. Blood splattered over the floorboards and Frank made a long guttural moan as he fell. She flipped the rifle and trained it down at his head. He wanted her dead. She should shoot him. He had drawn first — the law would side with her.

A muddy ravine choked with screaming bodies. Smoke in the air. Bullets on the breeze. *Again.* Charging and firing. *Again. Hit them again.*

Clara lowered her rifle. She looked at Frank's broken face. If he lived, he would never be the same. Did she have to hit him so hard? She never used to hesitate. Now it happened all the time. She walked to the bar. "You got a doctor in town?"

"Course," the barkeep said. "She lives up the street."

"Send for her."

"It's almost midnight, ma'am."

"Send for her. Kid will need help if he's going to talk again."

"On whose dime? He hasn't even paid for his drink."

She dug in her vest pocket and dropped a wad of bills on the bar. "See how many stitches that buys." She walked out. What might her life have been like, if she'd taken that other path? Would she still be beating up kids in bars?

The client was waiting on the porch, hands folded behind his back. "Excuse me, ma'am, but I do believe you're Clara Whitlock."

"Yep. And you ain't from around here."

"You're even more impressive in person."

"What do you want?" No sense hanging around Houck, especially if the kid woke up and decided to raise a fuss. She hadn't found work here in a week, and her rental at the stables was almost up. She would head south. There was always work closer to the border.

"You can call me John. I represent a consortium of scientists, philanthropists, and investors who have a considerable interest in seeing astronomy expanded in the West." When she didn't say anything, he continued. "I'd like to hire you — security detail for a train trip from here to Flagstaff tomorrow morning."

Clara slung her gun over her shoulder by its strap and buttoned her vest against the spring chill. "God Almighty, mister, but you take your sweet time getting to your point. We've been sharing a table for hours."

"I prefer to get to know a person before I engage their services. Do you fancy a night stroll? I'd like to explain."

"I'm going this way anyways." They walked down the dark street. It was a clear cold night in May, and the stars burned bright in the huge bowl overhead.

"I'm prepared to offer you a handsome sum for the safe arrival of the item in question." John named the sum.

Clara's eyebrows raised. "What the hell are you hauling? Munitions? Gold bricks?"

"A borrowed telescope."

In thirty years of being a hired gun, she had protected some interesting loads — dynamite, a cattle baron's private library, a dinosaur skeleton from the Bone Wars in Nebraska — but a telescope was a first. "Why do you want me?"

"They say that once you get a goal in your sights, you never slow down, never give up. That you are, well, relentless. We are on the cusp of a once-in-a-lifetime opportunity. Look up there." He pointed to a bright dot in the sky that burned more steadily than the others. "That's the planet Mars, named for the Roman God of War. In a few days, it will reach full opposition, meaning it will be the closest to Earth it will be in its orbit, and its face fully lit. Because of the ellipticity of Mars' orbit, this opposition is especially favorable, offering the best chance at astronomical viewing for the next seventeen years."

Clara usually avoided looking at the night sky because it reminded her too much of the long nights before battle. Both sides carried a banner sporting white stars on a blue field. "If you got a telescope, why not just look at it here in Houck? Why ship it to Flagstaff?"

John was excited now. This was clearly his favorite thing to talk about. "Because the seeing isn't as good here — the wind, temperature, humidity, dust, atmospheric turbulence, all the conditions that affect viewing quality. Flagstaff offers impeccable seeing, as scouted by my good friend Andrew Ellicott Douglass. A wealthy Bostonian named Percival Lowell is funding the construction of a new observatory on a hill outside Flagstaff, using his own funds. His team has spent the last five weeks building the observatory structure, and it's nearly finished, save for the installation of two borrowed telescopes, the larger of which, an eighteen-inch refractor on loan from John Alfred Brashear, is coming through here on the train tomorrow. On May twenty-eighth, one week from now, Mr. Lowell will arrive in Flagstaff to commence his formal observations of Mars."

Clara nodded. "And you need the big spyglass to beat him there or he don't get to peep on the Martians."

"I need it to beat him there *in one piece,* in fully functional condition. Mr. Lowell's associate, Professor Pickering, will be on the train in the forward passenger car, but we have no buffer of time for anything to go wrong. The heavens do not halt to accommodate our mishaps."

Clara hooked her hands on her hips. "Houck to Flagstaff ain't but a few hours by rail. You really expect trouble on the last leg? Who'd want to mess with a telescope?"

"Astronomy is experiencing a renaissance in this nation, and a town that boasts a telescope will assuredly experience a flow of people and resources as people travel to use it. Many nefarious individuals in this region might think to divert this instrument from its destination to their own towns, or worse, dismantle it and sell it in pieces. My associates and I are not prepared to gamble with the future of our field. We are adding this additional layer of caution to protect the Lowell vision. Can you keep it safe?"

"I can keep it safe. I'll be on the train come morning." She turned toward the stables.

"Do you have a horse liveried here?"

"I got myself liveried here."

"I see." John reached into his coat and pulled out an envelope. "An advance on your pay. In case it is useful."

Clara took it.

"Oh, and one more thing. You mustn't tell anyone about this job. This is a secret intervention. Not even Lowell himself will know I have thus engaged you."

"Sir, I have no idea what you're talking about."

John smiled. "Good. See the conductor at first light. He will direct you to your charge." He tipped his hat. "It was an honor meeting you, Miss Whitlock."

She nodded to him. He walked off down the street.

Clara thumbed through the bills in the envelope, enough to rent a room at the local inn for a month. She tapped it against her palm and glanced up at the night sky. Could a gander at whatever was up there really be this valuable? The job was deceptively simple. Short early morning ride on a passenger train, a heavy item only a few people would care about, let alone know what to do with. Still, sometimes seemingly easy tasks turned into nightmares.

Again! Again! Down into it once more!

She shook her head. She needed sleep. She tucked the envelope inside her vest and climbed the ladder to the loft.

The train bumped along the rail. Clara stood, rifle loaded and held across her body, leaning against the forward door frame of the cargo car. The enormous cargo box that held the telescope body mostly filled the car. It was secured to the walls and ceiling via thick leather straps in a sort of spiderweb fashion, preventing sliding when the train hit curves and grades or when it braked. A separate smaller box held the primary lens, removed from the telescope to protect it during transport, also tied down tight. There was still a bit of give in the straps, and the way the boxes shifted around made Clara feel like she was babysitting an ornery grizzly bear and its cub.

They were half an hour into the journey, with no issues so far, just a lot of pink sky and knobby red outcroppings gliding by the windows. On train jobs, she liked to post up by the exit, so she could quickly get outside if there was trouble. It was much more likely there'd be trouble from within — thieves might front as passengers or even workers on the train — so for every minute she spent eyeing the skyline for riders, she spent two minutes people-watching the adjacent cars. This cargo car was bringing up the rear, and the car ahead was the dining car. Through the windows, she could see a bunch of families were being served breakfast—tea in porcelain pots and wicker baskets of pastry and whatnot.

In the closest booth, a woman in a pink hat fought to keep her three young children seated while her male companion read the newspaper. She looked tired. One of the children, a toddler, climbed up to the window in the door. She made faces at Clara.

Clara made faces back. The child giggled.

The mother didn't seem to notice. Clara did not envy her. She had never wanted that domestic life, but it was the only option her parents gave her. It was what drove her to join the Confederate army when the fighting started in Tennessee. She didn't much like what the Confederates were fighting for, but she figured they would have less strict entry requirements, plus Tennessee had seceded and it felt right to defend the place where she lived. She cut her hair, stole her older brother's clothes, and snuck off to find adventure that didn't involve chasing chickens or children.

She found it, all right. The Battle of Shiloh was her first taste of combat. Her company was in bad shape. They had run out of supplies and hadn't eaten for twenty-four hours. Still, they managed to surprise Grant's army and send them on the run, but some Union soldiers holed up in a small ravine. Surrounded on all sides by rebel troops, they held for six hours. Clara's commanding officer sent her and scores of other soldiers down into the ravine again and again, in a dozen assaults, to try to break the enemy. Every charge, they killed more of them, while the Feds sent death flying back. Clara had not hesitated, not a single time. She had gotten a thrill from it, from following orders, from focusing on one thing, one job, a single goal. Just keep hammering till it's over. Her compatriots nicknamed that patch of fighting the Hornet's Nest from the stinging bullets whistling through the trees.

The Union eventually surrendered the Hornet's Nest, but won the battle when reinforcements arrived. There had been steep casualties on both sides, three and a half thousand dead. Her friend Jacob had fought beside her. He had to pull her back from the last charge. She was ready to go on shooting till she dropped.

Later that night, at the fire, her hands shook uncontrollably while she gazed into the flames. She had found something out about herself. Once she committed to a thing, she would do it till it was done. *Any* thing. Even killing. What kind of person did that make her?

A child screamed.

The toddler's sibling had come to the window, spotted Clara, and was shrieking, "Mother, there's a ghost in that car!" The mother came and dragged them both back to the table. The woman looked on the verge of tears. Still no help from the man.

No, Clara had no interest in domestic life. At least, not anymore. The only time she had ever been tempted was when Jacob had discovered her secret, that she was in fact not Clyde Whitehall, not a man at all. He hadn't reported her. The penalty for a woman impersonating a man in the army could be anything from a good laugh to a hanging. Instead, Jacob had told her about his uncle's property near Pigeon Forge. A cabin on a ridge. It would be his after the war was done. She could come. They could spend their days fighting a plow and bears and the chill of winter. Plenty of adventure still left in those mountains.

They never made it there. Jacob was staffing the armory the day it blew up. Clara was down at the river, washing alone, when she heard the explosion. There are times when a person just knows something in their bones. Clara knew instantly he was caught up in the blast. She took her time getting back to camp. They never even found his remains. She didn't speak to anyone for weeks. Where might she be right now, how might her life have gone differently, if she and Jacob had been able to carry out their plan? She'd had a shot at a different kind of life and missed it.

When the war ended in 1865, she headed west, hopping from job to job. Never thinking too hard about who she was or who she wanted to be. She was a hired gun. That was it. She'd been all over New Mexico and Arizona and partway up the Rockies. Been in range wars and joined search parties and was even temporarily deputized when a town was overrun with bandits. She'd brushed shoulders with all kinds of people. Felt less confident about gunning down the "enemy" without question than she had when she was twenty. Nowadays, she preferred being handed goods to guard.

This job felt different, though. This telescope was something new. It was 1894, nearly the dawning of a new century. What would Percival Lowell see up there on those other planets? What did it feel like to hold a whole world in your eye?

Someone was making their way through the dining car, showing off an open case, a very slight man in black wearing silver rings. Traveling merchant, likely, hocking pocket watches. She would keep an eye on him.

Clara saw movement outside. Something running parallel to the train. Could be a puma or a wild stallion. A closer look out the window didn't reveal anything.

A thud from above. Clara shouldered her rifle. There was definitely something afoot. She followed the footsteps along the roof of the car to the back end.

The intruder came busting through the glass, boots first, kicking her in the chest, knocking her back against the telescope box, but she held her footing. He looked her up and down and laughed. "Hey, Bobby," he yelled, "they got a goddamn lady guarding it!" He reached for his pistol. "And here I was looking forward to a real fi—"

Clara swept his feet and pulled a heavy barrel down on top of him, crushing his leg. He wailed something awful, screaming for Bobby.

"You can shut up or I can shoot you." She angled her rifle out the busted window at the second rider coming up from the woods, getting up to speed. She fired at him, but the bullet bounced off a passing telegraph pole. He heard it and backed off out of sight before she could get a good look at him. Her second shot whizzed through air. What was their plan, drag the telescope off a moving train onto horseback?

Someone put her in a headlock from behind. Bobby, no doubt. Her rifle fell and he kicked it away. She recognized the ringed fingers as belonging to the dining car merchant. "Would you like to be thrown off or kept for later?" he snarled. "I jammed the door of the forward car on my way out. Nobody's coming to help you." He grabbed at her waist for her pistol.

She remembered how slight a man he was, then threw all her weight forward at the shoulder. They toppled over together, the man's feet flying up over his head. Both scrambled to their knees to draw. They fired at the same time.

Clara's shot went into the man's chest. He slumped into a pile.

Bobby's shot lodged deep in Clara's left shoulder. It stung, a white-hot poker driven into flesh. She'd been shot three times during battle, never felt a thing until later in the hospital tent. A bullet had clipped her temple once on a job in Colorado Springs when a shootout broke out in the town square. It hadn't even been aimed at her. Such was the luck of a gunman.

Using right hand and teeth, she did her best to tie her handkerchief under her arm around the wound to slow the bleeding.

"I knew I should have brought more experienced men," a voice said behind her.

Clara turned. The man beneath the barrel whimpered. Standing over him was a ghost from the past.

The man's face was creased, ringed in gray hair, unfamiliar. But the eyes—the eyes gave him away. "Jacob?" she said.

"Clarabell?" His brows lifted in surprise. "What are you —"

They stared at each other for a long minute. Hot blood surged in her face. It felt like the train was tipping off the tracks, tumbling over a ravine. There was no one to pull her back from the edge. There hadn't been for thirty years.

The man under the barrel raised a pistol at Clara. She hadn't even seen him reach for it.

"No!" Jacob shot the man through the neck. "Idiot." His voice softened. "What are you doing out here?"

"Jacob . . . how are you still standing? You died in that munitions explosion in sixty-four."

He smiled but kept his shotgun ready. "I'm sorry, Clare. I didn't mean — it wasn't my intent to leave you. I needed out. I couldn't wait for the generals —"

He kept talking but Clara couldn't hear him. She was picking up splinters of wood and torn cloth, metal casings scattered in long grass. People were patting her shoulder, saying *We know you were close.* She was crying alone in her tent. She was piecing together a life from the wreckage of the only person she had ever trusted.

Jacob had faked the whole thing. She felt it, the shake starting deep in her core. She pulled her pistol, but the cylinder was empty. She needed to reload.

"None of that, now! I should have guessed they would pick you to guard this. The Relentless Mother. I've heard the stories. Not in a million years would I have guessed that was you, Clare." Jacob crouched in front of the lens box, keeping her at gunpoint with one hand, and undoing the latch with the other.

"Stop." The words sounded hollow. A cheap threat. She willed her voice to even out so she could say more, but the shake had reached her throat.

"I only need the lens. I have people waiting just up the line to haul it into one of the neighboring towns. Everybody's antsy to capitalize on this interest in the sky." Jacob lifted the heavy lid, revealing the wide glass lens packed tight. "Heavy son of a bitch, though. Bobby was supposed to uncouple the car. Guess I'll have to improvise."

"Don't touch it," Clara warned.

"There are wild geraniums all around the cabin," he said, inspecting the lens. "They bloom this time of year. I put in a little vegetable garden on the south hillside last summer. There's almost always fog rolling over the peaks. That's why they call them the Smoky Mountains, you know. Always blanketed in mist." He sighed. "I meant to come find you, Clare. After the war was done. But you never told me your real last name. And the only thing the guys from our company could tell me was that you headed west. It's a big country. I wanted to find you. I wanted to have a life with you."

"So you became a thief instead?" This couldn't be the same man. The Jacob she knew would never have robbed a train, pointed a weapon at her, shot his own man. Would he? Had she ever really known him at all?

"I was an infiltrator, remember? It was my job to sneak into Union depots and steal their ammo, their food, their maps. I was good at it, too. This is the same damn thing, it just pays more." He reached for the lens.

Clara glanced out the window, saw where they were in the journey: coming up on a curve.

"That life we dreamed about? We can still have it," Jacob said. "I wasn't expecting to find you today, but don't you see that the universe is drawing us together?"

A tight pang in her chest for what might have been. But that's not the way things worked out. And she could never be happy with it now.

The train hit the curve and the car shifted slightly. Clara dove for one of the leather straps connected to the lens box. Her weight on it popped the box up a bit, slamming the lid shut on the fingers of Jacob's left hand. He jerked them back, bloodied, and held them against his chest.

"You truly are relentless," he growled. "This is turning into more trouble than it's worth." The train braked, slowing down for the curve, and the contents of the car shifted again, entangling Clara's limbs in the spiderweb of straps. Jacob slid open the side door of the car, exposing the countryside streaming by. Dusty wind whipped through. He gripped the ladder on the exterior of the car with his good hand, started descending.

Clara untangled herself, hooked her boot under her rifle, flipped it into her good hand and had him in her sights at the end of the ladder. He froze. For the first time in a long time, there was no question of what she needed to do next.

"It's Whitlock," she said. "My real name. You have no more excuses for being a shitty person." She lowered her gun.

Jacob looked at her for a long moment, blue eyes searching. "I hope you find what you're looking for out here, Clara Whitlock." He jumped off and rolled down the hill toward the trees.

He would probably steal again. She understood that. But she didn't have it in her to murder him. That was a thing worth knowing about herself.

A week later, under a starry night sky, Clara leaned against the wall of the observatory. It was small, a squat wooden cylinder with a dome on top. John had told her to meet him here to receive the rest of her payment. Her shoulder was healing nicely. Mars Hill overlooked the growing town of Flagstaff, and Percival Lowell and his crew were just arriving up the new wagon road for his first night of viewing.

When the train pulled into the station in Flagstaff, Clara expected to have to explain the dead bodies and broken window to some very upset officials, but they seemed unfazed. "Mr. John warned us there might be trouble but that you'd handle it, ma'am." They refused to accept payment for the window, saying John had already covered it.

When John walked up to her on Mars Hill, he handed her the second envelope immediately. "I have a surprise for you." He called over his shoulder, "Mr. Lowell, there's someone I'd like you to meet. This is Miss Whitlock, a friend of mine. She has a budding interest in astronomy."

Clara raised an eyebrow. She had never expressed any such notion.

Trust me, John mouthed.

"Is that so?" Lowell came over and shook Clara's hand. He was a tall, well-groomed gentleman in a suit, with a bushy mustache and a strong, energetic presence. "We are about to observe the magnificent face of the Red Planet," he said. "Won't you join us?"

There was no reason to refuse. "I'd be honored, sir."

The dome was just large enough to hold the two telescopes, which shared a single central mount, plus a ring of people standing around the edge. One telescope — Clara recognized it as the one she'd guarded — was pointed out the slit in the dome at the bright point of light John had shown her the week before.

A man motioned for Lowell to ascend the ladder. "She's all yours, sir."

The telescope was massive, much more impressive set up in here than in its box. Its long brass-colored cylinder reminded Clara of the barrel of a cannon, except that instead of shooting out destruction, this cylinder was capturing light.

Lowell looked through the telescope for several minutes, murmuring, making adjustments, pausing to scribble in his sketchbook. "Remarkable," he said. "Truly remarkable."

Everyone in the party took a turn, while the others whispered to each other in the dark, chilly space. When all had gone up, John motioned for Clara to ascend.

She felt out of place in this dome of wealthy men, but she had already agreed, so she wasn't backing down now.

Nothing could have prepared her for what she saw through that eyepiece. A circle of reddish, grayish white, so close, *right there*, like a coin hanging in front of her eye. Its surface was scored with what looked like grooves. This was an entire world, whole, scarred, continuing to spin and spin through the years. Impossibly far away, but made clear to her, here on this quiet hilltop.

"Have you ever seen anything like it?" Lowell said in breathless wonder, helping her down.

"No, sir."

She went outside for air, but she couldn't tear her eyes from the sky. It was a new frontier out there past the sky. It was adventure beyond her wildest dreams.

"He will need workers, you know." John stood beside her.

"Guards, you mean."

"That, but also laborers to build things, assistants to record data, keepers to handle supplies. There are all kinds of possibilities here, Miss Whitlock."

"What makes you think I care about possibilities?"

"Everyone cares about possibilities. It's who we are as a species. It's why we look up at night."

The two envelopes in Clara's vest could buy half a year's worth of room and board. Or a cabin of her own. She wasn't sure yet what her first move would be, but she knew she wanted to find out.

She leaned her rifle carefully against a rock. "Fancy a night stroll, John?"

#

The historical event I chose to write about was the founding of the Lowell Observatory in Flagstaff, Arizona, in 1894. I selected this event because I've always been enamored with space and stargazing, and the true story behind this observatory includes many elements that make for a good tale: the excitement of a celestial alignment, the transport of valuable goods, and a race against time. I thoroughly enjoyed the research, particularly reading *The Explorers of Mars Hill: A Centennial History of Lowell Observatory, 1894-1994* by William Lowell Putnam, which chronicles the observatory's beginnings. Many of the details in my story surrounding Percival Lowell's launch of the

observatory, such as the Mars opposition, the
scouting mission, and shipping the telescopes by rail, are based on
actual events. Clara, John, and Jacob are fictional additions, as is the
attempted heist.

—Kelli Fitzpatrick

Kelli Fitzpatrick is a science fiction writer, editor, and educator. She is the author of *Captain Marvel: Carol Danvers Declassified*. Her *Star Trek* story "The Sunwalkers" won the 2016 Strange New Worlds Contest and is published by Simon and Schuster. Her space western story "The Rogue Tractor of Sunshine Gulch" is out from Baen Books. She is a contributing writer for the *Star Trek Adventures* role-playing game from Modiphius and has written for NASA's Hubble Space Telescope outreach team and Arizona State University's Interplanetary Initiative.

Chasing Fame

Aaron Rosenberg

Louis McGee was practicing with his lariat when he heard the mob. Coiling the rope back up with only a little fumbling, the lanky sixteen-year-old stepped to the stable doors and pulled one side open enough to stick his head out. The street was filled with people.

Since that never happened here in Solomonsville, Louis—Lou to his friends—stepped outside to see what had caused such a ruckus. He recognized almost everyone, of course. The town wasn't all that big. But the two men being escorted—that was a polite way to put it, his ma would have said—and the woman weeping between them, her arms wrapped protectively around several small children, those were all strangers to him.

Jeremiah Dorsett was just passing by on the outskirts, and Lou grabbed him by the arm. "What's going on?" he asked.

Jerry went to shake him off, but the old drunk's natural garrulousness won out over his irritation. "You ain't heard?" he asked, pulling his arm free but stopping long enough to let the rest of the crowd move on by. "Woman got herself dead up by Eagle Creek. They're sayin' the Devil himself did it, ridin' on a demon horse."

Lou stared at the man, but for once Jerry did not smell of whiskey, and his rheumy eyes were focused. "That can't be right," Lou finally managed, shaking his head. "There ain't no Devil."

"Is so," his informer insisted hotly. "And he done killed her. Stomped her flat. Least, that's what they're sayin'."

An older woman was just passing them, trailing the rest, and she paused long enough to deliver one of her trademark sneers—Mrs. Ogilvy ran the town school, and Lou was all too familiar with her disdain. "The story is ridiculous," she insisted in that high, sharp voice that still sent shivers through him. "Clearly one of the men killed her, or the other wife, and they concocted this story to conceal their guilt." She sniffed and stomped after the mob.

Lou and Jerry looked at each other, but neither wanted to risk contradicting Mrs. Ogilvy, even if they hadn't seen a switch or a ruler anywhere nearby. Still, Lou had to admit his interest was piqued, and he found himself following the rest. Sure as shooting, this was the most excitement to ever hit Solomonsville!

"We didn't hurt Sarah," the first man, Daniel Coulson, insisted. He was talking to the crowd he currently faced in the courthouse as much as the sheriff and doctor standing shoulder to shoulder behind him or even the magistrate and jury seated beyond them. "Trey and me, we were out all day checking the sheep. We came back to find her like that."

The "that" he gestured to had been delivered to the courthouse in the back of a wagon, and Lou could see from where it lay now that the lump under the rough blanket was awfully flat to be a person.

The second man, Trey Holt, nodded. Sarah had been his wife, Lou had gathered. "That's right," he insisted, clutching his hat in both hands. "Apaches came through day before, like they do. We had to see what livestock we had left."

All eyes turned then to the other woman, Martha Coulson. She looked like she'd been through the wringer already, Lou thought, with her blonde hair all blown about and her face all red, especially her eyes and nose. But when she spoke, her voice was clear, if trembling.

"Sarah went to get water from the spring," she stated, loud enough for all to hear. "Then the dog got to barking something awful. I looked out, and that's when I saw it." She shuddered. "It was big, and red, and riding it was the Devil himself."

That sparked a response from the crowd, murmurs of excitement mixed with fear and plenty of disbelief. A few voices raised in protest or query, but Sheriff Gleeson held up a hand for quiet and after a moment she continued.

"Then Sarah started screaming." Martha hugged herself. "I know I should've gone out, should've tried to help, but I was too scared. I fell to my knees and got to praying instead. I didn't stop till Dan and Trey came home."

"We found her by the spring," Daniel took up the tale. "Trampled flat. There's hoofprints all around and . . . across her, but big, and cloven. Found some long red hairs, too." Lou guessed by the man's tone that the dead woman hadn't had hair that color.

"Murderer!" someone shouted, and a few others took up the cry. Gleeson had to calm them down again. Beside him, the doctor, Zachary Minor, stood still as a statue and solemn as a grave, arms crossed over his narrow chest.

"We're looking into it," the sheriff promised in that low, grumbling voice of his, hands hooked in his gunbelt. "Judge'll reconvene once we know more." Lou hadn't ever seen the man draw his weapon in all the years he'd been here, but he had to admit, Gleeson was a calming presence. Standing there now, all quiet and competent, he quelled the discord. After another moment, folks began to disperse.

Lou wandered back toward the stables. His pa had been in the crowd too, so he wouldn't hear any trouble for leaving the place untended, but there were still stalls to muck and nags to feed. Same as always.

Still, he couldn't help but wonder about the strangers' story. What could've done for the woman like that, if it really had been how they said?

Whatever it was, he had a feeling it would be the biggest thing to come to this corner of the Arizona Territory in all his years.

And maybe, just maybe, that'd be something an enterprising young fella could use to get himself up and outta this dinky little town for good.

It was a full day before Doctor Minor was ready to release his findings. When he did, word spread and the whole town assembled once more in the courthouse to hear what he had to say. The aggrieved husband and the other couple were there as well, ready to either be charged or pitied, depending.

Minor had a flare for the dramatic, to be sure. Standing at the front of the room now, with his thick white hair floating up in a plume, he struck a pose. His voice, when he spoke, was the same rich, deep bass that always amazed Lou for having come from that skinny frame.

"I have examined the body of the late Sarah Holt," Minor declared loudly, glancing about him to make sure all were listening. "Her wounds are consistent with massive blows by something heavy, though whether an object or an animal I cannot be certain."

The judge, old Thomas Randall, leaned forward, wisps of white hair forming a halo around his bony scalp. "So you're saying it weren't done by human hands?"

The doctor frowned. "I cannot be certain," he replied slowly, "but no, I do not believe so. It is more consistent with an animal attack, such as a stampede, though the marks were made by no cow, bull, or buffalo."

Randall nodded before turning to the jury. "You heard the man. State your verdict."

The jurors huddled together, whispering, while the rest of the town waited eagerly. Finally they parted, and the foreman, Billy O'Dair, stepped forward, clearing his throat. "We find the cause of death to be death in some manner unknown," he all but shouted, "and the husband and the Coulsons to be not guilty."

A sound went through the crowd, half relief and half disappointment. Lou, however, was excited. Because that meant the real killer, this Devil or whatever, was still out there.

And he aimed to be the one who caught it.

"Don't be a fool," his pa said when Lou revealed his plan. "You wanna get crushed to death just like she did? That Red Ghost ain't nothing but trouble." That was what folks had started calling the murderous apparition. Lou rather liked it.

"I kin handle myself," he insisted, buckling his gunbelt a little tighter. "And the man who kills it'll be famous forever." Famous enough to never have to work in a stable again, that was for sure.

His pa shook his head. "Yer a dang fool," he opined, but he didn't block Lou when he made for the door. "Try not ta get yerself killed."

Lou nodded, waving a hand as he stepped outside. He took a deep breath.

It smelled like freedom.

He hired on with a wagoneer heading up through the White Mountains—the man was struggling to control an unruly quartet of horses, and was happy to have someone with Lou's wrangling experience. Their route took them up past Eagle Creek, and one night Lou was able to check out the Coulsons' and Holts' ranch, but saw no signs of the creature. A night or two later, however, he was in a saloon when he heard some men lamenting over "recent devilry."

"Sorry," Lou said, stopping at their table. "Did you say something about the Devil?"

The men studied him warily, with that hard-bitten look of folks who knew about living rough and guarding secrets, but their expressions brightened and their hands unclenched when he set the bottle down on their table. "'S right," one of them declared, helping himself to a drink. "Tore through our camp while we were panning the creek. Tents all shredded, everything knocked about, and long red hairs stuck in places."

The others all nodded.

"And where was this?" Lou asked.

"Up by Chase's Creek," another said, pouring himself a glass in trade. Lou thanked them and left the bottle behind. That was off the San Francisco River, less than a day's ride away.

He was getting closer.

He had no luck catching the Red Ghost there, however. And the next sighting, a few days later, was to the west. So that's where Lou went, hiring on to help ferry some settlers down the Black River.

But again he was too late. The creature had vanished once more, leaving behind only its description—over thirty feet tall, fast as lightning and red as flame—and the damage it had caused, knocking over several wagons.

The next tale came from up by Canon Butte, where it was said the Red Ghost had been spotted battling, defeating, and then partially consuming a grizzly. Lou met a government surveyor venturing north who desperately needed someone to manage his pack animals, and that took him as far as the site, though only the tale remained by the time they arrived.

By this time Lou had spent what little money he'd saved up back home, and most of what he'd earned so far. Fortunately, an outfit up in the Rabbit Hills needed a second horsemaster. Lou put his pa's training to good use and worked there several weeks, just socking away his pay and keeping an ear out for the Red Ghost.

When word reached him, he'd been gone nearly a month. This time the creature had been sighted down near the Salt River, so Lou packed his things and hired on with a caravan cutting back down that way, looking for a man named Cyrus Hamblin.

Hamblin proved to be a sociable sort, so Lou found him at a saloon, regaling folks with the tale. Pulling up a stool, he joined the audience to listen.

"That's when I heard a rustling across the ravine," the rancher was explaining. The glasses in front of him showed his listeners' appreciation, and the one in his hand was already half empty. "I looked over there, seeing something big and red moving through the brush, but couldn't make out anything more. So I figured I'd better get in closer, see what I was dealing with."

Draining the drink, he set it aside and was quickly handed another, which he gulped from before continuing. "Took time for me to get across, and then I still had to wait and hope whatever it was would move out into the open more. But finally it did, and you'll never guess what I saw —

"A camel."

Half the audience laughed. A few groaned. Some others shook their head in confusion. "The hell's that?" one man called out.

The storyteller nodded sagely, taking another sip. "Can't say I blame you for not knowing, friend," Hamblin stated in the exaggeratedly careful manner of someone well and truly drunk. "I wouldn't have known myself, 'cept I spent some time down by California, years back, and I seen 'em then. Big, ugly things, like weird hump-backed horses with strange, sneering faces. Great in the desert, though. Handle heat and thirst better'n any horse." He scratched at his neck. "Not sure why one'd be all the way up here, though."

"So it was just a camel?" someone else asked. "Not the Red Ghost at all?"

The rancher held up a hand — fortunately, not the one still cupping his drink. "Now, hold on a minute," he stated. "I didn't say that. See, here's the thing. This was a camel, no mistake. Redder than the ones I'd seen before, but the shape was right." He took a sip, and Lou thought the man was deliberately drawing things out. When Hamblin winked, he knew he was right, even before the man added:

"But that didn't explain the thing on its back. Because there was definitely a rider, but no man could flop about like that. No living one, anyways."

Lou frowned. So did some others in the audience. "What're you saying?" came the question. "That it had a rider, but he was dead?"

Hamblin shrugged. "Dead — or not a man. No idea. I wasn't getting close enough to find out."

Some of his listeners threw up their hands, then rose and walked away. Others nodded amongst themselves. Lou didn't know what to think. The description did fit with the Eagle Creek men's story of the Devil riding some sort of hellhorse, but could that really be true? A man seated near him expressed the same thought. "Yer just makin' this up!" he announced, staggering to his feet. Evidently Hamblin wasn't the only one drinking heavily this night.

But the barkeep was nearby and overheard. "I've known Cyrus our whole lives," he declared loudly. "You won't find an honester man this side of the Mississippi."

That caused more murmuring as people reconsidered. So did Lou. Regardless what it was, he did believe Hamblin had seen the Red Ghost. Which meant it had been here only a day or two ahead of him. It wasn't here no more, of course, but still —

He was getting closer.

An outfit came through looking to hire an extra hand to mind the horses, and with nowhere else in mind Lou signed on. They were headed for Prescott. The trek took them a week, and Lou was amazed when they reached the territory's capital. It was the biggest place he'd ever seen, a hundred times larger than old Solomonsville, and he goggled at the tall buildings, the wide streets, and the sheer number of people constantly walking or riding back and forth. The place was louder than he'd expected, though, especially after more than a month of tiny towns and quiet trails, and he soon found himself retreating to saloons on the outskirts, where the din was less noticeable.

One of the men he'd just traveled with found work guiding some prospectors back down toward Fort McDowell, and suggested Lou to them. He was happy to take the job, both because it kept him on the move and because he was finding Prescott too crowded. So after only a few days there, he hit the trails again, feeling a lot better with the city behind him and open plains ahead.

Besides which, no way was the Red Ghost dumb enough to venture into someplace as overwhelming as Prescott!

The prospectors turned out to be a friendly lot, once they accepted you. After their second night on the trail, both Lou and his buddy Dale were considered part of the group. That suited them just fine—it was a lot easier traveling together when your companions weren't clamming up around you and hugging their packs close like you meant to steal them. Not that any of them had anything worth stealing yet. Naturally, the plan was to fix that.

"There's gold all over these here hills," one of them, Jake Rutherford, liked to say—at every opportunity. "Just takes some vision and some staying power and it's there for the taking." He certainly had the staying power, if his ability to drink the rest under the table was any indication.

More than once, the little pack would stop by a random stream somewhere and the men would break out their pans to spend the day sifting clay and dirt, hoping for that telltale sparkle. When that happened, Lou and Dale set up the tents and the campfire, gathered water to boil, and then had the rest of the afternoon off. Dale was only a few years older, a short, stocky fellow with pale blonde hair and skin always red from the sun, and he liked to talk more than almost anyone Lou had ever met. And to dream.

"We could panhandle, too, y'know," he said one day as they watched the others standing in the stream below. "Find some gold, hit it rich, start a hotel somewhere." That was Dale's biggest ambition, to open a hotel with a saloon below and ladies up above. "Everything a man could ever want, all in one place," was how he put it.

Lou laughed. "Don't much fancy that," he answered, weaving two blades of grass together. He'd learned the trick for lariats, but it worked just fine here and gave his hands something to do. "The gold part, though, sure."

His friend glanced askance at him. "What're you aiming, then? Just ferry folks up and down the Territory forever?"

"Nah." Lou hadn't revealed his plan to anyone since his pa, but he figured it wouldn't hurt none. "I mean to catch the Red Ghost, become famous for it. Then I'll have my pick of jobs." Admittedly, that last part remained hazy, but he figured once he was famous it would work itself out.

Now it was Dale's turn to laugh. "The Red Ghost! You believe all that malarkey?"

Lou considered. "It's real, yeah. I believe that. Too many've seen it already for it not to be. The Devil? Who knows?" He grinned. "Guess I'll let you know once I catch it."

Most prospectors seemed to know each other, and whenever their group met others in a saloon there was a wary welcome, both sides eager to get information but not wanting to give away any secrets. So when they found another group of five near the Verde River, Lou's friends happily accepted the invite to pull up stools and share some drinks and some gossip.

The new group had been hard at it, given the bottle they'd already emptied, so their tongues were loose. In fact, they were eager to tell about their most recent adventure.

"We were up on a mesa off the river," one of them explained, leaning back in his chair and scratching his broad chest. "Getting the lay of the land and keeping an eye out for Injuns and coyotes. So when we heard something in the bushes, we figured it for one of them. But it weren't neither a' those." He shook his head. "In fact, it weren't nothing natural at all."

"It was the Red Ghost!" one of the others cut in. "Right there by the river!"

Now they had Lou's full attention. "The Red Ghost?" he asked. "Are you sure?"

All five nodded vigorously. "Oh, yeah," another chimed in. "We saw it, clear as day."

"Shot at it, too," the first one added. He grinned, showing blackened and broken teeth. "Even got ourselves a little souvenir." He gestured toward one of the others, who proudly placed a satchel on the table. Lou leaned in as the man flipped back the top flap, revealing — a human skull.

"The hell is that?" one of his friends demanded. "You go digging up some poor soul's grave?"

But the group of five all shook their heads. "It came off the Ghost, swear to God!" the first one insisted. "We shot it off that thing! Not that it slowed down any for it, just went crashing away through the bushes."

Lou leaned in closer to see. The skull was human, no doubt about that. It was old, too, with only shreds of flesh and hair left. Old or horribly weathered.

Hamblin had said the beast had a rider, either dead or unnatural. Could this have been its head? If it was just a dead man, that would fit, but what would a corpse be doing astride a camel? And why hadn't it fallen off in the months since?

As always, the sighting raised more questions than answers. But one thing was certain — whatever the Red Ghost really was, Lou was closing in on it.

Unfortunately, that thought proved less than prophetic. Despite venturing up to the Verde River, Lou found no trace of the creature anywhere. Nor, in the next few months, did he hear any more about it, beyond isolated accounts of something breaking into cabins, caving in mines, and stampeding horses and cattle. None of those were clear enough proof to make him chase them, and they were too scattered to provide any hint of where the creature might turn up next.

After a time, Lou grew tired of leading prospectors around. The railroad was coming through, and he worked for a while on that, laying down rail. That was hot, dusty work, though, and he soon moved on.

The government was building a canal through Scottsdale, and advertised a need for workers. Lou signed on, but digging proved even more exhausting than the railroad.

At one point he found himself in Pleasant Valley, where several ranching families had become prosperous enough to hire on additional hands. Only, Lou soon discovered that was partially because the two biggest outfits there, the Grahams and Tewksburys, were warring, and kept killing each other. He left that job quickly, and counted himself lucky to have made it out alive.

He passed through Bisbee in late December, but the town was still in mourning after the massacre that had occurred there, and no one was hiring.

Lou soon hired out as a cowhand, his experience with horses standing him in good stead. The work was decent and familiar and took him back down the Salt River toward Phoenix. That was how he found himself working at the Anchor-JOT ranch the following spring.

It was dusk, and he'd just finished checking the corrals when he spotted one with the gate open. Which was particularly odd because that happened to be a branding corral, and they only used it during roundup. So, slowing his horse to a walk, Lou ambled over to have a closer look.

The lowering light made it hard to see clearly, but he could make out some sort of creature in the corral beyond. Whatever it was, it was too big to be a horse but too narrow to be a buffalo. And the sun's fading glow made it out to be red as flame.

Lou felt his pulse quicken. It could only be the Red Ghost!

His first thought was simply to close the gate. A quick look told him that wouldn't work, however. The creature must have forced its way in because the gate was hanging by a single bent hinge. That wouldn't be secure any time soon!

Fortunately, Lou had his lariat. He reached for it just as the beast glanced up and saw him. It had big, dark eyes, and a wide mouth hooked into a permanent sneer. And even from here he could see that it did indeed have a headless rider on its back.

Then the Ghost shrieked, a terrible sound, and charged him.

Lou twirled and threw, and his lariat landed squarely around the creature's neck. Gotcha!

But that didn't slow the Red Ghost in the slightest. It raced toward him, bellowing in rage. Lou tugged on his reins, expertly rearing his horse to the side so the camel could slip past and he could tighten his loop once it had.

Except, instead of taking the opening, the Red Ghost lowered its head and smashed full into Lou and his horse!

The pair of them crashed to the ground, both crying out in shock and pain. Lou lost his hold on the lariat. The Red Ghost didn't even slow down. It sailed on past, all legs and fur and fury, and raced off into the night.

But not before Lou got a good look at the skeleton clinging to its back — or the straps holding the body in place.

Then the creature was gone. Lou managed to squirm out from under his horse, helping his steed back to its feet. Neither of them seemed seriously hurt, but both were badly shaken.

For Lou's part, he couldn't believe he'd finally caught up to the Red Ghost — and then let it escape. At the same time, a part of him was still quaking from its presence. That tall, gaunt form, those angry eyes, the shrieks of rage — he had never imagined it would be so terrifying.

Maybe it was for the best that it had got away.

Where did that leave him, though? Catching the creature had been his one chance at fame. What was he going to do now?

A few months later, Lou returned to Solomonsville. His father's stable was still there, and the man himself was mucking out a stall when Lou stepped inside, leading his horse by its reins.

"Stall for one?" his pa asked, glancing up. "For how many nights? Feed's included, of course, and I'll rub her down good, too."

"Pa." Lou moved closer, pushing his hat back off his head. "It's me."

He watched his father's eyes widen. "Lou?" Then the man had rushed forward to embrace him, something he hadn't done more than a handful of times in their life. "You're alive!" After that initial hug, his pa pulled back to study him. "You've grown some, too."

"Yeah." Lou knew he hadn't gotten much taller, but he'd filled out some, definitely, from all that work. "How've you been?"

His pa shrugged. "Eh. Fine. You?" He studied Lou. "You catch that Red Ghost of yours?"

"Sorta." Lou laughed. "Come on, I'll buy you dinner and tell you all about it." He saw the way his pa glanced around the stables. "And I'll help you finish up, after."

His father nodded. "All right. Let's get your horse squared away first, though. How long you staying?"

Lou had been pondering that the whole way back. "For good, I'm thinking," he admitted. "If you'll have me."

"Have you?" His pa wasn't much for showing emotion, but he smiled now, and his eyes seemed damp. "'Course. But what happened to all that talk of fame?"

Now it was Lou's turn to shrug. "Got tired of chasing it, I guess." And he had. He'd tried a bunch of different jobs along the way, but always found himself coming back to horses. That was what he knew best, and what he liked most. He'd also found Prescott and even Phoenix and Flagstaff too big and too busy for him, too crowded and too noisy by far. Solomonsville felt cozy now, where it had once seemed stifling. So, yes, he thought he'd stay a while.

As they headed out toward the saloon, several of the townsfolk saw them and stopped to say hi. All of them wanted to hear where Lou had been, what he'd seen. "You're famous," his pa said as they finally reached the saloon door. "Been farther and done more than most here ever will."

"Huh." Lou considered that. "I guess so." He smiled, following his father inside, where more surprised greetings arose.

If that was the fame he'd found, he thought it was the kind he could live with.

#

The Wild West always feels like it must have gone on for a century or more — it was, after all, an age packed with drama and daring, heroes and villains.

In reality, of course, it only lasted thirty years, from 1865 to 1895.

Which at least, when you're seeking inspiration — and a real-world event — for your story, narrows the field a bit.

I wasn't sure what I wanted to write about, only that I didn't want to do the more typical times and places and people. No Tombstone, no Billy the Kid, no James Gang, none of that. I was after something a little more esoteric. A little more Weird to go with the Wild. So I began researching weird sightings and not-quite-tall tales.

What I found was the Red Ghost. One of the stranger stories from that time — but one based entirely in reality.

All the events Lou hears of in this story are true, or at least were claimed as such. Most were written up in local papers. That includes the final encounter at the Anchor-JOT ranch.

And yes, the Red Ghost was a camel — and yes, it had a dead man strapped to its back. To this day, no one knows who he was or how he came to be there.

But it makes for one heck of a good Western tale.

—Aaron Rosenberg

Aaron Rosenberg is the best-selling, award-winning author of over 50 novels, including the *Twin Cities Cryptids* urban fantasy/cozy series, the *DuckBob* SF comedy series, the *Relicant Chronicles* epic fantasy series, the *Areyat Islands* fantasy pirate mystery series, and, with David Niall Wilson, the *O.C.L.T.* occult thriller series. His tie-in work contains novels for *Star Trek*, *Warhammer*, *World of WarCraft*, *Stargate: Atlantis*, Shadowrun, *Mutants & Masterminds*, and *Eureka* and short stories for *The X-Files*, *World of Darkness*, *Crusader Kings II*, *Deadlands*, *Master of Orion*, and *Europa Universalis IV*. He has written children's books (including the original series STEM *Squad and Pete and Penny's Pizza Puzzles*, the award-winning *Bandslam: The Junior Novel* and the #1 best-selling *42: The Jackie Robinson Story*), educational books, and roleplaying games (including the original games *Asylum*, *Spookshow*, and *Chosen*; work for White Wolf, Wizards of the Coast, Fantasy Flight, Pinnacle, and many others; the Origins Award-winning *Gamemastering Secrets*; and the Gold ENnie-winning *Lure of the Lich Lord*). He is a founding member of Crazy 8 Press. Aaron lives in New York with his family.

THE COWTOWN INFERNO

JAMES REASONER AND L.J. WASHBURN

[A Judge Earl Stark/Lucas Hallam Story]

Lucas Hallam was no bushwhacker, but Ben McNulty was just too dangerous to take any chances with him.

Hallam knelt behind some good-sized rocks along the edge of a bluff that sloped down about forty feet to the road between Fort Worth and Denton. Twenty years earlier, this area had been part of the stomping grounds of the legendary outlaw Sam Bass.

Old Sam had been dead and gone for a long time, but outlaws still roamed Texas, and that was one reason men such as Lucas Hallam wore the star-in-a-circle badge of the Texas Rangers.

Hallam heard a horse approaching from the south. He had already jacked a round into the chamber of his Winchester so as not to make any racket. He took the hat off his shaggy brown hair and eased his head up to peer over the limestone slab.

Ben McNulty, sure enough. Hallam was close enough to recognize the predatory face, the hawk nose, the drooping black mustache.

McNulty had shot a teller during a bank robbery he and his cousins pulled in Comanche about a year earlier. That fellow had recovered, but the deputy sheriff McNulty had gunned down in Coleman a few weeks later hadn't been as lucky. Neither had the son of a rich businessman from San Angelo. McNulty and the Grisham boys had kidnapped him and demanded a large ransom. They got the money, but the 14-year-old lad was found dead anyway. After that, the gang had stopped a train west of Weatherford, and McNulty had gunned down the conductor and the express messenger, brutally murdering both of them.

So that was four killings and numerous other crimes charged against McNulty. He was one of the most wanted men in the Rangers' doomsday book at the moment. Earlier that morning, Hallam had gotten a tip at a road ranch northwest of Fort Worth that McNulty was going to be headed for Denton later in the day, and traveling by himself to boot.

This might be Hallam's best chance to arrest the outlaw. The three Grisham brothers — Harley, Grover, and Teddy — were reputed to be just as mean and ruthless as McNulty. Grover was supposed to be the worst of the bunch. Hallam could understand why being saddled with a name like Grover Grisham might make a fella proddy.

He eased forward a little. From here it would be an easy shot for a man like Lucas Hallam. He could knock McNulty out of the saddle with his eyes closed.

He sighed. That would the most practical way of handling this problem, but he couldn't do it.

Instead, he raised himself higher and yelled, "Stop and put up your hands! In the name of the State of Texas, you're under arrest, Ben McNulty!"

As soon as the first few words were out of Hallam's mouth, McNulty was twisting in the saddle and whipping the gun he had drawn toward the bluff. By the time Hallam finished, the gun boomed and smoke gushed from its barrel. Shooting uphill like that, McNulty's bullet went low and kicked up dirt and gravel a good fifteen feet down the slope from Hallam's position.

Hallam stroked the Winchester's trigger, but McNulty kicked his horse in the sides and the animal leaped ahead at the same instant. When the Winchester cracked, dust jumped up just behind the horse's flashing hooves.

Hallam muttered a complaint and stood up to get a better second shot. McNulty threw more lead over his shoulder, but Hallam wasn't worried about the outlaw hitting anything from the back of a galloping horse. He squinted over the Winchester's barrel, lined the sights on McNulty's back, and squeezed the trigger again.

The horse veered slightly at just the wrong second. Instead of drilling McNulty's heart as Hallam intended, the rifle round sliced a gash on his left side under his arm. The bullet went through and clipped a piece off the horse's left ear. McNulty was already twisted in the saddle from the slug's impact. When the horse screamed in pain from its wounded ear and jumped and bucked wildly, McNulty flew from its back and crashed to the ground.

Hallam went down the slope in leaps and bounds, angling toward the fallen outlaw. Rocks slid under his boots, but he managed to stay upright. Just as he reached level ground, McNulty made it to hands and knees and scrambled after the gun he'd dropped. Hallam stopped short, jerked the rifle to his shoulder, and a well-aimed bullet knocked McNulty's gun out of reach and more than likely ruined it.

McNulty looked at Hallam, sighed, and rolled onto his back, where he lay there bleeding into the dust from the minor wound in his side.

He was caught, and he knew it.

Judge Earl Stark managed not to paw in annoyance at the tight collar around his neck, but it wasn't easy.

Back in the old days, he hadn't had to wear duds that dang near choked him. All that had been required of him as a shotgun guard was the ability to use a double-barreled Greener and the willingness to blow any no-good owlhoot who tried to hold up one of his stage-coaches clear to Kingdom Come.

Simpler times, indeed.

Now he sat on a bench just as uncomfortable as the driver's box of a Concord coach, except it didn't bounce around. He didn't have to breathe dust from a six-horse hitch, but he did have to listen to a bunch of slick-haired lawyers drone on and on. Stark kept a solemn expression on his bearded face and tried not to show how dadblasted bored he was.

"— and that's why I'm requesting a continuance, Your Honor," the attorney standing in front of him concluded at long last.

"It's late," Stark said. "I'll take your request under advisement, counselor, and make my ruling in the morning." He picked up the gavel in front of him. "For today, court is —"

The door at the back of the courtroom opened and U.S. Marshal Eli Nickerson stuck his head in. Eli looked excited about something, so

Stark hesitated before bringing the gavel down and banging the court into adjournment for the day.

"What is it, Marshal?" Stark asked.

"Permission to approach the bench, Your Honor?"

Stark wanted to ask Nickerson since when did he need permission to talk to him, since they'd known each other for fifteen years, ever since Nickerson was a deputy sheriff down in Llano. But the decorum of the court had to be preserved, Stark supposed, so he said, "Permission granted, Marshal."

He shooed the lawyer who'd been harping at him away from the bench. Nickerson took off his hat, opened the little gate in the railing, and walked up to the high podium where Stark sat.

Stark leaned forward and lowered his voice so that the hangers-on in the courtroom couldn't overhear. "What is it, Eli?"

"A Texas Ranger just brought in a prisoner and stuck him in our jail. He wants the fella held to face charges of murder and robbery."

"What does that have to do with me?"

"Well, you see, one of the deputies dealing with this Ranger happened to notice that the prisoner has federal warrants out on him, too."

Stark frowned. "As a federal circuit court judge, that would give me jurisdiction over the case against this man. What are the federal charges?"

"Mail robbery and the commission of a felony — in this case, murder — during that robbery. McNulty killed the conductor and an express messenger when he and his gang robbed a train a while back."

"McNulty," Stark repeated. "Ben McNulty?"

"You know him, Your Honor?" Nickerson asked.

"I know of him. He comes from a good family out in Buffalo Flat, but he was the black sheep, that's for sure. Fell in with some cousins of his from Winchell who were bad company, and he soon proved to be the worst of the bunch." Stark cleared his throat and sat back. "Very well. Hold this man for arraignment in my court tomorrow morning, Sheriff."

"Yes, sir, Your Honor." Nickerson hesitated. "What do I tell that Texas Ranger?"

"Tell him he's lost his prisoner and will get him back when the federal government is through with him, if then."

The sheriff made a face and shook his head. "He's liable not to like that."

"I don't care whether he does or not," Stark said. "I have bigger things to worry about than a Ranger's hurt feelings."

"Is that so, Your Honor?" Nickerson cocked his head slightly to the side, clearly curious.

Stark sighed and nodded. "That's right. I have to get dressed up and go to a blasted fancy dress ball tonight."

Lucas Hallam's big fist pounded on the hotel room door.

"What?" the man inside the room demanded as he jerked the door open and pointed a pistol at Hallam's face.

Hallam didn't step back, but the gaping maw of that gun muzzle did stir a few feelings of unease in him. He got a good enough look at the weapon to realize it was an old LeMat, a Civil War-era .36 caliber cap-and-ball revolver with an extra smooth bore barrel under the regular barrel for firing shotgun shells. It was a hellacious weapon at close range like this.

"Lower that gun, mister," Hallam said. "That's an order."

"And who are you to be giving me orders?"

"A Texas Ranger."

"Well, I'm a federal judge," the stocky, bearded man snapped.

"That doesn't make you above the law."

The man hesitated a moment and then lowered the LeMat. He eased the hammer off-cock and said, "Your name wouldn't be Lucas Hallam, would it?"

"It would," Hallam said. "And you're Judge Stark?"

"That's right. I can guess why you're here." Stark stepped back and used his empty left hand to gesture Hallam into the room. "You might as well come in so we can talk, but I'll tell you right now, it's not going to do you any good."

Hallam stepped into the room. Out of habitual courtesy, he took off his broad-brimmed brown hat.

"How are you at bow ties?" Stark asked.

Hallam shook his head. "Not good."

Stark set the LeMat on a dresser and picked up what looked like a ribbon of black silk. "These short, fat fingers of mine aren't made for such a delicate operation."

"I'm afraid I can't help you, Your Honor. But you can do me a favor, if you would."

"Release Ben McNulty from federal custody so he can face state charges?"

Hallam wasn't surprised that Stark had figured out why he was here. He said, "It's only fair. Texas has got a lot bigger grudge against McNulty than Washington, D.C., does."

"I'm a Texan born, bred, and forever, my boy," Stark declared, "and that part of me agrees completely with your sentiment. But these days I work for Uncle Sam, so I have to abide by his rules. The state charges against McNulty still stand; it's just that he has to face justice for the federal crimes he committed first."

Hallam shook his head. "It just doesn't seem right."

"It's the legal system, son. Right doesn't always have as much to do with it as it ought to."

Hallam knew that from experience. Several years earlier, when his father had been killed, he hadn't found any help by turning to the law. So he had tracked down the men who'd done it on his own and dealt with them. He could have easily wound up on the wrong side of the law himself if he hadn't fallen in with the Rangers — and all because he had done the right thing.

He pushed that thought out of his mind as he became aware that Stark was dressed up for some sort of occasion. The judge wore black trousers, a snowy white shirt, and a black vest. His collar was buttoned tightly around his throat. Evidently, he'd been trying to fasten that bow tie around his neck when Hallam's knock on the door interrupted him.

"Where are you going in that monkey suit, Judge?"

"There's some sort of fancy ball at the Spring Palace tonight, and the society folks who are giving it think it would be a good idea for me to be there." Stark shook his head. "I'd rather walk a few blocks north into Hell's Half Acre, to tell you the truth. More entertainment to be found there."

Hallam frowned. "You know about Hell's Half Acre?"

"I wasn't always a judge, son. I used to be a lawyer, of all things, and before that I was a shotgun guard on stagecoaches that ran all over West Texas. Fella left a set of law books on the stage one day, and I started reading 'em out of curiosity. All that led eventually to —" He gestured at the fancy suit. "This."

Despite the annoyance he felt, Hallam grinned. He felt an instinctive liking for this judge, who was unlike any Hallam had ever run into before.

"Are you sure you don't know how to tie a bow tie?" Stark added. "You wouldn't be lying to me because you have a burr under your saddle about McNulty, would you?"

"No, Judge, I'm afraid you're on your own. If I can't change your mind, I don't reckon we have any more business."

Stark shook his head. "I'm sorry."

Hallam sighed and said, "Maybe I'll take a *pasear* over to Hell's Half Acre myself."

"Drink a beer for me if you do, son. I hear they're going to be serving lemonade at this ball I'm going to!"

Hell's Half Acre was the roughest, rowdiest part of Fort Worth. A several-square-block area at the southern end of downtown, it may well have had more saloons, whorehouses, and gambling dens than the rest of the city's neighborhoods put together. Hallam didn't feel out of place here, although he made sure his Ranger badge was tucked away in his pocket and not pinned to his vest. No point in painting a big target on himself.

He was leaning on the bar in the Alhambra Saloon, hat thumbed back on his head, nursing a beer, when three men came in and headed for an empty table in a rear corner. Hallam saw them from the corner of his eye but barely paid attention to them at first.

Then something stirred in the back of his mind and caused him to start straightening up.

He stopped short and maintained his casual pose instead so that he didn't reveal the surprise he felt. He turned his head just enough to get a better look at the newcomers as they flagged down one of the serving girls and told her to bring them a bottle. Hallam made out enough of what the spokesman said to hear the order.

The air in here was a blue haze of tobacco smoke, of course, with the smells of sweat, spilled booze, cheap perfume, bay rum, and vomit underlying it. Not a particularly pleasant place to be, although the customers seemed to be enjoying it, judging by the raucous uproar going on. A piano player in the corner tickled the ivories in counterpoint to the boisterousness.

Harley, Grover, and Teddy Grisham weren't out of place in surroundings such as these. It was a little surprising that such wanted men would show their faces in public, but Hallam knew the Fort Worth police and other law enforcement agents didn't venture down here too often. It was possible he was the only star packer in Hell's Half Acre tonight, and he wasn't flaunting his badge.

He considered the odds and the possible outcomes if he tried to take those three outlaws into custody. Assuming he was able to capture them and make it out of the Alhambra alive with them, Judge Earl Stark would just take them away from him. Big Earl, as he was sometimes called, Hallam had remembered. He could have come up with some other names for the jurist, even though he knew, deep down, that Stark was right.

He wondered if the Grisham brothers knew that Ben McNulty had been arrested. They were talking animatedly among themselves as they began putting away the bottle the girl brought to them. They looked upset about something, and their cousin and leader being behind bars was the most likely explanation for that.

Hallam decided he'd try to find out more.

He drained the last of the beer in his mug and pulled his hat down so the brim obscured more of his face. He knew what Harley, Grover, and Teddy looked like because he had seen reward dodgers with their pictures on them. But he had never laid eyes on them in the flesh, which meant they had never seen him. They wouldn't know he was a Texas Ranger.

The door leading to the outhouse in back of the saloon was near the table where the three outlaws sat. Hallam started toward that door, not looking at the Grishams as he did so. He made his steps just slightly unsteady, the gait of a man who'd had too much to drink but wasn't quite drunk yet. Such individuals were very common in a place like this. One of the Grishams glanced at him but then paid him no mind. The other two never even looked in his direction.

As Hallam passed the table, he listened intently, although he tried not to look like he was doing that. He couldn't pick up much of the conversation, but the words he did distinguish were like fists in his belly. His heart began to slug harder in his chest.

Stark . . . Spring Palace. . . .

They were going after Big Earl.

Stark had finally gotten the clerk at the hotel's front desk to tie that blasted bow tie for him, and just in time, too, because a few minutes later the carriage that was supposed to take him to the Spring Palace had arrived.

Stark had seen the huge building when he stepped off the train a few days earlier. The Spring Palace dominated the entire southern end of downtown Fort Worth. Occupying a space equivalent to three city blocks, it was an ornate structure with eight pointed towers rising high above the street around its outer walls, and the dome in the center of the building rose even higher. Stark had heard proud Fort Worthians proclaim that it was the second largest dome in the whole country, taking a back seat only to the one on the United States Capitol in Washington.

It was worthy of the name "Palace", all right, no doubt about that. Stark also thought it was gaudy and even a mite ugly, but with the exposition staged there the previous year and the one going on now, it had brought visitors from all of the world to Fort Worth and presented an appealing picture of everything Texas had to offer industrially, agriculturally, and otherwise. All the newspaper writers agreed it was a great boon to the Texas economy.

To Stark it represented a place to escape from as quickly as possible, filled as it was with men in fancy suits and women in elaborate gowns that probably cost more than he was paid in a month. Most of the women had their hair pinned up so that it towered above their heads, and some wore feathers in it that made them appear even taller.

"Judge Stark!" one of those middle-aged ladies trilled at him. "It's so wonderful to see you again."

"Mrs. Guthrie," Stark greeted her as he took the white-gloved hand she extended to him. He squeezed it in both of his hands. Then he shook hands with the lady's husband and said, "Hello, Alexander. Thanks for inviting me tonight."

"Of course," Alexander Guthrie said with a smile. "We're pleased to have you as our guest, Your Honor."

"Please," Stark said as he made a dismissive little gesture. "Tonight it's just Earl. We'll dispense with that *Your Honor* business."

"Certainly," Mrs. Guthrie said. "Although it won't be easy to forget that you're such a distinguished jurist, Earl."

Stark's smile never slipped even though he knew that if he had encountered Mrs. Guthrie during his days as a stagecoach guard, she wouldn't have even glanced at him, let alone been pleased to be in his company.

But those days were long in the past, he reminded himself. No point in even thinking about them now.

"Let me get you a drink," Guthrie offered.

"I won't say no to that," Stark said.

Guthrie didn't fetch the drink himself, of course; he just signaled to one of the waiters to bring it. Stark hid his disappointment when he found that the concoction in a crystal glass was indeed lemonade. If it had been spiked, it might have been tolerable, but he recalled that Mrs. Frances Wiggins Guthrie was a leading light in the local Women's Christian Temperance Union. The ball at the Spring Palace tonight was as dry as a West Texas desert.

Stark sipped lemonade, chatted with the Guthries, and greeted a dozen other couples who wandered past, all of them members of the upper level of Fort Worth society.

Then the orchestra that had gathered at one end of the vast ballroom began to play, and Mrs. Guthrie insisted that Stark dance with her dear friend Violet Shannon, who was recently widowed.

Stark sensed that maybe Mrs. Guthrie was trying to line up a new husband for the Widow Shannon, but the lady in question, although somewhat horse-faced, had a willowy figure and danced well. She was more attractive when she smiled, too, and her melodic voice didn't put Stark's teeth on edge. To his surprise, he found himself enjoying the dance. He was a little disappointed when the tune came to an end and Mrs. Guthrie swooped in to take Violet away and push her into the arms of some other bachelor she considered a potential husband.

Shaking his head slightly at his reaction, Stark snagged another glass of lemonade from a passing waiter and moved over to one side of the ballroom to drink and look around.

This wide chamber was under the great dome, so the ceiling was high and impressive. A balcony with ornately carved railings ran all around the inside on the second floor. Staircases with gleaming banisters curved up to it. Many of the guests were up there, strolling around.

Display halls ran in all four directions from this central ballroom. One was filled with farming equipment, another with industrial machinery. Some fine art was on display as well; a huge mural attempted to depict all facets of Texas, from cattle ranges to fields lush with wheat and corn to cities with new-fangled skyscrapers reaching toward the sky.

Another hall was full of hay bales, sheaves of wheat and corn, barrels of sorghum and molasses, and cotton plants with the white bolls still on them. If it grew or was manufactured in Texas, the exhibitors in the Spring Palace put it on display. It was an impressive spectacle, Stark mused. He could see why Fort Worth—indeed, all of Texas — was proud of the Spring Palace.

With his thoughts taken up by that, he could almost forgive himself for being taken unawares.

Almost.

But he cursed himself roundly and fluently for letting it happen when somebody stuck a gun in his back and said in a harsh undertone, "Don't move, Judge, or I'll blow your backbone right out through your belly."

Once again, Hallam had debated the wisdom of trying to take the three outlaws inside the saloon. His chances would be better out on the street, he decided. He stepped into the alley behind the Alhambra but didn't visit the outhouse. Instead, he circled the building and waited in the shadows where he could see the saloon's front door.

He was taking a chance and he knew it. The Grisham brothers could leave through the back, just as he had. If they did, he might lose them completely. But he couldn't be in two places at once and figured this was the best bet.

He listened intently, though, thinking that if they did go out the back, he might hear them talking and would be alerted that way.

While he waited, he pondered on what the three outlaws might be planning. If they knew Judge Stark was at the Spring Palace tonight, their most likely move was to grab him and try to force him to have Ben McNulty released. Killing Stark wouldn't do McNulty any good. Murder only made sense if their only goal was revenge.

Minutes dragged by. Hallam was about to go back into the saloon just to make sure the Grisham brothers were still there when the door opened and the three of them stepped out onto the brick-paved street. They headed south toward the Spring Palace.

Hallam started to follow them, hanging back so they wouldn't notice him. He had gone about a block when a running figure suddenly burst out of a doorway to his left and crashed into him.

Taken by surprise, without his feet set, Hallam went down even though he was much larger than the person who had collided with him. He realized after a few seconds that the squirming armful of flesh that had landed on top of him was female. The woman was weighing him down. He grabbed her shoulders—she didn't seem to be wearing much — and was about to shove her to the side when a man yelled and loomed over them, brandishing a butcher knife.

"I'll teach you to try to cheat me!" the knife-wielder yelled.

The doorway from which the woman had emerged was dimly lit by a red-tinted lantern. A sign above the opening read MISS LIZZY'S BOARDING HOUSE, ONE FLIGHT UP. That was a brothel, of course, not an actual boarding house, and the woman who had fled from it and run into Hallam was almost certainly a soiled dove. The man pursuing her with the knife might be her pimp, or maybe a dissatisfied customer. Either way, Hallam didn't have time for this.

He drew his Colt, angled it up, and pulled the trigger. The blast made the woman scream and throw herself to the side. That got her off of Hallam, which was one of his goals. The man with the knife staggered back into the doorway, howling and clutching the bloody arm Hallam had just drilled with a .45 slug. He had dropped the knife, and it clattered on the bricks as he inadvertently kicked it away.

Hallam rolled, slapped his free hand on the ground to brace himself, and shoved to his feet.

"Leave her alone," he told the wounded man, but the woman was already hovering over her former assailant, fussing over him and asking if he was all right. She turned her head, frizzy hair swinging around her painted face, and glared at Hallam.

He sighed, pouched the iron, and looked around for the Grisham brothers.

Nowhere in sight, of course.

He broke into a long-legged run toward the Spring Palace.

"Are you completely loco?" Stark said over his shoulder to the man pressing the gun against his back. "You're trying to pull a holdup in the middle of a fancy party like this?"

"This ain't no holdup," the man said. "You're comin' with us, Stark."

"You have a grudge against me? Did I throw you in jail sometime?"

"Shut up. You're the one who's gonna come to the jail with us and make 'em turn Ben McNulty loose."

"Ah," Stark said. He had found out more about this McNulty after Eli Nickerson visited his courtroom that afternoon. "You must be one of the Grisham brothers."

"I'm Grover, and if you don't shut your mouth and do what you're told, I'm gonna kill you."

"That won't get your cousin McNulty free, will it? You need me alive for that."

Grover didn't say anything. He was probably trying to think and not finding it easy.

"Tell you what, then," Grover said after a moment. "I won't kill you, but I'll give the nod to my brothers and they'll start shootin' these fancy dans and their ladies. How about that? Just you look up on that balcony, Judge, and see what you see."

Stark raised his eyes to the balcony and surveyed around the ballroom. He spotted a roughly dressed man on either side. They were looking intently at Stark and the man with him, clearly watching for a signal. They would be the other two Grisham brothers, Stark knew, and they had to be well-armed under those long dusters they wore.

Waiters were working their way toward the outlaws, no doubt sent to escort them out of this ball where they so obviously didn't belong. Stark wasn't sure how they'd managed to sneak inside in the first place. Not that that mattered at the moment. They were here, and they were vicious enough — and dumb enough — to represent a deadly threat.

"I'll go with you," Stark said, "but I'm not going to turn McNulty loose —"

Two things happened at that moment to interrupt him.

Lucas Hallam ran into the ballroom with a Colt in his hand, causing several frightened shouts as people noticed the gun.

And on the far side of the room, somebody screamed, *"Fire!"*

There was no more feared word on the frontier than *fire*. An uncontrolled blaze could burn an entire settlement to the ground in a short time. Even in the larger cities that had actual fire departments with equipment to battle such blazes, the devastation could be immense. What had happened in Chicago some years earlier was proof of that.

So even though he was worried about Judge Stark and wanted to find the Grisham brothers, when Lucas Hallam heard that shouted warning, he stopped and looked for smoke and flames.

He didn't see either of those things, but he did spot Stark near the wall to his right. The judge whirled around and to one side, revealing Grover Grisham standing behind him. Grover had a gun in his hand and Hallam might have tried a shot at the outlaw, but Stark didn't give him a chance. Moving with surprising grace and speed for his age and size, Stark brought his left arm up under Grover's gun hand. The revolver fired, but the bullet went almost straight up into the dome.

A split-second later, Stark's fist crashed into Grover's jaw with such force that the outlaw flew backward and crashed into the wall. As he slid down, Stark kicked him in the face for good measure.

Since Grover was here, it was likely Harley and Teddy were, too, Hallam knew. He looked around as shouts and screams filled the air to a deafening level.

Despite the racket, he heard the shots that came from somewhere higher on his left. He raised his eyes to the balcony and saw Teddy Grisham there, leaning over the railing and firing a Colt at Stark. Hallam's gun roared and Teddy rocked back, then pitched forward. His midsection struck the rail and he flipped over it to plunge to the gleaming parquet floor below.

Now Hallam smelled smoke. He still couldn't see any flames, but he knew they were somewhere in the building, eating away at its structure. The smoke thickened amazingly fast, stinging his eyes, nose, and throat as he pushed through the panic-stricken crowd toward Stark.

The judge had a gun in his hand as Hallam came up to him. Hallam saw to his surprise that Stark held the old LeMat. The judge had brought it with him, even to a fancy dress ball.

"Judge, we need to get out of here!" Hallam shouted over the chaos as he reached Stark's side. "As much dry produce is stuffed in this place, it's liable to go up like tinder!"

"Let's get to the doors and make sure people don't get bottled up in them," Stark said, raising his voice as well.

The two of them turned toward the entrance, only to be confronted by Harley Grisham, whose face twisted in a hate-filled grimace as he started blasting at them. Hallam thought he heard a slug rip through the air next to his head, but in all the excitement, that could have been his imagination.

It was plenty real, though, when his Colt and Stark's LeMat boomed at the same time and the two bullets punching into Harley's chest flung him back like a rag doll. Hallam knew he wouldn't be getting back up.

"Is that all of them?" Stark asked.

"All that I know of," Hallam replied.

"Then let's do what we can to help these people."

Both men pouched their irons and got to work saving as many of Fort Worth's elite as they could.

The Spring Palace, magnificent edifice that it was, burned to the ground in fifteen minutes. Of the approximately five thousand people inside when it caught fire, only one man died — officially. That was an

English immigrant, a civil engineer named Al Hayne, who stationed himself at a second-floor window and lowered women to safety outside until he was overcome by smoke.

Two bodies, both ventilated by gunfire, were found in the rubble, but the influence of a federal judge and a Texas Ranger kept both of them from being listed in the official records. The fact that there was only one fatality was miraculous for a disaster of this size.

"Think they'll build it back?" Lucas Hallam asked the next day as he and Judge Earl Stark surveyed the rubble.

"Doubtful," Stark said. "I hope if they do, they don't make it such a firetrap next time." The judge scraped a thumbnail along his bearded jawline. "You have any idea what happened to the other one? Grover, you said his name was?"

Hallam shook his head. "No idea. He'll come to a bad end one of these days, I reckon we can count on that. I just hope he doesn't hurt too many other folks before that happens."

"He might hold a grudge," Stark said. "You'd best watch your back."

Hallam grunted. "I always do. That goes for you, too, Judge."

"How do you think I got to be this old?" Stark asked, chuckling.

"You know, you could still turn McNulty back over to me to face state charges."

"No, I can't, but once he's been found guilty in federal court, how about if I allow him to be tried for the state charges then, instead of waiting until he gets out of Leavenworth?"

"Texas is liable to hang him if you do that," Hallam warned.

"I damned well hope so."

Hallam laughed and said, "You know, for a judge, you're not too bad, Your Honor."

"Forget that," Stark said. "Just call me Big Earl."

#

The Spring Palace was never rebuilt, but in its brief existence, it was credited with bringing worldwide attention to Fort Worth and inspiring the State Fair of Texas, held every year in Dallas.

Ben McNulty was hanged at the state prison in Huntsville eight months later. Grover Grisham did hold a grudge, just as Hallam predicted, and Lucas Hallam and Judge Earl Stark met again.

But those are stories for another time.

—James Reasoner and L.J. Washburn

Writing separately and together over the past fifty years, husband and wife James Reasoner and L.J. Washburn have produced more than four hundred popular novels in a wide variety of genres — Western, historical, mystery, and romance, among others. Their books have won awards and appeared on the New York Times, USA Today, and Publishers Weekly bestseller lists. In addition to their writing, both have been editors and publishers for various imprints. They live and work in the same small town in Texas where they grew up.

THE LEOPARD

GORD ROLLO

*"Can the Ethiopian change the color of his skin, or the leopard its spots?
Then may ye also do good, that are accustomed to doing evil?"*

-- Jeremiah 13.23

From the Journal of William Boone
Sun River, Montana
November 8, 1889

Today was a happy day for the citizens of the small town of Sun River — hell, for every citizen in every town in Montana Territory, I suppose — celebrating the day Montana officially became the 41st State in the Union. It was a day many of the townsfolk thought would never happen. For many years the Democrat-controlled House of Representatives had been pushing to admit more Democratic-voting territories as states, but the Republican-led Senate fought to allow only Republican territories to join. Same old political song and dance, with the result being no new state had entered the Union since Colorado back in 1876. Sanity eventually prevailed when President Grover Cleveland allowed not just Montana, but three other territories — Washington, North Dakota, and South Dakota — to follow into the Union within a short period of time.

Those other territories would have to wait their turn, though. Today, November 8th, was Montana's time to shine, and throughout the land I'm sure the news was being greeted with tremendous joy. It certainly was here. The tiny community of Sun River, which sits high on the northern border of Montana, with a population of less than 500 (a handful over 300 registered voters) had come out in droves to celebrate this special day. The powers that be had managed to pull together a small parade complete with horses bearing saddles fashioned out of wildflowers, a local marching band and the town's mayor — Frank Tasker — riding in a horse-drawn carriage covered in red, white, and blue ribbons, waving a flag to the beat of the marching band's drums. If anyone had taken a closer look at the flag, it still only had 38 stars on it, but at the time no one in Sun River seemed to give a damn about that. The people were too busy drinking whiskey, rum, and beer, hooting and hollering as the parade went past.

The business owners had gotten into the act, too, with ribbons and flowers all over the front verandas of the butcher shop, the general store, the Riverboat Saloon, Mason's Livery, and the steps of the First Lutheran church at the far end of Main Street. There had even been a public execution earlier in the day — business before pleasure, I suppose — but someone had the gumption to pretty-up the unsightly gallows with another American flag and a large poster that had the word **FINALLY** *written on it in dark, capital letters.*

I was new to these parts, so you might wonder how I fit into this celebration or why me and my brothers — Alex and Brett — found ourselves in this tiny town a long ways from Helena, the city we'd been born in down south. It's a hell of a story, truth be told, and today has been the most eventful day of my life. And not all of it in a good way. Some of it has been terrible. I watched one of my brothers die about three hours ago — a bullet through his neck — but I'm getting too far ahead of myself. I need to slow down or whoever reads this — if anyone ever does — they won't understand the reasons I ended up doing what I did. It's easy for me to claim that God put me here in Sun River today, and maybe He did, but the devil probably played his part in this craziness too.

Regardless, to tell this right, we need to go back several days. Back before the Fletcher Gang's train robbery, the bank heist which started the chain of events that followed, outsmarting the posse, watching the public execution of innocent men — well . . . sort-of innocent men — the attack that would end up killing my brother, and how fate finally stepped in to change my life, perhaps forever. Just re-reading all that, it sounds a little overly dramatic. And maybe it is, but it's also true. . . .

Fletcher Gang Train Robbery
Gallatin Valley, Montana Territory,
November 5, 1889

Hauling three boxcars and a caboose, the steam-puffing iron horse chugged along the shining rails of the Great Northern Railway. The first boxcar was loaded with an expensive shipment of brand-new

Winchester rifles bound for Fort Ellis and the 2nd Cavalry guarding the mouth of Gallatin Valley. A detachment of ten men from the 5th Cavalry, horses and all, were crammed inside the second and third cars to ensure the safe arrival of the much-improved weaponry — the reliable repeating rifles much more effective against renegade Crow and Blackfeet war parties terrorizing settlers throughout the area.

Winding through the high alpine meadows, the train continued through the canyon. Two of the boxcars were partially open to allow fresh air inside the crowded space; some troopers enjoyed a fleeting glimpse of the passing scenery and smelling the fragrant aroma of pine needles alongside the seemingly endless tracks. Emerging from the stony heights, the glistening rails followed the meandering Gallatin River through a corridor of exceptionally tall pines, the sun streaking through staggered gaps in the trees reflecting a spectacular mirror image of their train on the sparkling calm waters as they passed.

If nothing else, it was a beautiful place to die.

Approaching a curve in the tracks, an explosion shattered the still air, sending twisted rails slicing through the nearby foliage before smashing into the unmovable pines. The brakeman, unable to slow the train's momentum, jumped clear as the iron monster careened off the suddenly railless track with a thunderous squeal of steel on bedrock and slid forward before turning on its side and jarring to a stop amongst a stretch of broken timbers. The boxcars and caboose followed in its wake, toppling on their sides and slithering down the embankment silent before breaking up — each car ploughing unchecked into the car ahead of it.

Many of the men and horses died in the crash. A few surviving horses struggled free of the wreckage then bolted in terror down the empty track, but the troopers weren't as lucky. The surviving cavalrymen exited the cars in disarray and were immediately cut down by a barrage of bullets from the trees. When the shooting ceased and the smoke cleared, the scene revealed was one of total carnage. Twisted bodies of men and beasts lay strewn amongst the shattered debris of the train and the splintered remains of the wooden railroad ties. Other than the hissing of steam from the crippled engine, an eerie silence hung in the afternoon air.

Five sinister figures brandishing Winchesters cautiously emerged from cover. Sam Fletcher, the leader of this gang of outlaws, scanned his handiwork, a smile of satisfaction spread across his pockmarked face. "Let's move these rifles, boys . . . before another train rumbles through."

It took four trips to transfer the rifles to a buckboard waiting on a nearby trail, but once the big wagon was loaded, the men wasted little time remaining at the scene of the crime.

Sam Fletcher was an imposing figure, with wild hair and eyes as dark as his cowboy hat. He was a white man, but he hated the US Cavalry and its government-backed policy of *stealing* Indian land and herding them onto reservations. It was only a matter of time until the natives were all but exterminated, and neither the Crow nor Blackfeet had the weapons to take on the US forces. Not on their own, anyway. Sam glanced back at the loaded buckboard and smiled.

This should help even the score, he mused.

Two weeks had passed since he had traded a dozen horses to the Blackfeet, led by a fierce warrior named *White Cloud*, who promised him gold in exchange for these new repeating rifles he'd heard about. Should Sam be successful in procuring such a shipment, he'd promised to meet White Cloud in two days. It was an appointment he meant to keep, even though he was slightly intimidated dealing with White Cloud, a man known for being violent and ruthless.

Fletcher had no qualms about placing advanced weaponry in White Cloud's hands; he was tired of seeing one injustice after another against the natives and the army never being held accountable. As far as he was concerned, the army deserved whatever it had coming. Any other feelings of guilt on his conscience vanished with thoughts of all the gold he and his men were about to receive. . . .

From the Journal of William Boone
Sun River, Montana
November 8, 1889

I loved my brothers. Let's start with that. Basically, Alex and Brett were all I had. Dad died when I was only six. He had consumption and I never really got to know him. The only father figure I had growing up was my grandfather on my mother's side — Gramps, we used to call him. He was a good man, but maybe a bit over-religious for his own good. He helped Ma run our small farm, but what he really wanted to be was a preacher. Not the kind who stood up at the front of a church on Sunday mornings, but the kind who stood on the street and tried to teach the gospel to the unclean men and women (his terms, not mine) going in and out of the saloons and brothels downtown.

Gramps wasn't making too many friends back in those days, and he often came home dripping blood from his mouth or nose from where someone had clocked him a good one for getting in their face and shouting things they clearly didn't want to hear. I think that's what started to put a wedge between me and my brothers. Alex was only one year older than me, and he liked Gramps okay. He'd still joke around with him and treated him with respect, but he kept his distance.

Brett, on the other hand, hated Gramps. Well, hate might be too strong of a word, but Brett — who was three years older than me — wouldn't tolerate the old man's constant sermons, growing colder and more distant with every passing year. It came as no surprise that he'd eventually become an outlaw and drag Alex and me into a life of crime alongside him.

By the time Gramps finally died in the spring of '81, Brett had become a big, strong, hard man, and in my opinion, a cruel and vicious bully. Especially to me. Alex he tolerated and continually tried to mold into a younger, slightly less violent version of himself, but he saw way too much of our grandfather in me, and always pushed me around whenever he could.

That's what caused the fight between us on the night before we robbed the bank in Sun River. When I look back on it now, I can clearly see that me standing my ground at that campfire was the straw that finally broke the camel's back.

The beginning of the end. . . .

Boone Brothers' Campsite
Five Miles West of Sun River, Montana Territory
November 5, 1889

William Boone had grown into a strapping young cowboy. At twenty-two years of age, he'd put on twenty pounds of solid muscle in the last year to help fill out what had been an admittedly thin, six-foot frame. As his body had filled out, his acne-spotted face had cleared up and he'd let his dark brown hair grow almost to his shoulders, making him handsome in a rugged, working-man kind of way. He didn't have to drive the young ladies off — not yet, anyway — but there was a quiet confidence and presence to him that hadn't been there six months ago.

He was enjoying his ride out of Sun River, letting *Wyatt* — Will's loyal Palomino stallion — set his own leisurely pace. Will was riding alone, having done a reconnaissance mission into town the night before, and was now en route to join the boys to plan tomorrow's bank job. It was an important meeting, but he was in no hurry to get there.

They'll be on higher ground, Will thought. *Always on guard. . . .*

Within a few miles, he saw smoke rising from a nearby bluff pinpointing the location of his brothers. Soon, he recognized the familiar, skinny frame of young Chad Morgan scanning the approach from his observation post overlooking the bluff. Will gave Chad a friendly wave and approached without worry. As he entered the camp, Will could see that the previous night's rain had not been kind to his brethren, evidenced by the clothes drying beside the open fire.

The clouds had long since shed their tears and a warming sun now had the morning sky to itself, the still air offering no resistance to the upward wisps of smoke. Alex Boone, looking tired, disheveled, and in need of a shave, offered his younger brother a mug of steaming hot brew. Of the three brothers, Alex was the smallest, but he'd always had a good heart and he was stronger than he looked.

"Must be nice," Alex said, his voice dripping with sarcasm.

"What?"

"Staying in town, obviously. Having a hot bath and comfy bed beats a wet blanket roll and hard tack, don't you think?"

"Can't argue with that. No hot bath for me . . . but the bed was decent. Don't be angry, though. Things are about to change for all of us. I have great news."

"Good, 'cause Brett's in one of his moods. Best to stay out of his hair . . . hear?"

"What else is new? But yeah, thanks for the heads up."

Will walked back to where he'd tied up his mount and started removing the saddle from Wyatt's back. He made sure the animal had a bucket of water to drink and some long grass to chew on before turning his attention back on the camp. Brett was over by the fire now, using his cowboy hat to fan the glowing embers, setting up a trio of sticks to roast some meat on. He gave Will a nod of his head, acknowledging his arrival, but turned back to the campfire without uttering a word. There was a pot of beans sitting in the coals already, and it looked like Brett — who had always been a good hunter — had managed to catch and skin a couple of rabbits earlier in the day. While his oldest brother busied himself with dinner, Will took Alex's advice and left him alone.

While supper cooked, Will sat quietly reading his Bible, lost in some of the passages he'd read many times before but that still fascinated him. He failed to notice Brett glancing in his direction with obvious distain, and it wasn't until his oldest brother walked up to him and yanked the treasured book from his hands that Will knew anything was wrong.

"What's this crap you're reading?" Brett asked, knowing full well what the book was. "Who gave you this nonsense?"

"Ma gave it to me after Gramps died," Will said, standing up and holding out his hand. "It was his. Gimme it back."

"Gramps was a madman. I can't let you follow the path he took. I'd never forgive myself."

"He was a good man. He —"

"He was a *nutcase* who failed our family. And this damn book's the main reason why. It's good for only one thing. . . ." Brett suddenly turned and tossed the old Bible into the glowing embers of the campfire.

Will gasped and ran, dropping to his knees to pull the book from the fire before it could ignite. The cover was smoking and singed black in places, but for the most part it was fine. Without thinking, Will climbed to his feet, turned, and while still protectively holding it with two hands, swung the Bible at Brett, the heavy book striking him solidly on the side of his chin. Brett spun backwards with the force of the blow but stayed on his feet.

Brett faced Will with a murderous look on his scruffy face. He was several inches taller than Will and at least thirty pounds heavier. "Why you little, . . . " he said through clenched teeth, and charged, plowing his weight into his youngest brother's chest and knocking them both flying. Rolling in the dirt, Brett ended up on top, and started punching Will in the face.

Will dropped the Bible to defend himself and swung a left hook from the ground that caught Brett under the chin and snapped his head back. With a little distance between them now, Will threw his knee into his brother's groin, and it connected solidly, causing Brett to roll off onto his side. Will scurried to his feet, fists raised, ready for the next attack, but by the time Brett had regained his feet, Alex had stepped between them.

"Stop it," Alex said. "Both of you. We're here to plan the bank job, not kill each other."

Alex was right, of course, and both Brett and Will knew it. It didn't stop Brett from tossing in one last jab, saying, "Reading that book don't make you better than me, hear?"

"You sure?" Will said. "Maybe if you'd ever taken the time to read it rather than bitching about it, you might know the answer."

Brett pulled out his Colt revolver and held it toward the sky. "This here gun gives me all the answers I need. And you know that, Will. You're the best damn gunslinger I've ever known, but something has you messed up lately. What's happening to you? You going soft on me?"

"Nothin' is happening. And I'm no gunslinger. I only shoot if I have to defend myself. I'm not like you. I'll *never* be like you."

"That's right . . . 'cause you're a coward."

Alex watched Will clench his fists in anger and stepped in once more, before his brothers came to blows again . . . or worse. "I said stop it, and I meant it. Now's not the time. You two wanna beat each other up, fine, but save it until after tomorrow. Let's eat and get down to business, hear?"

The three brothers and Chad Morgan sat around finishing their meals in silence. Tensions were still high among the group, and although Chad had been on watch and missed the fight earlier, he knew something bad had happened and he was smart enough to keep his mouth shut.

"Okay," Brett spoke. "Enough is enough. Let's talk about how we take the cash out of the National Bank in Sun River tomorrow. I say we keep it simple. Will and Chad keep watch outside while Alex and I go in and bust a few heads. Rough a few people up and the rest will do what they're told. If we have to pop someone to get the message through, that's what we'll do. Will and Chad watch our backs from the street and shoot any heroes who might not like us withdrawing their funds and come looking for trouble."

"What about the sheriff?" Chad said.

"Shoot him, too," Brett said. "Simple, like I said. Get in and get out in ten minutes."

"No," Will said.

"What do you mean, *no*?" Brett said.

"Even if we manage to shoot our way out of the bank and then fight our way out of town, an angry posse will be on our tail a minute later, hunting us down. It's a terrible plan."

"You have a better one?" Alex asked.

"We won't need to kill the sheriff or worry about a posse."

The others — even Brett — wanted to hear more. Alex was first to ask, "And why's that?"

"Because I'll ride into town ahead of us and inform the sheriff that the Double G ranch east of there is being threatened by a bunch of Blackfeet. If my hunch is correct, the lawman and all the men he can gather will ride to the rescue."

"Why?" Brett asked, his interest peaked. "What's so special about the Double G ranch?"

"It's where his wife grew up. George Gentry is her father. There's a chance the sheriff's wife might even be out there visiting, but even if she isn't, he'll ride out to try save her parents. His wife would never forgive him if he didn't."

"And how do you know all this?"

"I heard the sheriff... Charlie Houghton is his name, talking about his in-laws at the saloon last night. The place was crowded; everyone shouting over each other to be heard. I slid in next to his table and no one paid any attention to me. I got out quick as you please after I heard what I needed to hear. This'll work, Brett. Trust me for once. We don't always need to shoot the place up and kill people."

"Maybe . . . maybe not," Brett says. "I like your diversion idea, but we send Chad into town to tell Sheriff Houghton, not you."

"Why? No offense, but Chad gets flustered if he tries talking to a pretty girl, never mind trying to pull the wool over a seasoned lawman."

"I'm counting on it. Someone reporting a *real* Blackfoot attack would be flustered plenty, right? Besides, even though you laid low, there still might be someone who remembers your face. No one in Sun River knows Chad."

"So what? There are lots of visitors in town for the admission to the union celebration in a few days. I'm just another guy in the crowd. No big deal."

"We send Chad. End of discussion."

"That doesn't make any —"

"Don't push it, little brother. We're going with your plan, but I still call the shots around here. Unless you have a problem with that, too?"

From the Journal of William Boone
Sun River, Montana
November 8, 1889

I kept my mouth shut. I'd pushed Brett far enough for one day and there would be nothing but grief if I tried to push him any further. I'd made some progress by standing up to him as much as I had. He'd been right that something was different about me lately, but even I wasn't quite sure what it was yet. I just didn't like the way violence and killing was his first and apparently only option, and a big part of me wasn't interesting in being part of that anymore. There had to be a better way to live, right?

I hoped so, anyway. . . .

The Bank Job
Sun River, Montana Territory
November 6, 1889

Sun River had been a typical cowboy town until the arrival of the Northern Railroad, but now new homesteaders were flooding the fertile valley and the town was booming. Carpenters were in great demand as new buildings seemed to spring up out of the dust to cloud the once-open range. The constant sawing of timber and repetitive hammering of nails filled all hours of the day, not letting up until it was too dark to use the saws or swing the hammers.

As he reached the outskirts of town, seventeen-year-old Chad Morgan passed the livery stable and blacksmith shop before pointing the nose of his horse onto Main Street with its conglomeration of two-story commercial buildings framing the downtown area. The sidewalks were busy today, filled with men and children, but it was the fancy ladies in long dresses and lace-trimmed hats that caught Chad's eye. The young outlaw swallowed heavily, hardly able to even look at the pretty women, much less have the courage to speak to any of them. He kept moving, trying to stay focused and remember the things Brett and Will had told him to say.

Keeping his horse at a slow gait, he continued to edge along the street. Without glancing inside Chad managed to pass the front doors of the National Bank, congratulating himself for not looking, a smile on his face as he thought, *later. . . .*

Up ahead, the brightly painted, wooden structure of the Riverboat Saloon caught his eye, its hanging sign swaying in a freshening breeze. That was where Will had learned about the sheriff's connection to the Double G ranch. Past the saloon was a smaller building with metal bars on the windows. No official sign hung that said *"Sun River Jail"* or *"Sheriff's Office,"* but Chad knew he had found his destination all the same.

It was just shy of two o'clock in the afternoon when he tied his mustang to a post and stood taking a few deep breaths, preparing to enter the building. The sun was past its zenith for the day, but it was still shining brightly in the blue sky above. The temperature was surprisingly mild for this time of year, but that played no part in why the young man was sweating.

There was a blond-haired man sitting outside the doorway with his eyes closed, but he looked too young to be the seasoned lawman Will had told him about, so Chad walked right past him. Sheriff Charlie Houghton was sitting in his chair with his feet up on the desk when the outlaw walked in, and it didn't take a genius to see that both the lawman and his friend outside were having afternoon siestas.

Houghton was a broad-shouldered man, with dark hair and a thick, curling mustache under his prominent nose. For a big man, though, he was quick to react. The sudden intrusion of a stranger brought the lawman out of his languid state in a hurry.

"What the —?" Sheriff Houghton stammered, dropping his feet to the floor and sitting up straight. "Who the heck are you, boy?"

"Name's Vincent Hardy, sir," Chad said, lying. "There's big trouble, sheriff. You gotta help. The injuns are attacking. They're everywhere . . . hollering, screaming, and shooting. Thought they were gonna kill me, but I slipped away."

"Whoa, whoa. Slow down a bit, son," Houghton said, taking a moment to look the young man up and down. "What Indians? Where are they attacking?"

"Blackfeet raiders. Covered in war paint and everything, waving rifles in the air and whooping themselves into a frenzy. Had to be twenty of them. They were setting fire to the barn when I slipped past them to come get you. You gotta help those poor people, sheriff. Something awful is gonna happen."

"Where, boy? How far from town?"

"The Double G ranch. I just started working there and — "

"Oh my god!" Sheriff Houghton interrupted, shooting to his feet and racing for the door. "Mitch . . . *Mitch*," he screamed to his deputy sitting in the chair outside. "George Gentry's ranch is under attack by the Blackfeet. Round up the boys. *Hurry!*"

Ten minutes later eighteen men mounted up, and under Sheriff Houghton's lead, dashed off down Main Street, riding like they didn't have a moment to waste. And as far as they all knew, they didn't.

Chad Morgan finally let out a deep breath, watching the last of the posse ride out of sight. He'd pulled off the performance of his life, and he knew the Boone brothers would be pleased. Things had gone off without a hitch, and now practically every man in town who knew how to use a gun was off on a wild goose chase. The National Bank was practically theirs for the taking. Chad laughed and walked back inside the abandoned Sheriff's office. He grabbed the pot from the stove, poured himself a mug of coffee, and waited for his associates to arrive. . . .

The afternoon sun was sitting lower on the horizon as George Gentry, the spry, older owner of the Double G ranch finished repairing a section of his fence line, then pulled out a soiled handkerchief to dab the perspiration from his creased brow.

The sound of thundering hooves broke the stillness. Gentry looked up to see a band of horsemen crest the hill at a gallop and head in his direction. He started to look around in panic, thinking rustlers were about to thin out his herd, but to his surprise the riders were none other than Sheriff Houghton and his men.

"What brings you out here, Charlie?" George asked. "Don't often see you through the week. Everything okay with Sarah?"

Houghton looked around carefully, eyes and ears wide open. Except for a barking hound the place was quiet as a graveyard. "Never mind Sarah, George. Your daughter's fine. Where's all the injuns?"

Gentry looked at him as if the sun had affected his mind. "What injuns?"

"Your new worker, Vincent, rode into town to tell me you were under attack."

"I ain't got no new workers, and I don't know anyone named Vincent. You on the sauce again, Charlie?"

Houghton knew he'd been duped, but at the time the youngster's plight had seemed all too real. Now he wished he'd questioned the stranger in more detail.

"I got a bad feeling about this. We need to get back to town, boys." Tipping his Stetson in respect, Houghton turned away from his father-in-law and led his posse back toward Sun River as fast as their horses could run . . . .

Chad Morgan emerged from the sheriff's office not long after the posse left town. He mounted his horse and joined the three familiar riders slowly making their way along Main Street. Brett Boone took the lead with his brother Alex, and Chad joined Will behind them.

Brett turned to whisper to the youngster, "You're coming inside with me, Chad."

Everything had been worked out in detail the night before, but Brett was rewarding Chad for doing a fine job convincing the sheriff he was needed elsewhere. Nothing to it now other than to get in and out of the bank as fast as they could and be long gone before Sheriff Houghton caught wind of what they were up to.

The four riders pulled up outside the bank, where they split up — Will and Alex waiting patiently out front while Brett and Chad casually entered the bank through the oak doors, their guns hidden beneath their long, leather dusters. Inside, a lone, male teller was busy with a fashionably attractive female who made what appeared to be a small withdrawal inside her purse before taking her leave. On her way out, she gave Chad a warm, inviting smile. He nervously smiled back, holding the door for her as she left.

The bank now cleared of customers, both Brett and Chad pulled their bandanas up from their necks over their mouths and noses to conceal their identities. An opaque glass door inscribed with the words *Steven Holbrook – Manager,* isolated the bank's financial head from his staff. As Brett entered the manager's office unannounced, he gave the nod to Chad, who entered the swing gates and overpowered the teller with a single forty-five butt blow to the head. Not too hard — just enough to get his undivided attention.

With the muzzle of his Colt stuck in Holbrook's ear, Brett asked the startled financier to kindly hand over the key to the safe. "Best losing other people's money . . . than losing your life. Giddy-up and get at it, boss."

Before emptying the safe, Brett quickly frisked the bank manager and found a derringer in the inside pocket of his jacket. He didn't think Holbrook looked like the hero type, but Brett took the gun with him, just in case. Better safe than sorry.

It took only seven minutes to decrease the bank's assets, straddle their waiting mounts outside and nonchalantly make their way out of town. The whole gang was happy, but out of the four of them, Will was smiling the most. His plan to pull off the bank job quietly had worked. And they hadn't even fired a shot. . . .

Ten minutes later — the exact amount of time he'd been warned to stay inside — a shaky, disheveled Holbrook emerged from the bank and hurried down Main Street to the sheriff's office to report the robbery. To his astonishment and growing dismay, he found the building strangely unoccupied. Forty-five minutes later, he was still sitting there in a much-agitated state when Sheriff Houghton and his men finally arrived back in town.

From the Journal of William Boone
Sun River, Montana
November 8, 1889

The bank job went perfectly . . . like I knew it would. Brett and Chad were in and out of there in minutes and we all trotted out of town smiling, like we had no worries in the whole world. But things wouldn't stay that way for long, of course.

None of us knew it, but fate was about to start an unexpected series of events in motion that would eventually bring us back to Sun River.

Most of us, anyway. . . .

Pursuing the Outlaws
Sun River, Montana Territory
November 6, 1889

His worst fears realized; Sheriff Houghton listened to Holbrook's account of the holdup at the National Bank. He felt like a first-class fool for the way he'd been tricked by the robbers, but there was nothing he could do about that right now. "How much of a head start do they have?"

"I'd say they left town about an hour ago."

"Which way did they go?"

"Sorry, Sheriff . . . can't help you there. They warned me if I stuck my head out the door before ten minutes had lapsed, they'd blow it off."

Houghton was perplexed. "How many could you account for?"

"One son of bitch emptied the safe, and another one conked my teller, Tom Avery, on the head, emptied the counter drawers, and grabbed the day's float."

"Only two men?"

"Not sure. It all happened pretty fast. Maybe there was a third by the door, I don't know. Probably a few outside, too."

"Anything unusual about them?"

"The two I saw were both wearing kerchiefs. I was looking more at the man's gun than his face, ya know? I suppose I was struck a bit by their strange garb."

"What do you mean?"

"They were both dressed in long, leather coats, which seemed unusual for a warm afternoon like today. Who knows?"

"Would you recognize them if you saw them again?"

The bank manager shrugged his shoulders. "Not sure. I might recognize the leader's voice more than his face. He had a deep, raspy tone."

. "That's something, at least. Thanks for the information."

"Aren't you guys gonna go after them?"

Houghton tried to remain composed. "Which direction should I take, Holbrook?"

There was no response from the financier.

"That's what I thought. Regardless, we'll definitely go after the bastards. I'm not giving up the town's cash that easily. But seeing as they already have a huge head start, a few more hours isn't going to hurt. These horses need rest."

Houghton addressed his posse. "Going off half-cocked in ten different directions will spread us too thin, but I think we need to split up into at least three groups to up our chances of finding them. We'll cover a wider area that way, but still have numbers to take them down if it comes to that. Gets some rest tonight and some food in your belly. We leave first thing in the morning."

"Bring 'em back alive if you can, Sheriff," Holbrook said. "Nothing I'd like better than to see them swinging from a noose on Main Street."

"We'll do our best. That's all I can promise right now."

Houghton spent a few minutes dividing his men into groups for the morning, giving instruction for one group to head north, the second, south, and the men with him were going to head east. Hopefully somebody would get lucky.

It would certainly help ease his conscience if they did.

Brett Boone and his newly richer companions galloped east, distancing themselves from Sun River and any posse that might be coming in pursuit. Three hours later, they sighted Eagle Point rising above the tall ponderosa pines, an ideal spot to make camp and rest their sweating mounts. Brett picked a flat plateau about halfway up the slope; a quick glance below showed no dust trail and no one crowding their rear.

They could rest easy here. For now.

The evening air began to cool as the dying sun dipped below the horizon, leaving a brilliant, red-orange hue across the western sky. Settling around a crackling fire, all four of them sipping a steaming hot brew, it was time to divide the spoils of the day. Brett gathered the saddlebags and emptied their contents in full view of the others. They gathered around the pile of cash, eager to receive their share.

By the time Brett had counted the take, each man received close to seven hundred dollars, not too shabby for a quick trip to the bank and a stress-free unauthorized withdrawal. Having received a fistful of greenbacks, the group's restless mood changed to one of lightheartedness — everyone smiling and jovial — which was exactly what Brett had been hoping for. He took advantage of the moment and told them what he thought they all wanted to hear. Wagging his share of bank notes, he said, "This is peanuts, boys. Stick with me and I'll make you rich."

Will considered saying something about money not being everything, but when he saw how happy his brothers were and looked at the smile on young Chad's face, he decided to keep his thoughts to himself. Not for the first time, he questioned why he couldn't just accept the life he was living and be content the way everyone else seemed to be. Why did he always have to complicate everything?

With a sigh, Will spread his bedroll near the toasty fire. The others were climbing into their blankets as well. It had been an eventful day and sleep would be a welcome relief. Will glanced skyward and let his thoughts drift on the wind. Above, a white moon lit up the starry canopy and the last thing he heard before drifting off was the sound of a lone coyote baying in the distance, calling him toward a destiny he still couldn't comprehend.

Blood and Gold
Eagle Point, Montana Territory
November 7, 1889

The sun took over from the dying moon and slowly rose above the eastern horizon, its fiery orb lighting the dawn sky. Will and his brothers huddled around a small fire, waiting on a slow-boiling pot and an early caffeine rush. A breakfast of beans and dried jerky was gorged without much conversation.

No sooner had they doused the dying embers than they heard the distinctive sound of approaching horses in the valley below. A lone, somber looking rider was leading a covered buckboard, his expression revealing little emotion as he prodded his mount in a monotonous gait. Apart from his older appearance, he looked every inch a professional gunman, dressed in black and holstering two forty-fives. Will sensed he was a man of purpose.

And he wasn't alone.

There were five of them, two on the buckboard and two more gunslingers guarding the rear.

"A posse from Sun River?" Alex asked.

"I don't think so," Brett said, eyeing the covered wagon. "With that kind of escort there must be hauling something of value."

Chad, reaching for his gun, said, "We have the high ground, Brett, we can take 'em out."

"We could . . . but we're not gonna. I can smell gunrunners a mile away; take a look at the weight of that wagon. Bet my bottom dollar that buckboard's loaded with rifles. All we have to do is follow them and when the transaction is made we relieve them of their ill-gotten gains. Easy pickings. If we take them now, all we'll have is a load of stolen rifles."

"He's right," Alex agreed.

"Makes sense to me," added Chad.

Will kept his opinion to himself, but already he wasn't liking the way this was heading.

They allowed the gunrunners a lengthy head start, keeping to the high ground and trailing their quarry for most of the morning. The sun was high overhead when they noticed the riders ahead had stopped and smoke was drifting up from a newly lit fire. Forced to wait, they dismounted and seated themselves in the long grass. Not wanting to spook their unsuspecting prey, they resisted lighting a fire, settled for a few biscuits and some not-so-cool water.

An hour later, they were once again tailing the slow-moving group as it continued northeast. Will was trying to figure where they were heading, but way out here was Indian land, so he had a good idea who they'd eventually be seeing. Sure enough, the buckboard driver soon pulled on the reins and brought the snorting horses to a halt. Up ahead, a bunch of riders kicking up a dust storm emerged from the slopes and closed in on the waiting gunrunners. As they drew nearer there was no mistaking the painted Blackfeet war party, and their infamous, feathered leader.

Will stated the obvious. "Oh, no. That's White Cloud down there. These sons of bitches are trading with the Blackfeet, and we all know what they're gonna do with those rifles."

"Easy, Will," Alex said. "We can't do much about the redskins, but we can make sure these traitors are done gunrunning. Right now we sit tight and see what happens. Maybe the injuns will take the rifles *and* keep the money too."

Chad wiped sweat from his brow. "Hope not, otherwise we've wasted most of the day."

"Ain't that the truth," agreed Brett. Grabbing a tarnished brass telescope from his saddlebag, he focused on the rendezvous. One of the gunrunners had partially removed the tarp and their head honcho was demonstrating the simplicity of the repeating rifle. White Cloud unleashed five shots before a smile creased his painted features. He nodded his approval before one of his warriors handed over a canvas bag. It was too small to contain cash, so he deduced it was gold.

"They're paying with *gold*!" Brett said, excitement in his voice.

After a short exchange, White Cloud raised his feathered staff, shrieked some form of war cry and turned about. His painted warriors, escorting their newly acquired buckboard and arsenal, followed their leader toward the safety of their village. The gunrunners, fully compensated for their treasonable act and free from the encumbrance of the slow-moving buckboard, quickly distanced themselves from the painted horde and were heading straight back toward them, much to the delight of Brett and his gold-hungry friends.

"What do we do?" Chad asked, turning to Brett for the answer.

"We let them pass close . . . then let the *turkey* shoot begin."

"Hold on," Will said, jumping into the conversation. "There has to be a better way?"

"Now's not the time, Will . . . it's them or us if we want that gold."

"Then let them keep it. My pockets are already full."

Brett turned and looked intensely at his youngest brother, disgust showing on his scruffy face. "I'm gonna pretend I didn't hear that. We do it my way, hear? So shut your mouth and be ready when I make my move."

Sam Fletcher and his henchmen never saw it coming. With thoughts of how much cash the gold from selling the rifles might bring each of them, they blindly rode into the waiting barrage and were unceremoniously blown from their saddles. Three of the men were killed instantly — the older gunslinger who'd been leading the wagon, and the pair of hired guns who'd been guarding the rear. Fletcher and one other young man were grazed and bleeding, knocked painfully from their horses, but still able to fight. Unfortunately, they'd just sold all of their rifles and the gang had just lost their best shooters. They had to make do with the guns at their sides and quickly ran out of ammo in their six-shooters, only managing to take down one of the men who hid among the trees. With no more bullets, Fletcher tossed his useless weapon to the ground and put his hands in the air. His young friend obediently did the same. Whatever happened next — and Sam didn't figure it would be anything good — it was out of their hands now. Together they watched three angry men exit the trees, their guns pointed toward them, obviously loaded.

Brett walked toward the two remaining gunrunners, one of which he assumed was the leader by his age and fearless disposition. Not that it mattered, he intended to send both men to eternity to join their friends soon enough. First, he wanted to hear their story, though, and find out where they'd managed to get their hands on dozens of brand-new repeating rifles. He hated that they were stealing from the army to give weapons to the fierce Blackfeet, but part of him could acknowledge it was a damn good job they'd pulled off. The fact that Chad had taken a bullet in the chest during the exchange made Brett furious — he'd been a good kid and a better than average shooter — but if that sack of gold White Cloud had handed over was as heavy as Brett suspected it was, he'd find a way to get over it.

"You hear that?" Alex said, stopping to turn to his left.

"What?" Brett asked, never taking his eyes, or gun, off of the two men he had in his sights.

"Horses," Alex said, running toward the crest of the hill to get a better look. A moment later he was scurrying back toward his brothers "We got trouble. More riders coming hard . . . seven or eight men."

"The posse from Sun River. Gotta be," Will said.

"What do we do?" Alex asked, turning to Brett for the answer.

"I'm not leaving without the gold. Shoot these fools, grab the gold and hightail it out of here." Brett walked two steps closer and aimed his revolver at the younger man first.

"Don't do it, Brett." Will said.

"Stay out of it, boy. I'm warning you."

"Don't kill 'em or you'll be signing our death warrant too."

"Dammit . . . why? You have a better idea?" Brett said, his anger rising once again.

"Actually, yeah. Grab the sack of gold and get into the trees. Alex . . . drag Chad's body over here. Make it quick . . . we're almost out of time."

Sheriff Houghton and his posse came over the rise in the trail and saw six men laying on the ground in puddles of drying blood. They'd been patrolling south of here but had heard a flurry of shots from this direction and had come to investigate.

"They all dead?" Houghton asked the deputy beside him, a tall blonde man by the name of Mitch Harris. "Check 'em out."

It only took a moment to determine that there were four dead and two men who'd either been faking or had been knocked unconscious for real. Both living men had blood and scratches on them from bullet fire, and neither was too happy to see the law when they opened their eyes. Both men seemed reluctant to answer any of Sheriff Houghton's questions about their whereabouts in the last few days, but nothing they had to say mattered once Deputy Harris turned over one of the dead men and hollered for the sheriff's attention.

"Charlie . . . come look at this guy."

Sheriff Houghton walked over and once he looked down at the familiar young man, he started to smile. "That's the man who sent us on our wild goose chase to the Double G."

"Sure is." Deputy Harris reached into Chad Morgan's open jacket and pulled out a thick wad of greenbacks, holding them out for his boss to see.

"Good work, Mitch. Check the rest of them . . . see if we can collect all the money."

Ultimately, collecting the National Bank's stolen cash fell short, but between the six men they did find enough loose bills to cover about half of what had been taken. There was some discussion about there being more men here than had been thought to have pulled off the robbery, but they didn't pay Sheriff Houghton to be good at math, they paid him to bring the men who'd robbed their town to justice. And no matter how much the captures protested they knew nothing of a bank robbery in Sun River, that was exactly what Charlie intended to do.

"Round the two rascals up that are still breathin' and let's get back to town. They can either tell us where they stashed the rest of the cash, or they can tell it to the hangman. Choice is theirs. Let's move. . . ."

From the Journal of William Boone
Sun River, Montana
November 8, 1889

I don't know why we decided to go back to Sun River. It was a stupid thing to do, obviously, but Brett got a real kick out of my plan to set the gunrunners up to take the fall for our bank robbery. As soon as the deputy got a good look at our Chad, I knew my plan was going to work, but going back to watch those two men hang for a crime my brothers and I had committed . . . well, I wasn't too sure about that.

I couldn't blame it all on Brett, though. I wanted to go to Sun River, too. I can't really describe it other than I felt compelled to be there. Not for the same crazy, twisted reasons as my oldest brother, but still . . . something was calling me back there.

If only I knew back then what would happen, maybe I'd have been smart enough to stay far, far away. Or maybe not. . . .

Admission to the Union Day
Sun River, Montana
November 8, 1889

Will had no facts to base his opinion on, but he was relatively sure no other towns and cities in the brand new State of Montana were celebrating being admitted into the Union by staging a quick double hanging before the start of their parades. But in Sun River, people were angry from losing some — or all — of their meager savings to the two accused hooligans, and somehow handing out a little small-town justice didn't seem out of place on an important day such as this. In its own bizarre way, the executions of Sam Fletcher and Toby Kennedy were seen as a cleansing of downtrodden ways and bad luck, and the beginning of better days to come.

Will couldn't watch as the two men they'd knocked unconscious with the butts of their guns and left for the posse to find yesterday were led up a set of wooden stairs and presented to the cheering crowd.

Alex had no issues watching the hangings, and Brett absolutely loved the whole show, but for Will it hit too close to home for comfort.

"We should stop this," he said to his brothers. "It's not right. Those men are innocent, and we damn well know it."

"Yeah," Brett said. "Go tell the sheriff how you know they're innocent. See how that works out for ya. Besides . . . they're far from innocent. They maybe didn't rob the bank, but they deserve to swing for selling those rifles to the Blackfeet. That's treason, or *somethin'*. Worse than robbing, right? Don't go feeling sorry for the likes of them."

Will considered Brett's words, and as strange as it sounded, they actually made sense. A bit self-serving, of course, but also not without truth. In the end, he still looked away when the lever was pulled and the trap doors opened beneath the condemned men's feet. He'd accepted that their fate was justified enough, but that didn't mean he had to watch it play out.

After the bodies were cut down and dragged away and the crowd dispersed to prepare for the celebration, the Boone brothers gathered to decide what to do next. The parade didn't excite them much, but the saloons and brothels would be filled tonight, and no doubt there was fun to be had for three young men whose pockets were filled with money and gold.

"We're pushing our luck, hanging around," Alex said, and Will agreed with him, but as usual Brett saw things differently.

"Nothing to worry about. They just hung the men they were all mad at. Nobody's looking for us. And even if they were, we're the Boone brothers. We ain't running scared from *nobody*."

The parade wasn't really the brothers' thing, but it was entertaining enough to pass the time with its colorful wagons and flower-decorated horses, and even the marching band was good and loud and reasonably in tune. Brett took it all in with a smile on his face, but as soon as Sun River's Mayor, Frank Tasker, passed by waving the flag, he'd apparently seen enough. Brett put his arms around both his younger brothers' necks and shouted to be heard over the din of the crowd, "Okay, That's it for me. Let's get drunk."

For the next hour, Will, Alex, and Brett drank whisky and beer at two separated drinking establishments (Murray's Restaurant, and the Riverboat Saloon), and were preparing to walk down the street to a brothel that had come highly recommended when they heard the first volley of gunfire. A shot or two in a town like this was never much cause for concern — usually just a few good ol' boys letting off some steam — but twenty rapid-fire shots in coordinated bursts was another matter entirely. Everyone inside the saloon stopped talking, their eyes turning toward the windows looking out onto Main Street.

An elderly man with wild, grey hair, ran into the saloon screaming, "Help . . . help! The damn injuns are killing everyone."

Sure enough, when Will and his brothers shoved their way to the front windows, they could see several dead bodies lying in the street, and a horde of face-painted Indians on horseback at the north end of Main Street shooting at anyone they could see. It only took one look at their tall, savage leader for Will to instantly know what was going on.

"It's White Cloud," he said to his brothers. "Him and his Blackfeet warriors with a whole slew of brand-new repeater rifles, I'll bet."

"I reckon," Alex said. "I told you we shouldn't have hung around."

Several men were loading their guns and the bartender passed out three rifles he had stored behind the bar, then the men started heading outside to face the attackers in the street. The Boone brothers moved to join the fray, but a stocky man in a fancy suit was blocking the doorway, peeking outside. Brett wasn't about to miss out on all the fun, so he shoved the frightened man in the back trying to move him out of the way. "Come on fella," he said. "We got some injuns to kill. Giddy-up and get at it, boss."

The man at the saloon door turned to face Brett, and even after gulping down seven or eight whiskeys this afternoon, he recognized the man as the manager of the National Bank he'd met several days ago. The man cocked his head just a little, a strange look in his eyes.

"What did you just say?" Steven Holbrook said, his eyes darting back and forth between the three Boone brothers.

"I said get outta my way, fool. The town's under attack."

"I'm moving," Holbrook said, finally dashing out of the saloon and heading for a group of men who had managed to turn over a wagon and were using it as a shield while firing back at the Blackfeet warriors.

"Who was that?" Will asked.

"The bank manager," Brett said. "Knew it was him the minute he turned around."

"Do you think he recognized you?"

"Nothing to worry about. I was masked up before I met him."

"Nothing to worry about, huh?" Alex said, pointing out into the street, where the bank manager was now talking into Sheriff Houghton's ear as the lawman reloaded his rifle.

"That's not good," Will said.

"No, it's not," Brett said. "Follow me and stay close."

Brett charged into the street; his brothers close on his tail. Will thought they might quietly slide out of town while the sheriff and his men were busy dealing with White Cloud, but what happened next happened so fast there was nothing Will or Alex could do about it. Brett raised his revolver and amid all the chaos and screaming, fired into the crowd of Sun River citizens, putting a bullet into the head of Sheriff Houghton and another into Steven Holbrook's chest.

Both men fell to the dirt in a spray of blood, and the only man who witnessed what had happened — the tall, blonde deputy — took a bullet in the side from one of the attacking warriors as he stood up and exposed himself over the lip of the overturned wagon. The bullet turned him around, just as two more rifle shots pieced his heart. The deputy dropped to the ground beside his former boss and the lifeless bank manager.

Even Brett couldn't believe his luck, first off that he'd made those two tricky shots from a decent distance away, but also that the only person who'd watched what happened had been taken out of the picture too. It was almost like it was preordained, somehow fated to happen. What happened next might be the same.

Brett turned to look at his brothers, a big smile starting to form on his bearded face, when out of nowhere a bullet caught him in the throat, blowing a large hole out the back of his neck. Will and Alex both ran to catch their brother, but they both knew Brett was dead before his body thudded into the dirt in the center of Main Street.

The rest of the battle was a blur for Will and Alex. The Blackfeet warriors were brave and fearless, but soon more men from Sun River exited the bars, restaurants, and homes to fill the street with people protecting their town. White Cloud was no fool, and as his men were being picked off, he eventually shrieked out the order to retreat back into the wilderness. They'd fought well, and proved their point that they could match the white man in strength now that they had the same advanced weapons to fight with. Best to retreat today, pass along the news of their great victory to the other members of his tribe, and live to fight another day.

Later that afternoon, back in the Riverboat Saloon, Will and Alex sipped on a mug of lukewarm beer, trying their best to blend in with the understandably agitated crowd. The place was filled with even more people than had been here earlier, gathered for a town meeting that had been hastily called by Mayor Tasker. Will and Alex would have left already, but Sun River was in crisis mode, everyone on high alert, and they were worried it might look strange if they were spotted trying to skip town. Best to sit in the back of the room and lay low until later. If all went well, the plan was to quietly slip away tonight under the cover of darkness.

Tasker was a short, stocky man with salt-and-pepper hair that was thinning badly on the top. He was still dressed in the fancy suit he'd worn in the parade earlier, but there was blood staining the grey fabric around a small rip high on his right arm. The mayor ignored his injury and got right to the point.

"Thanks for coming, folks. First and foremost, I wanted to say how proud I am of all of you for standing up to those redskins. We lost ten citizens today . . . nine men, and one fine lady who'd been spooked and tried to run across the street at the wrong time. Tomorrow we'll pray for them and give them all a decent Christian burial. Far as I'm concerned, each and every one of them is a hero."

There was a scattering of cheers and a round of applause.

"The biggest issue we have now is not knowing if those damn injuns will be coming back for another poke at us, and here we stand without our sheriff or his deputy. Charlie Houghton and Mitch Harris were both good men, and excellent lawmen. They've kept us safe for the past four years . . . let us sleep easy in our beds when they were on the job, but now what are we gonna do to protect ourselves?"

Some discussion broke out as to who among them should be selected as the next sheriff, or if they should send a telegraph to the larger settlements nearby and ask if another experienced lawman might come hang his hat in Sun River. Both ideas had merit, but the overwhelming worry shared by the citizens represented in the room was that it might be dangerous taking the slower route of waiting for someone from parts unknown to come to their aid. After all, it was argued, if word got out that Sun River was currently without a lawman, there was no telling what sort of riffraff and trouble might come riding into town.

"Okay . . . quiet down," Mayor Tasker said. "I agree a man from right here works best all the way around . . . but which one of you is set on stepping up to the task?"

The room suddenly went quiet.

"Come on, now. The role of sheriff is a highly respected position, and now that we officially belong in the great State of Montana, the job is even more prestigious. Maybe even pays a bit more, but we'll have to work that out."

Still, no one came forward.

"I'd do it, but I'm a bit old for all the running around. Besides, I'm already mayor. Come on now . . . surely one of you fine men is willing to take the job?"

Tasker looked the crowd over, and just as he was about to give up, one of the men beside him tugged on his suit jacket and said, "Over there, Frank . . . someone has their hand raised near the back."

Mayor Tasker and the rest of the room — including Alex Boone — turned to see who was volunteering for the job. People started clapping and cheering, and the bartender called for a round of drinks on the house, but Alex just sat there with a stunned look on his face. The man with his arm in the air, and a shy smile on his face, was his brother Will.

From the Journal of William Boone
Sun River, Montana
November 8, 1889

That catches me up to date, but in the days and years ahead I'll try to keep filling in these pages, more so for myself than anyone who might read it.

I won't lie and say I knew exactly what I was doing in the saloon this afternoon, because I didn't. I'd raised my hand to be the next sheriff of Sun River on a spur-of-the moment decision once I saw that none of the other men were willing to take the job. Did that mean that I had to do it? No, of course not, but here's the kicker. I wanted to.

That's right. I wanted to be sheriff.

I'd spent my entire life doing the wrong thing, using my skills with a gun for no one's benefit other than my own. I'd lived a life of crime ever since I could remember and what good had it ever done me? What good had it done anyone? Brett was the man I'd followed, and look where all his cheating and scheming had gotten him. Dead with a hole through his throat.

I'm not saying I'm better than my brother; this decision was about me and had nothing to do with Brett. He made his own choices, but I've always wanted to be a better man and live a better life than I had up until that point. And that voice, that conscience, that . . . something inside me called out and demanded I do something about it today. Lying, cheating, stealing, killing . . . I didn't want any of it anymore.

So I'd raised my hand.

It's a few hours of drinking and celebrating later, and it's been a long, exhausting day, full of happiness as well as heartache. Truthfully, all I want to do is curl up and sleep, but I can't do that quite yet. There's still one more important thing I have to take care of tonight. . . .

Sheriff William Boone's Office
Sun River, Montana
November 8, 1889

Will sat at what had previously been Sheriff Houghton's desk, writing in his journal. Outside, the last vestiges of sunlight were gone, and he could no longer see well enough to keep writing. He tucked the journal away in the top drawer of his desk. The timing was good; when he looked up his brother Alex was entering his new office.

Just the man he wanted to see.

Will had been whisked away by the joyous crowd in the saloon for drinks after his unanimous selection as Sun River's new sheriff and the brothers hadn't had a chance to be alone and talk until now. Will struggled to find the words to start this important conversation, but Alex had some words of his own to say.

"What the hell is wrong with you, Will? Have you lost your mind?"

"No. I've finally found it. I think . . . ?"

"You *think*? Jesus. Sheriff William Boone. You've got to be kidding me!"

"Why? What's so wrong with that? It beats robbing and stealing and always looking behind me to see when the reaper might be sneaking up."

"Yeah, but sheriff? Even worse, the *sheriff of Sun River*? Do I need to remind you we played a part in getting the last sheriff killed? We robbed the damn bank here. It was us that let the gunrunners sell those fancy rifles to White Cloud. It was *your* plan to set those two men up to swing at the end of that rope rather than us. And it was *your* brother who shot and killed Sheriff Houghton and the manager of the National Bank to save our asses. And then you decide the appropriate action is to volunteer to take the dead lawman's job? What were you thinking?"

"Maybe I wasn't. Not clearly, and I'll admit the whisky might not have helped, but I'm happy with my decision. My gut's telling me it was the right thing to do."

"Why?"

"I don't know. I'm sick and tired of being an outlaw. Living by the gun never made anyone happy. Look at Brett, for God's sake, and you know damn well we'd be following him to the grave in no time. Maybe not today or tomorrow, but one of these days we'd pay the price."

"Nothing's carved in stone."

"Come on, Alex. If we don't change . . . we'll end up dead."

"And you think being a lawman isn't dangerous? That badge doesn't make you bulletproof. Being sheriff is probably even *more* dangerous. White Cloud and his warriors will be coming back to town . . . and he's just the start of your worries."

"Probably, but at least I'll be able to hold my head up for the first time in ages. That's gotta make some sense to you, doesn't it? You can't hate me for wanting to be a decent man."

"'Course not, but this is going a bit far. Brett would be ashamed of you."

"Maybe, but Ma and Gramps would be proud. And right now, that means a lot more to me."

"And what about my opinion? Does my opinion matter to you?"

"Your opinion means everything to me . . . which is why I wanted to talk to you tonight. I have something for you."

Will opened another drawer, reached in to grab something, and dropped a small, shiny star-shaped badge on top of the wooden desk. The star had the word, **"DEPUTY"**, engraved into the center of it. Will waited for his brother's reaction without saying a word.

"What the hell is that?" Alex said. "You want *me* to be your deputy?"

"Who else would I choose? I need your help to train this mob so they're ready for White Cloud. I can't do it without you."

"You're joking, right? I can't be a lawman."

"Why not? You're a good man, and better with a gun than anyone around here. Besides, it comes with a decent wage, and you and I can share quarters here with a roof over our heads for once. It's the best offer we're gonna get. Better than we deserve, to be honest, and maybe the last chance we'll ever get to stop running and finally have peace in our lives. We can make this change together, Alex. I know we can."

Alex stood in silence, staring down at the small metal star on the desk, thinking things through. And then he reached out and grabbed the star, taking a moment to pin it on his jacket directly over his heart. Even once it was on, and his hands dropped to his side again, it still took him time to find his voice.

"Thank you."

"For what?" Will asked.

"For not forgetting that family sticks together, no matter what."

Will stood up and went over to put his arms around his brother. Together they hugged, tears in both of their eyes. Eventually, they separated, and Will returned to his chair. Alex only had one last question to ask, and it put a smile on both of their faces.

"Are we *really* gonna do this?"

"We're gonna try, Alex. We're gonna try. . . ."

#

My story, "The Leopard," takes place on and around November 8, 1889, the day that Montana officially become the 41st state in the Union. This may seem strange, but living in Canada, as I do, we are always hearing debates (and sometimes arguments) about whether or not we will eventually become just another part of the United States. Some are in favor of this move, and many are not, but I had recently been part of one of these discussions, and for whatever reason I started looking at when some of the U.S. states joined. Not being taught any of this U.S. history in school, I was under the impression that most of the states were brought together around the same time, or at least grouped together within their geographical areas. So I was just looking around and I noticed that there was a 13-year gap between Colorado joining the Union in 1876 and Montana in 1889. I can't tell you why it struck me as strange for there to be that gap but it did, and I had a thought that there was probably a huge celebration that took place in Montana after they were finally given the green light to join. So I started thinking about a story built around that celebration, but that was also filled with chaos, danger, and excitement. From there, all I needed was a young outlaw main character who wanted to change his wicked ways, and *The Leopard* was born. . . .

—Gord Rollo

Gord Rollo was born in St. Andrews, Scotland, but now lives in Ontario, Canada. His short stories and novella-length work have appeared in many professional publications throughout the horror genre. His novels include: *The Jigsaw Man, Crimson,Strange Magic, Valley Of The Scarecrow, The Translators, TheCrucifixion Experiments, Between the Devil and the Deep Blue Sea,* and*The Dark Side of Heaven.* Two other novels: *Beasts of Copan,* a time-travel fantasy/horror, and *Voodoo Cowboys: The Life, Death, and Resurrection of Butch Cassidy and the Sundance Kid,* a weird western/horror/adventure novel, were co-written with the legendary Gene O'Neill. Besides novels, Gord has edited the acclaimed evolutionary horror anthology *Unnatural Selection: A Collection of Darwinian Nightmares* and co-edited *Dreaming of Angels*, a horror/fantasy anthology.

READ

CRAZY GOOD BOOKS

By Crazy Good Authors

WE all love books. But we each have our own particular tastes. And sometimes we can't find the books we want to read, or can't find them fast enough. Then we wonder why our favorite authors don't just write the books we want to read, all the time, as quick as we'd like.

Now the Wait Is Over!

Here at Crazy 8 Press, we write the books YOU want to read—the books WE want to write. We're not a big publisher. We don't have to answer to shareholders or marketing departments. We concentrate on writing fun and exciting and unique books because we know that those are the things you really want, too.

And because we produce the books ourselves, you don't have to wait two years between when we start a book and when you get to read it. When we have an idea for a cool new book, we sit down and write it, and get it out to you nice and quick, so you don't have to wait forever.

Check Us Out!

We have over 80 titles now, ranging from SF comedy to epic fantasy to superheroes to alternate history to mystery and more. Find us at one of the many conventions we attend, take a look at our website—or both! We're always happy to show off our books, and we hope you'll find something you like.

www.crazy8press.com